SILENCED

SILENCED

❖

KELLY BARTLETT

L & B

Lawler & Britton Publishing House

This novel is a work of fiction. Any references to historical events, real people, or real places are used fictitiously. Other names, characters, places and events are products of the author's imagination, and any resemblance to actual persons, living or dead, events or localities is entirely coincidental.

Cover design by Richard Ljoenes
Interior design by Phillip Gessert

ISBN 979-8-9866552-0-8 (pbk)
ISBN 979-8-9866552-1-5 (ebook)

For Molly, Heather, Meghan, and Colleen,
May you live beautifully ever after

TABLE OF CONTENTS

FLASH FORWARD

MAY 2014

IT'S NOT LIKE I want a smackdown by cops.

This isn't my choice. Far from asking for trouble, I had been trying my best to keep the secret on the down low. But events had spiraled out of control and I had to make a split decision: Follow the rules, or save Olivia.

I stagger into the Burlington police station, gingerly feeling the back of my skull, checking for blood. No oozing, thank God. I pat my long hair back into place, which is a bit awkward with handcuffs. At least my wrists aren't trussed up behind my back, as in the movies. Probably because I had been lying smack on my back when the cops nabbed me, and I moaned like a cow when they tried to roll me over.

"Wait here." Officer Thornberg points to a chair screwed to the floor, before lumbering through the doorway to the inner sanctum.

As I shuffle towards the metal chair, I hear *cheep, cheep, cheep.* I peek inside the large cardboard box next to the dispatcher's desk. Baby chicks! The pleasant dispatcher says they're homeless and offers them to me for free.

Tempting as it is, I realize I'm in no shape to take on additional responsibilities. I murmur a polite, "No thank you," although I agree to hold one.

I cradle it gently. My quivering fingers begin to relax around the downy, breathing body. The chick's tiny claws are harmless and its bright black eyes look at me curiously, without judgement. The golden down feels warm and peaceful as I stroke my cheek with the chick. I smell a delicately funky odor, like aged manure, a November vintage, buried under snow until the spring thaw. I award myself one last fuzzy caress, then hand the birdie back to the happy dispatcher, who holds it to her own face, murmuring *ooh*.

Thornberg reappears and calls my name in a loud growl. I wish I'd never met him. No doubt these chicks will soon be nestled in some cozy kitchen, while I have to outplay the law and get home before mom finds out.

Arrested?

Seriously?

I trudge behind the giant into the interrogation room and sigh, steadily, so as not to jar my pounding head. I flop onto the chair Thornberg holds out and bang my handcuffs on the table with a rebellious whack.

Unperturbed, he saunters around the table and presses a button on a device between us before settling into his own chair. Thornberg leans back, rests his head in clasped hands with his elbows triangulating out, and stretches his ginormous tree-trunk legs straight out as if he has all the time in the world to hear a good yarn. "Okay. Let's start at the beginning."

They say the truth will set you free, which is funny because when I finally mustered the courage to speak up, they arrested me.

But where to start? Today?

Three months ago?

Genesis?

Like many fiascos, this one began with lies.

ONE
MARCH 2014

ONCE UPON A time, a row of cars headed west to affluential careers in Burlington, while Annie Mulligan drove in the opposite direction, toward the mountain. Ahead of her arose a picturesque postcard of Vermont: snow frosting the peak in the distance, meadows white with snowfall on either side of the salty-gray road, here a quaint country store, there a curlicue of smoke wafting up from, yup, a sugar house, which puffed the scent of boiling maple sap rippling outwards, lending the atmosphere a syrupy sweetness.

Her windshield displayed a panorama of fertile forests concealing scampering squirrels and chittering birds and deer bending their heads to whisper secrets through the blanket of snow to the earth. Her car chugged past the dairy farm, the cows munching reliably, their four stomachs magically spinning straw into milk, a feat that would render Rumpelstiltskin a greedy green.

Annie felt ineffably fortunate to live in a land so magnificent that tourists flew zillions of miles to gaze upon the unshakable mountain that steadfastly greeted her every morning, arrayed in seasonal splendor, bounteous hues of green in spring, rollicking red and orange in autumn. And now, in March, the mountain's shadows of purples and blues shared prominence with dazzling white snow. Annie drove directly into and through this life-size poster of bucolic life.

She passed the old cottage on the left, built with hopes and dreams long, long ago, now weather-beaten into grizzled splintering slats, ramshackling towards the ground under gravity's spell. With a huff and a puff you could blow that house down. Annie mentally photoshopped the dilapidated wreck out of her virtual postcard.

She zoomed a few more minutes and swung right into the parking lot. Climbing out of the car, she spotted an empty yogurt cup, which must have tumbled out of one of the vans yesterday while a mom wedged her child into his car seat. To keep the Green Mountain State picture perfect, Annie snapped up the rogue plastic container.

She jangled her keys jauntily. Unlocking the school gave her the sense that she was not only the teacher, but the proprietor as well. She had the best job ever; she literally got paid to play with children. Every day offered a new opportunity to share another nursery rhyme or build a bigger marble run. And she never knew when she'd be called upon to save a child ... from ignorance, a classmate's ire, boredom. She rescued one from the garbage bin, another from being outcast, another from picking his nose. Just yesterday she had saved Nora, their tiniest toddler. If that snow sliding off the school's red metal roof had landed on top of her, Nora would have disappeared completely. Not even her little red woolen cap would have been visible under the heavy white avalanche. Luckily Annie was on guard and had plucked her away from danger.

Yes, the kiddos needed her. A former cheerleader, Annie was still cheering, but instead of urging gangly, leggy basketball players to shoot the ball, now she was coaching three and four-year-olds in life skills such as gathering acorns, counting lima beans, and sharing the sand table.

And saving the planet from plastic! Annie tossed the yogurt cup in the blue recycling receptacle, stepped out of her boots, hung her jacket up and set her purse on a high shelf in the kitchen area.

She spied a strip of crumpled waxed paper near the electrical cords on the floor. They had to be careful to keep the school clean not just for health inspections, but because it had been built in the 1800s and the attic was leaky, creaky, and prone to foraging mice.

As Annie picked up the trash to throw it away, she noticed a speckled pattern in the translucent paper. Lifting it closer, she spied white stripes ribbing one side and mottled brown tessellations on the other. She suddenly realized it was not waxed paper she was holding—it was a snakeskin.

Annie yelped and her fingers reflexively flicked it away. She stared in horror while it gently wafted down, circling back to where she found it.

Since the snake had outgrown its skin, was it now too large to squeeze back out whatever hole it had slithered in through? Was it still inside the schoolhouse?

She swallowed a big gulp of air and picked up the shed skin with pincer fingers, *ick,* and dropped it in the garbage. She grabbed a plastic sword from the dress up area. Wielding it in front of her, Annie began tracing the perimeter of the room methodically, probing corners and swiping underneath shelves with the flat of the weapon. Thanks to Willy, she knew that snakes didn't have ears per se, theirs was a silent world. *Serpentes* felt vibrations through a thingamajig attached to their jawbones. Annie tiptoed cautiously across the carpet, a samurai soldier, dressed in black, stealthily searching. She dreaded spying a forked tongue or reptilian eyes staring at her from under the sink, but not locating the beast would be even worse. She would never know where it was or when it would strike.

Step by step by step she hunted, muttering under her breath:

"Sneaky snake, freaky snake, I'll break you with a shake, shake, shake."

It was a gift she had—whipping up songs off the cuff. Her rhymes, riffs, and rhythms delighted the children. Someday she would compile her lyrics into a songbook to teach singing using her proprietary Murphy Method. She would include illustrations so the picture book would double as a read aloud for her preschoolers.

"What are you doing?"

Annie shrieked and dropped her sword. She pivoted and saw Bobbie, the teacher's assistant, taking off her coat in the mudroom.

"You startled me! I'm just—" Annie bent down to grasp the rapier—"just tidying up." She stabbed the blade into the bin brimming with capes, antlers, fake fur, and a yellow taffeta ballgown.

"Having a black day?"

Annie looked down. She wore slenderizing black pants as usual; she had eight pairs to get her through the week. Over her bright green tee shirt, she had donned a black hoodie. "I was chilly this morning."

"Yeah. Cold snap."

It might be cold, but it wasn't a black day. Annie was determined to have a fantabulous day.

She considered telling Bobbie about the fugitive snake, but quickly discarded the notion. A hardy Vermonter, Bobbie could be relied upon to organize their annual rummage sale, set mousetraps, and cobble forest forts together, but she was also a blabbermouth. If Bobbie got wind of this, before the day was out, every mother in the village would hear Play and Learn Preschool had an infestation of snakes. Nah, Annie would confide in Dan; he could keep a secret.

To Bobbie, she announced, "Hey, I have great news—Cara was accepted at Coolidge University!"

It was the American Dream come true—getting your child into college. Yesterday they had received the luscious thick creamy envelope holding the cherished letter of acceptance. Cara received a merit scholarship, an unsubsidized student loan, a negligible grant, and work-study. This fall, Cara would begin adulting by accruing her very own student debt.

V-I-C-T-O-R-Y! We're gonna win the game and you wanna know why?

They had toasted Cara over and over last night. "Cool U sure is lucky to get you!" If Annie's goblet had been a pompom, she would have proudly waved it back and forth.

Dan had offered, "Cara, would you like a glass? To mark the occasion?"

Annie smiled to herself, remembering her daughter's beautiful blue eyes shining more and more brightly with each sip. So cute, her first wine.

Before you know it, Willy would be off at college also, and then Annie and Dan could enjoy their empty nest years as second honeymooners. They could revisit the Bahamas. After nineteen years of marriage, Annie knew so many more maneuvers. She would love to practice them on Dan in that grass hut they reserved back when they were newlyweds. Someday soon she would join a gym to get in shape, maybe next week. Or next year.

Bobbie said, "Coolidge was her top choice, right? Congratulations!" She reached over to slap Annie a high five.

Annie sighed happily. Everything was going exactly according to plan.

'Cause we've got spirit and we're riding high, so V-I-C-T-O-R-Y!

TWO

CARA THOUGHT THEY'D outgrown pinkie swears way back in middle school. But Olivia extended her little finger, her face like snow, her grip like a ski binding. Cara knew only drastic news would make Olivia pull her into the secluded Staff Only lavatory in the abandoned art hallway. "What?" she whispered even though they were alone.

Olivia plunked her backpack on the counter and fumbled through it. "I just took the test. Look. It's positive." She thrust a short white stick at Cara. A vibrant pink plus sign shimmered on the end of it. "What am I going to do?"

Cara swallowed a gasp. She paused a beat ... then said with more assurance than she felt, "You're going to graduate in three months and go to college, just like you planned."

Olivia flipped the flap on the waste can and dropped the test stick in. She pressed both hands on her abdomen and shook her head back and forth. "I can't do this."

"What about Nate? What did he say?"

From her backpack Olivia fished out a snack-size Ziploc bag. "I'm afraid to tell him." She blew out a long breath. "He's so psyched about going to UVM. I can't hold him back. You know he got that lacrosse scholarship—practically a free ride."

Yesterday Cara had received her own acceptance letter from Calvin Coolidge University. But it would be premature to share this fantastic news with her stunned friend. Olivia needed moral support right now. Based on her pallid face, perhaps she needed life support.

Years ago their health teacher had described morning sickness so extreme that the mom-to-be had to be hospitalized to prevent death by dehydration. Cara had pictured it—a girl curled up in the fetal position on the bed with safety rails, attached to a plastic siphon pulsing with liquid nutrition, an external umbilical cord keeping her alive. Cara assumed the teacher had purposely exaggerated to scare the students into condoms, or abstinence. But maybe he'd been telling the truth? Right now, her bestie looked like she needed an IV.

Olivia ... pregnant? This was the sort of thing that happened to other kids, at other schools. This was a cheap cliché in a low-budget movie or a cautionary tale of what-not-to-do from sex ed class. This couldn't be happening to Olivia.

But then again, why not? Olivia had been going out with Nate since freshman year. What did she expect?

Olivia plucked a small joint out of the baggie. "My life is over."

"Via! Since when do you smoke?"

"I don't. Nate asked me to hold it for him." She slipped the joint between her lips and mumbled, "But now I need it." Olivia struck a match, lit the joint, closed her eyes and sucked in deeply.

She coughed. The joint bobbled up and down like a diving board. *Boing, boing.*

"What the—?" Cara grabbed the joint away from Olivia's spluttering lips. "You can't smoke."

"I don't care if I get caught."

"What about the baby?"

Cara put the joint to her own mouth inquisitively. She didn't need to protect a little one. She took a tentative inhalation. The hot dry smoke constricted her throat and she coughed.

Olivia slumped against the putty-colored wall of the teacher's bathroom. Her complexion matched the pale tiles, her blond hair was the color of grout. Her eyelids dropped down covering her brown eyes. "Like I said, my life is over." She started to sink, her shoulder blades sloping down the slippery wall of tiles.

"Your life is so not over, it's just begin—"

A metallic clink echoed in the cramped room as the bathroom lock jiggled.

Cara and Olivia gaped at each other. Only employees had keys to the adult facilities. Olivia had one because she had secretly borrowed a key from her mother and made a copy when they were freshmen.

Without thinking Cara pushed Olivia into the nearest stall and swung the door closed. "What—?" asked Olivia.

"Shh!" Cara turned and faced Ms. Purnell, who bustled in on high heels, huffy with importance and authority.

"What are you doing in here?" The guidance counselor sniffed suspiciously. "What's that smell?" Her small eyes lasered in on the weed. "What is *that*?"

Cara looked down. She was as shocked and appalled as Purnell was to see her hand holding a joint. A wispy trail of smoke lazily drifted upwards from the end. Shit. Shit. Shit.

"Nothing." Cara whipped her hand behind her back. Stupid. Stupid. Stupid.

"Give me that."

Cara froze.

"Now!" Purnell barked.

Cara jumped at the ferocity. She feared Purnell might notice Olivia's Ugg boots below the door of the other stall or that her friend would pop out and needlessly give herself away. No sense in Purnell nailing both of them. Cara handed over the evidence.

Purnell turned on the faucet and doused the joint, shooting a look of supreme disapproval at Cara. "Drugs," she pursed her lips. "You're going to the office."

Cara swooped up Olivia's backpack, slung it on her shoulder, and shuffled out of the teacher's restroom. Her steps slowed until she was taking baby steps. Purnell grabbed her arm to hustle her forward. The bell rang, doors opened, and chattering students streamed into the hallway, feet shuffling on autopilot, commuting to their second period class. A couple of friends turned their heads, curiously watching Purnell escort Cara.

She couldn't face them. Her cheeks felt hot with embarrassment. She yanked her arm away from Purnell, who wobbled on her high heels and bumped into a student's artwork in charcoal hanging on the wall.

"Look what you've done." Purnell angrily swiped at the black charcoal, which had rubbed onto her sleeve. "Wait until I tell Mr. Day."

How did her world tank so fast? Cara's stomach twisted.

THREE

At Play And Learn Preschool, toddlers built tippy towers with red, blue, and yellow blocks, dabbled in the sand and water tables, and scaled the three-foot high rock-climbing wall molded from repurposed plastic. In the dress up corner, Nora plugged the stethoscope in her ears and listened intently to the heartbeat of the naked baby doll held by Cannon, who had discarded his red cape to become a stay-at-home dad. Xander flicked a CD like a frisbee into the Nature Corner full of stones and burdocks and miscellaneous treasures collected during guided hikes.

"That's an outside choice," Annie informed him firmly. "You may choose an indoor choice." Xander jumped like a kangaroo over to the woodworking area, turned a bottle of glue upside down over a wood chip, and squeezed, his face as scrunched as his fists.

The CD had *Backhoe Girl,* which was Cara's favorite song when she was five. Swiping spruce needles off the silver disk, Annie spotted scratches and mournfully laid it to rest in the Art tub full of colorful yarn scraps and mangled pipe cleaners. Back when Cara was little, Annie knew everything she listened to. Now it was hard to keep up with her teen's playlist streaming through earbuds and iPod, although Annie did her best.

She closed her eyes, marveling at the passage of years. When she had held Cara in her arms for the first time, her skin a vibrant rosy pink, her eyes full of unseeing yet calm trust, her mouth, an *oh,* ready to grab hold and suck life, Annie had gasped in wonderment. She stroked Cara's velvety cheek and her fingers, wrinkly in that newborn, room-to-grow way. She cradled her child with a joy so complete she felt her heartsong overflow and flood the room with a reverberating, throbbing love. Tears dripped down Annie's cheeks, falling in soft spatters on Cara's pink blanket cocoon. Annie resolved to protect this child, as tenaciously as a mama bear. She bent close and murmured in her baby's perfect tiny ear, "I'll be a good mother to you, I promise."

With desperate devotion, Annie had redirected her darling from scraped knees to shoe-tying, from bony limbs to budding puberty, from last-minute middle school science projects to confident high school Power Point presentations. And now, here was her baby, on the brink of matriculation at college. Cara's imminent graduation from high school was proof that Annie had succeeded, that she had kept the solemn vow whispered to her daughter years ago.

Annie's eyes pooled. She felt as if *she* were graduating alongside Cara, shedding an old role that was no longer needed. Her tears were a cocktail of pride and wistfulness.

Annie blinked and shook her head. She couldn't get all maudlin here when she had a job to do. Cara didn't need her anymore, but the preschoolers did. She flipped open the teacher's log and finished writing her notes:

Order new Even Kids Get the Blues CD

Sew rip in crotch of beaver costume

Call Cannon's mother—collection of scabs must stay at home, health code

She put her pen down and gazed benevolently at her little kingdom. A toddler was scared-stuck on the top of a "ski mountain" of beanbag chairs and Annie slalomed over to lift him to safety.

The parent helper was sneaking peeks at her phone over at the woodworking table. Xander squirted glue into a pool on his slab of wood and then stirred the white puddle with his finger. The parent helper grabbed a paper towel and wiped his fingers. Xander promptly stuck his finger back in the glue and began drawing designs on the wood. The parent helper held out a paintbrush to the child, who studiously ignored it.

Annie schussed over and coached the woman, "Let's not interrupt his work."

"He's playing with the glue."

"'A child's job *is* to play.'"

"He's not using the brush."

"Scientists have discovered that play is crucial to a child's development. They learn by doing. It's on page two of the PAL handout."

From the guilty look on her face, Annie realized this woman had never read the manual, had skipped reading the guidelines regarding their mandatory Parent Helper Volunteer Program on page five. She had probably discarded the packet as soon as the orientation meeting was over.

And folks think preschool is just for kids. *Sheesh,* half the job is educating adults. That was one of the reasons they required parents to volunteer in class, so the staff could model effective teaching.

"Hm, could I get your help over here in the reading corner?" Annie ushered the mother away from the messy woodworking table.

Annie had taught at Play And Learn since Cara was two and had taken maternity leave when Willy was a baby, before happily returning to her job. Now Willy was in fifth grade, pulling good grades, while Cara was acing high school and due to graduate in three months. How time flies when you're having fun.

She glanced at the hickory dickory clock with the stuffed animal mouse perched on the peak and announced brightly, "Circle time." Today she would read *Hansel and Gretel.* The toddlers were always horrified but thrilled at how sneaky the witch was to lure Hansel and Gretel with a house made of sweets. Annie loved the reassuring message that the heroes outwit the witch and make it back home safely. As a bonus, Annie would throw in a lesson about the importance of brushing your teeth after eating candy, and choosing healthier foods to begin with.

Cara held her phone and wondered who to call.

Would her mom panic?

Or overhelp?

Both?

Ugh.

Her mother's "help" often came in the form of baked goods. No one denied mom was a great cook, but sometimes Cara needed calm assurance that everything was going to work out, not an overblown reaction followed by a warm chocolate chip cookie.

But Dad, he was steady ... as unfazed and reliable as Betsy Clunker, the decrepit van they bought for her to practice driving when she got her learner's permit. You could scrape Betsy trying to park in a narrow spot and no one would notice the new line scratched into the rusty rocker panel. And if her dad did happen to spot it, Cara would say, "mums," their secret decoder for, "Don't tell mom." If her mother overheard them, they would talk about chrysanthemums.

So when Principal Day asked her to call a parent, Cara tapped her Dad's number.

The last time Cara had been in this office, she was part of a student council delegation presenting their Project Graduation ideas to Mr. Day. He had the same fake potted plant in the corner lending faux greenery to his beige decor. He had a ginormous metal desk to settle behind in his swivel chair. The same crummy artwork on the wall, probably from that silent auction to raise funds for the ski team to field trip it to the Alps.

The student council had suggested a ropes course, a day at Jay Peak, or Smuggler's Notch. Cara had been rooting for the ropes course, she loved ziplines.

Principal Day had "regretfully" said "too expensive" to each request and suggested bowling instead.

From years of practice, the seniors kept their gazes polite and attentive and assured him they would think about it and get back to him ... they were after all, the good kids. But *bowling?* Could it get any more lame? In a coordinated group effort, they refrained from looking at each other and rolling their eyes until *after* they filed out of his office.

Cara's dad didn't answer his phone. He had recently gotten a promotion and was forever busy going to meetings. She listened to his recorded voice asking her to leave a message.

This was no time for a voice message! She clicked out instead.

Ugh.

She had to call her mom.

UGH.

There was a chance that her mom wouldn't pick up either. They weren't supposed to call her at work unless there was an emergency.

Let's see. Her best friend was pregnant, but Cara promised not to tell. And the principal was making noises about expelling her. *How could she go to college if she didn't graduate from high school????* This was definitely an emergency.

She fought back tears. No way was she going to shed tears in front of

Purnell, wedged in the chair next to her, sniffing huffily as if Cara had taken the last maple glazed doughnut at a buffet.

Cara squeezed her eyes tight, damming the tears.

She sighed, opened her eyes, swiped her phone, and poked her mom's number.

Annie helped the preschoolers stash their woodwork on the drying shelf and put away the paint pots. The kids zigzagged to the corner and plunked down on the soft blue shag rug for Circle Time. Nora climbed into Bobbie's lap. While Annie washed glue off her hands, her cell phone chimed. She recognized Cara's ringtone. She had trained her kids not to call during work unless it was an emergency. Annie quickly fished her phone out of her purse. "Hey Cara ... What?"

Her handbag slipped out of her grasp and splatted onto the wood constructions, causing gluey chunks of chips to scatter. She switched her cell to her left hand. "What?" She picked up her handbag and stuffed it underneath her arm. She grabbed paper towels from the kitchen area to wipe off the glue, but her pocketbook squeezed out of her armpit and landed on the pot of red paint. Annie swabbed her purse with paper towels, which smeared red all over the bottom and side of her jewel-toned quilted bag.

Bobbie gently undraped Nora and set her on the carpet. She heaved herself up off the floor and edged towards the kitchen with head tilted and eyebrows raised.

"I'll be right there," Annie said before clicking off the phone. She turned toward Bobbie. "It's Cara."

"She okay?"

"No. I mean, yes. She's not hurt or anything." Annie pressed her hand to her forehead. "Cara—" She stopped. She couldn't admit to three-year-olds that her daughter was caught with pot. And it would be far worse to admit that to Bobbie, or the parent helper, sitting in the circle, watching.

"Cara needs help. Um, she's not feeling well. I have to pick her up. Can you cover for me and call for a sub?"

"Of course. No problem." Bobbie turned back to the circle. "Okay friends, let's start our 'Recycle Song.' I need to make a phone call."

The parent helper gamely chanted the song, "Reduce, reuse, recycle, repeat," but her starting note wasn't low enough and by the second repeat, it was a high-pitched screech and kids were dropping out, their fingers exploring boogers in their noses while they stared at Cannon's sneakers which lit up in neon green every time he slapped them on the floor, which he did in rhythm to the ditty.

Annie dropped her phone in her purse, grabbed her parka, shoved her feet in her boots, dashed out the door, and scrambled into her car. And then she remembered that she forgot about the snake on the loose in the schoolroom. She gunned the accelerator. Cara came first.

FOUR

CARA WOULD NEVER break the rules like this. Obviously there was a big misunderstanding and Annie was determined to get to the bottom of it. She slammed on her brakes as the car ahead of her slowed down to turn into Mapleville Recreational Park.

Years ago the family had hiked there on a surprisingly warm morning in early May. Dan, Cara, and Willy had each held a dog by the leash. The golden retrievers pulled their lines tight, eager to sniff all the fresh, exciting aromas. The Mulligans had ventured off the woodsy trail to catch some sun, wading through tall moist ferns that tickled their knees. Suddenly, Curly had barked, ripped the leash out of Willy's hand, and barreled towards a knoll.

The other dogs had yipped and yanked their lines hoping to join the rush. As Curly streaked up, a deer popped up from the grass, bounded a couple yards left, and then, instead of leaping lightly away to freedom, the deer faced the dog, planting itself with front legs splayed and rump end high, ready to pounce. Curly galloped closer, yapping excitedly. Then the deer charged Curly, who yelped and dodged and circled back to his litter mates who snuffled him curiously. Willy grabbed the leash that was dragging behind.

"Wow. That must be a buck." Annie had never heard of a deer attacking a dog before.

"A buck would've run," Dan informed her. "That's gotta be a doe protecting her fawn."

"A fawn? I want to see it." Annie tiptoed closer to the meadow.

Dan grabbed her arm. "Give 'em space. Let's get back to the trail."

"But I want to see the fawn!"

"Leave 'em alone."

As the family trekked back to the path, Annie had marveled, *How can an herbivore with spindly legs, a narrow snout, and no claws, have the courage to stand her ground and do battle with a dog armed with sharp canines, shredder paws, and powerful momentum?*

Now, the car ahead of her completed its turn and Annie stepped on the gas. Minutes later she buzzed into an empty handicapped parking spot near the entrance of Camels Hump Union High School. Her fingers shook as she pulled the keys out of the ignition and shoved them into her purse. She jogged to the heavy double doors, yanked hard, then hurried to the main office, breathing heavily.

"Hi, I'm Annie Mulligan. I'm here to pick up Cara."

The secretary stared rudely at Annie's forehead, unwilling to meet her eyes. "This way." She led Annie to an inner office and poked her head in. "Mrs. Mulligan here to see you, Al."

Annie charged in, arm outthrust for a polite handshake. Mr. Day stood up and extended his hand, then paused, flummoxed.

"Mom," Cara whispered, "what's with the red?"

Annie swiveled and saw her daughter sitting in a chair next to a lady with big hair. Cara pointed to her head.

Annie fingered her forehead and felt a dried up puckered patch. "Paint," she explained. "I'm a preschool teacher." She directed this to Mr. Day who nodded in understanding.

"This is Ms. Purnell." He indicated the lady in peach polyester with matching hair. Her fingernails, plastered with thick peach nail gel, drummed on the desk: *Dum dum da dum.*

"Have a seat," offered Mr. Day.

Annie perched on the chair next to Cara. Above Mr. Day's head was a rustic wooden sign, painted china blue with black words in calligraphy that read:

I DON'T CARE HOW MUCH YOU KNOW
UNTIL I KNOW HOW MUCH YOU CARE

Mr. Day's face was rumpled and dimpled by acne scars. His nose was bulbous, not bony. Instead of high cheekbones, he had jowls. There were no sharp edges to knock up against. No jutting jaw to stub your education on. It was all accommodating bumps and a backpedaling hairline. He looked like he cared.

But disturbing words streamed out of the principal's mouth: staff only, school property, marijuana, illegal, expulsion.

"Expulsion?" Annie's head swiveled, looking for answers.

Cara drooped in her chair like a mylar balloon deflating.

"Your daughter is in serious trouble. Ms. Purnell found her smoking marijuana and we found more in her backpack. I've gone over school policy and I gotta tell ya, it's not looking good."

"What about my Senior Project?" Cara asked. She was still debating between volunteering with Special Olympics or Vermont Legal Aid.

"I am very surprised at your behavior, Cara. You've been an exemplary student up until now." Mr. Day leaned toward her and spoke kindly, almost apologetically. "But unless I can find a loophole, I will have no choice. You will have to make other arrangements for completing your senior year, or you can come back next year."

Cara slid an inch lower in her chair.

None of this made sense. Cara was an A+ student. Annie swallowed, but her throat was suddenly thick and it hurt to speak. "Expulsion?" she repeated, again.

"Seriously?" Cara backed her up. "It's just weed."

Mr. Day counted off with his fingers, this time addressing Annie and referring to Cara in third person. "One, she was out of bounds in the teacher's bathroom. Two, the marijuana. Three, she had a baggie of it ready to sell in her backpack. Four, assaulted Ms. Purnell."

Stunned, all Annie could manage was to repeat words. "Assaulted?" She turned to her daughter. Cara hadn't smacked anyone since she was seven years old and was shielding her school project, a poster about puppies, from Willy's squirt gun spray.

Cara crossed her arms over her chest. "I didn't assault her."

"She knocked me into the wall," claimed Ms. Purnell.

"You grabbed me first!" Cara defended herself.

Annie had been nurturing and grooming Cara for seventeen years, to prepare her for college and a career. All those flashcards and Mozart cassette tapes and playdates. All those stupid, messy science projects and the late nights helping with term papers and student council dilemmas. And now this stranger, this Purnell, was ripping it all away? Stealing the coveted diploma out of their grasp when it was a mere three months away? Annie leaned forward, jaw clenched, ready to pounce. "We've never had trouble like this before. There must be a mistake."

"Oh, yes, there's been a mistake and it was Cara's." Ms. Purnell's gaze bored into the top of Cara's bent head. "She was smoking marijuana in the teacher's bathroom and she shoved me into a wall."

"Cara," said Annie, straining to maintain a reasonable tone, "please explain to everyone that you don't do drugs and would never hurt—" she gestured towards the guidance counselor.

"It was an accident."

"Of course it was." Annie faced Mr. Day. "There you have it."

"What about the marijuana?" he asked, as if it pained him.

Annie smiled encouragingly to Cara, willing her to spell out to everyone's satisfaction that this was all a colossal misunderstanding.

There was a pause.

Annie nodded supportively.

Cara took a deep breath as if deliberating. Annie was relieved her daughter was choosing her words with care; much was at stake here.

But then, in an unfamiliar belligerent tone, Cara said, "Yes. I had the joint. Can we go now?"

Shocked, Annie sat back hard in her chair. The black hoodie had been a mistake; she felt hot and flushed and she could hardly breathe. She pulled at the stretchy fabric strangling her throat.

"*You* can wait outside my office." Mr. Day pointed to the door. Head down, Cara shuffled out.

"Something's wrong here," Annie said. "Cara's on the track team. She doesn't even smoke."

"I saw her with my own eyes," said Ms. Purnell.

"Cara has been an honor student all four years. This is a complete aberration. She's always followed the rules. Can't you give her a second chance?"

"A mulligan?" Mr. Day sighed. He tented his hands, clasped them, then rested his un-cleft chin on them. "I wish I could."

"She's on the student council! Project Graduation! Track!"

Ms. Purnell cleared her throat loudly and raised her eyebrows. "But we need to follow school regulations. That's what they're for."

"But—" said Annie.

Mr. Day sighed. "I'm sorry. I wish I could give Cara another chance. I really do. But that's what we did last year. With Callum Ladue."

Annie shuddered. She remembered Callum.

Mr. Day continued. "We thought—honor student, soccer captain, student council. Kid had everything going for him. So when we caught him with meth, we let him off easy with a two-week suspension. Next thing you know a freshman ODs and we find out Callum was dealing in the boys' restroom. I'm sure you remember what happened after that."

Last year Annie brought a plate of cookies and a candle to the vigil on the town green for the freshman in the hospital. Last year she had *tsk tsked* in pity for Ladue and his parents. Last year she had congratulated herself for being the kind of mother who didn't raise drug addicts.

Annie slid an inch lower in her chair. She finger-combed her bangs to release them, but they were too short to hide her face. They just sproinged back up.

"The media had a field day with the incident and the parents got organized and petitioned the school board. I have never seen the board mobilize that fast before." Mr. Day shook his wobbly cheeks, still incredulous that bureaucracy could be that speedy. "Fortunately, our student survived the overdose, but by the time he got off life support, they'd already enacted the Zero Drug, Zero Death policy."

"ZDZD," Annie chanted. She remembered the slogan's initials on posters and mass mailings. In fact, she and her neighbor Wendy had earnestly passed out flyers at Town Meeting Day. Annie opened her mouth and her breath escaped in a long sigh.

When she was growing up, Annie's dad used to say in his authoritative lawyerly voice, "Exceptions make lousy law." Now Annie suddenly understood exactly what he was talking about. Was every rule in the world an overreaction to an exception? Those blasted know-it-all parents and their idiotic rules and regulations. *Just because Callum nearly killed a kid with meth, our darling daughter has to get booted?*

This was a totally different situation from Callum's! It was just pot! No one was going to OD in his basement simply because Cara inadvertently toked up in the teacher's bathroom. Was it even *possible* to overdose on pot? And how in the world could Cara go to Coolidge University if she got kicked out of high school? And if she didn't go to college, how could she ever get a decent job?

"But you can't kick her out!" Annie pleaded. "She needs to graduate so she can go to college!"

Mr. Day looked genuinely pained. "I'm sorry, but like it or not, marijuana is still an illegal substance in this state."

Ms. Purnell added, "How can we expect our students to respect our regulations if we don't enforce them? It's our duty to expel Cara for doing drugs in total violation of the ZDZD guidelines."

Annie felt her hackles rise and her haunches rear up until she found herself erect, looming over them. She braced her hands on the desk. "You can't kick her out!"

Ms. Purnell said, "Oh yes we can and we will!"

"No you can't because I'm pulling her out! If my daughter's not good enough for you, she can go to another school and graduate!" Annie spun on her heels and stormed out of the office.

FIVE

ANNIE PLOPPED INTO the front seat of her car. The queasy quagmire in her gut was deeply regretting her impulsive reaction to pull Cara out of school.

Cara slipped silently into the passenger seat.

"We'll find another school." Annie wrenched on the steering wheel to turn left onto Route 15 towards Mapleville.

"Okay," said Cara woodenly.

Okay? That's it? "And," said Annie, "you are so grounded."

"Okay."

"That means no going out, no TV, no internet."

"Okay."

As if they were on opposite ends of a teeter-totter, Annie's voice escalated in direct proportion to Cara's impassiveness. "No phones. No friends. No boyfriend."

"Okay."

"What is wrong with you, Cara? Nothing about this is okay. Don't you understand? You are grounded for—" with a final burst of frustration Annie shot out, "forever!"

Cara's lips formed on "O," but she caught herself before the "kay" came out. She drew her lips closed with an invisible drawstring.

Annie would have appreciated the sudden silence in the car, except there wasn't any. The air around them reverberated with noise.

Was that a police siren wailing? In the rearview mirror Annie saw flashing blue lights on top of the car directly behind her. She checked her speed. "Crap!"

Annie pulled over to the side of the road and rolled down her window. She rested her forehead against the steering wheel. *What if one of the moms from the preschool sees me pulled over for speeding?*

"Good morning, ma'am."

She turned her head and saw a huge beige and green uniform hulking next to her car. His chest looked as large and heavy as a refrigerator, making his name badge, Thornberg, shrink to the size of a fridge logo. He cradled his ticket book with one meaty hand and flipped the pages open with a pen, grasped by fingers the size of cigars. This cop could stamp out crime with one fist.

He pointed with his pen toward the red smear on Annie's forehead. "Head injury?"

"Preschool teacher."

He nodded in understanding, as if the two were synonymous. "Know why I stopped you?"

"Um, was I going a little bit fast? ...Sir."

"I clocked you at fifty-one miles an hour in a thirty-five mile an hour zone."

"I'm sorry ... sir," she added again.

"License, registration, and proof of insurance, please."

Duh. Annie lurched towards the glove compartment but the shoulder strap of her seatbelt slammed her back against the seat. "Cara, could you open the glove box and get the insurance and registration?"

Annie pulled her purse onto her lap and extracted her license. Cara pulled out a business-size envelope with Dan's handwriting, all capital block letters reading: REGISTRATION. Annie handed both to the giant who hunched over to peer through the open window.

He asked, "Why aren't you in school, young lady?"

Annie's heartbeat hiccupped. Would Cara actually admit to Officer Thornberg that she had just been busted for doing drugs at school? Was her darling daughter about to get hauled off to jail?

"She's sick," Annie blurted as Cara explained, "I have a dentist appointment."

"What's that?" asked Thornberg.

"Dentist," said Annie while Cara switched to, "I'm sick."

He looked from one to the other. Ping. Pong.

"I picked her up at school for a dentist appointment, but she isn't feeling well, so we decided we better bring her home." Annie nudged the corners of her mouth up, hoping that would pass for a smile.

Thornberg took the envelope and whistled on his way to his cruiser to run their numbers through his Big Brother computer to make sure Annie was speeding through Underhill Center in a car that she hadn't stolen.

"Cara, when he comes back, rub your stomach and moan a little."

"Mom," protested Cara.

"Oh, sure, you can smoke pot at school but can't fake a bellyache? Do you realize how much trouble you're in? This is really going to mess things up. And now a flipping speeding ticket on top of everything else. How am I going to explain this to your father?"

"Explain what? Me or the ticket?"

Annie stared at her daughter. She was so befuddled, she couldn't tell if Cara was being snotty or sincere. She heard the crunch of gravel and glanced in the rearview mirror. "Sh. He's coming back."

"Here you go, ma'am."

"Ugh." Cara uttered a weak groan and pretended to look wan.

"Thank you." Annie obediently accepted her ticket and tucked it in her red-stained pocketbook. She leaned her head out the window to holler, "Sir!" as the giant tromped back to his cruiser.

Instead of harassing a preschool teacher suffering from shock, why isn't he apprehending real criminals like goons in ski masks holding up Cumberland Farms stores, or rapists preying on joggers, or the drug dealers pushing their wares on Cara? Annie maneuvered her steel blue Subaru back onto Route 15 and kept to a slow crawl, quickly accumulating a convoy of cars behind her.

She had raised her kids the Play And Learn Preschool way. Motto: *Education is PALpable.* Foster friendship. Provide a stimulating environment. Keep those hands busy. Ignore the bad as much as possible and focus kids on good choices. Use snacks strategically, as in dog obedience class where you bribe your pet with chips of fake bacon from pouches clipped to your belt.

It worked for Willy, their youngest. He was breezing through fifth grade. Academically, he was golden. His only problem was that the girls were bigger than he was, by eleven inches and forty pounds.

It had worked for Cara, too. Straight-A student, track team, student council, accepted to college. Cara had recently been spending hours on their latest project, the senior prom. Annie's child-rearing methodology of rewarding good behavior with motherly smiles and chocolate chip cookies had worked like a charm, until this morning when Cara senselessly blew it by toking up in the teacher's bathroom. "Honestly Cara, what were you thinking?"

"I'm sorry, Mom. I don't know what I was thinking." Cara turned her head to stare out the window.

The silence was weird, but Annie couldn't think of anything to say, which was weirder. Normally she would ask about the prom committee, but now that Cara couldn't go, that would rub salt in the wound. Normally Cara would fill her in about her friends or her weekend plans or how many miles she had run that day, but now she was grounded. Without school as a home base, there was nothing left to talk about.

Annie slumped as if all the air had been sucked out of her body. Her arms barely had the strength to navigate the steering wheel. She had no energy left for yelling at Cara. It was Dan's turn.

She poked the radio dial on for some uplifting music. But instead of a soothing sonata, it was VPR Classical's periodic news update: "California passed the Reproductive FACT Act requiring pregnancy shelters to inform patients of all their options, including abortion. Religious rights organizations vow to challenge this legislation in court, claiming it violates their freedom of spee—" Annie jabbed the dial off and they continued home in thick and sticky silence.

SIX

At the house, Annie waited until Cara trundled up to her bedroom, out of earshot, before she picked up the phone to call Dan. She punched in his number and put the phone to her ear.

"Hello. International Security Support. Dan Mulligan speaking."

Annie's knees buckled when she heard Dan's voice: deep, strong, masculine. He would know what to do. He could fix companies' software issues and the washing machine and the fuse when it blew. He could solve this problem. "It's Annie." This was followed by a blip of a sob.

"Is everything okay? Are you hurt?"

Annie gulped. "No, we're not hurt. But Cara got kicked out of school today for smoking pot in the bathroom."

"What?"

"They caught her with a joint in the teacher's bathroom," said Annie.

"You shitting me?"

"I wish."

"What the hell is Cara doing with pot?"

"I don't know!"

"Where is she now?"

"She's upstairs in her room."

"Okay, let's calm down. You sit tight and hold down the fort. I'm in the middle of scheduling some face time with my upper level. After I hear back from him, I'll head right home and together we'll go to Camels Hump and talk them into re-enrolling Cara."

Dan paused for a response but only heard a sniffle. "Annie? You okay?"

"Um." Annie wondered if she should tell him about withdrawing Cara.

"I'll get there as soon as I can. Don't do anything cra—well, just don't do *anything* until I get home."

Annie opted not to tell him about her rash, regrettable reaction to yank Cara out of school. He had enough on his plate. And she figured, for *his* sake, she should keep her speeding ticket to herself as well. "Okay."

Cara heard her mother pacing the floor downstairs. No doubt she had the phone in hand to call her dad. They would discuss her and wonder where the hell they went wrong and totally freak out about her. Cara ached to rush down and explain that there was nothing wrong with her, aside from her sick belly for getting kicked out of school.

She wished she could reassure her mother that no, she wasn't a stoner, the weed wasn't hers, it was Olivia's, but she couldn't rat out her best friend. Now that she was pregnant, Olivia needed all the help she could get. As soon as school got out, she would call Olivia and somehow they would figure out how to get her un-expelled without giving away the secret.

Cara slapped Olivia's bag onto her bed. Stupid backpack with its blue and purple butterflies. There was a vapid saying scrolled across it in silver glitter: "Just when the caterpillar thought the world was over, she became a butterfly." *Glitter.* Getting kicked out was humiliating enough. But then she had to slink out the front double doors escorted by the pernicious Purnell, her mom with a red blotch on her face, and a purple plastic butterfly bag on her back.

The only reason Olivia even used such a babyish backpack was because Nate won it by shooting plastic yellow duckies at the Champlain Valley Fair last year. So it was sweet when Olivia toted it around at school. Way dorky for Cara.

She ripped open all the zippers and fished through the compartments to make sure it didn't have Olivia's cell phone. Or any food that would rot. She pulled out Olivia's dog-eared paperback copy of *The Scarlet Letter*. She also found a comb, packet of bobby pins, hairnet, elastics, a fruit and nut bar, lip gloss, pens, and a sticky note: "Pick up Nelson, 4:30." Her fingers felt something dry and oddly squishy. She extracted not one, but two pairs of convertible ballet tights, rolled into tidy balls.

Would Olivia have to drop dance? How fast do babies grow? Would the baby bump show at Olivia's ballet recitals and dance team competitions? Leotards are so revealing.

Cara sighed, closed her eyes, and slumped backwards onto her pillow. How could she defend herself *and* keep Olivia's secret? Whose future was more screwed? Her bestie's or her own?

Annie slapped butter on bread. She sliced squares of cheese from the brick of Cabot cheddar. She twisted the knob on the stove to medium-low and assembled the grilled cheese sandwiches in the frying pan. She put a spoonful of salsa on Cara's before pressing the top piece of bread down on it lightly to weld it together.

How could Cara be smoking pot, without her knowing it? What else was going on under the radar?

Just last night the family had celebrated her acceptance at Cool U. Annie and Dan even gave Cara her own glass of wine. Jeesum crow, if they'd had an inkling that she was messing with recreational drugs, they wouldn't have introduced her to alcohol.

Annie heard sizzling sounds and looked down. She had pressed the sandwich so firmly that salsa seeped out the sides and was bubbling on the pan. She wiped it briskly with a washcloth so the salsa wouldn't get on Dan's grilled cheese.

The dogs barked and scampered over to greet Dan at the kitchen door. Automatically, he lowered his hand to rub Curly's head, then Moe's. But his gaze was trained on Annie. His brilliant blue eyes were a concerned searchlight scanning her face for clues.

"Did you get hurt?" He reached out and tenderly probed Annie's forehead.

"It's paint from the preschool. I forgot to wash it off." She wiped her buttery hands on her apron and hugged Dan.

"It's okay, Annie," he whispered in her hair. "Everything's gonna be okay." He stroked her back.

Her body relaxed, melding into his. Holding on to his sheer bulk was already helping her feel steadier.

"Where's Cara?" he asked.

"I'll get her." Annie went to the bottom of the stairs and called to Cara who slumped silently down the stairs and took her place at the kitchen table while Dan shrugged out of his jacket and slipped off his shoes.

Annie cut the sandwiches crosswise and they sat in their usual chairs. It almost looked like an ordinary dinner, except it was lunch. And Willy was gone, at school where he belonged. And everything was different now.

"Where'd you get the marijuana?" Dan asked.

"Mums," said Cara.

Annie's eyebrows furrowed. What did flowers have to do with this fiasco?

"That's not gonna fly, Cara," Dan said sternly.

Cara wiggled her triangular sandwich. Salsa juice dripped onto her plate in faint pink splatters.

"How long have you been smoking?"

Cara licked the salsa from the hypotenuse of her triangle.

"Who gave you the pot?"

Cara bit one corner and started chewing.

"Cara, I'm talking to you. Where'd you get that shit?"

She looked down at her plate and shook her head.

"Was it John?" asked Dan.

Cara looked up. "No. No, it wasn't John."

"Then who got you started?"

"It wasn't John."

Dan slammed his fist on the table. The pickles bounced on the plates and the plates rattled on the table. Annie grabbed Dan's tumbler of ice water as it wobbled.

"What the hell is going on here, Cara?"

"I have the right to remain silent!"

"This isn't a courtroom, it's a kitchen!"

"It wasn't John!" Cara stood up, stamped her foot, and threw her sandwich down. It bounced off her plate and landed in the salad bowl like an oversized crouton.

Dan turned to Annie with narrowed eyes. "I knew it. It's that dirtbag boyfriend." He dropped his sandwich on his plate. "I'm not hungry. I'll finish this later."

"Me too." Annie set her sandwich down.

Cara plucked her triangle off the salad and dropped it on her plate. She crossed her arms defiantly across her chest.

Dan stood up. "Let's go talk to Mr. Day now."

"Um." Annie remained seated.

"Aren't you coming?"

"Um."

Dan extended his arms, palms up, ready to receive an explanation.

"Before you go, I need to tell you something."

"Yeah?"

"Um." Annie couldn't face them. She squeezed her eyes shut. "So, right before I left the principal's office, I sort of told them I was pulling Cara out of school."

"Mom!"

"Annie!"

She opened her eyes and explained to Dan, "I didn't want them to expel her, so I withdrew her before they could."

"Annie!"

"Mom!"

Annie addressed Cara, "They were going to kick you out anyway. I just beat them to the punch. I didn't want 'expelled' on your record."

"I can't believe you did that!" Cara shouted.

"You realize you screwed this screwup even worse?" Dan tried unsuccessfully to keep his voice restrained.

Annie said, "I'm sorry, it came out before I knew what I was doing."

"Let's go." Dan turned to fetch his jacket.

"Maybe I should stay here with Cara."

"Maybe you don't want to face the principal." Dan spoke over his shoulder, giving Annie a hard look.

Cara said, "Maybe my chances are better if you go alone, Daddy."

"Good point." Dan grabbed his coat off the hook and left.

SEVEN

UPSTAIRS CARA KNOCKED Olivia's backpack onto the floor and flopped onto her bed. She was furious at her mother for withdrawing her without permission. She was miffed at Olivia for lighting up to begin with. She was pissed at Nate for dumping it on his girlfriend. Most of all, Cara was mad at herself.

As for her dad's suspicion that John had turned her on to weed, not hardly. Her boyfriend was obsessed with organic food, lifting weights, running trails, water filters, and air purifiers. No way would he ingest drugs. "You never know what fillers they put in it; the weed could be totally toxic. And don't go near that synthetic crap like Spice. You could go comatose." John wouldn't even eat a non-organic granola bar. Think he would put trash like THC inside his running machine?

At the Essex Cinema after *The Hunger Games* had begun, John insisted they change seats when latecomers reeking of cigarettes parked in front of them. They had fumbled their way over laps and kneecaps, sticking their butts in other spectators' faces on their way to fresher seats. Super awk.

Her parents thought John introduced her to weed? For one, John didn't smoke. For two, she didn't smoke. For three, her parents knew jack shit. For four, it was Nate's shit!

Cara's brain kept replaying the Restroom Disaster. Olivia, pale with desperation, the pregnancy stick glowing, striking the match, the key in the lock, the metallic tumbling of the gears, Cara pushing Olivia into a bathroom stall, turning, Purnell in all her horrified glory, staring at the smoke!

Smoke!

Smoke!

It was like the skip in her Adele CD, which replayed the same angsty note over and over.

How could she be so stupid? All she had to do was flick the joint in the toilet. Then flush!

Flush!

Flush!

Purnell would have chewed her out for being in the teacher's lavatory, Cara would have apologized profusely, and blamed it on that-time-of-the-month and that the bathroom door was inexplicably ajar, and convinced Purnell that she would never make that mistake again, and complimented her while leading her out the door.

In her imagination that's what Cara did. She adroitly flipped the joint in the toilet, kicked the flushing lever, turned, and told Purnell, "Oh, I'm sorry. The *teacher's* restroom? My bad, but it was a feminine emergency. By the way, love your heels. Where'd you get them?"

But even when she revised her memory, the truth intruded.

Joint!

Joint!

Joint!

Purnell's grip. Principal's office. Phone call to mom.

If her dad couldn't talk CHU into letting her back in, she would miss the state track meet. She'd be banned from the prom. She'd be excluded from graduation. No diploma. Which meant no college. Nate wasn't the only one with a great scholarship; she got one too. How could she graduate? How could she become a lawyer if she didn't complete high school?

Olivia's life wasn't over—*her* life was.

Her stomach felt sour. Cara had intended to take the heat for hanging out in the teacher's restroom—not for the joint, which was completely overshadowed by the baby news. She needed to clear this up. Via was her best friend. She would fully understand that they had to come clean. Cara pulled her phone out of her sweatshirt pouch and pressed Olivia's number.

Olivia spoke in a flood of words and relief. "Hey, Cara! I can't believe you did that for me, that was so sweet of you, but I can't let you get in trouble for something I did. I'll come over and explain the weed to your parents, but first you have to make them promise not to tell my parents because if they're riding me and find out I'm you-know-what they'll freak out and then they'll kill Nate and then *his* parents will find out and then—"

"Chill. Everything's going to work out. You can explain it all to my parents tonight, okay?" Cara breathed out a big sigh of relief.

"Sorry, but we have an away game tonight."

"Tomorrow?"

"Oh, I'm so sorry." Olivia's voice was pitched high with apology. "That's our date night. Do you want me to cancel? Of course," she said, answering her own question. "Yeah, I'll tell Nate." Her voice lowered and firmed up. "I'll tell him I can't go tomorrow. Yeah."

"No, it's okay. Go ahead and see Nate tomorrow." Cara could hold off one extra day. "You can tell my parents on Saturday." One day won't make any difference, in fact, it would allow her a day off from school and she could catch up on her homework. She was behind in chemistry and math. "You can pick up your backpack then." Her voice dropped to a whisper. "I forgot. My parents grounded me, so they'll take my phone away as soon as they think of it, so don't text me anything incriminating. Know what I'm saying?" She glanced around her bedroom as if searching for a wiretap. "We'll have to figure out a way to talk in case they snag my cell before Saturday."

"Okay. Hey, there's the bell. Algebra. Sorry, I gotta go."

"Okay, bye."

Cara stared at her phone. Her lifeline to friends. She skimmed through the texts and deleted everything from Olivia. Then she checked John's. His texts were terse. "Run?" "2nite?" "Study together?" The running dude emoji. Cara clicked delete and her phone inquired, "Delete All?" That's when she hesitated. If her parents thought John was leading her astray, then they wouldn't be snooping around suspecting Olivia. That would give her wiggle room until the weekend.

Cara hit cancel, leaving all of John's texts on her phone. She pulled her algebra 2 book out of her beat up backpack and flipped to chapter thirteen, complex numbers.

Olivia will clear everything up on Saturday. Only one more day of laying low and lying, then everything will get back to normal. By Monday morning, she'd be back in school where she belonged. Problem solved.

Cara refocused her attention on her math.

"We can solve equations that involve the square roots of negative numbers by utilizing the imaginary number 'i.'"

EIGHT

WHILE DAN WENT to negotiate with Mr. Day, Annie cleaned the kitchen by stress-eating all three leftover grilled cheese sandwiches. This is why she had trouble reaching her ideal weight; she was too tidy.

But her worry increased when Dan was gone for over an hour. CHU was only ten minutes away. How long does it take to apologize for your daughter's behavior (and your wife's), then persuade a school to allow an honor student back in?

Dan called around two o'clock.

"How'd it go with Mr. Day?" Annie asked.

"Couldn't get him to budge. Kept talking about a kid named Callum and a freshman named Trevor and that asinine ZDZD ruling. You go talk to him."

"Me?"

"I'm working on an important project here. I can't afford any more time off."

"What if I just mess it up even more?"

"How can this get worse?"

The Mulligans shared a brief and intense discussion about who had more free time versus who was better qualified to talk to the principal.

Annie lost the debate. The congealed cheese sandwiches battled her stomach acid, making her queasy. She sighed and shouldered her purse.

Annie slumped back down in the principal's office. She humbly withdrew her withdrawal, and Mr. Day accepted it matter-of-factly, but Cara remained expelled. Despite treating him to all her preschool redirection tricks and her cheerleading enthusiasm as well as her substantial personal charm, Annie got nowhere. She was a cog in the machinery of school boards and drug safety goals. Mr. Day clung to ZDZD like his pension depended on it. Rules are rules.

"What'll we do?" It spilled out in a horrified whisper, sounding rhetorical, but it was a genuine question.

The principal swiveled in his office chair and scooched over to a filing cabinet. He rifled through folders and held one up. "Here it is. A list of—" he paused, "—alternative schools." He extracted a sheet and passed it to Annie.

She stared at the list. She flipped the paper over to look on the other side. It was blank. "Are any of these schools in Vermont?"

"No, Vermont doesn't have any of these facilities."

Facility? Annie winced. "We weren't planning on sending Cara out of state."

"I'm sorry." Mr. Day spread his hands apart expansively. "But rules are—"

"Rules," Annie chimed in. "Look," she whispered to the smooth gray desk top. "Cara is a good student. I don't know what happened this morning, but it is totally uncharacteristic of her. Isn't there anything else we can do to ensure she graduates on time?"

"The only other choice is to homeschool," said Mr. Day in a voice dripping with skepticism. Like, sure, you could, but who would want to? Like you could just say "No" when the oral surgeon offers anesthesia for your root canal. But who would be crazy enough to do that?

"Home ... school?" repeated Annie, stumbling over the words as if they were in a foreign language, like Finnish.

That evening Annie ordered pizza for dinner and asked Cara to bring Willy to go pick it up. She needed to talk to Dan privately.

"We can't enroll Cara in another school. This afternoon I called five schools and they all said no, it's too late in the year for a senior to transfer. In order for Cara to go to college, our only option left is to homeschool the rest of high school."

"How the hell do you homeschool?"

"You know, you just ... you teach her at home."

"Like she could graduate from here?" Dan swept his arms out, incredulous that his living room could be the scene of an academic classroom. The room had a brown overstuffed sofa flanked by floor lamps. Kitty-corner to the couch was the matching loveseat on one side, TV on the other, and in the middle was their old chipped coffee table, which still had yellowed rings, caused from sweating beer bottles the night they unexpectedly conceived Willy.

"Sure. People do it all the time."

"Like who?"

Annie cocked her head as if listening for an answer.

Dan frowned. "Name one family that homeschools."

"The Pendergrasts!" As soon as the name shot out of her mouth, she cringed. Dan recoiled in horror as well.

"Homeschooling Cara for three months doesn't mean we have to turn into weirdos," Annie placated Dan in a let's-calm-down-and-be-reasonable voice. "Regular people like us homeschool, too. Mr. Day suggested it. What the heck, I teach every day, I could do it here just as easily as at the preschool."

"But that's just ABCs and potty-training."

"No it's not and you know it!" Annie jumped off her stool with such force she knocked it over. "The kids need to be toilet-trained *before* they're accepted into our school." It was maddening that after all these years, people, including her own husband, continued to consider her no better than a babysitter. She planted her fists on her hips and yelled, "And we teach way more than the alphabet! We do numbers and colors and days of the week!"

Dan looked at her blankly.

Annie paused. To buy time, she bent over to pick up the stool. So maybe the *Sunday, Monday, Tuesday* song wasn't the best preparation for tackling high school algebra. Maybe she shouldn't have mentioned coloring. She lowered her voice to mask its brittleness. "Remember, I majored in education. I've been teaching for fifteen years. I could teach Cara, no problem."

"What about science?"

Ouch. Dan knew her weak spot. Then inspiration struck Annie. "Simple. *You* teach science."

"Me? I've got a job already!"

"So do I!"

Why were they shouting at each other? This was all wrong. They should be yelling at Cara, as soon as she arrived home with the pizza.

Annie blew out a long breath. "Dan, we can do this. It would be like helping her with her homework, except first you tell her what the homework is, and then you make her do it."

Dan shook his head, unconvinced.

Annie looked him squarely in the eye. "We've got to do this. If she doesn't graduate, then she can't go to college and she'll never get a decent job. She'll wind up flipping burgers at McDonalds for life."

During dinner Dan and Annie told Willy that Cara was going to be homeschooled.

"Why?"

Cara hung her head a fraction lower.

Before dinner Annie had pointed out to her that the less Willy knew about the mishap at school the better. Cara was quite amenable to the notion of keeping that under wraps. Apparently Annie's brief lecture about how Cara was supposed to be a good role model for Willy had been highly effective.

Annie was also determined to appeal to the school board and Cara had readily agreed to keep up with her classes until CHU took her back. In fact, she had been surprisingly compliant considering her recent shenanigans. Cara had nodded her head emphatically and promised sincerely she would do whatever it took to get back to school, the sooner the better.

Now Dan turned to Annie who had rehearsed their story. She explained to Willy nonchalantly, "Cara's had so much pressure filling out college applications and writing college essays and working on the student council and prom ... she needs a break from CHU."

"Can I homeschool, too?"

"No!" Annie's voice was louder than she intended. Willy's eyebrows puckered in alarm.

Cara picked up her head to scrutinize him, as if wondering why anyone would *want* to homeschool.

Dan rested a hand on Willy's shoulder. "It's like an experiment in education. We're not sure how well it'll work out."

Annie slitted her eyes in Dan's direction while Cara slid another inch lower in her chair.

"You stay at Chittenden Middle School where you're sure to get a good education. Besides," he informed Willy as he ruffled his hair, "you love school."

NINE

ANNIE CLOSED THE lid on the white plastic garbage bin. It was Friday afternoon. She had rushed home after work to sniff the air and inspect all their wastebaskets for drug residue or matches. Nothing so far. Annie worked in a safety bubble of preschoolers. As for Dan, well, security clearance was so tight at ISS that he couldn't even afford to spill beer on his polo shirt. Any whiff of recreational use at work and he'd have to pee in a cup, pronto.

Cara maintained she'd done nothing but stay home and study all day, but can you believe the word of a seventeen-year-old who suddenly starts smoking at school with no warning? Thank goodness tomorrow was Saturday so Annie could try a new recipe while surreptitiously monitoring Cara all day long.

Grimly, Annie eyed her daughter who was sprawled on the living room sofa with a humongous textbook in her lap. "What did you learn today?" Annie asked, angling for an apology for disrupting their entire lives by acting out at school yesterday.

"History. This chapter talks about the Fugitive Slave Act of 1850, which forced abolitionists in free states to return runaway slaves to the slave states. It was bad enough to have slavery in the South, now other states were being forced to enable it. Vermont said no freaking way. Within two months, we passed the Habeas Corpus Law, which ordered law officials to *assist* runaway slaves, rather than return them. Good for Vermont. I mean, seriously? Why should other states tell us what to do, right?"

"Right." *Was this homeschooling?*

"Especially when they're so wrong."

"Right." Through the front window Annie noticed a figure walking down the sidewalk. "Wendy's here."

Cara rolled up from the sofa. "I'll do my homework in my room." She took the stairs two at a time.

Annie pressed her fingertips against her temples. She rubbed hard, as if massaging her skull would solve her problems. Wendy Weinstein was a great friend for going to the movies, carpooling, or if you needed advice about a strange rash making your nether regions itchy. But a crisis like your child getting thrown out of school for smoking pot? Annie didn't want to talk to Wendy. She was a shrink.

Knock. Knock. "Hellooo?"

Annie could hear the greeting muffled by the door.

Wendy had emotional radar and only lived four houses down the road; she'd find out soon enough anyway. Annie let out her breath and opened the kitchen door. Wendy breezed in, ruffles fluttering, scarf trailing behind her, lavender wafting around her like an aura. "My afternoon client canceled," she announced gaily.

The golden retrievers circled and sniffed Wendy in short-lived excitement before curling back onto the living room rug.

"Tea?" asked Annie holding the kettle up.

"I'd love some. Do you have any green or white tea?"

"How about chamomile?"

"That'd be brilliant." Ever since Wendy counseled the Boyles from Ireland, she'd been overusing the word "brilliant." Sometimes she pronounced it with a British accent, head held high, eyes batting, as if she were a character in a BBC series.

Wendy opened the box of tea herself and dropped a bag in the mug proffered by Annie, who tossed an Earl Grey bag into her own cup and flumped onto a stool at the counter to wait for the kettle to whistle. She blew out her breath until her shoulders folded over her deflated lungs.

"I sense some disharmony here," said Wendy. "Everything okay?" She hopped off her stool and started massaging Annie's neck. "Are you getting enough vitamin D? Do you realize that everyone north of the 37th latitude is deficient in vitamin D during the winter? Do you take supplements?"

Annie admitted that no, she wasn't supplementing with vitamin D.

"And what about kefir, how are your little guys coming along?"

Wendy always called the kefir grains "little guys" as if they were alive. Which, actually, they were, according to Wendy. Annie had already killed three batches and felt guilty each time. She was surprised Wendy continued to trust her with another flock of fledgling kefir.

"I'm sorry, Wendy, this is bigger than kefir." Annie sighed. Why fight it—Wendy would eventually winkle it out of her anyway. "Cara was kicked out of school yesterday for smoking an 'illegal substance.' I checked out other schools, but it's too late in the year to enroll her anywhere else and of course she doesn't want to wait a year and graduate with juniors, so now we have to homeschool her."

"You sound upset."

"Of course I'm upset! Last I knew Cara was acing school and now she's expelled and messing around with drugs. How are we going to get her into college?"

"Annie, this sounds like catastrophizing."

"I'm telling you, the guidance counselor found her smoking a joint!"

"Weed?" Wendy paused her massage to give an incredulous shrug, both palms up. "This is Vermont. Everyone smokes."

"Dan and I don't." This was one of Annie's ongoing fears, that there was a party going on and she wasn't invited. In her more honest moments, she admitted that much as she loved cheerleading, part of the reason she had joined the squad was to gain access to parties. She had quickly discovered that by the '80s, the cool girls played soccer and basketball and so she had missed out on the fun raves despite her lusty cheers and zesty cartwheels. "And I didn't know Cara was smoking! And with that stupid new ZDZD regulation, they had to expel her!"

"I thought that was for real drugs?"

"Me too! But pot is still illegal so they have zero tolerance! Zero!"

The teakettle whistled. Wendy gave a gentle squeeze to Annie's shoulders. Annie stood up and vigorously twisted the knob to off. She poured the boiling water into both mugs and flopped back onto her stool. "I just want everything to go back to normal."

Wendy asked kindly, "Do you want me to talk to Cara?"

"Oh, you don't have to do that." Annie waved her arm vaguely. She knew Wendy's children: River and Brooke. River was nineteen, sported a ponytail that he decorated with beads or feathers on special occasions, like when Grace Potter and the Nocturnals played in town. He also had plugs in his earlobes, which were eye-catching, but grotesque and distracting. Annie always wondered if her pinky would fit through the hole.

What if he got impaled by low hanging branches? Meanwhile Brooke had sixteen piercings, one for each year. So if you forgot how old she was, you could count the metal spikes lacing her eyebrows, earlobes, nose, and lips. Her left ankle sported a tattoo that grew higher as inexorably as clematis in summer.

It's not that Wendy never said "no" to her kids. For example, Wendy wouldn't allow a tongue piercing—it could chip a tooth. But Annie was uncertain about trusting Cara with a one-on-one with Wendy. What if they ran off and got matching butterfly tattoos on their shoulders? What if Wendy, to establish rapport, smoked a joint with Cara?

"We can work things out," Annie said. She certainly wasn't like Wendy's clients who had to pay large sums of money to get advice on raising children, to hear Wendy Words such as: Name it to tame it. Feel it to heal it. Blame the shame, not the child.

"I'm just saying," said Wendy stirring a teaspoon of honey into her tea.

"But what about school?" asked Annie. "Think we can really homeschool Cara so she can graduate in time for college?"

"Absolutely. That's very intuitive of you and Dan to avoid making her wait a year, that would disrupt her social support group and her emerging personality. But to homeschool, how enriching! You and Cara will have oodles of time to reconnect. A mother-daughter sabbatical could be just the ticket. You might be surprised at what you learn."

Hello! I'm the teacher, not the student!

"You two can learn together, real things, important stuff. For example, you could join the Elemental Enviros and plant trees. Can you imagine thirty years from now, strolling down Mountainbury Center, gazing at rows of endangered hickories on either side of the street that you and Cara planted together?"

Planting trees is noble.

"Or you could start a business like a bakery and teach Cara something practical. You could call it." Wendy paused and inclined her head upwards, awaiting enlightenment from her muse, who must be British because it came out with an upper crust accent: "Full Again in Mulligan's. You adore pastries."

Of course I love pastries! Everyone does! But if I balloon out from gorging on scrumptious cupcakes all day, how will I pack myself into skinny jeans?

"I envy you," sighed Wendy. "There are so many possibilities."

"What about matching braids and pinafores?" countered Annie. "What's up with that?"

"What's this?"

"Cara says homeschoolers have twelve kids in pigtails and pinafores."

Wendy's laughter tinkled lightly throughout the kitchen. "Not in Vermont. Here the homeschoolers are very eclectic and current. They do sports and drama, start businesses, even take college classes."

"How do you know so much about homeschoolers?"

"Oh, I see quite a few at the office. You'd be surprised."

Annie's eyebrows flipped up to her hairline; she *was* surprised. What was she getting in for? "Are they crazy because they homeschool? Or do they homeschool because they're crazy?"

"Not 'crazy,'" Wendy gave her the eye. "There's a lot of abuse embedded in our culture which can lead to the spiral of trauma and shame. Secrecy is toxic. I provide a safe space for my clients to process their trauma. As they say, 'It takes a village to raise a child' and I'm grateful I can play a role in helping my clients take planful steps to acknowledge their feelings, speak their inner truth, and take responsibility for their actions, including their children's education. Some homeschoolers live right here in Mapleville."

"The Pendergrasts," said Annie. You couldn't peg *them* as normal.

The Pendergrasts lived on the edge of town in a nineteenth century farmhouse flanked on three sides by ugly outbuildings. Rumor was it had served as a commune packed with bongs and bunkmates from 1973 until 1975, when the gaunt and hungry hippies gave up, moved back to New York City, and found real jobs. The compound had changed hands several times (including a brief and unsuccessful stint as a bed and breakfast in the '80s) until the Pendergrasts snapped it up during its latest foreclosure. They built an underground garden, a vertical garden, and a garden on top of the outdated solar panels on the roof. They raised cows, chickens, rabbits, and children.

"I can't divulge who *is* a client, but it doesn't break confidentiality to let you know that I don't counsel the Pendergrasts. Some of the homeschoolers I see decided to educate at home because they want to spend more time with their kids and strengthen family relationships. Other families, like the rock star and trustfunder, travel a lot and don't want their children switching schools over and over. And a few families homeschool because of bullying."

As a psychologist, Wendy earned good money putting a positive spin on family crises, making them sound not only surmountable, but opportunities for growth. Likewise, Wendy made homeschooling look not just doable, but actually enticing. Much better than the principal's insinuation that homeschooling was as pleasurable as a colonoscopy.

Perhaps Wendy was right. Maybe homeschooling would be fun? Annie did enjoy cupcakes. She could use one right now. She sipped her Earl Grey. "Dan agreed to teach science and math."

Wendy nodded her head in approval. "Brilliant."

"You know Wendy, if you like it so much, why don't you homeschool?"

Wendy ran her fingers through her curly hair as if shedding the idea. "Grade my own children? Reduce them to a depersonalizing number? I could *ne-ver.*" She noticed the look on Annie's face. "Oh, but you could. After all, Cara's already an A student. Just give her As. Easy peasy."

The phone rang. Annie checked the caller ID. "It's Dan. I better take it." Annie picked up the phone. "Hey."

"Hey sweetheart. I've got some important news. I've been assigned to Cancun. I leave next week."

TEN

"THEY'RE SHIPPING YOU off to Mexico?" Annie's grip tightened on the phone.

"That's right," said Dan.

"How long?"

"Six weeks."

Annie groaned. "Didn't see that coming."

"Remember they told me to get ready for travel? Just didn't know the assignment would get lined up this soon."

Perched on her stool, Wendy sipped her herbal tea and sighed contentedly. She could afford to drink her chamomile in peace; she didn't have to deal with an expelled teenager and a husband flying out of the country.

Annie asked, "It's not dangerous down there, is it?"

"Nah."

"The news is always reporting some kidnapping. Or gangs beheading people."

"That's Mexico City. Not Cancun."

"Why do you have to leave next week?"

"Because I want to keep my job. Remember OBS?"

Annie resented the Organization of Business Systems ever since Dan got laid off years ago in one of their endless downsize actions. "Listen, Annie, we knew there was a risk of an overseas assignment when I accepted this promotion. You agreed this opportunity was too good to pass up, that we need to bank the extra income for college. With this job market it's either move up or move out."

When Annie hung up the phone she explained to Wendy that International Security Support was sending Dan to Cancun.

"Brilliant! I love Mexican food and music," Wendy gushed. "Ooh, make sure Dan brings back some pottery and jewelry. They're absolutely brilliant with silver down south."

"Mexico?" Annie muttered. "How can Dan help Cara with science and math if he's not here?"

"Hire it out. That's what I did when River was in third grade. He wouldn't go near a pencil and I didn't want him to associate me with homework. So I asked his babysitter to practice handwriting with him and by the end of the year it improved so much, his teacher could read it. Didn't hurt that he had a major crush on her."

"His teacher?"

"His sitter." Wendy glanced at the time on her phone then set her mug in the sink. "Gotta fly. Let me know if you want me to talk to Cara or if you want to brush up on your español!" Wendy gathered up her lavender ruffles and floated out the kitchen door.

Annie walked to the bottom of the staircase and called to her daughter, still hunkered down in her bedroom. "Cara, I need you to research Cancun for me."

"What for?"

"Basic information like where it is exactly, time zone and weather, how far away it is from Vermont." Annie wished she had the time to look it up herself, but she had to fix dinner.

Then Cara asked a question Annie had never heard her daughter ask before. A question her preschoolers never asked. A question that made Annie swell with power and possibility. "Am I getting graded on this?"

Annie had never thought about it that way. But she felt a light bulb turn on above her head. She glowed. *Graded?* "Yes!"

"What subject is this for?" Cara yelled.

Annie pulled up short. Obviously not history or chemistry or algebra. The light bulb flashed again. "Spanish!" Annie shouted.

A long pause ensued.

"But you can write it in English." After all, Annie wanted to read it.

Annie held her breath.

"How many pages?"

Annie's arm did a long slow lever pull in the air. Jackpot! She had her. Now she'd let her off easy. "Just two pages. That's all."

No response. No argument. No snappy comeback.

I don't know why Wendy is so anti-grading. This works better than goldfish crackers with preschoolers.

❖

That night when they sat down to dinner, Cara broke her code of silence to ask Willy, "What happened to your face?"

"Nothing. Just a scrape," Willy answered. "Gym class."

Annie leaned close to scrutinize the red welt marring Willy's face, which was pudgy in an adorable, waiting-for-a-growth-spurt way. "I'll get a Band-Aid."

Willy pulled his head in the opposite direction. "I'm okay."

"Well, kids, I have an important announcement." Dan set his knife and fork down and paused to let the suspense build. "ISS is assigning me to Cancun."

"Awesome," said Willy. "Where's that?"

"Mexico."

Cara flicked her gaze toward Annie. "Is this what that Cancun research paper was about?"

"What's wrong with learning more about the place where your dad will be stationed for the next six weeks? You two can practice Spanish together."

"Sí, sí!" said Dan.

Cara silently put her head in one hand and with her other hand practiced stirring her chili in slow circles. Or was she spelling "No, no" with her fork?

Annie sighed, remembering the good ole days when Cara used to talk. Like three days ago. Cara would chat about her lovely friend Olivia Towne, the A+ student and dance team captain who was applying to top schools like Yale and Columbia. Cara used to joke and laugh with Dan while going over her chemistry homework with him. And, Annie's favorite, Cara would happily keep her up-to-date on the status of the prom decorations. Annie shook her head sorrowfully. Unless the school gave them an exception to ZDZD, Cara wouldn't even be able to attend the prom she had lavished so much time on.

"Mexico! That's where monarch butterflies migrate every winter to hibernate!" said Willy.

Bugs weren't as fun as matching up prom couples, but at least Willy was still talking to them.

ELEVEN

EVERYONE ELSE HAD finished their meal and moved on to their laptops but Cara wasn't hungry, like at all. She looked down at her plate and discovered she had carved an infinity sign in her half-eaten chili. She sighed, scraped the leftovers into the garbage, rinsed her plate, lined it up in the dishwasher and announced, "I'll be in my room, doing homework." Her parents gave an automatic goodnight without looking up from their computers.

Upstairs, she lugged her backpack to her bed and extricated her history text. It had only been one day in exile, but already felt like she'd missed a month of school. She couldn't wait for Olivia to come by and set the story straight tomorrow.

Bleep!

Cara snatched her phone quickly before her parents heard and realized they forgot to confiscate it. They didn't know the first rule of grounding—take away cell phone privileges. Duh.

The text was from John. "Let's talk."

Most students complained about track practices, but John and Cara both enjoyed them. In fact, Cara already missed her daily runner's high. Maybe she could sneak in an early run with John tomorrow morning when her parents were busy packing for her dad's trip to Mexico. Or wait until after Olivia spilled all, then Cara and John could meet at the village green and do their customary five-mile loop up Dairy Lane and down Cheesefactory Road.

They had both run track since freshmen, but didn't link up until junior year. It had been a late October afternoon, with a blue sky and air as crisp as the crunch of apples. The lacrosse game had finished and Olivia drove off with a triumphant and sweaty Nate. The other spectators had scattered off to their rides. But Cara hadn't felt ready to head back home. She wandered into the woodsy area past the grassy knoll behind the field and plugged her earbuds in. She had downloaded Ed Sheeran's songs on her iPod and was listening to "Small Bump" when John came pounding down the cross country path.

They were both startled to see each other. Cara politely stepped to the side, into the brush and overgrowth, bending her head to avoid poky pine branches.

"Hey Cara." He smiled. John had sandy hair and sandy freckles and sand-colored hairy legs.

Cara took one of her snail-shaped speakers out of her ear. "Hey."

"What you listening to?"

"*Plus.*"

"Sheeran's the best."

As easy as that, they connected. Not only did they share music and workouts, Cara found it highly convenient to have a boyfriend, because then she could double date with Olivia and Nate. After two years she was overdone being their third wheel. And she was desperate to erase the memory of Nate at homecoming.

Now Cara clutched her phone, wondering how to break the news to John about yesterday's Restroom Disaster without giving away Olivia's secret. She squished herself into her closet and shut the door before tapping John's number.

"Cara?"

"Hey. What's up?" she whispered.

"I've been thinking ... about us ..."

Me too.

"Our senior year ... my last chance at the state championship ... graduation ... And I'll be super busy training this spring so I won't have a lot of time to hang out ..."

Cara's mouth dropped open.

John cleared his throat with a scratchy galumph. "So I thought it made sense for us to get some space and concentrate on—"

"Space?"

"You know ... from each other. So we can finish up the year strong before we go off to college."

Cara let the dead air grow between them. The silence stretched on, like a horror movie right before the axe-wielding psychopath strikes the innocent teenage girl three months before her graduation.

"Cara? You there? Can you hear me? Whacked cell phone. Did I lose reception?"

"You heard I got kicked out of school yesterday, didn't you?"

"Smoking shit in the teachers' bathroom? What's up with that?"

Cara was so pissed she couldn't speak. She jabbed end call. She kicked her closet door. "Ouch!" She grabbed her toe.

Cara limped out of the closet and hopped to her bed. She pounded her pillow with her fists. *Bam!* He just jumped to conclusions. *Bam!* He didn't even give her the benefit of the doubt. *Bam!* After this weekend he would learn she was clean and he would feel like a total tool for dumping her.

She wondered if John wasn't such a keen Sheeran fan after all. They never did go to that concert he alluded to. Also, he had a suspiciously high number of One Direction songs on his iPod. Maybe he synched his running stride to the tempo and ignored the lyrics, but still, it was definitely a girlie band.

Bam!

TWELVE

On Friday evening as Annie buttoned up her flannel pajama top, Dan hugged her from behind and nuzzled her neck. "How's Mimi?" he asked, calling her by one of her pet names. He brushed his lips lightly over her earlobe.

Her daughter was caught with pot and kicked out of school months before graduation and now college was on the line.

Dan's kisses shifted from Annie's ear to her shoulder.

He wants romance? Dan was about to zoom to 90-degree weather where he could lounge on the beach next to a turquoise-colored ocean during his lunch break. And she was stuck teaching a recalcitrant teen in snowy Vermont after a day of herding three and four-year-olds. How could such an intelligent guy be so flipping clueless? Annie was definitely in a mood. Just not the kind of mood Dan was hankering for.

"Not tonight." Annie whisked her head away and swept off to the bathroom to brush her teeth.

Early the next morning Dan went to Desso's Country Store and bought new batteries for the smoke alarms. When he returned he methodically installed them, beginning in the kitchen, while Annie plied him with questions. "Where are you staying?"

"La Buena Vida Hotel. I sent you a link."

"Is your passport all up to date?"

"Yup."

"Do you need any shots?"

"I'm all set. Remember ISS told me last month to get ready, just in case."

"Are we forgetting something? Anything?"

"I'll be fine. People travel all the time, Annie." He smiled at her and gave her a reassuring peck on the cheek. "I'll be back before you know it." He stepped on a chair and unscrewed another smoke alarm from the ceiling. Annie handed him a fresh battery. He told her, "Check out the list I taped next to the phone."

Annie read the list of phone contacts out loud: Dr. Tyler, the plumber, the car mechanic, the electrician, and Steve—the neighbor who plowed their driveway when they went on vacation.

"See? I thought of everything," said Dan. "It's only six weeks."

The doorbell rang and Annie headed to the living room. Before she reached the front door, she saw Cara galloping down the stairs as if her room was ablaze. Cara yanked the door wide open, shouting "Olivia!" as if she knew it would be her best friend standing there.

"Hey, Cara. Hey, Mrs. Mulligan."

"Hello," said Annie, stepping aside to usher her in. "Come on in."

"Thanks." Olivia glided onto the threshold and paused. At the foot of the stairs was Cara's purple backpack. It looked like it belonged to one of Annie's preschoolers, covered with loopy butterflies, as if the psychedelic Flower Power graphics from the '70s had reemerged, gaudy as ever.

Annie took another step backwards, but Olivia didn't advance further, she kept one hand on the doorknob, as if it were a barre. She swayed lightly from one foot to another. Her filmy cream-colored skirt wafted gently against her brown leggings. Every move she made looked graceful. Susan had been taking Olivia to ballet ever since she outgrew diapers.

"I don't know if Cara told you," Olivia's head was tilted down, but she lifted her gaze uncertainly in Cara's direction. Cara shook her head no slightly.

Good, thought Annie, at least Cara is remorseful. "Yes," said Annie. "We know all about it."

"Oh," Olivia let out a breath as if she'd been underwater for five minutes. "Good. So you already know all about the weed at school?"

Cara shook her head no, more vigorously.

Susan's daughter looked like she just floated off a *Swan Lake* stage, whereas her own daughter looked like a bobblehead on the dashboard of a jalopy clomping down an unpaved road during mud season.

"Yes," Annie assured her. "We already spoke with Principal Day."

"Really?" Olivia's smile was lovely. The girl looked lighter than air. Slip fairy wings on her shoulders and she could play Tinkerbell without using a flying harness.

"But could you do me a favor?" Annie asked. "Please don't tell your mother. Not yet."

Olivia nodded her head eagerly. "Sure thing. Not yet."

"We want to sort things out on our end first. We're hoping that Camels Hump will reconsider—"

BLAT! BLAT! BLAT! BLAT! BLAT!

"Just testing!" yelled Dan.

Annie rushed back to the kitchen to help. Dan dismantled the smoke alarm. "Sorry about the noise. Wanted to test them."

Annie brought a plate of snickerdoodles to the living room to offer Olivia, but she had already exited, stage left, her lacy skirt swishing. Still shaking her head, Cara stared out the window, watching her friend flounce off.

"Isn't that your new backpack?" asked Annie. Olivia was tossing it into the back seat of her car.

"It's hers. I was just borrowing it."

"Why?" It was the tackiest backpack Annie had ever seen. And she worked in a preschool.

"I don't know." Cara braced her forehead against the window. "I don't know why."

Teens were so weird and dramatic. Annie squeezed Cara's shoulder supportively and held the tray out. "Would you like a cookie?"

"No thanks."

Annie picked one up and began munching. She had added extra cinnamon and it was scrumptious. She watched Olivia drive away from the curb. "Has she heard back from Columbia yet?"

"Not yet. But she'll get accepted. She's got the grades, AP classes, captain of dance team, that clinic she interned for, she's got ... she's got everything."

"Wait a minute." Annie smacked her hand to her head. "You're grounded! Olivia's not even supposed to be here. Jeesum crow, and I let her in and all."

"It's okay, Mom. She's gone now." Cara pivoted and ascended the stairs, non-galloping, as if trudging upstairs to face her own funeral pyre.

Cara flopped backwards onto her bed, stifling a groan. Olivia had totally bombed that confession, grabbed her bag, and left before she could explain. But Cara's snarly frustration with her friend was matched by a tangle of guilt. She knew what it was like to muff it big time. Even though it happened over a year ago, Cara felt her face flush prickly-hot as she recalled the memory.

In fall of their junior year, Olivia had been feverish and clogged with a cold and couldn't make it to the homecoming celebration. Cara had hitched a ride to the bonfire that night with Danielle, who soon paired off with her boyfriend, leaving Cara to small talk her way in the dark around the fiery blaze at the edge of the football field.

When she found Nate he gave her an enthusiastic greeting and a sloppy hug, instantly raising her status among his buddies. Cara latched on, relieved to have a group to hang out with. Already tanked, Nate did most of the talking and soon, craving another brew, he wrapped his arm around her shoulders and steered her to his truck in the far corner of the parking lot and climbed in. After checking all directions for an adult, he snapped open a can and gentlemanly handed it to Cara before popping another for himself. She didn't like beer to begin with, and this was a Budweiser. But still, no one says no to Nate. She tipped the can up and swigged it, ignoring the aluminum-malted taste.

She asked about lacrosse and gave Nate ideas about fun dates to take Olivia on and what to do for her birthday. Cara suggested surprising her with horseback riding and Nate called it a baller idea, although maybe that was the beer talking.

Away from the bonfire, the damp Vermont chill had seeped up Cara's back and shoulders and she shivered on the truck's cold seat. Nate pulled her close and flopped his arm around her shoulders. He felt like a big brother, generously sharing his expansive warmth and Cara leaned in to him gratefully. They joked about what if a stray chaperone discovered them with alcohol? They heard something in the woods skirting the parking lot ... wind whistling through leaves? Or a coy dog? Bear? Laughing, they swapped synopses of the worst horror movies they had ever seen. But really, they felt safe and removed in the Chevy and the black night enveloped them in a screen of safety.

All their little noises felt loud in the quiet truck. His breathing, the creaking of the leather seat, the liquid sounds of Nate's sips, rustling crinkles of the jacket as they moved their arms, the swish of his sleeve against hers. The velvet darkness surrounding the vehicle invited confidences. Nate got slurrily sentimental telling her about losing his dad when he was nine. Heart attack. Cara had known his father was gone, but didn't know it happened so suddenly or when Nate was so young, and she murmured a heartfelt, "Sorry," and she, in turn, wanted to tell a story of loss, but all she could come up with was Larry, her golden retriever, getting hit by a car, which paled compared to losing a dad, but it was the best she had, and he said, "sorry," and Cara was surprised to feel tears swell in her eyes; she hadn't realized grief was still lurking underneath, and then, (did he forget it was Cara and not Olivia?), then he had turned his head, and Cara didn't turn away, but surprised and curious, she turned her face up to his questioningly, and then his lips leaned in to hers.

And now curled up on her bed, Cara cringed, scrunched into a ball, remembering that she had let him use tongue ... a slow, swollen slug exploring her mouth. Ugh.

Cara had pulled away and scooched to the passenger side, pressing against the frigid door, her arms wrapped around herself, belatedly protecting herself from the cold. Nate had brushed it off, with a slurpy laugh and helpless, careless happy-drunk question, "The fuck?" as if *she* had been the one who came on to him.

Everything about that kiss had been jank, ratchet, and shady. It had tasted of beer and smelled of hot breath and felt prickly from midnight stubble and it poisoned the whispered revelations and closeness they had just shared. Worst of all, it had been a monstrous betrayal and all Cara could see the rest of the night, as she miserably circled the bonfire searching the dark for Danielle to beg her to drive her home, was Olivia, in her soft pink jammies, on the sofa in her living room, surrounded by tissues and hot tea, watching a rom-com and trusting, never-suspecting, her best friend.

THIRTEEN

IN THE CHURCH hall after Mass, Susan bustled over with a doughnut and coffee. Annie tried to make a run for the Ladies Room, but Susan was quicker. "Hello, Annie!" she intercepted. "How are you?"

"Good."

Susan tilted her head and peered kindly at her. "And how is Cara doing?"

Annie's shoulders drooped. Just yesterday Olivia had promised not to tell her mother.

Susan continued, "When I heard Ms. Purnell talk about catching a student with pot, Cara was the last one I suspected." Of course Susan already knew about the joint; she was an administrative assistant at CHU.

"Yeah, surprised us too." Annie was still shocked that Cara was expelled for smoking. She wished she could believe her daughter when she denied taking more than one toke.

"So what are you going to do?"

"We're going to homeschool so she can start college this fall."

Susan's eyebrows lifted, paused, hovered near her hairline, searching futilely for a polite response.

Annie gazed around the room and saw Olivia pick up an apple cider doughnut, wrinkle her nose, and set the confection back on her plate, unbitten. No wonder the girl had such a nice figure. She could say no to sweets. Apparently she could just say no to drugs, too; after all, *she* wasn't expelled from CHU. Maybe Olivia would be a good influence on Cara? Should Annie bend the grounding rules and allow Cara to hang out with her? Cara and Olivia were best friends and if she permitted this, perhaps Cara would rustle up a healthier outlook on drugs? She had been unexpectedly cooperative about not being allowed to see her boyfriend.

"How about Olivia?" Annie asked Susan. "Has she heard from Yale or Columbia yet?"

"Yes—she got accepted at Columbia, *and* she got a scholarship to UVM. Still waiting on Yale. She certainly has a difficult choice ahead of her. A topnotch Ivy or one of the best state universities in the country. Tough decision. I don't envy her."

I do.

Oops, did I say that out loud? Annie peeked at her friend. But Susan was stirring her coffee and gazing at Olivia with the kind of pride and adoration shown only by the mother of a senior headed off to college with a four-year financial aid package that made young parents sign their kids up for preschool while they were still gurgling in their bassinets, batting their arms about, trying to figure out what hands were.

"Anyhoo, I'd love to talk longer," said Annie, "but we really need to get home and get Dan's packing all squared away. He just got assigned to Mexico."

"Let me know if I can help with anything."

Like what, a mac and cheese?

But her mother had always insisted that manners matter. So Annie chirped, "Thanks." She shoved the rest of her doughnut in her mouth, gathered Dan, Cara, and Willy and ushered them to the car.

During dinner, the Mulligans talked about Mexico and beaches and who to call to clear the driveway when it snowed if Steve wasn't available and how delicious the roast beef was and, like a normal family, they never mentioned the words *expulsion, graduation*, or *marijuana*.

That evening Annie took a long bath scented with essential oils that Wendy had given her when she turned forty, a combination of ylang ylang, patchouli, and grapefruit in a tiny pink bottle labeled *Closer!* She slipped into her saucy black teddy and pinched the lock shut on their bedroom door. "Mimi's here to see you, Monsieur," she whispered in a nasal French accent.

"Oui, oui," growled Dan, arms outstretched.

Annie tried to memorize every move, every murmur, every muscle because, let's face it, Dan would be gone for six weeks and so much could happen. The plane's engine could blow, triggering an emergency landing and he could be stuck drifting in a lifeboat to Cuba and get detained by the black hole of communist red tape. Or the Buena Vida hotel could be attacked by one of those drug cartels they keep talking about on the news.

Or Mexico could be split asunder by an earthquake causing Cancun to simply slip into the sea.

She sniffled.

"Ah, my little French minx is going to miss me, non?" Dan asked.

Annie dropped all pretense of an accent. "Tell me everything's going to be fine."

"Everything's going to be fine, Annie. Scout's honor."

Annie felt reassured even though she knew full well he couldn't guarantee that. He had never even made it to Scouts. He quit shortly after Cubs because he didn't want to deal with meetings and badges and selling popcorn and Christmas trees; all he really wanted was to hike mountains and build wicked forts and campfires in the woods. But just hearing Dan say everything would be fine made it feel better.

She fell asleep with Dan's arm wrapped around her waist.

Early Monday morning, Dan said goodbye to Willy. He grabbed his son in his arms and lifted him in a bear hug. Willy's legs dangled, his black chunky sneakers swinging around Dan's ankles. Dan set Willy down and swiped his son's head with a gesture that bordered between a caress and a noogie. Willy grinned and smoothed his hair down.

Annie didn't trust Cara home alone. "Cara, you're coming with us."

Cara clomped her book shut and stood up from the sofa.

Willy asked, "Can I come too?"

"You have to stay here to catch the bus."

Willy hopped from one foot to the other, demanding, "Why can't I come to the airport with you, like Cara? It's not fair that I have to go to school and she doesn't."

"This is only temporary." In a reassuring voice, as if offering to buy a new video game for his son, Dan added, "*You* get to go to a *real* school."

"It's not fair," insisted Willy.

Dan gave Willy a one-armed man-hug and explained, "Sometimes life isn't fair."

Annie and Cara shuttled to the car, while Dan swung his luggage into the way back, one suitcase at a time. As they backed out of the driveway, Cara noted, "There's Willy."

They all waved and shouted goodbye at Willy's small white face watching them from the living room window, shrinking as they drove away.

There were two cars stopped ahead of them at the red light on Williston Road. "Damn traffic," said Dan, trying to lighten the mood.

"Ha, ha," said Annie.

Dan liked to tease her ever since she had complained about the congestion when trying to make a left turn on Route 15 one morning. She had waited for fourteen cars to pass. "You haven't seen traffic 'til you've been in Boston during rush hour," he'd said at the time.

Cara kept quiet the whole ride until after they parked and she offered to wheel in a suitcase. They waited in the check-in line together while Dan received his boarding pass. Then they paused at the security gate. "You can't go any further," Dan said. "We have to say goodbye here."

Dan hugged Cara and said, "You behave yourself now, Care Bear."

"Don't worry, Daddy. I will." And she smiled at him.

Annie did a double take. It had been days since she had seen Cara smile. It was breathtaking.

All too soon, it was Annie's turn. She gave Dan a brief hug then took a step backwards. "You behave *yourself* down there, Mr. Mulligan." He gave her a grin and a wink, then kissed her long and intensely. She sniffed deeply, trying to inhale six weeks' worth of Dan's manly scent to tide her over until she saw him again. He smelled like smart and strong testosterone with a touch of spicy aftershave. Cara stood nearby pretending to read the framed advertisements decorating the cement wall. *8 Ways to Enjoy Winter in Vermont!*

"It's time," said Dan and he stepped into the security line. He set his bag down and took off his shoes. His big toe poked out of a hole in his black sock. With a pang, Annie realized she wouldn't see that toe again until May. She found her eyes suddenly brimming with tears.

Annie waved goodbye, blew Dan a kiss and turned around resolutely.

"Come on, Care. Time to go." Annie trudged down the gray hall plastered with *America's Family Fun Resort!* and *Got Snow?* posters and turned the corner to wait for Cara to catch up.

Buck up, Annie coached herself. *You have to be strong for the kids.*

Cara rounded the corner. Tears streamed down her face.

Annie peeled back strands of brown hair stuck on Cara's wet cheeks and draped her arm around Cara's shoulders. "It's okay, sweetie. He'll be fine. He'll be back before you know it. What can go wrong in six weeks?"

"You don't understand!" Cara jerked away from Annie's embrace. "Everything already *is* wrong!"

FOURTEEN

AFTER BUCKLING HER seatbelt, Annie glanced over at Cara, her cheeks still wet with tears. *What else was wrong?* "You know you can talk to me, right?" Annie said gently.

"Sure."

Annie waited for Cara to spill. After a couple of beats, she encouraged her daughter again, "You can tell me anything."

"Okay."

She waited again, but Cara was stonewalling her. What was she hiding?

Cara used to confide in her. Just last week she had admitted how annoying it was that John sprinted ahead at the tail end of their runs. Annie had commiserated, "Guys hate to lose. Especially to girls!" They had shared a good laugh over obnoxious man pride.

Annie twisted the ignition and the motor rumbled. She didn't know who Cara had become. In Annie's day, the potheads waited until after seventh period ended before wandering out behind the baseball field to congregate in the gully at the edge of the woods, and they had the good sense to post a lookout in case a teacher stumbled upon them. *But suddenly Cara is so addicted she lights up in the teacher's room? Before first period? No sentinel? Not even a friend? Cara is so strung out that she smokes in the morning, alone? What if she calls her dealer and gets a fresh batch of pot and spends the day getting high in her bedroom while I teach preschoolers the "F" letter?* Annie better keep a close watch on her. She decided to bring Cara to work with her, figuring she could help out by refilling paint pots, wiping snotty noses, and wrassling kids into their snowsuits for outside time.

"We'll stop at The Muffin Man, you can get anything you want for breakfast," Annie said, hoping nourishment would cheer up Cara, who sniffled during the entire loop out of the airport parking garage. "Then I'll bring you to work with me."

"Can we stop at the house on the way in so I can get my homework?"

Annie had forgotten about homeschooling. "Good idea." Cara would have plenty of time to do chemistry while the preschoolers had circle time.

PAL was only a few miles away from their house. One more reason why Annie loved her job—a short commute. She hung her coat up on the high peg and hurried in to the schoolroom to search the perimeter. No sign of the molted snake. Hopefully it had squeezed through whatever hole it had snuck in from and slunk back out into the woods where it belonged.

"Cara, we have a couple minutes before the kids arrive. You can study in the kitchen area until they get here."

Bobbie stepped in, whisking cold air in with her. "Hey, Cara. Feeling better?"

Cara glanced at Annie who nodded slightly.

"Yes, Mrs. Andrews, I'm feeling much better, thank you." Cara looked back at Annie who smiled slightly.

Bobbie peered down at the book spread out on the low table Cara huddled over. "What's that? Chemistry?"

"Yeah. The mole."

Bobbie nodded. "Uh huh." She headed to the woodworking table to restock the glue. "Vacation day for Camels Hump High?" she asked.

Cara looked at Annie who shook her head no slightly. "Um, it's not a vacation day exactly ... but I'm taking today off to ..."

"She's working on a special project," Annie intercepted. "The school knows about it. In fact, CHU told her to take this time to work on her Community Service Senior Project."

"Lucky. When I was a kid I would've loved getting out of school to do a special project. To do *anything,* actually," said Bobbie. "What's your project?"

Cara raised her eyebrows and stared at Annie who answered for her. "She's studying ... um ... different forms of education. That's why she's here, in fact, to help out with the preschool and observe how young kids learn."

Bobbie nodded. "You're in the right place. Your mom is a whiz at teaching letters and numbers."

Annie shrugged modestly.

Cara bent her head, scratching something in her notebook while Bobbie replenished the art table with twigs and scrap yarn and filled Annie in on her weekend away at Jay Peak. "The skiing was stellar, but I had no internet. What did I miss?"

Annie's life had totally crapped out since last Thursday. "Nothing," she answered.

They could hear the kids before they saw them. Children popped through the door with excited shrieks, encased in jackets and snow pants, slathered with backpacks, mittens, and hats dangling off their extremities, with their moms trailing behind with younger siblings straddling their hips, lunchboxes and handbags belaying from the opposite arms. Like rock climbers, the babies clung to their mothers with a bond that defied gravity.

Carol Van Horn presented herself to Annie. "I'm the parent helper for today. Go ahead and put me to work."

Carol's hair was in a preppy bob, moussed to perfection. She wore a hunter green sweater, which looked like soft expensive cashmere. Her slacks had creases down the center, as if freshly pressed. Her fair isle socks looked handknit.

"Thank you," said Annie. She glanced around and spotted Carol's son Xander stomping snow in the mudroom. "Would you help Xander take off his snowsuit? We're about to begin."

"Sure." Carol spotted Cara at the table. "Hello, Cara."

"Hello, Mrs. Van Horn."

"Aren't you supposed to be in school?"

"I'm working on a special project."

Suddenly Carol sucked air like a noisy vacuum. "Weren't you—?" She clamped her mouth shut. "Never mind."

Carol went to the entryway. While she ordered Xander to pick his snowsuit up off the floor and hang it on a hook, she pulled her cell phone out of her purse and tapped on it.

Annie gathered the preschoolers in the kitchen area and said, "It's time to check on Carter the caterpillar to see if he has turned into Buddy the butterfly yet. Who can tell us the rule for observing the Butterfly Garden? Yes, Nora?"

"Use your eyes, not your hands!"

"Yes, that's right," Annie whispered. "Let's go."

The kids teeter-tottered on their tippy toes circling around the table where Carter had built his chrysalis in a cardboard box with see-through plastic portholes.

"So soon," Logan chanted the lyrics from the caterpillar song Annie wrote.

"Hurry up!" shouted Cannon.

"Hurry up!" echoed Xander.

"Let's use our inside voices so we don't scare him. Remember Carter is inside the chrysalis. Even though we can't see him, we know he's in there." Annie gave the kids a few more seconds to ooh and aah over Carter and then she ushered them to the window room for circle time. The secret to preschool was to stay one distraction ahead of the kids' attention spans.

The kids scooted over to the rug in the corner, plopping down in a sloppy amoeba-shape officially called "the circle." Xander eyed his mother, took his finger out of his nose, and wandered away toward the kitchen.

"Over here, Xander," Annie beckoned. "Crisscross applesauce." She pointed to an empty spot in the circle and he flopped, legs overlapped. He wedged his finger back up a nostril.

While Bobbie sat on the floor with Nora cuddled in her lap, and Carol swiped her son Xander's nose with a tissue, Annie led the singing. She had a beautiful voice and had considered majoring in music, but in her second year of college in Philadelphia, she decided to go with early education, because after she graduated she would need a job to pay off her student loans.

Annie sang slowly and e-nun-ci-a-ted so the children could keep up:

Caterpillar, caterpillar,
Safe in your cocoon,
Someday you'll be a butterfly,
Come out, come out, so soon!

Thanks to Willy, Annie was fully aware that butterflies actually metamorphose in a *chrysalis,* but *cocoon* was much easier to rhyme with. Plus the kids could pronounce it.

The "caterpillar" was the index finger wiggling up and down. Then the kids wrapped their left hand around their right finger for the cocoon. The trick was the grand finale: switching from the cocoon to the butterfly. Every morning for the past two weeks, Annie had modeled how to hook her thumbs with her hands crossed and facing herself. She fluttered her fingers to make the butterfly flap its wings.

The kids' scrunched fists waved up and down. Cannon linked his pinkies instead of his thumbs. Nora didn't even bother trying to clasp her thumbs; she wrapped her arms around herself and rocked side-to-side, setting Bobbie's boobs swaying in stereo behind her. Xander's butterfly rammed Logan's shoulder. Logan's butterfly swooped out and bopped Xander's. Annie took pity on Carol, who had wedged herself between Logan and Xander's battling butterflies. Kids always acted up most on the days their mothers had to volunteer to be the parent helper.

Carol's hand hijacked Xander's butterfly's flight and pressed it forcefully to a landing on his knee.

Annie smoothly deployed the distraction technique. "Okay, friends, time for a story." She held up the colorful picture book and opened it in front of her chest. She could read these rhymes upside down.

The Snowball was a tall tale about a young scalawag named Jack who sneaks out of the one-room schoolhouse to play in the snow. He makes a snowball the size of his fist, then rolls it down the hill where it grows bigger and bigger until it pounds through the farmer's open barn door, scooping up chickens, pigs, sheep, and cows before it bounces out the door at the opposite end. When the farmer trudges up the hill to ask who started that snowball, the little lad lies because he doesn't want to get in trouble. But when the farmer accuses Becky of making the snowball, Jack musters his courage and fesses up. To Jack's surprise, he is awarded with a badge the size of a dinner plate because he had unwittingly saved all the farmers' animals from an avalanche that flattened the barn after the snowball rolled them out of the way.

The kids reveled in the rambunctious illustrations. The final snowball, the size of a Ferris wheel, dribbled to a stop in the valley. It was studded with pink pig snouts, wooly sheep butts, golden chicken wings, and black and white cow legs sticking out all over it. At the last page Annie paused for a beat and all the preschoolers chimed in as she chanted: "If you are brave like me, the truth will set you free!"

FIFTEEN

ANNIE PICKED UP the next read aloud, *The Three Little Pigs.* She loved fairy tales because it was always ridiculously obvious who the villain was, and the hero always won. As she squealed in her high-pitched piglet voice, "Not by the hairs on my chinny, chin, chin!" the mudroom door opened and Leslie, PAL's school board president, breezed through as if she had blown it open with her breath. Leslie spotted Cara hunched studiously over her books in the kitchen area. Annie noticed Leslie nod to Carol who nodded back. Then Carol quickly averted her face from Annie's.

Leslie asked Bobbie to take over the circle while she spoke with Annie. "It was brought to my attention that you brought your daughter to our preschool today."

"Yes."

"I've also heard that Cara was expelled from CHU for substance abuse? Is that correct?"

Annie's breakfast muffin flip-flopped in her belly. Her answer dragged out reluctantly, "Yeah."

"For the safety of our students, I must ask you to send Cara home."

Annie looked at Cara, bent diligently over her notebook. Annie was afraid to leave her at home. She did that last Friday and then worried all through choice time and circle time. While passing apple slices and ants on a log around the tiny table. While plucking Xander out of the garbage bin. While stuffing Ryder's chubby legs, one at a time, into his spare sweatpants after he peed his pants. While lying flat on her back, having her blood drawn by Nora ... Annie kept picturing Cara, in her bedroom, braced against her headboard, huddled over a bong, stray ashes burning tiny holes in her green and navy plaid flannel duvet cover.

"We're homeschooling Cara," Annie explained to Leslie. "She's working on her chemistry right now."

"If she's homeschooling, shouldn't she be at *home*?"

"The kids are safe. I can supervise Cara here. You know I would never put the students at risk."

"Then you'll cooperate by sending Cara home. *You* are welcome to work here, but we haven't cleared Cara."

"You didn't clear Carol Van Horn, either, but she's helping out with the kids!"

"I'm not going to argue with you. You and Cara are not a package deal. We hired *you* and we want you to continue here. The kids love you, the parents love you, the board … appreciates you. But you have to leave Cara at home."

"Or else?"

"Or else we'll find another teacher."

"I need to work out some logistics. Can I get back to you?"

"Yes, but Cara needs to leave the premises now."

Annie felt her stomach drop. "She can take my car home and then pick me up at three. Okay?"

"For today. In the future we don't expect her on the premises."

"I'll talk to her."

"I'll cover for you while you do."

Cover for me? Humph. Like Leslie knows how to be a preschool teacher.

Leslie sat stiffly cross-legged in the circle while Bobbie continued reading about the big bad wolf who tries to outsmart the pigs. Leslie reached out to pat Nora who scooted away and scrunched closer to her friend JoJo on the right. Carol avoided Annie's gaze.

Annie slid over to Cara, who looked like a giant jammed into the tiny plastic red chair. Her chemistry textbook was spread out on the manila-colored tabletop and she was scribbling mysterious abbreviations in her notebook. Annie leaned over and put her hand on Cara's shoulder. "Hey Care Bear. Good news. You don't have to study here; you can take the car home and do your homework there. Just be sure to pick me up at three. Okay?"

"What about my 'Special Project?'" The corners of Cara's lips inched up a fraction.

"Turns out they're not too thrilled with the idea of you doing a special project on their special kids."

They looked over at Leslie who was trying to drag Cannon onto her lap. He spread eagled his body and refused to bend. *Go Cannon!* Annie cheered mentally.

Annie dangled her car keys over Cara's outstretched hand.

What if Cara drove straight to some sketchy neighborhood and bought an illegal substance from some dude with dirty dreadlocks and vacant eyes and then Cara overdosed? Or what if she got high and got into a car accident and Officer Thornberg nabbed her with a DUI?

The keys jangled above Cara's hand, but Annie didn't let go. She looked over at the kids in the circle. Nora was still self-hugging and swaying, Logan was sucking his thumb, and Xander had his finger back up his nose, digging for treasure. Leslie had given up on snaring a child in her lap; she stood arms akimbo, watching them.

"You can let go, Mom," said Cara.

But Annie's fingers gripped the keys. The preschoolers would be fine. The most they would sniff was Elmer's glue. The closest they got to drugs was a spoonful of children's Benadryl at 7 p.m. when their parents were dying for a good night's sleep. The preschoolers were safe and sound.

Annie looked back at Cara, her beautiful daughter who last week had been planning for the prom, graduation, college, a career ... and now was a homeschooling dropout grounded for the rest of her life.

"Hold on," she told Cara.

Annie slipped over to Leslie and whispered, "I need to take a leave of absence for a couple of weeks."

Leslie folded her arms over her chest. "You can't just take a leave of absence like that."

Annie aped her, crossing her arms defiantly over her chest. "Yes, I can."

"No, you can't."

"Watch me," she whispered fiercely and turned to leave.

Leslie warned quietly, "If you go now, you're fired."

Annie's jaw clenched. She swung around to face her opponent. She would do anything for Cara, absolutely anything. Yet even she was surprised to hear her own response. "Too late. I quit."

Annie marched to the kitchen area and grabbed her coat and Cara's. "Let's go."

Cara scooped up her textbooks and they bolted outside.

In the car Cara asked, "Did I just get kicked out of *pre*school?"

Annie said, "I got kicked out, too. Now we're in the same boat, thanks to you."

"They fired you?"

"Yup." Annie scanned the sides of the road in case Thornberg's patrol car crouched in the woods, waiting.

"I'm sorry about your job, Mom, I really am. But that isn't my fault."

"Yes it is! If you hadn't smoked pot at school and pushed that woman, they wouldn't have fired me!"

"I told you, I didn't push her! If there was any 'assault' it was hers—she grabbed me!"

"And we're supposed to believe you when you've been running around behind our backs, smoking?"

"Mr. Day was looking for a loophole! If you hadn't pissed them off by withdrawing me, they might have given me a short suspension!"

"Seriously? Take it from me, kiddo, life always catches up with you! You think you can break the rules and get away with it?" Cara was dreaming, except this was a big hairy nightmare. "We gave you everything! Why did you blow it?"

There was a pause.

Annie waited, like a volcano building up magma.

Finally, tentatively, Cara asked, "Didn't you ever want to try weed when you were in school?"

"The smell alone gives me a headache! And I'm a singer! Remember your great uncle Howard?"

Cara had heard about this distant relative who passed away before she was born. He had smoked a pack of cigarettes a day, contracted throat cancer, and had his larynx surgically removed. Annie had been four years old when she met him. She had watched curiously as he pressed a small black box to his throat. But when she heard his voice disembodied into the little machine and come out all staticky, as if there were a miniature robot in his neck, "Hello. Nice to meet you, Annie," she had shrieked, darted away, and hid behind the rhododendron bushes edging the garage, sobbing.

Cara's voice sounded utterly discouraged. "Don't worry, Mom, I can't get cancer from one stupid inhale."

This failed to lessen Annie's outrage. But she clamped her lips shut, afraid lava would erupt.

SIXTEEN

AT HOME, CARA shouldered her backpack and trudged upstairs. She belly-flopped onto her bed, opened up her history book, and stared.

In 1857 the Supreme Court ruled against Dred Scott, a slave who had sued for his freedom after his owners had brought him from the South to live in a free state. Chief Justice Taney asserted Scott was still a slave and not entitled to the rights of a US citizen. Furthermore, he ruled that Congress did not have the power to prohibit slavery in the territories. The Court's convoluted reasoning and judicial overreach on a political problem inflamed the North. Far from settling the controversy, the Scott decision drove the wedge deeper between north and south, hastening civil war.

With this perspective, Cara's problems shrank. Homeschooling was nothing compared to the "peculiar institution" of slavery. So what if she was wrongly accused of selling Nate's drugs at school? And as scary as Olivia's situation was, at least she was free. She had equality. She had rights.

Cara realized they couldn't keep Olivia's secret forever. True, her bestie had royally screwed up her first attempt at coming clean—Olivia had readily agreed not to tell her mother, grabbed her backpack, and fled during the smoke alarm, not realizing that when Cara's mom claimed she knew "all about" the weed, she only knew the lies about it, not the truth.

But Olivia had to wear leotards at ballet. Soon the baby bump would show on her size four frame. That would be Olivia's cue to own up to the pregnancy, the weed, and the Restroom Disaster. Cara only had to hold out until then. Before she knew it, she'd be back at school, catching up on news with Olivia and pointedly ghosting John instead of eating lunch with him. Cara could learn on her own until then. She wasn't about to betray her own BFF. Let time be the bad guy. How long could it possibly take for the baby to reveal itself?

And what about Nate, when he finds out? Would he be able to keep his mouth shut?

Maybe.

At least he never ratted her out about the kiss.

Hot shame flooded Cara's face as she recalled that night. A shadowed part of her had wondered if he really did like her—Nate, the popular lacrosse jock! She hated this about herself. Daydreaming about him was traitorous, too. Cara had studied him the following week, afraid he would tell Olivia, and almost, almost but not quite, hoping he would. She hated this too. But he definitely didn't spill. The It Couple was as tight as ever and there wasn't even a blip of tension between Olivia and her.

Maybe Nate had never told because he didn't remember it? He had been completely wasted. She had convinced his friend to pocket Nate's keys and promise to drive him home. Cara quelled her guilt by telling herself she hadn't kissed Olivia's boyfriend, she had smooched Budweiser.

Cara blinked hard and moved on to Abraham Lincoln: "In this great struggle, this form of government and every form of human right is endangered if our enemies succeed."

After she read the same sentence three times, Cara heaved a sigh and slammed her heavy text shut and dropped it on the floor with a thunk. She climbed off her bed, went over to her desk, opened up her laptop, and googled "baby bump." She clicked on Your Baby Week-By-Week and then paused, her middle finger hovering over the choices. Cara took a guess and pressed Week 6. She learned that Olivia's baby had grown from the size of an apple seed to a pea and was about to grow facial features. She might be wiggling her teeny hands and feet right now. Next week she would be blueberry-sized and generating 100 new brain cells per minute.

Cara clicked on "baby photos" and started scrolling. One newborn was lying naked on a white towel placed in an old-fashioned gray washtub with a yellow rubber ducky next to it. She scrolled to an older infant smiling a gummy, toothless smile while her pink bow propped up a nearly invisible fountain of hair. Aw. Twins in footed pajamas clasped each other, one sucking on the other's nose. Double aw. She clicked on a video and saw a baby laughing hysterically because her dad was ripping paper.

She hated to admit it, but Cara was a teeny-tiny, itsy bitsy bit jealous that instead of flat photos on a screen, her best friend was going to have a real baby to cuddle and adore in 3D.

SEVENTEEN

Annie cracked two eggs in a large mixing bowl and whipped them into a frenzy. She scooped King Arthur flour into a separate bowl of dry ingredients. She had decided to bake a devil's food cake to perk everyone up. Thanks to Leslie and Carol Van Busybody, Annie had all afternoon to play with frosting and sprinkles. Maybe a snowman theme? Willy would prefer a beetle or praying mantis, but Annie wasn't about to put those on her cake. Maybe a ladybug? She had some all-natural food coloring and ladybugs were cute.

She and Dan had provided Cara with everything she ever needed, and then some. From a solid start at Play and Learn Preschool to reading aloud at bedtime, playdates, swim lessons, soccer cleats, back-to-school shopping, and endless nitpicking during the horrible summer of lice, why, they even buckled when she begged for horseback riding lessons. Annie drove Cara to the stable four weeks in a row, and then claimed they ran out of money for lessons, because she heard from Susan who heard it from a friend that horseback riding was the fastest way to turn money into manure. But even then Annie compensated by turning on the TV so Cara could satisfy her longing with Saddle Club reruns. Why did Cara ever start messing with drugs? Her life used to be practically perfect!

While the cake was in the oven, Annie fetched the mail. In the mailbox was a weighty 9 x 12 envelope. Annie glanced at the return address: Camels Hump Union High School. Did Mr. Day change his mind? Did he come to his senses and realize the folly of expelling Cara, the honor-student-track-team-star? Was this the necessary paperwork to reenroll her? Once Cara was back at school, Annie would talk her way back to her Play And Learn job and regain her life!

Annie rushed to the house, wedged out of her boots, and jumped on the sofa. Eagerly she unfolded the flimsy golden fastener and tilted the envelope. A thick packet of papers slid out. Annie picked up the top sheet.

Dear Mr. and Mrs. Mulligan:

This note serves to formally advise you that your daughter, Cara Mulligan, is expelled from Camels Hump Union High School effective March 21 due to her being discovered by staff with an illegal substance and exposing school premises to the risk of fire. This action is required by Code F, Sections C and J. We regret the necessity of taking this step. Cara has had an otherwise exemplary record at CHUHS, in particular her academic achievements and participation in student government.

Please be advised that state truancy laws require that Cara enroll within ten days at another school. Please inform us of her new educational institution by April 6 so we can update our records and notify Vermont's Department of Education. Thank you for your prompt attention to this matter. The necessary forms are enclosed.

Sincerely,

Mr. Alfred Day

At the bottom of the letter, on a pastel yellow sticky note, in black voluminous cursive: *Hope all goes well for Cara. Call me if you have any questions.* This was followed by the signature, *Martha Purnell* in matching fat, loopy handwriting.

What unmitigated hypocrisy! First they kick Cara out, then they pretend to care about her?

Annie flipped through the ream of papers. Most Vermont professionals would send an online link in order to save the environment. Purnell had dispatched half a tree, pulverized and printed into a bureaucratic hot mess. *Questions?* Annie wanted to ask, *Don't you care about pine trees? Have you never heard of global warming or carbon dioxide emissions?*

As Annie shuffled through the papers, she discovered the bottom half had nothing to do with truancy. It was information about drugs: brochures, newsletters, support groups, healthcare, locations of methadone clinics ...

Methadone? Annie shuddered.

One pamphlet warned that Vermont had the highest incidence of marijuana use in the country. In fact, the plant grew wild on the banks of the Winooski River. Annie made a mental note to discard this brochure before Cara read it. Wasn't that counter-productive for the state to advertise free marijuana in their anti-drug literature?

She continued reading and learned this wasn't just a pot problem. Her home state ranked number one overall for substance abuse, with 15% of Vermonters admitting to using illicit drugs in the previous month. Located between Montreal and metropolitan hubs such as Boston and New York City, it was easy for drug runners to drop some dope here and there in the bucolic state of Vermont, creating a serious heroin epidemic. The number of residents seeking treatment for opiate addictions grew by 770% since the year 2000. Whether caused by ultra-tolerance, the laid-back hippies, or small-town ennui, Vermont had a receptive audience for mood-enhancing drugs. Annie's top suspect was the frigid rigid winter. Cabin fever was a legitimate danger.

She popped a couple of aspirins and kept reading. One recent newspaper clipping detailed the downfall of a local teacher charged with breaking and entering and possession of stolen property. She had been raiding medicine cabinets for painkillers. The unfortunate woman had lost her job teaching social studies at the high school because she had back surgery last year with opiate addiction as a side effect.

Annie had been going to preschool for the past fifteen years where the most dangerous chemical they encountered was the occasional red food dye from parents who didn't read the healthy snack protocol. She launched off the sofa and locked the front and back doors to keep her medicine cabinet safe, leaving the kitchen door exit through the garage unlocked so Willy could return from school unimpeded.

Annie was grateful that Cara wasn't hooked on heroin; fortunately she was only messing with marijuana. And despite the school's alarmist propaganda, many people considered pot benign. Like Canadians and Coloradans and Wendy. Seventy percent of Burlington voters supported legalization. Vermont even had a political party devoted to it. Previously, Annie had deemed it a ridiculous platform, but now with Cara's graduation at risk, she reconsidered. If the drug wasn't outlawed, her darling daughter would still be in school.

She googled The Marijuana Party website and subscribed to their newsletter. Who knows how many kids she could save from ruined lives if marijuana were legalized?

EIGHTEEN

Mission: Be a stellar mother and get Cara into college

Goal: High school diploma for Cara

Lesson Plan: Day 1

1. Review Cara's homework and assign more homework
2. Brainstorm ideas for a small business
3. Boost Cara's self-esteem so she won't turn to drugs
4. Cook dinner (hot dogs?)
5. Go over Willy's homework and make sure he puts it in his backpack before he loses it
6. Call Mom (do not mention marijuana, expulsion, or fired from PAL)
7. Schedule FaceTime with Dan

LAST FRIDAY ANNIE was shellshocked and Monday morning was a mangled mess of dropping Dan off at the airport, working a couple of hours at PAL, then getting booted. She decided today was the real first official day of homeschooling. Now that she didn't have a job to go to, Annie could pour all her time and energy and professional expertise into Cara's education.

At Play and Learn Preschool Annie would begin the year by reviewing the school's mission statement, then hammering out goals and objectives for each student. Writing a Lesson Plan for Cara helped Annie feel focused and professional about the whole homeschooling thingy. By the time she finished her morning cup of coffee, she had it all figured out. Cara would save oodles of time by getting her work done at home. The bus ride alone took almost an hour. Plus, Cara wouldn't have all the distractions at school: friends, boys, her boyfriend John, getting high in the restroom.

What with all the extra time she had, Cara could start her own business, as Wendy suggested, get credit for it, graduate from high school, then use her business earnings to pay for her freshman year at college. In September Annie would go back to work and get paid for teaching instead of doing it at home for free. As Wendy put it, easy peasy.

After Cara finished her milk and cereal, Annie said, "Sweetie, show me where you are in your books and we'll go over your assignments together. Then you can start on today's homework."

"Okay," said Cara dubiously, as if Annie had just said, "Today in chemistry we're going to discover a cure for breast cancer."

Annie smiled beatifically. This would be a snap. Cara was already an A student. No problemo.

Cara hauled her backpack over to the kitchen table. One by one she removed textbooks and notebooks, maintaining a running commentary throughout: "For English I have to finish reading *The Scarlet Letter* and write a paper on that, then we move on to *Huckleberry Finn.* In Algebra 2, we're on chapter thirteen, complex and imaginary numbers. American History, we're covering the Civil War, and we have to answer a bunch of questions about that. Spanish, we just had an exam, so we're going to start the next chapter. In art we're in the middle of a unit on value. For chemistry we're on module nineteen." She looked up. "Where do you want to start?"

Annie sat down hard in the chair opposite Cara's. "Let's start with English." This was familiar territory; she had been speaking English her whole life. "I thought you were reading *Pride and Prejudice.*" Annie loved the romance between Elizabeth Bennett and Mr. Darcy.

"That was last semester, British Lit. This semester it's American."

"Fun! And what do you have to write for your *Scarlet Letter* report?"

Pulling out a sheaf of papers, Cara flipped through them until she located what looked like a spreadsheet for an IRS audit of OBS. "Here's the grading rubric for my paper."

Annie stared at the grid filled with numbers, plus signs, percentage symbols, capital letters, and acronyms. How did Cara's English suddenly transmogrify into math? For a brief moment Annie wished Willy had been the one caught with pot; homeschooling him would be so much easier. At least she understood fifth grade math and English.

But that was crazy talk. Of course she didn't want to homeschool Willy. He was much better off at a real school.

Annie drew her finger down the graphs and flipped the page. The codes continued. "Okay," she enthused. "Let me know when you're done with your report and I'll grade it then. In the meantime, let's look at your math."

Cara splayed open the spiral notebook she used for math homework. "Can you check my answers before I go on to the next lesson?"

Annie stared at the page in Cara's notebook. It was filled top to bottom with penciled numbers and x's and y's and equal signs funneling into polynomials that Cara had circled. Her solutions, presumably. How was Annie supposed to suddenly transform into Supermom and determine if Cara was doing Algebra 2 correctly?

"Hmm." Annie wiped her finger down the college-ruled page, as if she were skimming Cara's calculations. "It would save a lot of time if I had an answer key." About forty-eight hours per day.

"Can't you get one from school?"

"I'll give them a call. You work on *The Scarlet Letter* while I make this phone call."

Annie dialed the phone. She'd use this opportunity to get a feel for Cara's chance of getting accepted back into CHU.

The secretary said, in an unnecessarily snippy tone, "If we pass out answer keys to every parent, how do we know the students are actually doing their homework?"

"I see your point." Annie stepped into her bedroom and shut the door behind her. "However, we'll need the answer key to make sure Cara understands the concepts. Can we borrow it for a couple of weeks? Then we'll give it back."

"How do we know she won't xerox the answer key?"

"I won't let her have it."

"How do we know *you* won't xerox the answers?"

"May I please speak with Mr. Day?"

"He's not in his office right now. Would you like his voicemail?"

"Yes, please." Annie hoped that didn't come out too crisply. She couldn't afford to get snappy with the secretary, because who knows how soon she'd need more help from the school?

Annie concentrated on sounding pleasant and undesperate as she left a message, begging the principal to lend her an answer key so Cara could keep up with her classes and, by the way, how was their appeal coming along?

"Okay," Annie announced as she emerged from her bedroom and hung up the phone. "They'll get back to me. Let's move on to US history." Annie rubbed her hands together gleefully. She loved the Civil War, when right and wrong were so clearly demarcated.

Cara opened her history book. "William Tecumseh Sherman said, quote, 'There is many a boy here today who looks on war as all glory, but, boys, it is all hell.' Was Sherman's scorched earth policy justified because it ended the war quicker?"

"Hm. Good question."

Maybe it was the phrase "scorched earth" but suddenly Annie was parched. She wondered if Dan drank all their Sam Adams before he flew to Mexico. She preferred The Alchemist's Heady Topper, of course, but she had given up microbrews for Lent. She opened the fridge and fished in the bottom drawer ... ah, yes, two brown bottles of Sam Adams. She would have one beer tonight and save the other for tomorrow.

"Second question. Abraham Lincoln said, 'With public sentiment, nothing can fail; without it nothing can succeed. Consequently he who moulds public sentiment, goes deeper than he who enacts statutes or pronounces decisions.' Do you agree or disagree? Give specific examples in your answer."

Actually Annie had given up all beer for Lent but by Friday evening after Ash Wednesday, Dan had handed her a Long Trail and said, simply, "Please." His eyes so plaintive, his eyebrows so earnest ... he never once complained about her three-day nonstop bitching, so, for the greater good, Annie allowed herself mainstream brewskis and accepted the bottle with an appropriately pious attitude as an extra Lenten sacrifice.

"I think I agree. What about you, Mom?"

"I'm sorry." Annie shoved the crisper drawer closed and shut the refrigerator door. "What was the question again?"

After Cara repeated it, Annie agreed with Lincoln, not that she understood all the nuances of his position, but when was he ever wrong? And she assured Cara that she was doing a great job. Although, honestly, she wasn't sure. The older Cara grew, the more it looked like she knew more than Annie did, which was super awkward now that they were homeschooling.

While Cara worked on the War Between the States, Annie sat at the kitchen table and brushed up on chemistry. She figured she better get a jumpstart on it. She was tired of being ambushed by Cara's assignments. Annie flipped to module nineteen and started cramming.

Definition: Stoichiometry is the relationship between the relative quantities of reactants and products in chemical reactions. Stoichiometry builds upon the lessons from earlier chapters including The Law of Conservation of Mass, the Law of Constant Composition, the Law of Multiple Proportions, and the Law of Reciprocal Proportions (see Module One).

Who knew there were so many dang laws? Maybe this gobbledygook would help when Cara went to law school, assuming she ever graduated from home school.

Annie turned the page. *Stoichiometry is used to determine the quantity of a product yielded by a reaction. See Chart 19.1 below:*

Write and balance equation

Convert grams of reactant to moles

Determine moles of product yielded by reaction

Convert moles of product to grams of product

Bonk!

Startled, Annie's head jerked up. She glanced at Cara. Her daughter was calmly perusing her history and didn't seem to notice that Annie had dozed. No wonder kids at CHU walk around the halls with screensaver faces. They've been bored into zombies.

Wendy lied. This wasn't easy or peasy.

Annie clapped the chemistry book shut. "Care Bear, let's take a break. You fix yourself some lunch; I'll run out and buy some milk."

"It's only 10:30."

"Really? Well, I'm famished." Annie grabbed her purse and scrabbled for her keys. "I'll get milk."

Cara was already at the fridge. She pulled out the white plastic jug and tilted it. Milk sloshed softly against the translucent sides. "We still have half a gallon."

"Right. Well. We don't want to run out. You know how much Willy likes milk with cereal and cookies. I'll be back in a jiff."

NINETEEN

ANNIE PEELED OUT of the driveway with one hand pressed against her forehead. How could everything deteriorate so quickly? One day she was a professional teacher, getting paid to tell stories to preschoolers, the next thing she knew she was stuck at home teaching a high school senior without pay or a teacher assistant or a parent helper. She was all alone.

Annie didn't even want to homeschool in the first place. She had to talk herself into it. And then Dan.

What if he hears how horrendous it is? What if he hears that I got fired from PAL? How can I help Cara with chemistry? That petrifying grading rubric? I can't do this!

There was a time when Annie dreamed of changing the whole world, one song at a time. Her plan was genius, yet elementary. She would teach children how to sing—like a vocal counterpart to the Suzuki method. In fact, it would be even *more* successful than Suzuki, because although low-income families couldn't afford violins, each child, no matter how many food stamps they qualified for, had a voice. Every child could join the chorus. She would save the future of America, one child, one song at a time!

She called it the Murphy Method (this was before she became Mrs. Mulligan). *Anything that can go wrong can become a new song.* And once audiences heard these innocent children lisping out delightful melodies and harmonizing beautifully, their hearts would expand, like the Grinch's shriveled heart that grew three sizes bigger after hearing the little Who people sing their joyful song of celebration despite being robbed of Christmas. Yes, crusty career criminals would open up their hearts like the Grinch, and lay down their manifestos, machetes, and machine guns, and clasp hands in solidarity, and join in crooning "Twinkle Twinkle!"

However, one thing Annie learned from PAL, is that teaching children to sing was really, really hard. Even the "Butterfly Song," simple as it was, (five notes, major key, 4/4 time) over-challenged them. The preschoolers flubbed the lyrics, the tune, and the timing. All they had left was their cuteness. And adorability wasn't enough to stop a baby-kissing politician from voting for war.

Annie scrunched her lips together. Nope. She blinked her eyes. Nope. She would not cry. Nope.

Taillights flashed bright red ahead of her and she slammed on her brakes. What clod is stopping in the middle of the road?

Annie peered ahead. A few cars beyond, cows were placidly picking their way across the road. It looked as if a Woody Jackson print had come to life ... in syrupy slow motion.

Of course Annie admired Holsteins, the black and white backbone of the dairy industry. They were good for agriculture and tourism, which Vermont sorely needed since all the jobs at ski resorts and microbreweries were taken. Annie appreciated cows as much as the next loyal Vermonter. Just not today. Not when her husband was in sunny Mexico and she had to stay at home and relive Algebra 2 again.

And fail.

Again.

Annie massaged her temples. Damn, cows were sluggish.

She turned her head to the right and noticed a layer of snow frosting the archway over the granite statue in front of Holy Family Church. The Christ child nestled on Mary's lap, while she smiled serenely at him. Joseph stood beside them both, paternally and perpetually protecting them from danger, staff in hand to keep wolves at bay. The infant's stone-gray eyes stared straight at her.

At *her*. At Annie. She blinked. Jesus was watching her.

Honk!

Annie jumped. The cars ahead of her had resumed their commutes. She obediently released her foot from the brake to cruise her Subaru forward. Annie glanced again at the statue and saw Jesus's baby eyes patiently following her.

That's it—she needed help. She'd been trying to do everything all by herself, without Dan, without Wendy's help, without an Answer Key. Time to call for backup. Annie would recruit the entire Church Triumphant, especially that saint her mother followed, Saint Catherine of

Somewhere who urged, "Be who God meant you to be and you will set the world on fire." What the hell, Annie was desperate.

She flicked her right blinker on and pulled into Holy Family's parking lot. Annie wasn't familiar with this church since she and Dan belonged to the parish in Mapleville. She twisted the key in the ignition and glanced around, scouring the area for prying church ladies. None.

Head bent, Annie scurried in to the stone building. She picked a random pew, knelt, and pleaded: *I'm trying to do the right thing with Cara. I even quit my job to homeschool. I stayed faithful to Dan during those six months between jobs when OBS dropped him and he was a crankypants every single day and I kept telling him he would find a job soon, even though I was secretly afraid he would never in a million years find another job in this state. And remember the time he bought a security system for the house and called it my birthday gift? Don't I deserve extra credit for not filing for divorce right then and there?*

But my precious Cara? Last I knew she was nailing high school. Expelled for marijuana? How could this happen?

She waited.

And this homeschooling thing? I can't do this by myself. I need help to help Cara!

She waited.

Please, God, please send help, for Cara's sake if not for mine.

Annie shifted on her knees. They were not accustomed to bearing her weight for this length of time.

Is this because of that thing in college?

Whoosh. Annie hunched over until her head rested heavily on her hands gripping the back of the pew in front of her. "I'm sorry," she breathed. "I'm so sorry."

A soft crunch signaled that the heavy church doors had opened. Annie turned her head and watched a mother and a passel of kids process in, quietly and devoutly, their small noises reverberating in the church: the genuflections, the dip of their hands in the holy water, the rustle of their pants and skirts, the kneeler unfolded with a muffled thud. The mother knelt in a pew while her children veered off toward the altar. The mother saw her and smiled in a way that said, *I don't mean to interrupt your privacy, but hello.*

Annie swiveled her head forward. She squinched her eyes shut and pressed her palms together. She was supposed to be concentrating, not getting sidetracked by others. Here she was, praying very fervently, maybe on the brink of a miracle, which is precisely what she needed to fix her life, but this family up and barges in.

Then Annie felt like a social cretin for not smiling back at the mom. She blotted her eyes with her scarf in case she had any telltale tears on her face, climbed back onto the pew, and rubbed her knees. Once she figured she could stand without keeling over, she walked over to the mom kneeling in a pew. Annie flashed her a smile and whispered, "Hi."

"I hope we didn't disturb you," the woman whispered back.

"Not at all."

"I'm Maggie Boucher. My kids and I are here to drop off lunch for Fr. Dan and we couldn't resist coming in to church to say a quick hello to Jesus."

Annie glanced at the row of kids kneeling directly in front of the altar.

"I'm Annie Mulligan and I came here—" She was ashamed to admit she didn't have a hot lasagna in her car for the priest. And she definitely didn't want to tell Maggie-with-the-angelic-children the truth—that she was escaping her grade-A-student-turned-juvenile-delinquent at home. "Well, actually I just came to pray," she said apologetically.

"Praying." Maggie nodded. "That's the perfect reason to come here."

"Um, I notice you have your kids with you ..." Annie's voice trailed off.

"So why aren't they in school?" Maggie's blue eyes twinkled. "Don't worry, they *are* in school. We homeschool. Lots of times they learn on the road."

Annie's mouth dropped open. "You homeschool?"

"Yes, we started when Zachary, my oldest, was in second grade and it fit so well we just kept going. Been about ten years now."

"I just started homeschooling myself."

"Have you heard about our meetings on Fridays?"

"Cara!" Her mom shouted as she barged through the kitchen door stomping snow off her boots onto the mat. The dogs circled her, tails wagging, noses snuffling. "Good news! Guess what?"

"You got milk?"

"No, you said we didn't need any." It looked like her mother had forgotten her original errand and then kinda blamed Cara. "This is better than milk."

"Mr. Day decided not to kick me out after all?"

"No, but I just found a different kind of school that could help—it's a bunch of homeschoolers. They meet every Friday in Burlington at Faith United and they'll let us join in. You can take chemistry there."

"Chemistry on Fridays? Y'mean I don't have to do it the rest of the week?"

She didn't seem to hear Cara's question. "I just met the nicest family." Her face glowed. "They live right nearby in Richmond, and they've been homeschooling all along so they know exactly what to do. The mother, Mrs. Boucher, used to be a nurse, but now she's nothing, she just stays home and homeschools. They have six kids. They even have a boy your age."

"Mom!"

"I'm just saying."

Ugh. Cara wished her mom would stop pretending she knew everything. She was clueless, especially when it came to chemistry and algebra and guys. Cara groaned and dropped her head in her hands.

Could my life get any worse? My best friend is pregnant and when I cover for her, I get kicked out of school. In order to get into college, I have to fake some type of homeschooling shit. John dumps me before I even think of ditching him. And now my mother handpicks some homeschooled dweeb for me?

Cara pictured a geek wearing a pale yellow polo buttoned all the way up to his bony Adam's apple and pasty complexion, and tucked all the way down into his too-short pants. She shook her head and, sighing, turned back to her computer. A matchmaking mother would only make everything worse. She would have to keep a close watch on her mom.

TWENTY

WHILE WILLY WAS busy getting educated at a real school that Friday, Annie reminded Cara they would be going to the homeschool group that afternoon. All morning she could feel her daughter's frustration simmer until Cara erupted, "I wouldn't have to go to this stupid homeschool thing if you hadn't yanked me out of school!"

"You got kicked out, I was trying to save your record!"

Cara's blue eyes pooled and Annie immediately regretted her outburst. "I'm sorry, Cara." She reached out to smooth a brown strand of hair that had escaped from her ponytail. But she was too late, Cara was already turning to retreat to her upstairs bedroom. Annie attacked the carrots, celery, and lettuce with a chop, chop, chop.

Lunch was subdued. Cara answered Annie's questions with pronounced civility. The homeschool co-op could hardly be more punishing than this. Annie put the leftover salad in the fridge and announced, "Let's go."

Faith United Community Christ Memorial Church was a typical New England church with white clapboard, green shutters, gothic arched windows framing plain glazing, and a high belfry topped with a cross. The long appellation came after several weeks of intense committee negotiations by congregations financially forced to merge. One doctrine all three parishes readily agreed upon was inclusiveness, which extended to the new name. Cara shortened Faith United's nickname to FU, but Annie shushed her in case Willy heard it.

She had never seen so many vans and large junkers in one place before. Cara's old beater Betsy Clunker would blend right in here. This was certainly not the exorbitant "Subaru-bia," which is what Dan called PAL's parking lot full of Outbacks and Foresters. She glided in next to a vehicle the size of a small bus, pock-marked with rust.

As they descended the stairs to the church basement, they could hear the muffled thrum of voices. How appropriate that they met in a cellar, tucked away out of sight, the underground railroad of education, where officials like Ms. Purnell wouldn't discover them. Annie peeked through the windows in the double doors.

It looked like kids outnumbered adults by a ratio of twelve to one. Youngsters wrapped themselves around the poles holding up the ceiling, girls played intricate hand clapping games, older kids played cards at a table and toddlers tugged at the skirts of mothers milling about, wiping crumbs off tables and packing leftover lunch debris into canvas bags the size of bathtubs.

"Freaks on parade," whispered Cara.

"Shh," Annie hushed her. "Would you rather have *me* teach you chemistry?"

Cara sighed ... slowly, loudly, hopelessly.

From the safety of the hallway, Annie continued surveying the room. She expected homeschoolers to be at least a smidgeon exotic or exciting. A pinafore would be fun, or a pitchfork. What a disappointing tableau. These folks looked *normal.* Except for the child-to-mom ratio. And the ankle-length skirts. And was that kid by the water fountain wearing a fencing mask?

But Annie couldn't afford to be choosy. At least she wouldn't be home alone trying to look like she knew what she was doing. At least she could find some support here. At least she wouldn't have to talk to Cara about stoichiometry. Annie's responsibility would begin and end with the scientific inquiry, "Did you finish your chemistry homework?"

Like it or not, they were in this together. Annie pushed the door open and pulled Cara in by the hand.

Normally at 12:40, Cara would be sitting in algebra, next to John. While the teacher squeaked out ellipses in chalk on the blackboard, she and John would jot word problems in their notebooks, then slide them to the edge of their desks so they could read each other's.

"If the boy/girl ratio is 48/52, how many students would choose meatloaf for lunch today?" They didn't bother with answers, they only posed questions.

"If they run out of meatloaf, how many lacrosse players would it take to change a light bulb?" John always ragged on lacrosse. (Except not Nate. John gave Nate a pass since he was going out with Olivia.)

"If lacrosse wins their game today, how many spectators will show up for tomorrow's meet?" John was permanently pissed that other sports attracted much larger crowds than track and field.

If Cara could go back in time she would write: "After hearing rumors from lacrosse players about weed in the teacher's restroom, how many nanoseconds would it take for you to decide to dump your girlfriend!"

Why did her best friend have to get pregnant and toke up at school? This was all Olivia's fault. No, actually, Nate's. He got her pregnant. He told her to stash his weed in her backpack. Nate should be forced to homeschool, not Cara.

Now it was 12:40, and she had to hang out with a bunch of moms and homeschoolers. Teaching was one thing; homeschooling was completely different. Cara suspiciously spied on the dorkage before her. She feared she was approaching social hell. They might as well have a banner emblazoned above the entryway: *Abandon all hope ye who enter here.*

Her mother opened the door and dragged her into the room. "Mom," she whisper-yelled while pulling her hand away. She angled her head down and scoped out the people through her bangs, not abandoning hope that she wouldn't be recognized. She saw a teen sporting a trench coat with his messenger bag slung crosswise over it. No doubt he was trying to look like a hipster, but the strap bunched up the coat and made it puff out as if he were injected with helium and would float away like a hot air balloon. He was talking to a guy in a light blue button down who wore his pants so high, he had a Tweedle Dee look going. All he had to do was tug his pants two inches lower onto his hips and then his friends (*if* he had any) wouldn't be exposed to his white-sock-encased ankles. The problem with homeschoolers is they were clueless about style. Cara groaned inwardly and wondered which one of these nerds was the one her mom had raved about.

She noticed a couple dancing in the corner near an exit. The girl looked pretty, though it was hard to get a good visual on her since the guy was spinning and twirling her like crazy. He had curly brown wavy hair and looked like an American Eagle model in his jeans and burgundy polo. His partner looked way too young for him in her pleated skirt and tights and headband, as if she were twelve years old instead of in high school. The girl seemed to be doing all the work, while he mostly stood there and extended an arm now and then. Looking almost bored, as if he were demonstrating how to do old familiar tricks with a yoyo. Back and forth, in and out, a spin. Here comes walk-the-dog.

Meanwhile, the girl kept talking. Not to *him.* She would turn her head to address the girls surrounding them as if to say, "Look what I have." She was practically throwing herself at the guy. Like, she literally just jumped on him!

Luckily he was ready for it and simply hoisted her up and swung her around his shoulders before setting her back down. She laughed and hung onto his shoulder as if she were all that.

Cara scrunched her lips at the public display of affection. At that moment, the guy nonchalantly scanned the room and caught her staring. Cara instantly tilted her head back down, allowing her bangs to fall forward. She wished she had her cell phone to scroll on, but her mom had finally remembered to confiscate it.

Just then, a lady spotted them and with a warm smile headed their way, wading carefully through the infants and toddlers on the floor. "Hello! So glad you decided to come." They said hi and her mom introduced her to Mrs. Boucher.

Turning to the others Mrs. Boucher shouted, "Listen up!" No one heard except Annie and Cara and maybe that cute guy who had glanced her way, but Cara kept her gaze down and didn't know for sure. Undeterred, Mrs. Boucher slipped both pinkies into the corners of her mouth and whistled. The piercing shriek boomeranged off the industrial-strength walls. Everyone turned and stared.

TWENTY-ONE

ANNIE STRETCHED HER lips sideways into a smile. As uncomfortable as she was, she knew Cara would be a gazillion times more self-conscious. Were they going to have to introduce themselves?

Hello, my name is Anne Mulligan and I got fired from my job and my daughter got kicked out of school for doing drugs at school. Thanks for having us.

Fortunately, Maggie took charge. "We have a new family joining us. This is Annie Mulligan and her daughter, Cara. Let's be sure to welcome them into our group." She cast a meaningful glance at the cluster of girls in the dancing corner.

Dutifully, two of them trooped over to Cara and, after introducing themselves, Michelle and Charlene, offered to show her around.

Annie watched Cara follow the girls as they gave her a tour of the classrooms opening onto the cafeteria. These young ladies looked like Lands' End models in their plaid skirts and patterned tights and long hair pulled back with charming headbands. Not a single face piercing in the whole crew.

After a little small talk, Annie thanked Maggie and excused herself to go the ladies room. On her way back to the cafeteria, her phone bleeped. It was Wendy texting, asking if she wanted to grab a coffee since her patient was a no show. Annie explained she couldn't. While she selected emojis: a coffee cup, heart, and smiley face, she overhead a couple of boys talking in the kitchen behind the partition.

"— bet she thinks we're all geeks who sit around memorizing the dictionary so we can win spelling bees."

"And win science fairs."

"Write books about dragons."

"Read *Lord of the Rings* three times for fun."

"Shut up."

Annie was standing in the alcove to the restroom and couldn't see who was talking, but she heard a playful scuffle.

"Play in a Suzuki violin group," the other one countered.

"She probably thinks we can't play basketball."

"Or soccer."

"Or any sport."

"Or talk to girls."

Annie smiled. A bunch of kids too nerdy to do drugs, this group was perfect for Cara. She tapped on a final emoji, a mug of foamy beer, and zapped her text to Wendy.

She returned to Maggie who introduced her to the mothers and little kids. Annie was used to preschool where they wore their names on sticky labels in colorful bold block print for the first three weeks. Here there were no name tags. The only reason she remembered Paloma's name is because she was so short, Annie thought she was one of the students until the adorable little black-haired clones standing next to her were introduced as Paloma's daughters.

Annie wondered if the kids with the buzz cuts and khakis were the Pendergrasts, but she didn't want to insult them by asking. Their mother, Evelyn, wore a navy blue polo, no nonsense jeans, and short hair. Her husky voice and commanding posture reminded Annie of her gym teacher from elementary school.

One mom wore a tie-dye tee and ripped jeans and had long, fluffy hair. Her daughters had matching mermaid hair that rippled down to their shoulders. Even her boys had hanging fluff, like the mom was personally opposed to cutting hair. Like it was unnatural and would increase global warming, or something. Actually, Annie wasn't sure if any of her kids were girls, maybe they were all boys?

There was a beautiful young ginger woman speckled with freckles. She looked impossibly young to be pregnant, but there was her belly, bulging out in front of her as proof. She used her baby bump as a shelf, settling her daughter's elbow noodle necklace on it.

There was the obligatory farm family. Every town in Vermont has at least one of these, the mainstay of the food industry. Annie privately nicknamed them Little Homeschool on the Prairie. One of the older boys placed a stack of cardboard egg cartons on a side table with a hand printed sign that read *$3.00, Free Range, Organic.*

The Prairie kids probably didn't know what marijuana was. Probably the most dangerous substance they got close to was lye for their biannual soap making day.

Annie hoped that Cara would blend in and keep her recent escapade on the down low. In less than seven days, she had been kicked out of high school and preschool. The last straw would be getting rejected from Faith United.

There was no bell to mark the beginning of class, but in a secret synchronized movement, kids automatically shuffled off to different side rooms leaving mothers and little ones in the cafeteria. While Cara went to science, Annie took a seat in the circle with the leftover moms who weren't teaching classes.

Maggie asked, "Any announcements?"

"I'm looking for a Saxon math 5/4 book," said the tie-dye mother. "Does anyone have one they're not using that we can borrow for next year?"

Four ladies raised their hands.

While she negotiated a lending schedule with the mom closest to her, another announced, "I want to remind everyone that there's a contra dance at the Mapleville Community Center this Saturday. And because it was such a big hit last month, we're going to have another spelling bee during intermission. By the way," she smiled encouragingly at Annie, "you don't have to know how to contra dance. They'll teach you. Five dollars a person, or ten for the whole family. A real bargain for big families."

Evelyn said, "Speaking of family size, have you seen today's paper? There's a chart that shows Vermont has the lowest birth rate in the nation."

"Don't blame me," joked the red-haired mother as she patted her belly, which was the size of an award-winning watermelon. The tangled necklace had been joined by a toy car, and a smattering of Cheerios.

Diana said, "I wonder if it's because Vermont has more Planned Parenthood clinics per capita than any other state."

Annie squirmed, trying to get comfortable in her metal folding chair. To make a good first impression she had worn her skinny jeans, but the waistband was digging into her abdomen and she began to feel queasy.

"Plus Vermont is the least religious state in the union," Evelyn added.

"Atheists don't have as many kids. They think people ruin the environment."

According to the packet of anti-drug propaganda that Purnell had sent Annie, Vermont had a plethora of drugs. The state didn't need religion to be the opiate of the masses, they had genuine narcotics for that.

Maggie said, "We don't have enough business or affordable housing. Kids graduating from college these days can't find jobs here; they have to move out of state and raise their children somewhere else."

Before today, Annie hadn't realized that Vermont had a dwindling supply of children; PAL always had a lengthy waiting list. She looked around at the moms nursing their babies, the toddlers scribbling in coloring books on the floor, the doors to the classrooms full of students. No shortage here. One of the doors opened and a teenager came out carrying a couple of beakers. He passed through the cafeteria towards the kitchen.

"If Vermont's population is aging and our birth rate's declining, who's going to take care of us when we're all in nursing homes?" asked Paloma.

"Our kids will. And our grandchildren," said Maggie.

"In fact, our kids will also have to take care of the people without kids since they don't have any of their own."

"We oughta get a subsidy!"

"Oh no," warned Evelyn. "There's always strings attached to government money. No thanks."

Annie had no idea so many ultra conservatives lived in Vermont. And here they all were banded together. She had assumed her parents were an anomaly.

Paloma turned to her. "Are you new to homeschooling?"

Did it show? Annie discreetly fastened her top button and nodded yes.

The teen came back through the cafeteria holding the beakers in one hand, a pitcher full of water with the other, and a roll of paper towels tucked under his arm. He tapped the door with his foot and waited for someone on the other side to open it for him.

"What made you decide to homeschool?" Evelyn asked.

Annie skipped over the expulsion part of the story and said, "Cara is doing her Senior Project on different methods of education. Right now she's studying homeschooling."

The moms nodded in unison.

"I have tons of links that show homeschooling is just as effective as public school. Better, actually," said Paloma, swinging her black hair behind her shoulder. "I'd be happy to send them to you."

"Um. Thank you."

Annie's phone rang. "Excuse me," she said. She fished her cell out of her purse and checked the number. "It's my son's school. I better take it." *Did Willy forget his lunch again?*

Annie stood up and started walking away from the group of mothers. "Hello."

"Mrs. Mulligan?"

"Yes."

"This is the school nurse at Chittenden Middle School. I'm calling about your son, William. We had an incident here this afternoon."

Incident? Was he caught with an illegal substance like Cara? Were both her children into drugs? "What do you mean, an 'incident?'"

"There was an altercation."

Annie's anxiety jolted into alarm. "Is Willy okay?"

"Yes, he'll be fine. We'd like to take the precaution of asking you to pick him up and have him checked out by his physician. We believe he may have a broken nose."

"I'll be right there. Tell Willy I'll get there as soon as I can."

Annie turned back to the cluster of moms sprinkled with babies and toddlers. "I need to go. I have to pick up my son." What about Cara? Annie scanned the cafeteria, which had four classroom doors and two exits. "Which one's the science room?"

Maggie lifted a toddler off her lap and came over. She put her arm around Annie's shoulders. "Is everything okay?"

"There was a fight at Willy's school. He was injured."

"Ooh," said Maggie sympathetically. "I'm sorry."

"They think it's a broken nose."

"You go ahead and take care of him. I can drive Cara home after class."

"Oh, that's not necessary." Annie felt lightheaded, as if all her blood had plunged from her brain to her ankles.

"It's no problem at all."

"Well, all right," said Annie uncertainly. "We live right nearby. I'll call Cara later to explain." Annie plucked her coat off the back of her folding chair. She turned to Maggie, whispered a heartfelt, "Thank you," and dashed to the door.

TWENTY-TWO

Cara dutifully wrote down the observations in her chemistry notebook. She had already done a similar experiment at CHU. Here she was paired with two lab partners. One poured, one called out the measurements, and Cara became the secretary.

While waiting for the next mote of data to transcribe, she snuck a peek at the cute guy, the one with the brown wavy hair she had seen dancing. His bicep flexed as he adjusted his beaker. His limbs were all bent and folded to fit in the metal chair. One Nike sneaker tapped rhythmically against the floor, the blue swoosh logo winging up and down. Swoosh. Just like her breath.

His lab partner returned from fetching supplies in the kitchen and now they were whispering together. She couldn't pinpoint why, but she sensed they were talking about her. When both looked over at her, she nearly gasped. They were!

She immediately dropped her gaze towards her notebook. What were they saying? All they knew was her name. Unless her mother had said something when the partner got supplies from the kitchen! Ugh, her mother was a total blabbermouth. Cara felt her cheeks grow warm.

She hunched over her notes. Her nose was practically touching the lined paper. This was ridiculous. She steeled herself and turned to look casually in their direction. She caught Swoosh staring at her.

He immediately looked away towards their beaker.

Cara smiled and tried to concentrate on the chemistry experiment.

Finally, the predictable result was reached. Cara and her partners wiped their supplies with paper towels and put them in the cardboard box on the teacher's table.

Cara filed to the cafeteria ahead of the guys. She was dying to know if her mother had blabbed about her expulsion, even though it made no sense; her mom was more embarrassed than she was. Cara surveyed the room but didn't see her.

Mrs. Boucher approached and draped an arm around Cara's shoulders, calmly explaining that Annie had gone to the middle school to pick Willy up early—he hurt his nose, but he was okay—and that she would drive Cara home. "After classes are over we tidy up the rooms, and then we can leave."

Cara felt abandoned by her mother and highly suspicious that she had mentioned the weed or the expulsion because the guy and his friend were acting real shady. They were hanging around, emptying wastebaskets from different classrooms and stealing glances at Cara. Mrs. Boucher set her mop against the wall and said, "I'll go check the ladies' room."

"Anything I can do to help?" Cara asked politely.

She gestured toward the mop. "You could wipe up the melted snow in the hallway."

"Sure." Cara dragged the string mop back and forth, grateful for something to do to keep her from stalking Swoosh and company.

Soon Mrs. Boucher announced that everything was tidy and they could leave. She turned off the lights in the cafeteria and headed towards the exit.

The hot guy stalled. He asked his friend, "Watcha doing tonight?"

"Getting together with my girlfriend, Emily. You?"

"Same. Hanging with Ashley."

"Later." They did a chest bump, glanced at Cara, and parted ways.

Hm, Ashley wasn't the name of that girl he had danced with. She had introduced herself as Charlene. Was he cheating?

Cara went up the stairs out to the parking lot. As she followed Mrs. Boucher to a ginormous van, she noticed Swoosh following. He opened the driver's side door. Before getting in, Mrs. Boucher said, "Cara, you can ride in front, and Zachary, today you can hop in back."

So this is Mrs. Boucher's son? The one her mom picked? Gah!

Zachary walked around the front of their van and opened the door for Cara. He studied her as she climbed in.

"Thank you," she said, looking him squarely in the eyes. She couldn't figure out what game he was playing. Why was he acting the charmer by opening Cara's door, when he was going out with his girlfriend tonight? Not to mention dancing with a different girl in the lunchroom?

"Okay guys, time to go!" Zachary called to his brothers and sisters who were throwing slushy snowballs at each other. He opened the back seat door and stepped aside while his siblings climbed in.

Cara noticed his dancing partner got in the van. Okay, so Charlene must be his sister, good to know. But still. What about Ashley?

Zachary got in last and sat closest to the door, behind Cara's seat. As they drove off, he leaned forward and asked Cara, "Do you have any questions?"

"About chemistry?"

"About homeschooling. Figured you'd have some questions."

Cara cringed. What did her mother tell these people? "Um. What's the biggest difference between homeschool and public school?"

"We go at our own pace. We're not stuck in school all day long. As soon as we're done we can do whatever we want."

Maggie looked in the rearview mirror and asked, "Zachary, did you get your calculus done this morning before Friday group?"

"Word."

"Excuse me?"

"Yes."

"And are you visiting the nursing home again tomorrow?"

"Yeah."

Maggie turned to Cara. "Pet therapy. Zachary takes his dog Frodo to visit with patients at Burlington ElderCare. The residents love it."

"Frodo?" Cara smiled at him over her shoulder.

He seemed to wince. "I was eleven when I named him."

"What kind of dog?"

"Black lab." This time he couldn't hold back a smile, thinking about his dog made his lips swoosh and his eyes crinkle.

Cara had to turn her face forwards. She couldn't hold back a smile, thinking about this guy.

TWENTY-THREE

WILLY STOOD UP as soon as Annie walked into the nurse's office. His nose was an ugly red, and three times the size it had been that morning. Annie sucked her breath in hard, then gently cradled his head in her hands. "You okay?"

He twisted his head out of Annie's encircling hands. "I'm good."

Mrs. Walsh handed Annie a slip of paper. "This is just a precaution, Mrs. Mulligan," the nurse explained. "Mrs. Woodruff is checking into the incident. Our hands are tied since we don't have the full story yet."

"William," Mrs. Walsh rested her hand lightly on his shoulder and addressed him directly, "please tell us exactly what happened and who was involved."

Willy dropped his gaze and shook his head no.

The nurse threw her hands up and gave Annie an exasperated look as if to say, "See what I mean?"

How dare she blame Willy! As if it was his fault he was bullied and is too scared to give out names!

The nurse continued, "Mrs. Woodruff can talk to you as soon as she gets out of her meeting."

Annie couldn't stop staring at Willy's nose. Her heart felt as stretched and bruised as the skin surrounding his nose. "I'm not waiting. I'm taking him to the doctor now."

"Let us know what he says."

Annie and Willy already had their backs to the nurse. Annie linked her stride to his as he shuffled out of the office to their car.

After Dr. Tyler examined Willy, Annie plugged in Cara's number. The phone rang and rang and she left a message. After she clicked end call, Annie remembered that she had confiscated Cara's cell phone. Crap.

While walking to the parking lot, Annie called their home phone. No answer. Cara must still be at the homeschool group. Annie left a message on the answering machine. "Hi, Cara, Willy and I are heading out of the doctor's office. Willy has a broken nose, but other than that he's okay." She smiled ruefully at Willy who was tentatively fingering his swollen nose. "We'll be home soon. I need to stop at the pharmacy on the way. So, hey, I'll give you an extra A if you heat up some spaghetti or something for dinner."

Annie opened the car door for Willy and he crawled in. She got in the driver's side, started the car, and headed towards the drugstore for his meds.

"So what exactly happened, hon?" Annie asked.

Willy stared out the car window. The tree branches were black and gnarly against the white snow. "Some eighth graders jumped me."

"What?"

"A couple of jerks jumped me from behind."

"Why?"

"I don't know. They hate me. They're jerks. I don't know."

Annie shook her head.

"Usually I'm too fast for them. But I had to go to my locker for my science project and that's when they got me."

"You mean this has happened before?"

"No. Not like this."

"Who did this to you?

"You know if I tell they'll get me even worse."

"No, it doesn't work that way. We can't let them get away with this. Who are these boys?"

"You don't know them."

"Who would do this to you?"

Willy ignored that. He asked, "Can I stay home from school next week?"

Annie stole a quick glance at Willy. The nurse had cleaned up the abrasions but the angry red swelling had turned to queasy purple bruising. His nose was grotesque.

He turned his head, meeting her gaze, his blue eyes pleading, watery and bright. "Everyone will freak out when they see me."

Annie pressed her lips together. She couldn't blame them. *She* was freaking out and she was an adult. Annie faced forwards at the road winding ahead of them, wondering what to do. What would Dan say?

"You let Cara stay home. Why not me?"

There must be a good reason to say no. But Annie couldn't think of a single one. She was still in shock that anyone would assault her son.

"Please?"

"Sure, honey," she assured him, patting his arm and hoping she wasn't handling this the exact wrong way.

If she agreed to let him stay home for an entire week, would he ever learn to stand up to bullies? Would he ever go back to real school or would she have to homeschool him like Cara? If she homeschooled Willy would he actually be able to graduate and go to college, or was he doomed to flip burgers at a greasy joint like Cara for the rest of his life, working nonstop overtime to pay their bills?

Annie sighed. At least Maggie and the other moms were raising reliable kids. At least Cara's best friend was on track for becoming a nurse. Olivia Towne, RN, could provide care when she and Dan were both toothless and incontinent.

TWENTY-FOUR

Cara stirred slowly, watching the spaghetti noodles spiral around the ladle in the pot. As soon as she got home, she had tried stalking on Facebook. She typed in "Zachary Boucher." Nothing local. "Zach Boucher." Zip. She was dying to scope out his girlfriend, but she didn't know Ashley's last name. Hell, she didn't even know Eric's. The only reason she knew Zachary's was because of his mother, and talk about desperate, she had plugged in Maggie and Margaret Boucher, but got nowhere. She would have to do it the old school way.

Zachary had wowed her with his good looks and dancing skills. But then she found out he was Mrs. Boucher's son, the one her mother raved about. Ugh. Plus he had a girlfriend and she never ever wanted part of a Nate-like betrayal again. Double ugh.

And then Zachary was all weird, opening the car door for his mother and herself. This is Vermont, where girls live by the MO: I am fully capable of opening my own doors, thank you very much.

When was the last time John opened a door for me and let me go first?

Cara sighed, her breath plowing through the misty steam above the pot. She missed Olivia. When Cara got back from track practice, she would call her and they would fill each other in about the day: their classes, their sports, their guys. But now that she was grounded and her parents yanked her cell, Cara didn't even get to vent to Olivia about John breaking up with her. Cara was tempted to use the house phone, but her mom and brother could be back any minute.

Cara wondered what John was doing now. He'd have finished running his miles and probably already showered and snarfed up his protein shake with organic chia seeds. Then he would methodically do his homework in the order of his classes. English, AP History, Photography, all the way to his last class, Bio. He probably was *not* thinking about Cara right now. She slammed the lid back on the pot with a metallic clank.

She grabbed the landline phone and punched in Olivia's number. Before she answered, the dogs' ears poked up. Curly and Moe unfolded, stretched, then nosed towards the kitchen door. Cara immediately pressed the phone off and clicked it into its recharge station. She resumed stirring noodles.

By now the dogs were pacing in circles of anticipation. They snuffled all the strange new smells on Willy when he walked in the door and wagged their tails in frantic excitement.

"Your nose," said Cara.

"I know."

"What happened?"

Her mother shook her head slightly at Cara.

"We can talk about it later," said Cara. "Want me to make you some hot cocoa?"

"Sure." Willy sat at the kitchen table and pulled out some homework from his backpack.

Cara spooned cocoa mix into a mug, added tap water, then put it in the microwave. "Mom, what did you tell those homeschoolers about me?"

"Nothing. I said you were studying homeschooling for your Senior Project."

"Mom! So they think I'm, what—spying on them or something?"

"No, I just told them you're researching different forms of education. Calm down. They think homeschooling is the best thing since Ben & Jerry's came out with Phish Food. They're happy to show off."

"Ugh."

Her mother patted Cara's back and leaned over her shoulder to peer at the pot on the stove. "When will the spaghetti be done?"

"Couple minutes."

"Thanks. Good job." Annie wrote *March 29, Dinner: A+* on a sheet of paper and filed it on her desk. "By the way, I decided to give you your cell phone back. As a safety precaution." Annie climbed on a chair to fetch it down from above a kitchen cupboard. "It's important that we're able to stay in touch, especially with your dad away."

Cara extended her hand for her phone. "All right. If you think it's best." She suppressed a smile.

"But only use it for good reasons." Annie looked pointedly at Cara as if to say, *What I mean is, don't use your phone to contact dealers, but I can't say that in front of Willy.*

Cara nodded. "Okay, Mom. Got it." As if she couldn't use her laptop to contact the outside world.

The microwave beeped and Cara gave Willy his cocoa. "Here ya go."

"Thanks."

"Okay kids, it's Friday," said her mother. "After dinner, let's FaceTime your Dad."

"Tell him I say hi. I'll be upstairs studying," said Cara.

"Same for me," said Willy.

"What's wrong with you two? It's a Friday night. You have all weekend to study."

"I know but I have a lot of homework," said Cara. "I want to keep up with my classes in case CHU lets me back in."

"Guys, your dad doesn't just want to talk to *me.* He wants to talk to you two, too."

"I don't want him to see my nose," said Willy. "He'll freak."

"I don't want to talk about homeschooling," said Cara. "Or ... anything."

"Well, I don't want to tell him I got fired!" their mom shouted. Cara and Willy gaped at her.

She blew out a breath in weird puttering noises. "He can't do anything about it, and it would just make him worry. So here's the plan. We ask him how his job is going, and how warm Mexico is, and let him do all the talking. Willy, you stand in back so he doesn't see your nose."

After they cleared the dinner dishes, Annie set her laptop on the kitchen table and they gathered around. She dialed in and clicked. Dan's face popped onto the screen. His eyes twinkled and his dimple puckered when he smiled at her. Annie felt a pang of longing. She hadn't realized how much she missed him.

"Hi Dad."

"Hey kids. Hi Annie."

"You look tan already," said Annie.

"Yeah, weather's great here. In the nineties."

"It's thirty-three degrees here."

"How is everybody doing? Where's Willy?"

"I'm back here, Dad."

"I can't see you."

"Can you hear me?"

"Yeah."

"So how's the job?" Annie asked.

"It's a lot of new people and systems but it's pretty relaxed down here. We have an hour for lunch everyday so I eat outside. The hotel is terrific. Has an outdoor pool and an indoor gym. I think I'll survive." He smiled and smoothed his brown hair off his forehead. His eyes blazed bluer than ever in his freshly bronzed complexion. "How about you? How's the homeschool going, Cara?"

"Great."

"How are you doing, bud?"

"Great," said Willy, standing behind Cara and Annie with his head turned toward the left.

"How's PAL, Annie?"

"Great. Kiddos are fine." As far as she knew from last she had seen them.

A couple more minutes of chitchat and they said goodbye. Relieved, Annie clicked out of FaceTime. She was happy that Dan's new assignment was going well and that he could continue to work without worrying about them since he didn't know the preschool dumped her, homeschooling Cara was complete crap, and Willy's nose was the size of a Zeppelin.

Since she agreed to let Willy stay home and recover next week, Annie figured she might as well help him keep up with his schoolwork. It could be homeschooling practice for her. Not that she planned on continuing to keep Willy home after the swelling went down. In fact, the possibility of Willy dropping out of middle school for the rest of the year was so remote, she didn't bother mentioning it to Dan.

On Monday she would call Willy's teacher and get his homework for the week and inquire about the investigation of the bullies. Meanwhile, Annie called Maggie and left a message asking if they had any textbooks they could borrow temporarily to see what fifth grade homeschoolers do all day.

TWENTY-FIVE

As soon as FaceTime with her dad was over, Cara hugged her cell phone to her chest, ran upstairs to her bedroom, shut the door behind her, and stepped into her closet to call Olivia. As soon as she answered, Cara said, "John dumped me!"

"No!"

"Yes!"

"Douchebag!"

"I know, right?"

"Total bag! Why'd he end it?"

Cara paused with her phone pressed to her ear. She didn't want to tell Olivia that John ditched her because of the Restroom Disaster because she didn't want Olivia to feel guilty as if it were all her fault. Because it wasn't. Not *all* of it. There was plenty of blame left over for Nate.

"John said he wanted to focus on grades and running." Even as she said the words, they sounded suspiciously lame.

"That's weak. He's already accepted at UVM. What's really going on?"

"I don't know. How about *you*?" Cara changed the subject. "How are you doing? Have you told Nate about the baby yet?"

"I haven't told anyone except you."

"But he's your boyfriend."

"I know, I know." After a pause, Cara heard a breath whoosh out. Olivia's voice became small. "But I'm not sure I can go through with it."

"You have to tell him."

"No, not that. I mean ... go through with the pregnancy."

"Sure you can. People have babies all the time." Cara had seen the photos. She had set up an online account at BabyBumpz to get free weekly updates of Olivia's pregnancy. Of course she didn't use her name, or Olivia's. She had typed "Hester Prynne" and for the date of conception she typed March 5 (total guess, but it was Town Meeting Day, so school was out). While she was at it, she gave the baby a name and gender as well. Pearl, Female.

Cara slowed down her voice to sound calm. "School's almost over ... and you can take an easy course load at college, have the baby over Christmas break, and get right back into classes in January." Even as she said the words, they sounded suspiciously unrealistic.

"I don't know, Cara. It's not that simple. I don't want to walk around Columbia University full out preggers. I don't want to be *that* girl."

"But what else can you do? Take a gap year?"

"No. That would get me all off track. I've been thinking of, I know you won't like this, but I'm thinking of, you know ... getting rid of it."

"No, Via. That's your baby. She's as big as a raspberry now. She's got fingers and toes. Soon you can hear her heartbeat. You can't just ... stop. It's not fair to the baby."

"It's not fair to me, either!"

"It's not fair to me, either! You can't let me take the heat for smoking and get kicked out of school and then abort the baby anyway after my life is ruined!" *Damn. That is not what I meant to say.*

Click.

Cara stared at her phone. In nine years of friendship, Olivia had never hung up on her before. Ever.

Cara called right back, but Olivia didn't answer. She left a message. "Hey Via, it's me. Sorry I yelled. Seriously. I'm sorry. Call me back. Please?"

No response.

She switched to text messages and tapped in, "Sorry!"

She sent nine broken hearts.

She sent a crying emoji.

Nothing.

The next morning Cara pressed Olivia's name on her phone. No answer. She left a message. "Hey Via, it's me again. Just wanted to see how you're doing. Sorry I blew up on the phone yesterday. How is—" Cara paused. She didn't want to ask about the baby in case Olivia listened to her message in public. "How is everything? Call me."

Normally Cara would run a three-to-five-mile loop with John on Saturday. Now she was on her own. She chose a route that John never used and asked permission first. "I know I'm grounded, Mom, but it's Saturday and I'm caught up with my homework and I need to stay in condition in case CHU lets me back in." Her parents had sent a formal appeal to the school board and were waiting for their decision.

"Good point." Annie nodded. "Be back in an hour."

"Thanks."

Cara dressed in layers and slid her phone into her pocket in case Olivia called back. The air felt freshly washed and zinging with energy. Running always helped clear her head, like an internal shower.

She owed the running to Olivia, really. When they were freshmen, Cara had gone out for the soccer team, as usual. That year the pool of girls who came from the other middle schools all funneled into the same high school, all competing for one team. The previous summer, everyone else seemed to have gone to a killer soccer camp, whereas when Cara wasn't hanging with Olivia, she had earned money by house sitting and pet sitting. After the grueling week of tryouts, Cara couldn't find her name on the team roster posted on the bulletin board outside the soccer coach's office. It hadn't shocked her, but it had devastated her.

It had been Olivia who had pulled her into the teacher's restroom for privacy, the one where Purnell ambushed them three years later. Cara had literally cried on her shoulder, and Olivia just held on tight and listened while she sobbed and sobbed. Then Cara rinsed her face at the sink, and the girls meandered outside around the building in the warm September afternoon, avoiding the kids in tee shirts and shorts walking to field hockey practice or the guys' soccer field and definitely keeping away from the girls' soccer field. Instead they turned left and wandered up the path in the woods and sat on a fallen log and threw acorns at the leaves overhead. Olivia had invited her to an impromptu sleepover that night, just the two of them. They tried on outfits, practiced with makeup, and binge-watched YouTube. At 2:00 am, Olivia suggested track and field. Cara had been running ever since.

TWENTY-SIX

"NOTHING IS COVERED up that will not be uncovered, and nothing secret that will not become known…" In his homily that Sunday, Father McHolland linked the gospel reading from Luke to the weather, emphasizing the clarity that comes from the cold. "Winter makes the invisible visible and matter becomes crystalized until you can see your very breath. We can see much farther into the forest without leaves and underbrush, now that the woods are black and white. We must seek the big picture. If we only look through microscopes or telescopes, we compartmentalize our world into fragments. Scientists like Snowflake Bentley can photograph snowflakes to show us what they look like, but who can tell us why they are beautiful? A surgeon can transplant a heart from one body to another, but what doctor can elucidate why a heart loves?"

Annie would love to be with Dan in Mexico; that's what her heart was elucidating to her. But no. Here she was, trapped in a Vermont winter, which was skidding on and on, with no job and no Dan and no end in sight.

Annie brightened up at the communion song, a southern spiritual she'd always loved, *What Wondrous Love is This?* Annie went full soprano on it and felt her voice reverberating in the rafters, possibly beyond. She noticed Cara edging away from her and she reduced her volume.

At coffee hour in the church hall after Mass, Annie offered Susan an apple cider doughnut. Susan waved it away. "My weight's gaining on me. The Change is brutal on your waistline."

At least Annie didn't have to deal with that yet; she had enough on her plate, including the apple cider doughnut her friend had rebuffed. Annie picked it up and took a bite.

Susan took a sip of coffee from her Styrofoam cup and brushed her hair back from her flushed face. "Olivia still hasn't decided what to do."

"It's a tough choice."

"Mmm. Columbia or UVM. They're both great options. How about Cara. Has she decided yet? Is she going with Calvin Coolidge?"

"Not yet. She's um ... narrowing her choices. Process of elimination." By now Cara might have eliminated all of her options, including UVM, her safety school. Unwilling to talk to Susan about the Big Expulsion, Annie changed the subject. "How's Nelson?" He had stopped coming to church with the Townes as soon as he started at UVM. He had graduated last year and like zillions of other Millennials, Nelson was now living back home and applying for jobs.

"Still looking."

Brrrng! Brrrrng!

As Annie reached for the phone, she glanced at the caller ID: Murphy, Glen and Angela.

Annie drew in a deep breath, picked up the receiver, and forced out a cheery, "Hello Mom!"

"Dearie. Is everything okay? I didn't hear from you yesterday. Didn't know if you all dropped off the face of the earth, or what."

"Everything's fine, Mom. Sorry I didn't call. Kids and I are busy adjusting to, um ... life without Dan."

"Do you need anything? Shoveling? Groceries? Help with your tax return? I could send Glen over."

"We're fine." She wasn't about to worry her mother with news about an expulsion or bullies.

"How are the kids?"

"Good." Willy was nestled with his computer, hungrily compiling factoids for science. And Cara was doing well in ... Spanish ... as far as Annie could tell.

She changed the subject. "How's the convention coming?" For over thirty years Annie's mother had volunteered for Vermont Right to Life. Nowadays her primary duty was organizing refreshments for their annual event: tuna fish and egg salad sandwiches on white bread.

"Martha May had to drop out of the committee this year. She needs a hemorrhoidectomy. And I think Sylvia has Alzheimer's. She's supposed to take notes, but last month instead of sending us the minutes of our meeting, when I opened the file she attached, it turns out it was her bucket list. I had to google 'bucket list' 'cause I didn't know what it was. Then I wondered if maybe that wasn't an accident? Maybe Sylvia sent it to us on purpose? Anyway, I'm going to write out *my* bucket list and send it to Sylvia. She has some pretty nifty ideas. We don't have a lot of time left to get all this done. Women need to help each other. She wants to take flamenco lessons but I'm hoping I can talk her into Irish step dancing instead. And I've always wanted to be a redhead. We could hit the beauty parlor together. Get this—she wants a purple streak. Can you imagine?"

Annie pictured her petite white-haired mother with a bright copper-colored coiffure and Sylvia sporting a swath of purple mingling with her silver. She pulled out a mixing bowl and butter and sugar. She might as well whip up a batch of cookies while her mom chatted. Later she and Cara could feast on the goodies and drink tea while watching *Downton Abbey.*

On Sunday evening Olivia called Cara back. "Hey," whispered Olivia.

"Hey." Cara could hardly hear her friend; she pressed her cell phone flat against her ear.

"I'm so scared."

"I'm sorry, Via. I'm really really sorry. I shouldn't have said that. This isn't your fault."

"But you got kicked out because of me!"

"That wasn't your decision. No one wanted that. Except Purnell."

Olivia sniffed, trying to stifle her crying. "I can't deal with this. I don't want a baby."

"Want me come over?"

"Aren't you grounded?"

"Oh, yeah, I forgot. I've never been grounded before. So weird."

"I don't know what to do."

"Have you told Nate yet?"

"I'm afraid to."

"You have to tell him."

In a pained panic, Olivia squeaked, "Don't tell me what to do!"

The squeal pierced her ear and Cara jerked her phone away. She had never heard Olivia get so freaked so fast. She backed off instantly. "Okay, okay," she pacified her. "You don't have to. You don't have to do anything right now." Although Cara was desperate to get back to school, her predicament was minor compared to Olivia's. Patiently she listened to her bestie weep and whisper one fear after another.

Eventually Olivia was feeling better and sipping water and snacking on saltines. When she felt well enough to crack jokes about Nate, Cara almost told her about Zachary, but what was there to say? She barely knew the guy and he already had a girlfriend, and, worst of all, he was a homeschooler.

Instead Cara suggested they watch a chick flick together. Since she was grounded, they each holed up in their own bedrooms and watched the same movie at the same time while texting. She let Olivia choose and of course she picked her fave, *Step Up*.

When her mother knocked on her door and invited her to watch their weekly TV show while munching chocolate chip cookies, Cara politely declined. "I'm in the middle of something." She hid her cell phone under her duvet and gestured to her laptop, hoping her mother would assume it was homework.

"But we always watch *Downton Abbey* together," her mother countered, looking hurt.

"Sorry, Mom. You can fill me in later." Cara hated to disappoint her yet again, but Olivia needed her more. Her mother was a grown woman and could wait her turn; she used to spend all day teaching preschoolers how to do it.

TWENTY-SEVEN

"MOM, DID YOU know that butterflies have thousands of lenses in their eyes?" It was Tuesday morning and Willy was online, as usual.

"Really?" Annie sat at the kitchen table besieged by books and papers. With one finger marking her place in the answer key, Annie used her other hand to scribble "C" for correct in a red pen on Cara's math problem. It was easy to lose her place and mark an "X" on an answer that Cara actually got right.

"And that monarch butterflies fly one thousand seven hundred eighty-seven miles to get from here down to Mexico every year?"

"Mm hm." In fact, that's what Annie did yesterday. She marked an answer wrong and made Cara redo it and after five minutes of frustration, Cara asked her to double check the answer key and turns out Annie had incorrectly graded it wrong.

"Yeah, and scientists are analyzing butterflies' wings because they overlap in a way that lets light into the lower part which doubles the amount of light they get. Know what that means?"

"Mm hm." So then they had a loud discussion where Cara accused Annie of being incompetent. And Annie apologized. Then Cara said Annie didn't know what she was doing. And Annie said, sure she did. And then Cara went all hormonal and yelled, "No one in this family knows anything about what the hell is going on!"

"That's why butterflies stay warm—they have that extra layer of sun hitting their wings. And the cool thing is, scientists think we can use that design for solar energy panels and double the amount of energy they can store up."

"Mm hm." So Annie said that was uncalled for and ordered Cara to her room. And Cara asked in a snotty tone, "Or what? Gonna kick me out of *home*school?"

Annie couldn't remember the last time she had given Cara a time-out. When she was five years old? Out of practice, Annie had blundered the delivery yesterday; instead of sounding calm and commanding, she came off whiney. She cringed in embarrassment.

"So cool." Willy shook his head in awe.

Annie shook her head. Teaching preschoolers was way easier. What the heck did Cara mean—no one knew what was going on? Teenagers were so touchy.

"Mom, you ought to listen to Willy. He's got some great ideas," said Cara who was lounging on the sofa with her stocking feet propped up on the armrest and *The Scarlet Letter* propped on her lap.

"I *am* listening to him. He's talking about butterflies." Annie turned her head towards Willy. "Right?"

He glanced from Cara to Annie and nodded wordlessly.

Annie asked Cara, "And shouldn't you be reading your book right now?"

"I *am* reading."

"Good."

"Fine."

Annie's cell phone rang. It was sitting on the table and Willy checked the contact. "It's Dad. Want me pick up?"

"Sure, hon." With a pencil, Annie scratched a light line in the answer key to mark her place. She didn't want to repeat her past mistake. She set the pencil down next to the red pen and waited for her turn on the phone.

Willy accepted the call with an enthusiastic swipe. "Hi!"

"Sorry to bother you at work, Annie. I just have a quick question about our health insurance."

"Hey Dad, it's not mom. It's me, Willy."

"Willy?"

"Yeah."

"What are you doing at Play and Learn?"

"We're not at PAL. We're here at home."

"Someone sick?"

"No, we're good."

"Why aren't you in school?"

"Mom said I could homeschool this week."

"What the —? Put your mother on the phone."

Annie took the phone and went to her bedroom and shut the door behind her. This might be loud and she didn't want to disturb the kids while they were working so diligently on their homework. "Hello?"

"What's this? You're homeschooling Willy?"

Annie explained what little she knew about the bullying at middle school.

Dan yelled, "Why didn't you tell me?"

"I didn't want you to worry."

"What else is going on that I should know about?" Dan asked rhetorically in a snarkastic tone.

Annie swallowed. She might as well fill him in now and get it over with since he was already furious at her. "I lost my job."

"What?"

"They fired me because I brought Cara in to work and they found out about her little mishap at CHU."

"Annie!"

She held the phone away from her ear. She fancied she could hear his voice thundering one thousand seven hundred and eighty-seven miles from Mexico. A blast of sound waves rippling across state borders, over mountain ranges and prairies, flustering butterfly wings, possibly sending them off course from their migration.

When the noise died down, Annie put the phone back to her ear and said, "It's not my fault. How was I supposed to know I couldn't bring Cara in? That snooty Carol Van Horn got all up in my business and called Leslie and she up and fired me. Right in front of the kids, too."

Dan didn't say anything. Loud breathing crackled through the phone lines as if she were conversing with Darth Vader.

"But enough about me," said Annie. "What am I supposed to do about Willy?"

"Sign him up for karate."

"Karate?" That was a surprise. "You sure?"

"Yes, that's exactly what he needs. Next time those assholes jump Willy, I want him to be ready to take them down."

"Next time? I don't want there to even be the possibility of another incident."

"Annie, he's got to grow up. Shit happens. You can't baby him forever."

"If you had seen his face, his *nose*, you'd understand what we're up against here. They pounded him."

"I wish I were there. I'd pound the shit out of those little assholes."

"Dan, the school will handle it. No one's going to beat up anyone."

"Let me talk to Willy."

"Oh." Annie hesitated. "Just a minute."

She walked back to the kitchen and spoke to Willy. "Your dad wants to talk to you." She reluctantly handed the phone over.

"Hi Dad." Willy looked up and saw his mother standing there, listening. He climbed the stairs to his bedroom and shut the door. Annie tapped her red pen. She carefully found her place in the answer key and checked Cara's answer. It was mostly right. Annie gave her partial credit.

Soon Willy returned and set the cell phone on the table.

"What did your dad say?"

"He said to take karate classes and learn to defend myself."

"Do you want to take karate?"

"I guess." Willy shrugged his shoulders and stepped around Annie. He hefted his backpack onto one shoulder and tucked his tablet under his other arm. "Homework," he explained and marched upstairs to his bedroom.

Karate? Did Dan think it was that simple? Why do guys always turn to violence? How can a little guy like Willy ever beat down the bullies of the world?

Annie had just told Dan that beating up punks was no solution, but every time she saw Willy's bruised nose she felt heat come out her ears. Of course she would never strike a child herself, she had never even spanked her own kids, except for a safety-smack when Willy stuck his fingers in the electrical outlet and when Cara darted out to the busy street.

But now Annie closed her eyes and allowed herself to indulge in a fantasy where she had a black belt herself ... and the pudgy eighth-grade bullies were in front of her outside at recess ... and she skillfully flipped them to the grass, one by one by one.

Annie opened her eyes and looked down and found both her hands knotted into shaking fists. But who was she to punch?

TWENTY-EIGHT

CARA WAS MUNCHING on her sandwich when her mother announced, "Mrs. Boucher is coming over this afternoon with some books for Willy to borrow. After lunch be sure to clear your dishes and put your gear away."

"Is Mrs. Boucher bringing her kids?" asked Cara.

"I don't know. After I get dressed, I'll bake cookies just in case."

Cara put her plate in the dishwasher, grabbed her books from the kitchen table and zoomed upstairs to change, just in case. She stripped off her aqua-colored 802 sweatpants and Vermont State Parks "Play Outside" T-shirt in hot pink, a freebie she won at a race last year. She snapped on a bra, then rifled through her closet and selected jeans and an olive green top. She rushed them on and stood in front of her mirror. No. Too plain.

She peeled the top over her head and flung it onto her bed. She slipped into a navy cami and buttoned a burgundy shirt over it, half-tucked into her low waist jeans. She stood in front of her mirror. Yes. Good enough for homeschoolers. Cara smiled. In fact, she could wear this outfit to CHU, as soon as they let her back in, after reviewing their appeal.

She checked the time on her cell: 12:35. Cara jump-jogged in place, then stretched her quads one at a time, a brief ritual before every competition to calm her nerves and channel her energy.

She took her time brushing her hair in front of the mirror and popped a breath mint in her mouth. She didn't want to smell like a roast beef sandwich, just in case.

She went back downstairs to the living room, sat on the sofa with the view out the window, and worked on her history paper. But it felt majorly pointless to write about states' rights versus federal rights when everyone knew the real issue was slavery. That's what her assignment should be about, not stupid politics.

When the Bouchers arrived, the dogs went bonkers with delight. They barked and circled and wagged their gold and white fringed tails. Annie held the door open and they filed in, Mrs. Boucher first, then five kids, then Zachary holding a cardboard carton bringing up the rear. Homeschoolers seem to travel in family clans, like modern day tribes.

Zachary set the box on the kitchen table then squatted down, petting the retrievers and allowing them to sniff him and lick his hands. "What are their names?" he asked.

"This one's Moe and that one's Curly," said Cara, pointing.

"What, no Larry?"

"He got hit by a car two years ago."

Zachary looked up at Cara. "I'm sorry." His eyes were a deep, warm brown.

She already felt warmer. "It's okay. You didn't know." She shrugged her shoulders. "Pretty stupid names for dogs. We were bound to lose one before the others."

"These guys are beautiful." He continued stroking the golden retrievers. Curly and Moe sat at his feet, heads held high for easy access to caresses.

"So ... what's pet therapy all about?" asked Cara.

Holding a plate of cookies, Joey led the other Boucher kids to the game room in the cellar, while the mothers checked out the books. "This is a real mishmash," Maggie said, taking a stack from the box and spreading them out on the table. "I thought these books would be good for Willy. Most are 5th grade, but I also brought some leftover 6th grade books that Joey finished."

"Thanks," said Annie, flipping through the pages of *Exploring Creation Scientifically*. "Can Willy try them out for now and then we'll let you know if we want to borrow any long term?"

"Sure, no rush. How is Willy doing?"

"The swelling has gone down, but his nose is still all types of colors."

"Hm. And how does he like homeschooling?"

"Oh, he loves it. We made insects out of pipe cleaners and I whipped up a song and dance routine about verbs to help him with grammar." Annie sing-songed, "*Run, run, run, is a fun, fun, verb!* We even did art.

Check out our posters." Annie indicated the kitchen wall that displayed sheets of paper speckled with splatter paint. "At first he wasn't into it, but I made it look so fun he couldn't resist joining in. This one's his." Annie pointed to the one in variegated shades of mud: brown, black, gray.

"Yeah, sometimes kids expect to be entertained instead of taught." Maggie smiled understandingly. "Sometimes learning means *un*-learning first."

Annie felt her face flush. "I know, right?" As soon as the Bouchers left, she would take down the artwork. Only one was Willy's anyway; she would tuck that in his portfolio along with an A. "I'm all about facilitating learning. Mostly I give Willy assignments and he spends hours on the computer doing research. Happy as a clam. He's relieved not to have to face the bullies at school."

"A shame that ever happened."

"Yeah. My husband wants Willy to learn karate."

"Good idea."

"Yeah?"

"My kids take Tae Kwon Do classes three times a week. It counts for their gym class. You know that once you homeschool you need to document some type of Phys Ed, right?"

"Mr. Day never mentioned gym."

"Only up until ninth grade, so Cara doesn't need it. I'll send you a link to the state homestudy office. You can get the forms you need from them."

"Thanks. And what about the place where you send your kids for Tae Kwon Do? Would you recommend it?"

"Of course. If I didn't like it, I wouldn't have them go there. It's Jordan's Black Belt Academy."

Zachary slowly combed his fingers through Moe's fur. Cara noticed the muscles in his forearm rippling as he stroked the dog. She knelt down and patted Curly's head.

"If you follow the natural contours of the body, it feels sweet," he said. "Like a massage." Moe flapped his tail blissfully against the floor. It was ridiculous, but Cara was jealous of her dog.

She was close enough to Zachary to smell the fresh outdoors on him.

What did he do, hike through a pine forest before coming to their house? She breathed in deeply.

Stop, she cautioned herself. *This guy has a girlfriend.*

Cara stopped tapping Curly's head and brushed her hand down the length of his spine. "Like this?"

"Exactly." He flashed her a pristine smile. He could sign a modeling contract with Hollister. Because. Gorgeous.

Stop, she warned. *This guy is taken.*

"How often do you visit the nursing home?" she asked.

"I usually go on Saturdays. That way if the patients have their grandchildren visiting them and they're getting bored, the kids can play with Frodo. But my favorite visit was when I took him to a school with special ed kids. The teacher told me afterwards that she had never seen this one third grader smile before. But he really latched on to Frodo. He petted him for ten minutes straight." Zach rubbed Moe's chest and the retriever rolled onto his side and stretched out his legs luxuriously. "It's easier for kids to learn when they're relaxed."

"Does that apply to homeschoolers, also?" Cara asked with a smile.

Zachary dropped his hand and stood up abruptly. "Yeah. Sure." He headed towards the kitchen.

She followed him, wondering what put him off so suddenly. Was it because her mother told them she was studying homeschoolers? Why did her mom open her big mouth! "Um. Pet therapy would be fun to see. Could I come with you some time?" It wouldn't be horning in on Ashley, it would be community service.

Zachary paused for a beat. "All right."

"Let me know when you go. You can reach me on my cell." Cara pulled her phone out of her back pocket and clicked on New Contacts. "What's your cell phone number?"

"I don't have one."

She looked up, surprised. "You must be the only eighteen-year-old in the entire country who doesn't have a cell phone."

"Eric doesn't have one either."

Weird. At least that meant Zachary couldn't text his girlfriend all day long. For some reason Cara felt a bubble of happiness float inside her chest.

"Okay," she said. "What's your *home* number?"

TWENTY-NINE

ANNIE PAUSED AT the entrance of the homeschool cafeteria. She was determined to make a good second impression since her first visit had been cut short by Willy's broken nose. He had begged to get to the co-op early today so he could shadow Mrs. Boucher's son, Joey, and sit in on his class. Cara was in the car, still fussing with her hair. Which was silly, she was already lovely.

The families were sitting around tables eating their lunches. Most had been at the church for hours, teaching or taking morning classes. Annie was glad that Cara's chemistry class was in the afternoon, so they had time to get other important homeschooling tasks done first such as breakfast, lunch, and getting dressed.

Maggie bent her head and folded her hands, saying grace with her crew. Willy spotted Joey and bounded over to their table. Other moms spoon-fed their infants and passed around sandwiches to their kids. Beyond the half wall marking the kitchen, Annie could see the spelling bee mother untwisting the wire wrap at the end of a plastic bag enclosing a loaf of bread. The fluffy-haired mom was washing her hands at the sink. She caught Annie looking and gave her an airy smile, as if trying to remember her name, a concern they both shared. Annie smiled back. Then she pulled her phone out of her purse and checked her text messages so she wouldn't look stupid standing there doing nothing.

But who to text? Wendy was at work, helping her clients share their "truth." Susan still had her job at the high school, how could she possibly understand Annie's dilemma? And Dan? He felt so remote in Mexico. There he was, keeping companies secure and solvent, thereby saving the livelihoods of millions of employees. And here she was, desperately trying not to embarrass herself. She tapped out a brief text to Dan. *At homeschool group!* Her finger hovered over the send arrow.

Plump little Paloma bustled up, beaming. "Hello Annie! So glad you're here. I thought you might want to borrow this book of mine. I found it really helpful when I first started." She handed Annie a volume titled *Schooled: How to Train Your Child's Mind Without Losing Your Own.* "Tips to get you started."

"Thanks. I need all the help I can get." Curious, Annie scanned the Introduction:

This book is based on the premise that homeschooling is for everyone, because every parent teaches. You teach your child to walk and talk and share toys ...

"Here, skip to this chapter." Paloma reached over and flipped through the book. The pages automatically parted to a dog-eared chapter:

Homeschool Do's and Don'ts.

When your friends and neighbors ask, "What about socialization?" explain that you're relying on the community. "Can I pencil you in for Thursday afternoons to come socialize with the kids?"

Annie looked up. Paloma was watching her with a huge smile on her face, her eyes wide and happy, even her black hair was glossy with joy. "I can't even tell you how many people have asked me, 'What about socialization?'" Paloma said. "You can borrow this as long as you like."

Annie nodded gratefully. Yikes, she hadn't considered socialization in her lesson plan. Fortunately she needn't concern herself with Cara because her daughter had plenty of friends: Olivia and her boyfriend Nate, her other girlfriends like Taryn and Danielle, and John the Druggie. Cara was plenty socialized. Maybe *too* much? With the wrong kids? Good thing they grounded her. And then Willy ... poor kid, he got socialized by bullies. Fortunately Joey seemed like a well-behaved child.

One of Paloma's little clones came up with a chocolatey-brown smudge outlining her mouth. She was about to hug her mother's leg, but Paloma deftly intervened. "Here, let's get you cleaned up." She steered her daughter's face away and started walking towards the kitchen.

"Thank you for the book," Annie called after her. "I'll finish this at home."

Annie stepped around the corner and leaned against the wall separating the kitchen from the hallway to the restrooms. She skimmed randomly through different chapters: *Another advantage that homeschooling provides is the opportunity to select not only the curricula for your children, but their teachers, mentors, and friends as well ...*

Annie heard boys talking on the other side of the wall, "She's back. I thought she was only going to be here a week?"

Use socialization to benefit your child's specific talents, interests, and needs.

"She has a name," said another guy. "Cara."

Annie's ears pricked up at her daughter's name and she held still. She continued staring at the pages but didn't see any of the homeschooling advice; she was too busy straining to hear what the boys were saying.

"How long does it take to realize homeschooling is better than public school?"

"Actually, public school is better for some families. Not everyone is cut out for homeschooling."

"Give me one way public school is better than homeschooling."

"Football."

"Football players get concussions. They're brain damaged. That's why they play football."

"First of all, that's a circular argument. Secondly, basketball."

Annie didn't care about sports. What about *Cara?* She and Dan had grounded her from having a boyfriend, but they could reconsider if a squeaky-clean homeschooler asked her out.

"Dude, you want to shoot hoops? We got this." There was a pause. "I'll take Matt and Jon. You get Elliot and Josh." There was a longer pause. Annie imagined the boys surveying the cafeteria. "Okay, we could let the little guys in to get enough players."

The other guy lowered his voice, "Or let girls play."

Next came the longest pause. Annie held her breath, silently begging them to keep talking. And speak louder.

"How long is she going to be studying us?" Now both guys were whispering.

"I wonder if she plays basketball."

Yes! Annie wanted to assure them. Cara can play okay ... for a girl. At the very least she has stamina from all that jogging.

"If she keeps showing up here, let's keep the game going."

What game?

"Let's drop it."

"Dude, it's fun. How often do you get to design a girlfriend?"

Paloma's book dropped on the floor with a loud smack. Annie bent down, grabbed it, and skedaddled to the bathroom before the boys could come around the kitchen wall and find her eavesdropping.

She panted in the bathroom, catching her breath. She was dying to know which guys were talking about Cara. Although, did it really matter? Aren't all homeschoolers the same?

And what did that mean, "design a girlfriend"? Was that some new teenager video game? Jeesum crow, they were always coming up with crappy new apps.

During chemistry, Cara nonchalantly asked her lab partners if Ashley was part of their homeschool group and they said no, they didn't know any Ashleys. She asked if they had boyfriends and the girls giggled and said no, then showed off their purity rings.

After class ended, kids filed into the cafeteria to regroup into clans and beg their moms to let them stay longer so they could play outdoors since it was unusually sunny and warm for April. Cara grabbed her jacket and gloves and walked outside with Zach's sisters, Michelle and Charlene.

Plows had pushed snow into mountainous melting snowbanks in the corners of the parking lot and kids ran around, scooping up the softening snow and slapping it at each other. A basketball appeared and Zach, Eric and other guys quickly formed a loose three-on-three game at the hoop at the far end of the parking lot, near the tree line behind the church.

"Want to play ball?" Cara asked.

"Not in these shoes," said Michelle.

"Too cold," said Charlene. "Those guys are nuts."

"Bet their hands are freezing," Michelle added.

Cara didn't want to be the only girl playing. She wasn't impervious to peer pressure. But she was itching to get closer, at least to watch. As they chatted, Cara very gradually shuffled the conversation closer to the game.

The guys were hooting and ribbing each other. It was reassuring that homeschoolers could trash-talk. At least they weren't complete dweebs. Zach was good, it was evident right away. He was fast, aggressive, could finesse a fake, and he was a team player, often passing the ball to a teammate, instead of taking a shot.

Cara wondered what Ashley looked like. Probably short and curvy with long blond braids. She probably wore baggy sweaters with skirts to her calves. Clunky black shoes and ankle socks.

Okay now Cara was just being spiteful. Besides, Zach was way too cool for a derpy girl like that. Cara glanced at Charlene and Michelle to make sure they didn't notice her scoping out their brother. Nope. They were talking about their English homework with an enthusiasm that was dorky but kind of refreshing.

Suddenly their little sister ran over and latched onto Zach's leg while he was holding the ball. Marie should know better—she could have been knocked over!

Zach hesitated. He gripped the ball with both hands and squared his stance for stability so Marie wouldn't tumble. That pause, Cara knew, was his deciding moment: he could continue to play and ignore Marie, shuck her off his leg as easy as swatting a fly. But he didn't. He chose to interrupt his game. With a smooth underhand pass, he tossed the ball to a teammate, then turned and knelt. He put his hands on Marie's shoulders and leaned in to listen. Marie had the open vulnerable face of a four-year-old. Cara had no idea what the little girl was telling him. Some slight from the other kids?

Cara couldn't hear Zach's words, but she saw his expression. His brown earnest eyes gave his full attention to Marie. Silhouetted against the filmy layer of snow on the blacktop, they were face to face, his tall rectangular frame kneeling on the ground, his arms bracing her tiny upright body in her bright pink puffy jacket. He spoke to her as she sniffled and wiped her nose on her sleeve. His lips kept moving until she nodded, all big-eyed and attentive. He leaned his forehead to touch hers, like a prefrontal kiss.

It was the most beautiful moment Cara had seen in a very long time. Her throat constricted and ached the way it did when she cried. She pursed her lips and breathed slowly to let the pressure out.

Marie was beaming as she scampered off to rejoin her friends and Zach stood up, brushed slush off his knees, and extended his right hand wide, I'm open.

Cara was aware of teen paranoia, the feeling that everyone is watching you, even when they aren't, even when they couldn't care less about you. But sometimes it's in the most private moments that character is most clearly revealed. What do you do then? Do you ignore your little sister, or take the time to listen? When you assume no one is looking, it's easy to go low. In Zach's case, he took the high road even though it was so mundane to him that he never considered that anyone would care to watch.

Oh, but she did.

Cara knew she should pay attention to Michelle and Charlene who were kind enough to include her. But she couldn't focus on their conversation. It was like deplaning after a visit to a faraway country, a mystical land she had only dreamed of, with knights errant slaying evil dragons. Cara felt electrified and infused with the warmth of idealism. Chivalry is not dead. There's some good in the world and it's worth waiting for.

THIRTY

On Monday the Mulligans had reheated frozen pizza for dinner, again. "I didn't have much time to rustle up a meal tonight since it took so long to correct your homework. How is it?" Annie picked up a slice and peered at it, weighing her hunger against the edibility factor.

Willy shrugged.

Cara filled in the silence. "Great."

Annie nibbled a corner of her steaming piece of pizza. Total crapola. Liquified cheese on a petrified sponge with oil pooling on top. "Aren't the Bouchers wonderful? That is so nice of them to lend us books and drive you to Tae Kwon Do. How's it going, Willy?"

"Great! We do kicks and punches across the floor. And Joey said he'll help me memorize my first pattern. Can I hang out with Joey sometime? Can we invite him over here? We could do homework together."

Annie smiled fondly at her son. "Sure, hon." She turned to Cara. "Want me invite Zachary over, too?"

"Mom!"

"What? You're both seniors. You two could study together."

"Please. Don't even go there."

"Ouch!" Annie jerked a slice of sizzling pizza away from her mouth. Mozzarella cheese stretched like a tightrope between her teeth and the pizza she was drawing away. Hot tomato sauce dribbled down her chin onto her pajamas. "Crap! I hope this doesn't stain."

"You've been in your PJ's all day," Cara noted.

"What's the point in getting dressed when you're just at home all day long?" Annie said crossly, dabbing the pizza sauce with a paper napkin, which spread red glop around her plaid flannel top.

Silently Cara and Willy eyed each other. Annie glared at them both, daring them to challenge her. After a moment, Willy ventured a response, "Pajamas are cool."

Cara chimed in, "Lots of homeschoolers wear pajamas. All day. According to Eric, that's the second biggest advantage to homeschooling. The first is sleeping in. He's always raving about how much better homeschooling is than public school. Or, as he puts it, 'government school.'" Cara scratched finger quotes in the air. "He's so defensive about it. I don't know why he thinks he has to convince me. Like I have a choice."

"Can I wear pajamas all day tomorrow?" asked Willy.

"Sure," said Annie. How could she say no to him when she didn't bother getting dressed herself?

"You like Mozart, right?" Cara asked her mother. "Did you know he was homeschooled?"

"Really?"

"Eric told me. Every week he has a new list of homeschoolers he brags about. As if their talent can transfer to him. Like that'll help him play violin better, or something."

"I bet Eric wears his pajamas when he practices," joked Willy.

"Good one," said Cara, reaching over to give her little brother a fist bump.

Willy milked it, "Maybe I'll do better in English in my PJ's, right, Mom?"

"Right." Willy was absolutely adorable. Except for his nose, which had turned a sickly yellow-green.

After dinner the kids helped clean up the table, which was a snap since they ate on paper plates and didn't use forks or knives.

"I'm going to take a nice long bath," Annie announced, heading down the hallway towards her bedroom.

Cara flopped on the sofa and flicked on the TV. Willy stood in front of the mirror in the entryway, staring at his nose.

Cara asked, "You okay?"

"They jumped me from behind." Willy tentatively felt the bridge of his nose. "They called me a loser."

"You are not a loser."

"That's what the kids in school said."

"Are they the ones who entered the science fair?"

"Yeah."

"They're jealous you won and they're wimps for ganging up on you. *They're* the losers, not you. Get it?"

"Got it."

"Good."

Willy turned his head left and right in front of the mirror. "Zach said my nose was epic. And he's got a black belt."

"Zach's right. Your nose is wicked epic."

"For his black belt testing, he broke five boards with a sidekick! He did a jumping, flying straddle kick, broke two boards, one on either side!" To illustrate, Willy spread his arms out as far as he could. "He did take downs. Bam!" Willy threw an imaginary opponent to the living room rug. "He had to spar two blackbelts at once! Joey told me all about it. I wish I had seen."

BLAT! BLAT! BLAT! BLAT! BLAT!

Willy covered his ears with his hands. Cara launched off the sofa and dashed to the kitchen to get a cookie sheet, which she waved at the smoke alarm.

Annie stumbled out of the bathroom with a towel wrapped around her, dripping water on the hallway rug as she rushed to the kitchen. "SMOKE ALARM!" she yelled.

Willy, with his hands still protecting his ears, nodded.

"DID I FORGET TO TURN OFF THE OVEN?" Annie's wet feet slapped on the kitchen floor. She bent over the control panel and pressed *Off.*

"GET THE DOOR, WILLY!"

Willy yanked the kitchen door wide open. A blast of frosty air swept into the room. Cara used the cookie sheet to usher the fresh outside air into the frantic alarm screeching at the smoke emanating from cheese burning on the bottom of the oven.

The golden retrievers cowered in the living room corner, trembling. Their mournful eyes followed Annie piteously, like the starved, neglected dogs on the TV commercial for the animal shelter, wondering, *Why are you doing this to me?*

Annie shoved the kitchen door shut and hugged her towel tighter and shivered. "I'M HEADING BACK TO THE TUB BEFORE I CATCH COLD," she called. "SORRY ABOUT THE SMOKE ALARM!"

Back in the bathroom, Annie dropped her towel and slid into the soapy water. The alarm stopped blaring and Annie closed her eyes at the sudden silence. *That was a close one. I almost burned the house down.*

She told herself to calm down and think soothing thoughts like Dan stretched out on the beach soaking up a tan, and furry kittens, and orange popsicles in summer, and goose bumps, and ice skating, and ice fishing, and the way ice cubes stick to your damp fingers when you reach in to pull them out of their freezer's broken ice dispenser...

Wait a minute, this isn't warm or relaxing.

Annie twisted the outlet plug and let the tepid water glugg down. As she dried off with a towel, she wondered what would have happened if the house really had caught fire. She would have had to call 911 and rush outside in her terrycloth bathrobe and huddle in the black arctic night with Cara and Willy to watch helplessly while firefighters hosed her house down, forever ruining her furniture and rugs and favorite cookbooks and family photos and the new skinny jeans she bought on sale that will fit her as soon as she drops fifteen pounds.

And if the house burned, they would be homeless for a while and have to wear castoff clothes donated by do-gooders from local churches. She and the kids would go to the homeschool group at Faith United and the families there would recognize the holes in their jeans and wool Aran sweaters with frayed cuffs. Willy wouldn't care, in fact, he would wear anything that Joey or Zachary had previously touched, but Cara? She would be mortified to wear charity. Cara would rather become a hermit and never leave her room. Except, of course, she wouldn't have a bedroom if the house burned down.

Annie pulled on sweatpants, a turtleneck, and sweatshirt, and shoved her feet into furry slippers. She picked up her stained PJ's from the wet bathroom floor and shoved them into the hamper. She padded to the kitchen. "Kids?" she called, but they didn't answer. They must have already gone upstairs to their bedrooms.

Annie pulled a Long Trail from the fridge and settled on the sofa. She groaned and put her feet up on the armrest. After a long day watching Cara and Willy labor over their homework, Annie was exhausted. When she committed to homeschool, she didn't fully appreciate that she would never have privacy. Now her students were living with her nonstop and asking why the cicada nymphs stay burrowed underground for seventeen years and then only get five weeks of life in the sun before dying ... if imaginary numbers aren't real why do I have to study them ... what's for dinner?

She grabbed the remote and zapped on the TV. To reward herself for all the homeschooling she did, she would watch her favorite show, a blend between a talk show and a reality show. As Ula puts it in her warm southern drawl, "We take the talking to *your* home." The camera zooms up on a metallic golden globe which blooms tissues, like a lotus blossom.

Last week's episode featured a darling young girl who hand-sewed stuffed animals for kids to cuddle when they had to go to the time-out sofa in the back of her sixth-grade classroom. Ula offered the gold orb to the mother, who pulled out a tissue to dab at her tears of pride.

Annie had often imagined herself being featured on *At Home with Ula*, especially when she was baking. She would talk to the pretend camera and decorate her Nutella cheesecake with charming insouciance, tilting the platter so the audience could better admire her handiwork. She also invented complete conversations where she explained the inspirations for her preschool songs for a Murphy Method episode. And she passionately passed on parenting tips to an appropriately appreciative Ula for a segment titled "How to Raise Superlative Children."

Of course that was before Cara turned to drugs and some punks broke Willy's nose. Now that they were homeschooling, Annie didn't feel quite as prepared for primetime TV.

But at least Cara was dealing with normal teenage stuff like pot, unlike Ula's current guest, Tiffany, a pale slip of a girl. She looked as young as Cara, yet she'd been married three years already. Tiffany sorrowfully recounted her ordeal of four miscarriages in a row. She recited each infant's name: Franklin, Ulysses, Clinton, Kennedy. Ula plucked a filmy white tissue from her proprietary gold ball and passed it to the tiny girl who burrowed back into the gray loveseat, swiping at the tears glistening on her hollowed cheeks. Annie sighed in sympathy as Tiffany sniffed and blotted her eyelids.

Someone always wept: a neighbor, a formally estranged family member, the camera man. Annie much preferred the episodes when the interviewees cried tears of joy. Usually Ula could pull it all together into a happy ending, perhaps introducing a surprise guest, the mean girl from seventh grade or the long-lost lover from senior year of college, and they would all resolve the conflict with heartfelt hugs and apologies. But occasionally Ula's efforts failed and the ubiquitous tissues wiped up tears of separation and grief.

Oozing warmth and empathy, Ula enveloped Tiffany in her velvet voice and cooed comfortingly. They danced around feelings and bleedings and babies. Ula asked about morning sickness and midwives. Finally she touched Tiffany's knee and gently suggested adoption.

At this, Tiffany burst into sobs. "I can't!" she wailed. "Jackson wants a biological son and if I don't give him a baby he says he'll get a divorce!"

Annie gasped in horror and even Ula the unperturbable, swallowed a big audible breath. Annie grabbed the remote control and quickly clicked out of the show before Ula could turn to flint-faced Jackson wedged next to Tiffany on the loveseat to ask for his side of the story.

Who cares about his perspective or how sterling his genes are? There is no excuse for treating a girl like that. This is 2014, not the dark ages. Women are not baby-making machines. What could he possibly, possibly say to redeem this situation? Whether Tiffany successfully gives birth to a baby or not, Annie was convinced hubby would split, now that his dirty laundry was aired for all the world to see and judge and boo.

Tiffany's plight was sickening. The TV show was supposed to entertain Annie, not make her feel depressed and angry. She pulled the faux shearling blanket up to her chin.

This is when she missed Dan the most. If he were here, they would cuddle on the couch and she would discover if he was feeling frisky. Sometimes she would pretend to be Mimi, the saucy French maid. Sometimes she would be Lulu, the sultry lounge singer. Occasionally Annie would slip on her red silk kimono with the mysterious slits in strategic places and become Cio-Cio-san, the geisha girl with exotic moves, who was even exotic-er after a couple rounds of beer.

Although the kimono was tricky. One night Annie had accidentally slipped her leg through the wrong hole and got all tangled up. Dan had to unravel her. He didn't mind; he laughed his head off the whole time, making *ohsofunny* jokes about eating his "little egg roll." But she had been aiming for an alluring "come hither" look, not "come snicker" while you unwrap me. That was the first time she swore off vodka shots forever.

She wanted Dan. Damn ISS for sending him to Cancun. Why couldn't he telecommute like the guys at OBS?

Annie snapped the off button and stood up. She tilted her beer upside down over her open mouth and guzzled the dregs.

She missed Dan. She missed her job. She missed her life. She was sick of staying home and homeschooling. All because of a couple puffs of pot? Cancer patients used marijuana for medicinal purposes. So it couldn't be that bad, right? Not bad enough to kick a young girl out of high school and irretrievably screw up her life, right?

And her *mother's* life.

Right?

It was so stupid and unfair. Annie plucked a wrinkled, worn paperback from the bookshelf, *A Slice of Cake.* She would read in bed and keep the light on as long as she needed.

THIRTY-ONE

After they got back from church on Easter morning, Annie ran through the house, barking directions. "Cara, you take the bathrooms, Willy, you sweep the kitchen, be sure to get around the dog bowls, and for Pete's sake get your insect collection off the table, I need to set it for dinner."

Cara said, "I cleaned the bathrooms last week. It's Willy's turn."

"I don't have time to argue. I have to peel the potatoes. Willy needs to get his gear out of the dining room. You do the bathrooms."

"Do I get extra credit?"

"Yes, yes. Just get the job done." It was highly irrelevant. Cara didn't know it, but Annie planned on giving her all A's anyway, so what use was extra credit? Annie would have given Cara an A+ to infinity, as long as the loo was sparkling clean before her mother inspected it.

That afternoon Annie's parents showed up at their house with their traditional coleslaw and pineapple slush.

Cara raved about Grandma Murphy's copper hair. Grammy cupped her hair with her hands and smiled radiantly. She offered to show them all how to do flamenco arms; she had been unsuccessful in persuading Sylvia to take Irish dance. Laughing, Willy joined the arm tutorial, while Grandpa sat on the sofa, nursing his beer, critiquing. "More pizzazz." "Too robotic."

Afterwards Grandpa carved the ham. Dan joined them for dinner on the computer. The whole time, Annie was dreading the school question. She had asked the kids not to mention homeschool and just pretend they were still going to real school. "It's not exactly lying. You *have* been in school up until last month. I just don't want to worry my parents, is all." For extra credit, both kids agreed. But what if they flubbed it?

Thanks to her dad, Annie was well versed in Murphy's Law. In fact, he had a special corollary they called Dad's Addendum: If anything *can't* go wrong, it will anyway. Even if you have an ironclad case. For example, your client doesn't show. Your client lies through his teeth. A new piece of evidence pops up out of nowhere. Your client changes his mind. Your witness breaks down on the stand and changes her testimony entirely. Your client skips out without paying. Your client is bankrupt and can't pay. The judge is an asshole who is hungry for his lunch break.

Annie had spent her happy-go-lucky childhood preparing for the worst. It was the Irish version of prepping. So when her dad asked the kids how school was going, Annie closed her eyes and held her breath.

But Cara smoothly launched into her American history. "Grandpa, I think you'll like this quote from Abraham Lincoln. 'As a nation, we began by declaring that "all men are created equal." We now practically read it "all men are created equal except negroes." When the Know-Nothings get control, it will read "all men are created equal except negroes, foreigners and Catholics."'"

Annie's eyes snapped open.

Cara was reading from her cell phone. She continued, "'When it comes to this I should prefer emigrating to some country where they make no pretence of loving liberty – to Russia, for instance, where despotism can be taken pure, and without the base alloy of hypocracy.'"

Cara was rewarded with a short snort of laughter from her grandfather. She explained, "That's a direct quote from Lincoln to his friend and slave-holder Joshua Speed."

"Ha. Even in the 1800s Russia had that reputation," her grandfather said appreciatively.

"Did you know that slaves were only counted as three-fifths of a person in the Constitution? Talk about inequality!" Cara's eyes glittered with anger at the injustice.

"Life isn't fair. That's why this country needs good lawyers like us, right Cara?" her grandfather smiled proudly at her.

"Good job," Dan chimed in via computer screen.

Then Willy launched into his science project and before he could fully explain why the Morgan Sphinx Moth has a proboscis over twelve inches long, both grandparents were trying to change the subject to the weather—sloppy spring snow—while they shoveled in scalloped potatoes.

It just goes to show how easy it is to hide the truth when everyone cooperates. Although Annie had dreaded it for days, Easter turned out to be a miracle.

After scarfing dessert down, Cara and Willy said goodbye to their dad and disappeared upstairs while Annie served tea. As her mother stirred cream into her teacup, her scarf slipped down and Annie noticed a red welt on her neck. "Mom, do you have a rash on your neck?"

She quickly readjusted the colorful scarf. "It's nothing."

"It looks inflamed. That's not skin cancer, is it?"

"No, dear. I'm fine." She clutched her scarf to her throat and reached for a scoop of pineapple slush. "Perhaps my pin scratched me."

The pin was a life size replica of an unborn baby's feet at ten weeks, which were displayed at every pro-life convention, including the booth at the summer fair. Grammy had a gazillion tiny gold feet. She stuck feet on the lapel of every coat in her closet and she pressed them on all her grandkids. One summer she had poked the pin into the brim of Willy's Red Sox baseball cap, insisting, "Goes with everything." Actually, it didn't, and as soon as her mother left, Annie gave permission to Willy to unplug the feet from his hat.

Her mother swiveled the pin on her scarf so the toes were pointing up. But the pin was inches away from the contusion on her neck.

Annie crooked her finger and pulled the scarf away. "That looks like a—omigod, mom, is that a *hickey*?"

"Annie, what your father and I do is our own business." She flapped Annie's hand away and fiddled with the scarf, her fingers fluttering. "We gave up … you know … for Lent, and now it's Easter." She looked down at her scarf, as if explaining to the pastel flowers spattered on the light green filmy polyester. "We have every right to … to …"

Stop!" Annie held her hand up. "Don't tell me."

Her dad had stopped chewing his pie and was staring at his plate. His shoulders shimmied, causing his fork, halfway to his mouth, to wobble and the apple pastry clinging to it wiggled, precariously, closer to the edge. They stared, transfixed, as the jiggling pushed the apple over the cliff of tines. The apple glop fell in a soft wet splat on the fine china below. Annie thought she heard her dad chuckle.

"Hello?"

They all turned toward the laptop propped up at the head of the table.

Annie had forgotten him. "Hey, Dan."

"Listen, I'm going to sign off and get a little more work done. The more I get done now, the sooner I can come home."

They all agreed that was a good plan, said goodbye, Annie blew him a kiss, and he clicked out.

"So, Mom, what else is new?" asked Annie. "Aside from, from ..." All she could think of was *hickey*. "Aside from—" she stirred her tea—"flamenco lessons and the hair salon?"

"Yes, well, I have quite a few exciting ideas on my bucket list. Such as swimming with dolphins."

"You hate getting your hair wet," argued Annie's dad.

"Eiffel Tower," she continued.

"Overrated," he countered.

"Ice skating at Rockefeller Center, then watching the Christmas tree light up."

"You'll fall and break your wrist. I'll have to take you to the emergency room. There'll be traffic and it'll take forever to get to the hospital and you'll miss the tree lighting show."

The doorbell rang and Annie jumped up. "I'll get it."

It was Wendy at the front door. "Happy Equinox!" she announced, holding a tray of lemon cups.

"Thank you, come on in, my parents are visiting." Annie bent her head to Wendy's ear and whispered, "Don't mention marijuana, bullies, or homeschooling." She ushered Wendy into the dining room and re-introduced everyone and shoved the apple pie and pineapple slush aside to set Wendy's concoction in the center of the table.

"So nice to see you again, Mr. and Mrs. Murphy. Try a lemon cup. They're Paleo."

Annie's mother picked one up and slid her spoon into it. She tucked a dollop of lemon pudding into her mouth and gave an appreciative, "Mmm."

Her dad said, "You can check Paleo off your list."

"Very funny." Mrs. Murphy turned to Wendy. "Have you written out your bucket list? Probably not. You're so young, yet. You have plenty of time. I'm up to number sixty-nine: Rebuild homes for Habitat for Humanity. I wonder if there were any floods in Hawaii or Tahiti where they need new homes? Perhaps Aruba?"

Years ago Wendy had told Annie about the birthing classes she took when pregnant with River. The birthing expert explained how to avoid the risk of urinary incontinence after childbirth by strengthening the pelvic muscles with Kegel exercises. Wendy took this very seriously and practiced clenching whenever she was stuck listening to a boring person. Considering she was a counselor, Annie figured Wendy's levator muscles were lockjaw pliers by now.

Since then, Annie sometimes wondered, *Is she doing her Kegel exercises right now?* Annie would study Wendy's face for telltale signs, and sometimes she spotted a strained look in her eyes, as if she were combating boredom, but then Wendy would say something off topic that explained her expression, such as, "What's that smell? Did you just get a delivery of propane gas?" Or, "My Muladhara chakra feels disturbed," and she would twist her spine until it crackled.

And now here she was listening to her mother's bucket list. Annie peered closely at Wendy. Was she clenching? But of course Annie couldn't ask.

"Good for you!" Wendy exclaimed to Mrs. Murphy. "You've already completed sixty-nine goals? That's brilliant!"

"No, dearie," she patted Wendy's hand. "I haven't *completed* sixty-nine. I've *listed* them. I've only finished a few so far. These things take time. Sylvia and I got our hair colored and took dance lessons and now I'm trying to get Glen here to help me out with number fourteen: The mall walking club. But he says he'd rather watch a Hallmark movie than go window shopping with a 'bunch of hens' even though I told him it's not just for women ..."

After Wendy and her parents left, Annie put her special china back in the hutch. She went into the master bedroom and changed out of her dress clothes, putting on comfy PJ's and shuffling into her slippers. Unaccountably wistful, she flopped on Dan's side of the bed and sniffed.

Aside from the Horrible Hickey Disclosure, dinner had gone off without a hitch. The table setting had been festive; her ham was juicy; the desserts were lush and lavish. Wendy's lemon cups were surprisingly tasty. But something was missing.

Annie wiped a renegade tear that dribbled out the corner of her eye.

She had a love-hate relationship with ISS. She loved Dan's salary, because, as vital as teaching preschoolers is, the wages are lackluster. But she hated Dan's overtime and his assignment to Mexico. She blew her nose and dropped the crumpled tissue off the side of the bed.

How pathetic that her mother got more action than she did. Her parents were so old. Ew. She had assumed they had given up sex, not just for Lent, but for life.

It made Annie's sacrifice seem small in comparison. During Lent she had been sucking down mainstream beer, abstaining from the really good stuff like Heady Topper and Fiddlehead.

But this afternoon when her Lenten fast was finally over and she snapped open Sip of Sunshine's tall yellow cylinder, Dan wasn't there to clink cans with her. His head was trapped in their computer, with a disorienting time delay, and some watery sounds, and then the screen froze when he was talking, so they found themselves conversing with a still shot of his face with his lips garbled in a goofy way.

Annie felt cheated. Her mom and dad got credit for giving up ... whatever exactly they actually did give up. But she and Dan were separated by Mexico for six weeks and they got no Lenten credit at all for their abstinence.

Sure, Dan FaceTimed. After the connection reanimated, she could see his adorable eye crinkles when he laughed. She could see how handsome he looked with his dark tan. She could blow him a kiss before signing off. But FaceTime and phone calls simply weren't enough. She honked her nose again and lobbed her used tissue like a javelin. It lost momentum at takeoff and wafted lackadaisically towards the floor.

To hell with a virtual presence. Annie yearned to touch Dan and smell him and taste him. They had never been separated this long before. Aside from postpartum healing time, they had never abstained for this length of time. The celebration simply wasn't complete without Dan because the Easter feast is not really about food; it's all about family.

Annie clambered off the bed to open his top bureau drawer. She had to yank hard on the left handle; it was sticky there, which bothered her every time she put Dan's underwear away. She hadn't opened this drawer in weeks. The swollen wood squealed as she squeaked it open. Her heart echoed that squeal.

The drawer didn't have much in it, only the extras and rejects that were too tattered to pack into his Mexico suitcase. There were the standard black ankle socks rolled in tidy balls. His underwear. She fingered the folded double-sewn edges of his briefs longingly. The pointless fly pocket in front.

And then his tee shirts. Ah. She saw one with gray armpit stains and drew it to her face. She kissed it. She licked it. The dryness sucked the moisture out of her tongue. Sheesh, what did she expect?

She pressed it to her face and inhaled deeply. Yes. Oh yes. His specific and exquisite brand of testosterone with its unique undertone of sweat. She hugged his tee to her chest and tiptoed to the bed where she tucked it in on Dan's side, underneath the covers, next to where she would lie that night, lonely and cold.

THIRTY-TWO

"Hi, come on in!" Maggie beamed at Annie who stood at the doorstep with her arms full of borrowed books that Willy had nixed. Maggie held the door open while Annie stepped around her into the Boucher's black and white tiled mudroom.

There was an array of cardboard boxes lined up along one wall. They were in varying dimensions, from the size of a shoebox to large ones about three feet long and almost as high, and stacked in irregular piles, one upon another, halfway up the wall, as if they were propagating.

"Don't mind the clutter," said Maggie. "We just picked up a delivery from the food co-op and haven't had time to put it all away."

Annie peered at the labels: Koyo, Riceland, Aura Cacia, Seventh Generation, Vermont Coffee Company.

"You'd be amazed how much my crew can eat. We go through this monthly." Maggie waved an arm at an open box stacked near the kitchen. Annie peeked in and spied a large bag of oats bundled inside. "Sometimes it feels like feeding an army." Maggie's blue eyes sparkled. "But I wouldn't trade it for the world. Here, let me help you." Maggie took the top four books off Annie's stack and led the way. "Come on in to the kitchen."

The stove was flanked by a dark granite countertop glistering in the afternoon sun, which poured through the window framed by potted pink geraniums. The French colonial cupboards gleamed bright white and the floor sparkled as if Cinderella and her animated animal friends had just spruced it up. Annie's right middle finger twitched automatically to pin the room on her Pinterest board.

She heard a piano and violin practicing a Mozart duet in another room. On the oak floor in front of the woodstove, three little heads bent over a large mosaic formed out of colorful wood blocks. Maggie nodded toward them and explained, "Math."

Zachary was sprawled belly down on the area rug with his head propped in his hands. His dog lounged next to him, resting his snout on his back. The teen looked up from his thick book. "Hello, Mrs. Mulligan."

"Hello, Zachary. How are you?"

"Fine, thanks. And you?"

"I'm fine." And suddenly Annie *did* feel fine. Completely and sincerely. It was so peaceful here. The kids were all studying so ... so ... studiously.

With one finger, Zachary slid a yellow octagon piece over to the younger kids. "Try this."

Without looking up, his little brother picked it up and incorporated it into the pattern growing on the floor. "Thanks."

These children were delightful. Polite and helpful. And so studious. Annie felt the compressed hush of knowledge being exchanged, as if she were standing in a library, absorbing the thoughts of the great minds that wrote the classics. She inhaled deeply. She could smell the elegant scent of intelligence and wonder. She caught a whiff of Plato and Aristotle and eau de Einstein.

It looked so effortless. Maggie didn't have to do anything but entertain Annie and then start cooking dinner. No, she probably had a chore chart for meals. "Do your kids just teach themselves?" Annie wondered.

"Actually, we do use a lot of self-direction—the Montessori method."

Annie gazed at the tidy row of labeled potted herbs, the wooden bowl heaped with gleaming, healthful fruit, beautifully framed maps on the wall, the chore chart pasted on a scruffy brown repurposed washboard ... Of course Maggie had a chore chart! As soon as she got home, Annie would slap together a sticker chart for Willy and Cara.

She sighed happily. "What a beautiful kitchen. I love your countertop and all the windows."

"Thanks. The kitchen is what sold us on this house. They call it home schooling, but when it's not van-schooling, it's usually kitchen-schooling." Maggie smiled. "I'll just put these books in the library." She stepped past the little ones absorbed in their math. Annie followed her into the adjoining room. "This was listed as a living room, but we converted it to a library."

Maggie set the books down on a coffee table and Annie put her pile next to them. She turned and stared at the range of bookshelves lining three walls. A small plaque in Old English calligraphy with a colorful ornate border stated: *Fairy tales are more than true; not because they tell us that dragons exist, but because they tell us that dragons can be beaten.* ~ G. K. Chesterton. Annie had heard of this guy, but had never read any of his books.

"And that's where I do my daily workout." Maggie inclined her head toward the far corner.

She expected a stationary bike or elliptical machine, or a set of weights, or maybe a thick pink Pilates mat like Annie used. On the sporadic occasions when she did work out, Annie performed her exercises lying comfortably on her back with her legs in the air. One time Dan chanced upon her and if the kids hadn't been home at the time, they would have engaged in *his* favorite calisthenics.

Instead of a treadmill, Annie saw something that looked like one of those ergonometric chairs that she and Dan tried out at the ISS conference they attended at a ritzy New York City hotel a few years back. Except instead of constructed from recycled metal and remolded plastic, Maggie's contraption was made out of dark polished wood and a slab of fabric. It didn't look nearly as comfy.

Plus, how do you do a workout on such a low bench? Was Maggie stuck in a 1980s step aerobics routine? With her hair in a high ponytail contained by a floral scrunchie, wearing white chunky sneakers and ankle socks and poison green zebra print tights with a neon pink leotard cut high above her hips?

"It's our prie-dieu."

Annie looked at her blankly.

"A kneeler, for daily prayer."

Then Annie noticed the maroon velvet padding on the step and the Celtic cross carved into the wood. Right. *A kneeler.* Like the one that Julie Andrews would kneel on in *The Sound of Music* back when she was trying to be a nun, bargaining with God, before she gave up and married the Captain.

"Ha ha," trilled Annie, to show Maggie she understood her joke about her daily workout. But internally she wondered, is Maggie a religious fanatic? Do her kids come running when her husband whistles, like the Von Trapp children in the movie?

"What does your husband do?" Annie asked.

"Vermont Air National Guard."

"Oh. Is he on tour?"

"It's classified, but I think he's stationed in Afghanistan. Sh." Maggie briefly pressed a finger to her lips conspiratorially. "Don't tell anyone." She gave a thin, yet gentle smile, as if her lips were too threadbare to stretch into a full-fledged smile. "We have so much to pray for, hence the prie-dieu."

Maggie led the way back towards the kitchen. Her kids were still on the floor, fanned out around their pattern blocks. The atmosphere exuded the promise of cooperation and erudition. How did Maggie achieve this academic peace by herself while her husband was overseas?

"How long will Rich be gone?"

"He's coming home mid-May. It sounds so far away, but it'll be here before you know it."

"I had no idea your husband was in the military. Mine's in Mexico for business for six weeks and I hate it."

"Yeah," Maggie commiserated. "I miss Rich especially when we're celebrating, like Zachary's black belt testing. Joy is meant to be shared."

"I thought it was misery that loved company."

Maggie laughed as if Annie had cracked a joke. "Have a seat." She scooped up some papers on the kitchen table. "I was in the middle of paying our property tax bill."

"Speaking of misery. Don't you hate paying such high taxes when you don't even send your kids to school? You could be sending them to school for free."

"Not exactly 'free.'" Maggie rustled her bill. "But we need a good education system for children. That's why public schools and school choice are so important. Not all mothers are cut out for homeschooling."

Was Maggie referring to *her*? Did she hear about Annie's geography blunder when she told Willy that Sierra Leone was a mountain range in Nevada? Annie's fingers scrabbled to her bosom to fasten her top buttons, but her fingers fished in vain. She had no buttons today; she was wearing a scoop neck. Intent on getting her priorities straight, Annie tugged her stretchy top higher to cover all cleavage, inadvertently creating a swag from one boob to the other.

"So we need good schools in the community," Maggie went on. "But I want to be the one to choose our curricula because *what* we teach is as important as *how.* And of course who we are is more important than what we know." Maggie twinkled mischievously at Annie. "You might be surprised at what your kids learn about *you* as you homeschool."

Yikes, that was Annie's secret fear! She smoothly changed the topic. "But what about making sure they get a complete education? What about getting into college?"

"Haven't you heard? Colleges love homeschoolers. Statistically they do really well. But that's beside the point," Maggie waved her arm airily, "my job isn't to create geniuses who get accepted into elite colleges, it's to raise them to be saints."

Holy crap. How did Annie miss that memo? Everyone knows the goal is to send kids to college! Everyone knows that!

Zachary picked his head up from his book. "I heard that, Mom. Are you implying that I'm not a genius?"

"I'm not worried about your intelligence, darling, it's your soul I pray for."

"Hey, hey," said Zachary. "I'm working on my halo. Can't you see it?" He fanned his hands above his head, indicating an invisible circle.

"Saint Zachary." Maggie played along. "You're going to look so handsome on a stained-glass window someday."

"That's what I'm talking about." Zachary flashed them a mock-smug smile.

Annie sighed wistfully. She couldn't remember the last time she and Cara bantered back and forth like that ... maybe when she was plugging Vegas Nights and Cara was rooting for Underwater Delights for the prom theme?

If Maggie was worried about Zachary's holiness, she would be downright appalled at Cara. Annie tried not to be jealous of other peoples' kids. Working at a preschool repeatedly taught her not to compare children. But she couldn't completely quash her wish that Cara were more like the Boucher kids who enjoyed studying *and chatting with their mom!*

THIRTY-THREE

THEY PULLED INTO FU's parking lot, crowded as usual with old vans and minibuses. "Too bad they don't have stained glass windows at this church," Cara's mother said, shifting the car into park. "You would look so lovely on one. Saint Cara."

Cara stopped brushing her hair and tossed her hairbrush into the glove box. Her mother cupped her hands over her head, pretending to set an invisible crown there. "It's a halo. Get it?"

"Weird." Cara opened her car door and fled.

She gave Zach a casual, "Hey," before chemistry class started. And she said hello to his lab partner, Eric. She wondered if they double dated with Ashley and Emily. "So I know you don't have cell phones because of the EMF radiation, but are you guys on Facebook?" Cara asked.

"Of course," said Eric. "We get to surf the net all day long, another cool thing about homeschooling."

"What he said," said Zach.

"What name do you go by?" Cara didn't want to admit that she had plugged in every derivation of "Zachary" she could think of.

The guys looked at each other and smiled sheepishly.

"Boris," said Eric.

Zach's smile became sheepisher. "Sam Gamgee."

"Seriously?"

Zach explained, "My dad doesn't want us using our real names online. Privacy, tracking, and security risks and all. He's in the Guard and could be targeted, and doesn't want to put us in jeopardy."

"So you chose ... Sam Gamgee?"

"Samwise Gamgee, actually." Zach's voice intensified with conviction. "Sam was the real hero, anyway. Frodo never would have made it up Mount Doom without him."

Cara raised her eyebrows at him.

"Did you know Frodo homeschooled? The dude who played him?" asked Eric.

"That one I did know." Cara and Olivia had watched all the movies in middle school and afterwards begged for archery lessons. "Did you know Gandalf homeschooled?"

"The actor?" asked Eric, genuinely surprised.

"No, the wizard. His mother taught him to read and write and wave a wand." Eric looked bemused, but she could tell Zach got it because he smiled. "Anyway, now that I know your Facebook names, I'll friend you."

"Sure, but I hardly ever go on," said Zach. "Waste of time. What can you do online that isn't better in person?"

Eric said, "Facebook is wicked whacked. We're keeping it real right here in 802." He punched Zach's arm. "And gonna keep on keeping it real in college, right, bro?"

"Hey, speaking of college, I got accepted to St. Ambrose!" Zach turned to Cara. "They have an excellent pre-med program."

"You want to be a doctor?"

"Vet. I've always loved animals. It would be so cool to work with them. How about you? What do you want to go to school for?"

Cara looked down at her notebook and her voice shrank. "My grandfather is a lawyer. We don't have the death penalty here, but other states do and he's told me about getting convicts off death row using DNA evidence. That's what I want to do. Defend the innocent." She suddenly wondered if she'd said too much. She glanced up at Zach.

He was nodding. "Cool."

"A lawyer, huh? Did you know Sandra Day O'Connor was homeschooled?" Eric bragged.

"No, I did not know that," she admitted.

"I'm telling ya, made it all the way to the Supreme Court. But what I want to do," Eric paused and puffed out his chest. "I want to design computer games! Unfortunately my parents say that's not a career, that's a—" Eric scratched finger quotes in the air— "'fantasy.' They want me to go to tech school so I can be an electrician or plumber because plunging can't be outsourced to some dude in India." Eric pumped a pretend plunger into an imaginary toilet, with a disgusted expression. "But I don't want to unclog toilets, I'm a gamer. I'm going to get my degree in electrical engineering. That way I can make the chips that go into the games. And make bank so I can pay off my school loans. Am I right?" He slapped Zach on the back.

Cara put her hand on her hip. "I don't know why they treat us like little kids for years, tell us where to go, what to do, what to study, and then suddenly it's all, 'What do you want to do for the rest of your life?'" She squished her lips together. "Talk about pressure."

"My 'rents don't tell me what to do all day long," Eric said. "But I have heard that kids in public school can't even go to the bathroom without a hall pass." He slid his eyes sideways to catch Cara's reaction. "One more reason homeschooling is better."

"Let's see you homeschool your way through *college*."

Zach said, "Actually, many colleges offer online classes which is essentially the same thing as—"

"Oh shut up." Cara punched his bicep playfully. "What about Ashley?" she ventured. She didn't even know how old she was, but she was about to find out. "Is she going to college next year too?"

"Ashley?" asked Zach. His eyebrows puckered in puzzlement.

"Your girlfriend?" Cara inquired.

"Oh yeah." He shot a look at Eric who nodded energetically. "Um, yeah. Ashley's going to college."

"Same school as you?"

"Um. No."

Zach was acting fishy and sheepish at the same time. Cara studied him, then Eric, hunting for clues.

"Yeah," said Eric. "Emily's going to college next year too."

Why were these guys being so shady about their girlfriends? "What's up? Did you guys break up or something?"

Zach nodded as if he had just remembered they were no longer together.

"No," Eric corrected him. He slapped Zach's abs in solidarity. "No, they're still our girlfriends. We just haven't seen them lately. We've been busy, y'know."

How can homeschoolers possibly be too busy to hang with their girlfriends? According to Eric they lounge around at home all day long in their pajamas.

"I'm almost done!" said Willy from the back seat.

Annie rested her forehead against the steering wheel. She had tried reaching out to Cara on the car ride, but it fell flat. Homeschooling was bad enough when the entire world thought you were nuts. Now Cara did too? It's downright embarrassing to have your own daughter call you weird.

She wished she could FaceTime Dan right then and there. But how could she even explain this moment to him? There was so much going on in her life. A weekly online chat wasn't sufficient to fill him in on everything.

"Come on, Willy. Ready or not, it's time to go." Annie opened his car door and carried his backpack for him while he shuffled his papers into order.

When they got inside, the classes had already assembled, so Willy ran off to English. She took a seat between Maggie and Paloma.

For the past three weeks Annie had looked forward to the homeschool group. Someone else taught chemistry to Cara and English to Willy, while she got to hang out with the extra moms and learn something new about homeschooling.

At least these women didn't call her weird. These ladies were helpful. They passed on the names of teachers willing to do year-end assessments. They showed her the easy way to document learning for the state (xerox the Table of Contents in your textbooks). How to save money by shopping at the best thrift stores and liquidation centers so you can spend more money on classical curricula and piano lessons. How to homeschool using unit studies, which incorporate several different subjects at once. For example: geography, history, math, and poetry.

Unit studies sounded fun until she learned the topic the François family was in the middle of learning: covered bridges of Vermont. As far as Annie was concerned, covered bridges belong on post cards and calendars, not in curricula.

If your goal is to bore children to death, why not a 4-week unit study on nineteenth century door knockers? You could study metallurgy for science, the mass production of goods during the Industrial Revolution for history, and use *A Christmas Carol* as a literary tie-in. If the kids aren't already rendered comatose, top it all off with a hands-on art project for the kinesthetic learners: each student could fashion their own movable door knocker out of aluminum foil, while they swapped knock-knock jokes.

Actually ... making your own door knocker would be a blast. Her preschoolers would relish getting their hands on sheets of shiny foil that they could mash into any shape they like. And even if they did toss their contraptions at each other, no one would get hurt. Even Carol Van Busy-body would be hard pressed to see the danger in foil-balls. After Annie got her job back at Play And Learn, she would locate an environmental source of scrap foil. The kids were always game for a field trip to Recycle North.

"Ladies, I need your help." Linda scanned the large hall and looked behind her before she continued. "I just found out that Therese," Linda dropped her voice down to a whisper. "Therese is only one fourth of the way through her math book."

The women in the circle drew in a collective breath. Annie belatedly sucked in air loudly with them.

"I know," Linda agreed. "All along she'd been telling me she was doing her math while I worked with Athanasius, Vincent, and JP, too. Well, I finally got around to checking her work and she's only on lesson 37. And here we are in April!"

The ladies clucked in commiseration.

"What am I going to do?"

"What grade is Therese in this year?" asked Melanie, the fluffy haired mom.

"Seventh."

"Don't worry, Linda. She'll be fine. Just have her do two math lessons a day until she's caught up." Evelyn counted on her fingers. "In August."

"She already hates math."

"If she hates it, she'll need a break in the summer," said Tonya François, wagging her finger sagely.

The other women nodded their heads up and down.

"When you start up in September, start off where you ended in June," Tonya advised. "I did that a couple years ago with Halle and it all worked out just fine."

"But what'll we tell the state?"

"Tell the state what concepts Therese *has* learned," Maggie advised. "Don't mention the lessons that she didn't get to."

Linda nodded. "That could work."

Between Paloma's how to book, the homeschool group ladies, and the heavy stacks of curriculum catalogs they pressed on her, Annie discovered there were as many homeschool philosophies as diet strategies. Doubling up on math lessons was like trying to cram fifteen pounds of weight loss into four weeks like Annie's friend who came back from a cruise and stopped eating for a month so she could fit into a size six dress in time for her class reunion, which didn't work.

The unschoolers were as mysterious as the folks who ate what they wanted when they wanted and magically didn't gain weight. The ladies who bought prepackaged curricula were like dieters who had meals delivered to their door.

Maggie's friend Deb was a hybrid homeschooler. She rarely had time for Faith United meetings because she was continuously carting her kids back and forth to fencing (Hunter was an Olympic hopeful), music lessons, dance, and drama. Deb signed her kids up for classes at museums, pottery studios, libraries, as well as public school for sports, Spanish, and Driver's Ed. Annie hoped Deb's family could afford a hybrid car to go with all that chauffeuring. She filed Deb into the all-you-can-eat-buffet category.

As for herself, going cold turkey from real school to homeschool, Annie felt like she just got her stomach stapled.

THIRTY-FOUR

IT WAS STATISTICALLY improbable, but all the requisite doors opened at the same time creating a window of opportunity.

Annie let the dogs out the back door to do their business. Willy brought the trash out to the bin in the garage, leaving that door open. And Cara, on her way back from the "library," had used the remote control hanging on the visor in the car to open the garage door before going upstairs to "study." And then, sonofagun, a squirrel darted past the front yard.

Moe and Curly hightailed it from the fenced backyard, through the side door, out the garage door and galloped after the squirrel, who scampered up a tree across the street in Mr. Hans' yard. The dogs barreled across the suburban street, directly in front of a Green Energy truck whose driver was so high up he never saw them. Moe made it past, but Curly caught the bumper with his hindquarters and flew up and onto the snowy yard.

Willy dropped the trash bag and ran towards his dog, shouting for Annie who charged out, slippers flip flopping. Curly lay on his side, quivering in the snow.

A Lexus pulled over and a lady in a creamy cashmere coat climbed out. "I saw the whole thing. Let me take a look." She stripped off her brown leather driving gloves and extended one hand so the retriever could get acquainted with her smell. "No blood or bones that I can see. That's good." After Curly licked her hand, giving her the green light, she crouched next to him in the snow and gingerly felt his spine, flanks, and then each leg. She closed her eyes briefly, summoning all her senses to her fingers.

"Is he gonna die?" asked Willy. When a car had struck Larry years ago, Willy had been safe at school, so he hadn't seen the crash or the ugly aftermath, but he feared Curly was doomed to a similar fate.

"No one's going to die," the woman assured him. "She'll be fine."

"You're gonna be fine," Willy crooned into Curly's ear. "Gonna be fine."

The woman said to Willy, "You're very good with dogs."

"Thanks," said Annie, proudly putting her hand on Willy's head as he petted Curly.

"Why aren't you in school today? Are you sick?"

"We homeschool," Annie answered for him.

"What about socialization?"

That's what Annie wanted to know. She didn't know how to answer, but surely socializing with a Good Samaritan had to be better than being bullied by middle schoolers. "You're it for today."

Annie wasn't sure the do-gooder understood her joke. The woman nodded seriously, as if accepting the mission, and continued examining Curly. As she bent over the retriever, Annie could see the woman's caramel-colored hair, light and airy as maple cotton candy, fluffed back into a French twist, held in place by a slender black clip studded with sparkly gems. It was a very elegant look. Annie wondered if they were zirconia or actual diamonds.

You don't see a French twist every day. Annie decided then and there to grow her hair long enough to sweep it into a striking and sophisticated updo. She marveled at the woman's calm demeanor and skillful fingers, assessing Curly's limbs with confidence. "Thank you—" Annie said, pausing for her rescuer to fill in the blank.

"Dr. Higgins. Louise Higgins."

Her slender fingers continued probing gently. Suddenly Curly winced, raised his head and stared at Willy, as if asking for help. "It's this one. Could be a fracture. I'll help you get her into the car."

"Him," corrected Willy.

"Pull your car up alongside," she directed.

Annie ran inside, grabbed her purse, kicked off her slippers, and shoved her feet into boots. "Cara! We're taking Curly to the animal hospital!"

Cara bounded down the stairs. "What happened?"

"Curly got hit by a truck. Willy and I'll bring him in. You need to get Moe. He chased a squirrel up Mr. Hans' tree."

Cara ran outside. She checked in with Willy and Curly before fetching

Moe who had given up on the treed squirrel and was nosing Curly curiously. Meanwhile, Annie backed the car out and parked it next to the snowbank. She opened the way back and felt the plastic mat. It was frigid. She ran back into the house and scavenged through the rag bin under the sink until she found the old sleeping bag that Willy had outgrown. She was about to spread it in the back, but Louise asked her to bring it next to Curly. They slipped it under him and then lifted the four corners up, hefting Curly, scared, wide-eyed, and panting, into the back of the car. Willy consoled his retriever, the entire time murmuring, "You'll be okay, you'll be okay."

Annie turned to Louise. "Thank you so much!"

"You're welcome." She must have seen the panic in Annie's face because she paused a moment and said kindly, "She hurt her leg, but she'll be fine. And they can give her pain meds."

"Him," said Willy.

"We really appreciate this. Thank you."

"Can I ride in back with him?" Willy had already climbed in the back of the car, hunched over his dog, petting Curly's back slowly and steadily, careful to avoid the injured limb.

"No," Louise and Annie both replied. They smiled at each other.

Willy grudgingly clambered over the seat and buckled himself in. Annie slammed the hatchback shut and called, "Thanks again!"

Louise turned her head over her shoulder and called, "You're welcome!" She strode to her car, her creamy coat flapping sedately behind her long legs, her head held high. Instead of a veterinarian she could pass for the queen of a European country or the spokeswoman for a luxury travel service.

Dr. Higgins was right about the break. Luckily it was only a hairline fracture. The first thing the vet did was administer a pain reliever. Then he put a splint and cast on Curly. As soon as the retriever woke up from the medicine, he systematically began to gnaw at the bandage.

THIRTY-FIVE

CARA WAS SURPRISED when her phone bleeped. No one called her anymore. Having her phone confiscated for a week hadn't helped the communication flow. John hadn't called since he dumped her and she hung up on him. Olivia usually called late, so her mother wouldn't know. Her other friends didn't know what to say about her expulsion so they had gradually dwindled away, with noncommittal texts such as "What up?" Suffering from major FOMO, Cara periodically checked CHU's website and Facebook to stay in the loop.

Cara glanced at the contact. Olivia. Uh oh, she was supposed to be cheering Nate at his away game this afternoon. "Hey, Via."

"Nate dumped me!"

"No!"

"Yes!" Olivia sniffled. "He dumped me!"

"D-bag!"

"I know, right?"

"Major bag!" Cara switched her phone to her other ear. How could he do this? Nate and Olivia had been going together since spring of freshman year! "Why did he break up with you?"

"I did what you said. I told him I was pregnant. But he says he doesn't want to deal with this—this *shit*—as he put it." Olivia sobbed and coughed. "Cara, he called my baby 'shit.'"

"That's *his* baby, too, he's talking about."

"I know! But he doesn't want it! He says I have to take care of it."

"He's freaking. You know that, right? He just needs to get used to it. He'll come round."

"Not in time for the prom. He said I can keep his ticket. Or give it to someone else. He didn't care."

"Asshole." Cara's estimation of Nate had tanked when he slobber-kissed her in his truck at homecoming, but she never expected him to be this douchey.

"Maybe he's right. Maybe I *should* stop this." Olivia hiccupped.

Cara wished her grandmother were on hand to advise her. Grandma had volunteered for Vermont Right to Life for about a thousand years and would know exactly what to say to Olivia. But Cara was drawing a blank. Zip. She couldn't think of a single thing except for the fact that they were talking about a baby. According to BabyBumpz, Pearl was as big as a prune.

She knew it was a selfish motive and not entirely logical, but she couldn't help feeling that if Olivia got an abortion, then Cara's sacrifice—taking the heat for being in the staff bathroom with the weed, getting expelled, being homeschooled by her mom, risking her college scholarship, ruining her entire freaking life ... it would all be in vain if Olivia got rid of the baby.

But she couldn't breathe a word of that to Olivia—she didn't want her bestie to hang up on her again. Besides, Cara's life wasn't *entirely* ruined. She had met Zach.

"Don't do anything yet, Via. Promise me?"

Olivia snuffled.

"Just give me some time," Cara continued.

"Time for what?"

"I've got an idea." Cara had zero ideas. "Just promise me you won't do anything about the baby for one more week? Okay?"

Nothing.

"You've got time. In Vermont you have all nine months." This was one of several nuggets of information that her grandmother passed around as liberally as her baby feet pins.

Sniffle.

"Just a couple more days, okay?" In a week Pearl would be a lime.

It was very faint, but Cara heard Olivia whisper, "Okay."

Cara clicked her phone off. *Thank God I'm not pregnant.* If it hadn't been for John's flexibility she might have found herself in Olivia's predicament. A pregnant single teen. A statistic on some stupid census that solves nothing.

John had many faults, including outrunning her whenever they worked out (he always cheated near the end by sprinting the last few yards), a grating laugh, being paranoid about pesticides and drugs, and most of all breaking up with her. But at least he didn't get her pregnant. Early on in their relationship, she had told him she didn't want to go all out and he accepted it.

In fact, looking back on it now, he seemed downright relieved. Maybe John wasn't really respecting Cara's wishes so much as he was afraid of an STD? Or a baby? If John dumped her over a single joint, how quickly would he have ditched her for getting pregnant?

Cara and John had only been going out since October. But Nate and Olivia had been The Couple since freshman year. It was positively barbaric for Nate to drop Olivia now, mere weeks from graduation. Simply because she was pregnant. With *his* baby.

How could Cara convince Olivia to keep her baby?

She had to show Olivia that she didn't need Nate. That she was fine without him. If she could prove to Olivia that she could have a fantastic evening at the prom without him, then she could also have the baby without him. Cara was already lacing on her running shoes. She needed to think.

THIRTY-SIX

Tuesday the toilet overflowed. Annie FaceTimed Dan so he could troubleshoot it. She recruited Willy to hold the computer at the precise angle for Dan to see into the tank while Annie fiddled with the thingamajig inside which triggered the lever for the flush. Dan was all stressed out because she had pulled him from the middle of an important meeting and he kept rushing Annie. She finally got the plumbing cleared, Dan clicked out of FaceTime before she said goodbye, Willy went back to his homework, and Annie was left to mop the mucky puddle by herself.

The microwave clock read 3:00 pm. That's close enough to dinnertime and both kids were upstairs in their bedrooms. Annie grabbed a beer from her fridge, uncapped it, and turned it upside down over her open mouth. She heard a noise. She turned the bottle upright and turned to look.

Willy peeked his face around the corner of the kitchen.

Damn, there was no privacy! Homeschooling would be a lot easier if the kids weren't always underfoot. At PAL she had an hour of free time between morning and afternoon classes to tidy the room and collect herself.

"You okay, Mom?" Willy asked.

"Fine. Great." She saluted him with the bottle. "Just doing the recycling." She made a big show of disposing the beer bottle in the bin holding empties for returns. She nestled it in upright so it wouldn't spill. She could come back tonight and rescue it, after Willy was in bed.

"Okay," he replied, dubiously.

That night Annie dreamt she was working at the preschool. She heard the menacing measures of Beethoven's Fifth, then Purnell appeared in a white lab coat and enormous safety goggles, holding an official-looking clipboard, asking invasive questions for a health inspection, like what books was Willy reading and was he allergic to Long Trail beer? Next thing she knew Annie was standing in front of the Camels Hump Union

High School board while snooty and suspicious board members pelted her with questions about her art books and gym curriculum when suddenly they all started laughing at her. She looked down. She was wearing her pajamas with an oversized baby bib tied around her neck to hide the pizza stain underneath, but the sauce spread and oozed blood red onto the white bib and she feared her heart had erupted.

Annie woke up screaming and thrashing around. She grabbed for Dan's warm body next to her, but there was only cold empty bed space and one measly tee shirt. She draped his white cotton shirt over her face, but her heart thumped too fast to relax.

She crawled out of bed and zapped a glass of milk in the microwave. She sipped the warm milk and nibbled cookies and clicked through TV channels until *It's a Wonderful Life* popped on and she fell asleep on the sofa.

The next day she spent hours fussing over a lasagna with sausage and homemade marinara and driving it to Christine's house since she had just had a new baby, Henry, 8 pounds, 3 ounces. She even volunteered to watch the older brothers and sisters, all under age seven, while Christine took a nap with newborn Henry even though Annie would've loved a snooze herself.

By the time she got home she didn't have time to cook and she knew Cara and Willy were sick of reheated frozen pizza so she surprised them with popcorn and soda for dinner, which was supposed to be a jolly lark, but Cara and Willy grumbled until Annie peevishly tossed the popcorn out the back door and they all munched on milk and cereal in crunchy silence.

Unbeknownst to Annie, Moe and Curly devoured the popcorn when they went outside to pee. Curly was still limping with his cast halfway chewed off, but that didn't stop him from joining Moe in ralphing all over the living room rug after she let the dogs back in. As Annie swabbed up glops of popcorn, she wondered what Dan was doing. Drinking Dos Equis by a pristine pool?

On Thursday Annie surprised the kids with a brand-new set of pattern blocks. She had used her teacher's discount to get a 250-count package with a bonus set of Cuisenaire rods. According to the brightly colored label on the box, manipulatives such as blocks make math kinesthetic and visual and offer real-world applications, such as symmetry and measurement. Plus, the packaging promised: *FUN!*

Cara said, "You do realize I'm seventeen years old, right?"

"Zachary is your age and he uses pattern blocks and Mrs. Boucher says he's acing *his* math class."

Cara's face twisted into a question mark. She whispered, "Zach uses *blocks*?"

"Does Joey use them?" asked Willy who had already opened the see-through plastic tub and was pouring the tiles onto the rug.

"Yeah."

The blocks floated precariously on top of the carpet's polyester fibers. And when Willy nestled the triangles around the octagon, they tilted slightly away, leaving tiny slices of air between them.

"The Bouchers used them on a wooden floor," Annie pointed out helpfully.

She went into the kitchen to open up her new daily planner which she also used her teacher's discount on. It was a leather-bound deluxe journal with separate pages to mark each individual day for each student.

Ping.

Annie smiled and stripped the plastic wrap off eagerly. Her new homeschooling friends all stressed how important it was to document all the kids' activities and lessons to send to the state in June. Annie went to the first blank student page, and with her new ballpoint pen she entered the date, then wrote carefully in her legible preschool font, CARA.

Ping. Ping.

Underneath, she wrote MATH in the subject line. Pattern blocks, 10:30-11:30.

Ping. Ping. Ping.

She turned to a new section and wrote out a corresponding plan for Willy.

She heard a smattering of pings, like acorns hitting the ground when she rattled the oak branch during outside time at PAL. The kiddos loved this and would frolic under the tree *trying* to get hit by an acorn.

Annie tracked the sound to the living room. Willy and Cara were scooping up pattern blocks by the fistful and throwing them at each other. The blocks that missed their target tagged the wall and cascaded in wooden plinks on the hard floor, or softer landings on the sofa and area rug.

"Cara! Willy!" she shouted.

They froze, arms outstretched in catapult pose. Cara struggled to hold her wriggling lips in place. Willy tried to contain his smile, but it snuck out and he gave up and giggled.

Back when Annie was pregnant with Cara and reading the first of an onslaught of parenting books, she thought that "Choose your battles" was excellent advice. For example, would she allow Halloween candy in her house? How about Santa Claus? Barbie? At what age would she expose her tender child to her first PG-13 movie?

Annie was prepared to render a decision on manners (always) and hitchhiking (never) and boyfriends (how cute is he?). But little did she know how many battle lines would be drawn over the years, how many choices she would have to make. Little did she know that seventeen years later she would need to decide whether to engage with her children over the abuse of math manipulatives.

Should she draw her metaphorical sword and charge them? Or pretend she was cool with it? Should she chew them out or celebrate the fact that at least Cara and Willy were playing together, instead of in their separate bedrooms, plugged in to their individual computers? How did mothering become so damn complicated?

"Just don't hit the lamps," Annie commanded authoritatively.

Annie turned on her heel and marched back to the kitchen. She went to Cara's page and crossed out the time next to math. She wrote in a new entry, PHYS ED: 10:30—11:30. Throwing, catching, aiming, dodging.

Annie recalled her senior year of college when her boyfriend had caught her taking notes in class with a pencil. He had astonished her by confiscating her yellow No.2 and breaking it in half. She had gasped in awe when he lobbed her pink eraser towards the back of the room where it bounced off the concrete wall before flip flopping to a stop. "You're not a kid anymore," he had told her. "Use a pen." He had whipped an extra out of his backpack and handed it to her.

She had accepted his pen ceremoniously and pressed the top of it with an assertive click to stake her claim to emancipating adulthood.

Now Annie was *un*-learning. Unlike ballpoints, lead can be erased.

Next time Annie used her homeschooling planner, she would use a pencil instead of a pen.

When co-op day rolled around, Annie scurried into Faith United and crumpled into the folding chair next to Maggie and blew out a big sigh. After such a hellish week, Annie really needed support.

Linda announced that the older kids' English class would be presenting *A Midsummer Night's Dream* in three weeks in the Mapleville Elementary School gym and they were still looking for a donkey head they could borrow for Bottom. One of the older moms, in an archaic jean jumper and white turtleneck, offered her Easter bunny costume. A lively discussion ensued about the feasibility of turning a rabbit head into a convincing jackass face.

Annie voted full bore in favor. To enjoy Shakespeare's play you must suspend belief enough to pretend a rustic can be magically transformed into a donkey. Surely going from fake bunny to fake donkey required even less mental pixie dust.

The field trip to the llama farm had to be postponed because Tonya was still recovering from the flu.

Flatcher Free Library offered a free rug hooking class (Happy Hookers), which could count towards the state's Fine Arts requirement. "And," Melanie pointed out, "Phys Ed. Fine motor skills." This seemed to be an ongoing game with these ladies—to see how many subjects a specific class qualified for.

Paloma gave an update on Christine. "Mother and baby are doing fine. I organized a Meal Train for them, so you can sign up online."

"I already brought over a meal," Annie volunteered. "Henry is adorable and has regained his birth weight!"

Maggie said, "Speaking of babies growing, I just read a fascinating article that researchers discovered cells with a Y chromosome in the brains of deceased women. What happens is when a baby develops inside the uterus, fetal cells can pass through the placenta from the baby into the mother."

Annie wondered if she had some Willy cells floating in her head. And what were they up to?

"In a different study, researchers discovered hundreds of fetal cells in an alcoholic woman's *liver.* Because fetal cells are malleable, scientists believe they might help us resist certain diseases. They call it fetomaternal microchimerism."

The circle of ladies smiled, no doubt imagining all their offsprings' cells inside like emergency medical technicians, zooming where needed to assist. Annie mentally channeled her incipient cells to her right ventricle.

Maggie gestured to the toddlers playing with blocks and dolls in the middle of the circle of moms in folding chairs. "And the placenta is a two-way street, that is, our children could have some of our cells inside them."

Annie's chest trembled. She put her hand to her heart to feel the warmth exuding from it. Science had confirmed her gut feeling that she had lost pieces of herself years ago.

THIRTY-SEVEN

"Hi Mrs. Boucher, this is Cara." She felt awkward calling their house phone. "May I please speak with Zach?" Cara paced back and forth in her bedroom, like a prisoner in a cell.

"Certainly, Cara. I'll go get him."

Cara passed her bed six times before she heard, "Hello."

Zach's voice was deeper on the phone than she remembered it being in person. She had become accustomed to being mesmerized by his gorgeousness, which was one reason she was calling him on a Saturday, instead of asking him yesterday at FU. But even without a visual hypnotizing her, she was stunned—his voice was so deep and warm, it resonated on her skin. She felt hot and flushed, and was relieved that he couldn't see.

"Hey Zach, how ya doing?"

"Great. You?"

His voice rumbled down the back of her neck and her knees felt crumbly. Swoosh. Cara plopped on her bed so she wouldn't crumple into a pile on her rug. Only three words and he had already made her collapse. *Focus!* "I'm good." *Just Do It.* "Um, I was wondering if you could do a huge favor? I have this friend who has tickets to the prom but her boyfriend just dumped her so she has no one to go with? She needs a date? I know you already have a girlfriend, so this would just be as friends." Cara rattled it out quickly before she lost her nerve.

"You want me to take her to the prom?"

"Yeah. I mean, if that's okay with Ashley?"

"Your friend?"

"No, your girlfriend."

"Oh, right." He coughed. "Right." He cleared his throat. "Nah, she wouldn't care."

"How do you know?"

"Because she trusts me. I'll explain it's for a friend of a friend."

Cara's heart thumped. He had just called her his *friend!* "Okay, great! Her name is Olivia and she's been my best friend for ages. And you don't have to pay for tickets, she already has those."

"Is this a double date?"

I wish! "No, I'm not going to the prom this year."

"So you're talking about a blind date?"

"Yeah. I've seen you dance, Zach. I know you can do this."

"Was this your idea, or did Olivia ask you to call?"

Totally Cara's idea.

Her first plan was to have John escort Olivia to the prom, but her bestie trashed that idea. In fact, Olivia's exact words were: "No way! I wouldn't even go to the New York City Ballet with that douche who ditched you."

Cara didn't dare ask Olivia about Zach. She would arrange it with *him* first, and then pitch it to Olivia. After all, he had a girlfriend and he might say no. Cara spoke nonchalantly into the phone, "I already talked to her and she really wants to go to the prom."

He didn't answer. All she heard was his breathing and even that was attractive. Her skin tingled.

"The thing is," Cara continued. "Olivia's in a real tough spot. She and this guy Nate have been going out for years. So for him to dump her now, when ... um, when they're both seniors, right before our last prom, it's just so harsh." Cara wished she could tell Zach about Olivia's baby, but it wasn't her secret to tell. "She shouldn't have to miss out on her own prom just because her boyfriend bailed. Can you please take her to the prom?"

More breathing. Cara's skin sizzled and she rubbed her arms to flatten the goosebumps.

More breathing.

More goosebumps.

Finally Zach said, "I'll pray about it. I'll get back to you."

Pray about it? "Oh." *How do you argue with prayer?* "Okay."

"See you Friday, Cara."

"Okay. Bye."

Mystified, Cara clicked her phone off. Sometimes she thought Zach was the coolest guy she ever met. Then moments like this made her suspect he actually dropped from a wormhole conduit to a staticky black and white 1950s TV show.

THIRTY-EIGHT

"MY NEW BOOK came out and I'm so excited I just had to share it with you!" Wendy displayed her paperback in front of her chest, like a superhero logo. The orange block letters on the cover read: *When you Hurry and Worry: Coping with ADD and OCD.* "I knew you would want your own copy. Go ahead and open it. I'll sign." Wendy handed the book to Annie and whipped out an orange ultra-fine point Sharpie from her handbag while her daughter Brooke paused on the mat to unlace her black ankle boots.

Jeesum crow, does Wendy think I'm nuts?

While Wendy signed the inside front cover, Annie poured tea and asked Brooke, "Would you like a scone?"

Unlike Wendy with her colorful scarves and ruffles, Brooke wore black leggings and a black T-shirt with a white silhouette of a kitty on it. "Is it vegan?"

"No." Annie glanced around her kitchen and spied the fruit bowl. "How about an apple?"

"Is it organic?"

"No, but I can wash it for you."

"I'll pass."

Annie said, "Cara's doing her homework in the living room."

Brooke wandered out of the kitchen to the adjacent room.

Wendy finished her signature with a flourish and capped the marker. "How's homeschooling going?" she asked.

Annie blew on her cup of tea to make it cool faster. "It's much harder than preschool."

"Mm hm."

"Cara has all these questions about math, but I don't know how to do any of that stuff anymore. Not that I ever did. She keeps getting mad at me when I try to help her. Dan was supposed to teach math, but now he's in Mexico. Besides, will Cara ever use algebra again? Do you ever use it?"

"Haven't touched it since high school."

"Me neither. Do you think we could just let it slide?" Annie's eyebrows slid upwards, begging.

"Let me ask you a question. Which is more important, Cara or algebra?"

Was this a trick question? Of course Annie loved Cara more. Way more, like infinity squared. But surely math was important to the world, to society, for the greater good. Didn't scientists need calculus to get rockets to land on the moon instead of veering off into space and knocking into Pluto? Didn't Derrick, their tax guy, need it every spring to navigate zillions of tax code computations before April 15? And how would credit cards work without formulas? What about online shopping?

"Algebra?" Annie hazarded a guess.

Wendy closed her eyes briefly and pushed a long breath out of her mouth. She reopened her eyes, inclined her head gently and looked kindly at Annie. "Attachment parenting recognizes that the relationship with the child is paramount. Before you can teach a child effectively, first you need to engage her and foster a thriving relationship. See what I'm saying?"

"Cara is more important!" Annie should have stuck with her first answer. That's what teachers advise on multiple-choice tests—trust your gut. "I knew that!"

Wendy nodded softly and smiled wisely, like Yoda, but with soft blond curls.

Annie's eyes brightened. "So, what you're saying is, we can ignore math for the rest of the year?"

The Yoda smile was imperturbable. "I'm saying, do whatever works best for Cara. For your *relationship* with her."

Annie nodded thoughtfully. No wonder people paid Wendy by the hour. She gave such good advice. "Also, Cara's been so darn touchy lately."

"Hm."

"She said I didn't know what I was doing. And something else really odd—that I didn't know what the hell was going on around here. Now what is *that* supposed to mean?"

"Remember high school?"

"It's been a while."

"Adolescents go through transformational changes and traumatic experiences, but sometimes they are afraid to talk about them. The problem is that shame leads to secrecy. Studies show that silence surrounding trauma can be more detrimental to our psychological health than the initial event itself. Speaking up is vital. Teens need to hear that what they're going through is normal. They're growing in several different directions at once." Wendy extended her arms in step with her words. "Physically, mentally, emotionally, socially, sexually ..."

Did Wendy just say 'sexually'? Annie felt a gush of relief that Cara was just a pothead and not sleeping around. At least she hoped she wasn't. How could Cara possibly be messing around? She couldn't see John because she was grounded.

Wendy continued, "It's a lot for them to process. When I talk to young patients, I listen beyond their words and hear their emotion. What do you think Cara is *feeling*?"

"I think she's frustrated about being stuck at home and she's taking it out on me. But it's her own damn fault. It's not like I woke up one day and said, 'Gee whillikers, I want to quit my paying job so I can stay home and homeschool Cara for free.'"

"I have something that will help." Wendy reached into her bag and pulled out a small vial. "My current favorite. It's called *Mindfulness.* It's a blend of orange, spruce, and patchouli."

"What I need is an essential oil called 'Cure for a Crappy Day.'"

"Annie, allow yourself to open up your throat chakra. This will help you speak your truth. Here, I'll put some on the back of your neck." Wendy unscrewed the cap and upended the miniature bottle over the palm of her left hand. After she collected a few drops, she stirred the teeny puddle clockwise with her index finger. "You want the electrons to align," she explained. "We all have a frequency and to achieve health, our bodies want to sing in harmony with the earth's hertz of 7.83." She floated her palm under Annie's nose. "Doesn't it smell celestial?"

Annie sniffed. "Mm." It smelled fruity, woodsy, and sensual. Much better than the oil Wendy pushed last time called "Abundant Joy" which smelled musky in a smarmy way like the overeager car salesman who wore too much cologne and stood too close and called her Angie and pushed for way too much for a used Taurus.

"Pull your hair up and I'll apply it directly to your neck."

With both hands, Annie lifted her hair. She felt Wendy's warm hand massage the liquid into her skin.

"How's that feel?"

"Great. Can you keep massaging?" Annie sighed. "I miss Dan."

Wendy said soothingly. "Of course you do, luv."

"Wendy?" Brooke wandered back into the kitchen. "Time for herb class." She stepped into her boots and tied the laces.

"Thank you for the massage and the book," Annie said.

"You're welcome. I'm already working on my next book: *Are You MAADDD? Mothers Against Attention Deficit Disorder Drugs*."

"Sounds like the group against drunk driving."

"It's M-A-A-D-D-D. Get it? Isn't that fun?"

After Wendy and Brooke left, Annie put the teacups in the dishwasher and joined Cara in the living room. "Do you think I have OCD?"

"No. You worry a lot, but you're a mom. You're supposed to."

"How about ADD?"

"No. You're a preschool teacher. You have to pivot."

"Thank goodness. I have enough to deal with."

"Did Mrs. Weinstein say you have OCD or ADD?"

"Not explicitly. But she said I ought to have the book she wrote about how to cope with it." She held up the big orange hardcover book.

"Mom." Cara lowered her book slightly and eyed Annie. "She just wanted to autograph it. Mrs. Weinstein doesn't know everything, y'know. She thinks Brooke goes to class and is going to become a radical social worker and change the world someday."

"What do you mean *thinks* she goes to class? Is Brooke skipping school?"

"You didn't hear it from me."

"Now what am I supposed to do? Tell Wendy her daughter is playing hooky?"

Cara picked her book back up.

"How's *The Scarlet Letter* going?"

Cara lowered the book. "I don't know how Dimmesdale can stand being such a jerk, letting Hester take all the blame."

"He *can't* take it."

"What do you mean?"

"I don't want to spoil the ending for you. Just keep reading."

"If this book were written nowadays, it wouldn't be about adultery. Hester would've gotten rid of Pearl and she would be branded with an 'A' for 'Abortion.'"

Annie felt her eyes widen in alarm. Woozy, she reached out a hand to lean on the back of the armchair. She looked left and right to ensure Willy wasn't in the room. She didn't want him to learn that nowadays children in America were expendable. She whispered to Cara, "No, we wouldn't ever *brand* her. That's not the answer."

"But you know what I mean. They keep telling us that guys and girls are equal. Girls can do anything guys can do, blah, blah, blah. That's a lie. In reality, we're different. When it comes to hooking up, girls bear the brunt of it. Girls get pregnant, while the guy is totally off the hook. It's totally unfair."

"I wouldn't blame the guy either. He's probably as young and scared as the girl."

"Who are you talking about? Dimmesdale was old enough to know what he was doing."

"But that was adultery. You're talking about something different."

"I know! But can you imagine if abortions were legal back then? Would Dimmesdale pay for Hester to get an abortion? It's such an easy out for the guy."

"No, I don't think Dimmesdale would've done that. He's a minister. Plus, Hester wouldn't allow it." Annie tilted her head. "Are you going to write that in your paper?" Her brain felt foggy and she feared something crucial was slipping out of her grasp. Annie was willing to give extra points for thinking creatively about the story, but she wasn't sure how legit Cara's analysis was.

"Mom! No!" Cara climbed off the sofa and stabbed the air with her arm. "This isn't about my paper! I'm just saying sometimes guys force their girlfriends into getting rid of the baby when they don't really want to and it's not fair! Guys get off scot-free! There should be some accountability!"

"Blaming the guy isn't going to help."

"I can't believe you're defending the *guy*! Whose side are you on anyway?" Cara clamped her lips in a tight line and stamped up the stairs pounding each tread as she went. *Stomp!*

"We're on the same side!"

Stomp!

"I'm on your side!" Annie insisted.

Stomp!

"It's legal so guys assume it's okay!"

But Cara wasn't listening. The bedroom door slammed shut, smacking the doorjamb with a harsh thwack.

Annie shuddered, as if the sound waves from the door had blasted through her. She crumpled into the soft easy chair and the rip on the side of the brown cushion yawned open and white fluff plumped out, like a hernia. Annie poked the white stuffing back in, but as soon as she released her finger, it popped back out.

How did this go so wrong so fast? Why was it so hard to connect with her own daughter? Why did it keep backfiring on her? She asked a simple question about her English assignment and Cara started shouting and retreated upstairs with a stomp, stomp, stomp.

Annie pushed out a long melancholy breath. She wasn't sure she'd be able to keep up with the homeschooling shtick for two more months. But what else could she do? She had run out of choices.

By the time graduation rolled around, would Cara be giving her the silent treatment permanently?

THIRTY-NINE

"I wish I'd known," said Annie after parking in the Shellbrook Museum parking lot. "We could have dressed up, too." She got out of the car and removed the hefty monogrammed canvas bag she had recently ordered, now filled with notebooks, pencils, and lunch.

Cara caught her gazing wistfully at Mrs. Pendergrast in mutton sleeves and an ankle-length skirt, looking like a Gibson Girl, except older and heavier and her hair was too short to put in a triangular bun.

Cara smiled in relief. Thank God her mother didn't know, or she might have tried to force Cara into a bonnet and calico. It was supposed to be educational, but she wondered if the field trip was simply an excuse for the moms to dress up. Halloween only comes once a year, but many of these homeschoolers bought family passes to the museum so they could pretend to live in the 1800s and churn butter in long skirts and then drive their rust-pocked vans home to post photos of themselves churning butter in long skirts on Facebook.

"I see the Bouchers," said Cara. "Okay if I head over?"

"Me too," said Willy.

"Me three," said Annie. "We'll come back for our lunch later." She returned the cavernous bag to the car and slammed the back door down. They strolled across the parking lot to The Barge where the Boucher family was disembarking.

"Hey Zach," Cara greeted him, secretly disappointed that *he* wasn't in costume. It would have been interesting to see him in suspenders and breeches. As they chatted, she inched her way towards the vintage carousel, gradually, so he wouldn't realize he was following her. She couldn't wait to ask what he had decided about taking Olivia to the prom but she didn't want to discuss it in front of the others.

"Haieuken!" Eric came from behind and slapped Zach on the back by way of greeting.

So much for privacy.

"Yo," said Zach, pounding Eric's shoulder in return. "Sick top."

Eric was wearing an olive drab tee with an outline of the state of Vermont. Inside the border were the words: *KEEP VERMONT WEIRD.*

"Thanks, bro." Eric beat his chest and gave a sideways peace sign.

"Don't move out of state. Mission accomplished."

Unfortunately, this reminded Eric of one of his video games. He could segue from any topic to a video game or movie. "So my mission was to take down FatChopsticks ..."

Cara never enjoyed updates on Eric's games, but especially not today when she needed to talk to Zach about Olivia. But Eric kept going on and on.

"I built a lava pit and just when FatChopsticks thought he was going to get my trapped chest, BAM, down he goes. Totally torched! I completely pwned him!"

Cara smiled and nodded, smiled and nodded, waiting for Eric to leave so she could talk to Zach.

If these kids enrolled at CHU, Cara wondered which clique they would sift into. Eric and his trusty violin would definitely hang out in the band hallway with other music and art fans. But with his games and all that trivia he kept trying to impress her with, would he lunch with the nerds? Hunter, with his mad fencing skills was definitely an athlete, but Cara couldn't picture him with the soccer team, or lacrosse ... maybe he could throw the javelin for track and field?

Cara herself had been a library card carrying member of the preppy college bound crowd. At least she used to be. What about now? Her status on the track team was iffy and she feared she would be labeled an outcast because of her exile to Homeschool Land.

And Zach? Where would he fit in? He was too homeschoolery to be popular. Or was he? Maybe too smooth for student council? Despite his stellar SAT score, he was definitely too gorgeous to mesh with the math club. He needed a posse of models who visited nursing homes with pets and secretly solved algebraic equations on the side. No, that wasn't right either. She studied Zach for another clue.

Eric had been playing his game online on a global level and gloating because he was beating Asian players. As he yammered on about Questcraft, Zach turned to Cara, locked eyes with her and raised his eyebrows.

Stunned, she stopped breathing. She and Zach were sharing a special bonding moment! Together! Just the two of them! Apparently Zach cared as much about Eric's castle-building and fortress-guarding as she did.

Joy bubbled up inside Cara. A buzz of excitement sparkled throughout her body like carbonated water rippling through her veins. Her heart was effervescent, light enough to float away.

Cara nodded and smiled, for real this time. Eric could babble on all he wanted about virtual bricks and treasure while she floated on the fizz of Zach's root beer eyes.

"Eric!" His mother called from across the parking lot. "I need your help!" His mother was trying to extract a stroller from the back of their car. Their cooler and canvas bag were already set out on the curb.

"Catch up to yuz, later," Eric said.

"I'm gonna check out the barn," said Zach. "See you there."

As Zach and Cara ambled down the gravel path to the post and beam barn, she popped the question. "So what did you decide about Olivia and the prom?" Cara smiled as winsomely and persuasively as she could.

"Yeah," he answered. "I'll do it for ya."

"Thanks!" For *me?* Cara's heart tingled.

"I'll need her number. Give her a call tonight."

"Tomorrow." Cara hadn't told Olivia about her plan yet. "She has dance team practice tonight. Call her tomorrow, okay?" That would give Cara all of tonight to talk her into it. She gave him Olivia's name, number, and address.

At the barn, he asked tons of questions about the livestock, much to the delight of the retired farmer volunteering at the museum. But Cara tuned out their conversation. She gazed at Zach, admiring his strong arms stroking the heifers, and she laughed when he took a turn milking, and she made the appropriate *oohs* at the piglets snuffling about the huge sow splayed on a bed of straw; but Cara's heart was feeling darker and heavier at each stall they explored.

She was supposed to be happy for her best friend; she had smoothly solved the dilemma of getting Olivia to the prom. And Zach already had a girlfriend. He made it clear that Cara was just a friend. So why did her heart feel as sucky and sludgy as the brown mud surrounding the trough?

FORTY

ANNIE WOKE UP in a cold bedroom. She climbed out of bed and pulled up the shade. The Snow Queen had traveled through the night freezing everything in her path. Ice encircled boughs with beautiful tubular glaze. Encased by heavy silvery ice, the branches of maples, birches, flimsy poplars and bristling pines sank onto electric lines triggering power outages across Chittenden County.

After taping *Do Not Flush* signs on their toilets, Annie stood with her arms crossed across her bosom, staring wistfully at the electric burners on the kitchen stove. She couldn't have a cup of tea. No coffee either. No lights. No internet. No heat. No Dan.

She picked up the kitchen phone. Nothing.

She pulled her cell out of her pocketbook. She had neglected to charge it overnight.

Annie stepped gingerly onto the slick front stoop. The mountain glittered white with frozen crystals reflecting the sun. She couldn't see the ski trails slaloming across the slopes or the cozy lodges stocked with fireplaces and tidy woodpiles for tourists. Annie saluted the alp with her phone, hoping to beckon power from its far-off cell phone tower.

One bar.

Annie hurried back inside, shivering. She shuffled to the closet, pulled on her puffy winter coat, and wedged herself into the living room La-Z-Boy to wait morosely for the lights to come on.

When Willy got up and discovered they had no electricity, he jumped up and down shouting, "Snow day! Snow day!"

Annie informed him, "You can't get online, but you can still do your homework from your books."

"Oh." Crushed, Willy immediately understood that snow days have no power to stop learning.

Annie felt exactly the same. Crushed. That was one of many problems with homeschooling—it was endless! There was no morning circle time or leaving PAL to go home. She was always at work, always teaching, even when she wasn't aware of it.

Willy's face brightened. "Hey, can I get together with Joey and do my homework at their house?"

"Great idea." Annie pushed herself out of the recliner and scuttled to her cell phone, her down coat wafting behind her. "Maybe they have power? We could all hang out there."

Annie clicked on Maggie's number and kept her conversation short to save juice. Maggie explained that they had no electricity. "If we don't get electricity by tomorrow afternoon, we'll go to Evelyn's for showers. She's been prepping for years. The Pendergrasts have a generator and a solar powered well."

Annie made plans to drive Willy to the Boucher's house once their driveway got cleared. At least Maggie had a woodstove so he could warm up.

She heard a knock on the kitchen door and opened it.

"Hello. I figured your power was out and with Dan gone, I thought you might need sustenance." Wendy held out a tray full of gray, nubby squares. "Homemade coconut and flaxseed granola bars. They're vegan." She kicked her boots on the stoop to shake off residual snow, stepped into Annie's kitchen, and removed her boots. "Great for breakfast."

"Thanks," said Annie. "I wish I could offer you a cup of tea. Let's go in the living room. With the morning sun coming in, it might be a bit warmer in there." Annie put some paper napkins on the tray of goodies and set it on the mantel where the dogs couldn't reach. She picked one up and sampled it.

"Hm, it's very," Wendy looked around.

"Cold?"

"No ... what's the word?"

"Dark?"

"*Red.* For me to speak my truth, I must say Annie, it's very red in here."

First of all, it wasn't red. The walls were painted a deep, rich *burgundy*, which evoked the wealth of royalty, the enlightenment of libraries, and the upperclassness of a sommelier.

Second of all, what's wrong with that?

Cara tromped down the stairs with her arms wrapped tightly around herself, holding her sleep-warmth close. One hand clutched her cell phone. "My phone is dead!"

"We lost power," Annie explained.

"What the—? How am I going to charge it if we don't have power?"

"Say hello to Mrs. Weinstein. She brought us breakfast." Annie gestured to the bars on the mantel.

"Hello." Cara picked up a granola bar and stared at it. "Thanks."

"You're welcome," said Wendy. "I would offer my house, but we lost power too."

"I need my phone," said Cara.

"Your phone's grounded, except for emergencies," Annie reminded her.

"Oh, this is an emergency," Cara smoothly assured her. "I need to do research for history and I wanted to call the library and see if they have the book I need."

"I'm sure the ice will melt soon. It's the end of April; can't last long."

"Can I take the car to Quarternote Café and charge my phone there?"

"We can't get out until Mr. Hans clears the driveway."

"Ugh." Cara stomped back up the stairs. "Let me know when the driveway's done."

Annie smiled apologetically at Wendy. "I'm sorry Cara is so cranky."

"Perhaps it's the walls."

"Cabin fever. Of course. She's dying to get out of here."

"No, I mean the color. Red is so ... so angry. If you want to promote joy, you might consider painting your living room yellow. Or purple for creativity."

Annie put her head in her hands. "I wish Dan were here."

"Oh pish. What can Dan do here that you can't do?"

"Hook up the kerosene heater."

"I'm sure the electric crews will get the power turned on soon." Wendy smiled encouragingly at Annie. "I better scoot home and see if Levi got our woodstove going."

Annie escorted Wendy to the kitchen door. "Bye! Thanks for the granola bars."

She slumped back into the living room and surveyed the walls critically.

The tiny paint chip was called Wine and Dine. Annie had thought the shade would be perfect for their living room walls, which flowed directly into their dining room. She hadn't known it fostered anger. If only she had gone with Tuscany Gold, would Cara still be at CHU? Would Annie still be earning good money at Play And Learn?

Being a stay-at-home mom was inglorious. And it's not like homeschooling raised her status any. It simply made others think she was weird. On top of being too lazy or stupid to get a job, she was a freak.

Annie missed her little kiddos. Did the new teacher remember that JoJo's language development was delayed and she needed extra verbal practice and that the dress up area was perfect for that? And that for snack time, she must seat Xander and Logan at opposite ends of the table so they wouldn't start another food fight "on accident." Or that Nora needed extra cuddles because her parents were in the middle of a divorce?

One morning she had noticed Nora looking big-eyed and scared as she flipped through a book of fairy tales during choice time. Annie rushed over. Nora pointed to the colorful illustration of Rumpelstiltskin in his red cape, green cone hat, and blue breeches. In his wrath he had stomped one booted foot into the floorboards—stuck and enraged—he grabbed his other foot and dismembered himself.

Ugh. No child ever needed to see that gruesome ending. Ever.

Annie had put her arm around Nora and explained what the little imp did was impossible and make-believe and why don't we read *Corduroy* together?

Nora nodded and got cozy in Annie's lap.

At home that night, Annie had lifted her X-Acto knife from its safety container and with the studied precision of a surgeon, she excised the illustrated page near the seam and discarded it. The rest of the book was child-friendly, but Rumpel was better suited for feminists to bemoan the injustice of a father who lied to a greedy and powerful king, putting his hapless daughter and future grandchild into mortal danger.

Although Annie believed that all preschoolers were special snowflakes, she couldn't help recognizing that some were specialer than others. Since teachers weren't supposed to have favorites, she never told anyone that her secret nickname for Nora was Anorable.

Annie selected another gray bar and nibbled at it. She wondered if Anorable and the other kiddos got to witness Carter the Caterpillar turn into Buddy the Butterfly. Or did the magical metamorphosis happen overnight when no one was watching? Annie sighed and zipped up her coat and flopped into the easy chair to wait for power.

FORTY-ONE

THE NEXT DAY, after eating room-temperature leftover pizza for breakfast, Annie stepped on the take-out box and shoved it into the recycling bin in their garage. Luckily the power had been reconnected at Rise High Bakery. The Mulligans had spent an hour there the previous night, basking in the light and warmth, hobnobbing with other Vermonters stranded from home. Annie had spent forty bucks on pizza and drinks, and it was well worth it to charge their cells and laptops. She had kept a close watch on Cara, to ensure she wasn't scoring marijuana from the waiter with the dreadlocks.

Tired of living in fifty-five degree weather indoors, Annie called Evelyn. She would join the queue of homeschoolers at the Pendergrast's house.

Evelyn was in her element, passing out towels and washcloths with a constant pot of coffee burbling in her kitchen. She had a stopwatch slung around her neck and she banged on the bathroom door if you took more than your allotted ten minutes.

There was a festive flavor and the families enjoyed exploring the warm, funky farmhouse. Evelyn broke open one of their Bug Out Bags and the boys sat around a blanket on the floor, critiquing the MRE fare, as if they were military experts or restaurant reviewers. The kids were in high spirits; it was like camping indoors and the moms were too busy talking to each other to make them do school.

Everyone enjoyed it, except Cara. Annie's seventeen-year-old daughter hated the idea of taking a shower at someone else's house. Before they went, Cara kept asking who else would be there. As if Annie knew! She wasn't psychic.

The Boucher clan arrived at Evelyn's shortly after the Mulligans. Willy ran directly to Joey and Zach and his dog, Frodo, who was a big hit.

But when Cara emerged from the bathroom wrapped in a towel with her wet hair dripping and she spotted the Bouchers, she ducked her head and bolted to the master bedroom, which Evelyn had helpfully made over into a changing room, complete with sheets hung up for privacy. Cara was in there for twenty minutes. Good thing Evelyn wasn't timing the bedroom with her stopwatch.

Then Paloma proposed a group photo. "This is our chance to prove that we *do* socialize!" She nudged all the kids into a condensed mob and held her cell phone in front of her face, about to shoot, when Annie said, "Hold up! Let me get Cara!"

Annie hurried to the master bedroom, rapped on the door, and called for Cara who slipped out quietly with her head hunched into her shoulders. "Hurry," Annie urged, plucking Cara's sleeve and escorting her to the living room. "Look, there's room in the back next to Zachary." Annie prodded Cara in his direction.

Annie noticed Cara's cheeks were a lovely pink, probably from the hot shower. "Get closer," Annie directed. She gestured with her palms drawing towards each other. "A little closer!"

Cara leaned her head in, which accentuated the awkward gap between her and Zachary. That wouldn't work for Paloma's proof that homeschoolers socialize. Looking meaningfully at Cara, Annie forcefully squeezed the air between her hands again. At that point, Zachary draped his arm across Cara's shoulders and ushered her into the group picture. Paloma snapped away.

As the kids disbanded, Zachary's friend gave him a fist bump and they did other complicated hand gestures. Annie hoped Paloma got that on video for proof that homeschoolers have friends.

Paloma assured the moms she would send the pics to them via the group email list. The ladies started calling out subject suggestions for sending the photos to the state homestudy office. The freeze-dried food qualified for Science, Nutrition, and Vermont Citizenship. Frodo counted towards Health and Natural Science. Melanie suggested that Frodo also counted for Literature, but the other moms said that was a stretch.

Evelyn gave the kids a nine-and-a-half-minute tutorial (Cara timed it) on their solar powered well, which Willy loved but Cara texted the whole time. Annie was surprised that Cara had to text so many libraries for books.

Paloma made them all surround the well so she could document it for Environmental Science and Field Trip. Everyone agreed that the day also counted toward Vermont History since it was the most damaging ice storm on record in April.

Cara didn't seem to appreciate history, though. Beyond a stony "Please pass the salad" at dinner, Cara didn't talk to Annie for the rest of the day. As if it was Annie's fault that they lost power and had to shower at Evelyn's, who forced the kids to listen to her boring solar power lecture.

At least Willy was still willing to talk to Annie. A mile a minute, in fact. Always science, but at least he wasn't all teenagery and incommunicado.

Three hours after they returned home from their field trip to Pendergrasts' the lights came on. Oh, that magical moment when the house started buzzing with electricity, the fridge began to hum, and lights flashed friendly-like on the stove and coffeepot and microwave clocks. They were all thrilled to be in a heated house with a functional kitchen and internet and phone chargers. Annie danced from one bathroom to another, relieved to catch up on flushing.

FORTY-TWO

"DEFINITELY."

"Ya think so?" Olivia twirled in the tiny dressing room. The shimmery chiffon material wrapped itself around her legs, spiraling up towards her perfectly sculpted thighs.

"You look gorgeous!" Cara stood outside the open dressing room door and concentrated on not feeling envious. After all, setting up Olivia and Zach had been her idea.

But Cara couldn't help it. She wanted to be the one picking out a new gown. She wanted to be the one going to the prom. She had been anticipating it since she was a freshman.

Four weeks ago Cara had been a solid member of the track team, pulling A's at CHU, going out with John, and looking forward to college and a lucrative career saving innocent victims from injustice. She had spent days selecting her senior photo before submitting it to the yearbook club. She had spent twelve years tackling books, studying for exams, collaborating on projects and presentations. All that work, up in smoke. Now she was ghosted.

She was dumped by John and banned from school, from the prom, from fun, from her entire effing life. The only reason her mother permitted this shopping trip was because she thought Olivia would be a good influence on her. The irony was almost funny. Ha.

Now Cara was forced to spend every day watching her mom pretend she knew how to teach high school. Now Cara had to play along to keep Olivia's secret and get a stupid homemade transcript. Now she was watching her best friend spin like a fairy in a sea-green cocktail dress.

She couldn't stop wondering what Zach would think when he saw Olivia's beautiful ballet body adorned in this filmy, flattering dress? Would he recall the last time he saw Cara at the Pendergrasts, with her wet hair hideously plastered to her head? Would Olivia make him forget all about Ashley?

It wasn't Cara's fault that Olivia was preggers. It wasn't Cara's fault that Nate asked Olivia to stash his weed in her backpack. It wasn't Cara's idea to toke up in the teacher's lavatory. Not her baby. Not her weed. Not her fault. This was all Nate's fault but the wrong people kept getting punished. Olivia was stuck with his baby. Cara was stuck homeschooling because of his stupid joint.

Your entire life trajectory can shift because of one simple mistake.

Cara thought she was helping, but what if she was just messing things up? They couldn't keep this secret forever. Someone had to tell eventually. As Grammy always said, "The truth will out." Why not now? Why put off the inevitable? They could come clean and get Cara out of homeschool hell.

Cara cleared her throat. "Olivia," she began gingerly.

Registering the serious tone, Olivia stopped rotating. The skirt of her dress fell softly, the ruffles waving around her knees. Olivia turned sideways and stared at her silhouette in the full-length mirror. She pressed her hands on her belly. "It doesn't show, does it?" she whispered. Olivia's eyes, big and watery in the mirror's reflection, pleaded with Cara.

Years ago Willy's pet bunny escaped from his cage and Larry had grabbed him by the neck while Moe and Curly growled jealously. Everyone rushed at the dogs and pulled them away. Willy cradled his pet tenderly in his arms, but the bunny's body grew limp. It wasn't the dog's bite that had killed the bunny, it was the fright.

Olivia's wide brown eyes looked like that rabbit's: trapped and terrified.

"No," said Cara. She was imploding inside but she wouldn't let Olivia know. "No, it doesn't show. No one will know. No worries, you look absolutely drop dead gorgeous."

Annie felt she was getting the hang of homeschooling. Willy was very independent, cruising through his math and science and English. And history in fifth grade was fun—they watched National Geographic and

PBS specials. He borrowed a coonskin cap from Joey and dressed up like Davy Crockett and they printed a hard copy photo to submit to the state.

Cara was cooperating. No more outbursts about Annie's lack of knowledge or intelligence or cooking skills. Cara slogged through her chemistry homework thanks to the co-op, dutifully researched Harriet Tubman and the Underground Railroad, and watched soap operas in Spanish.

But she seemed distracted and melancholy. Feeling sorry for grounding her, Annie inquired sympathetically about John, but Cara just gave monosyllabic answers. Most began with the letter N. It would be rough to not know if your boyfriend was taking someone else to the prom you were banned from. To cheer her up, Annie had allowed her to go dress shopping with Olivia.

Annie wasn't too concerned that Cara dropped down to C's on her math homework this week since Wendy said algebra was irrelevant and they had lost power for one and a half days.

They FaceTimed Dan on Thursday afternoon because he had a company function to attend that Friday evening. Annie slipped on her slinky blue blouse, swiped on mascara, and dabbed on some blush. She didn't change out of her pajama pants, because ... why bother?

Annie set her laptop on the dining room table and called the kids to join. Cara pointed to the disconnect between Annie's makeup and her PJs. "Party on top, homeschool on bottom."

Was Cara mocking her? These days it was hard to tell. Annie shrugged it off. "Whatever." She was excited to see Dan and refused to get embroiled in a squabble over her fashion choices. There's no pleasing teenagers anyway.

Dan looked tanner and handsomer than ever. The sunshine glinted off the top of his brown hair, making it glow as if he were blond.

"You look great," she said.

"So do you," he said appreciatively.

Annie was glad she had dolled up. She shot Cara a victorious look. Her daughter was gazing morosely at Dan the screen, over a thousand miles away. "How's it going Daddy?"

"Hey Care Bear. Hey Willy! How are you two doing?"

"Great," said Cara, in the tone she used when Annie told her she had to take an algebra quiz.

"I'm going fishing with Joey and his brother!" said Willy.

Annie let the kids hold center stage for a bit. When Dan mentioned that he was wrapping things up in Mexico quicker than ISS expected, she suggested they indulge in a drink to celebrate. Dan grabbed a Dos Equis from his hotel minifridge. Annie scooted carefully away from the dining table so he wouldn't see her ratty pajama pants while she fixed herself a girlie margarita. They toasted carefully so as not to spill their drinks on their mutual computer keyboards.

"I could really go for a little *egg roll* with this beer." Dan winked.

"Dan!" Annie glanced left. Cara was balancing on one foot, she held her other leg bent behind her to stretch her quad. She was staring desultorily out the window.

"Or maybe a fortune cookie," Dan added.

Annie peeked at Willy. He was smiling open-faced and innocently. Annie leaned in to the screen and mouthed, "Not in front of the kids." She wasn't sure Dan could lip read. He smiled hungrily at her.

"Is the Chinese food good in Mexico?" asked Willy.

"Not like at home." Dan was practically licking his chops.

Annie felt her cheeks flush and her insides shiver. She shook her head no, but she was smiling yes. "Cara and Willy, you two can go do your homework, now. Your Dad and I need to talk about ... um ... health insurance."

FORTY-THREE

May is magical in Vermont. One day the lawns are ugly patches of droopy damp husks in shades of wheat and chaff poking through leftover snow. Then overnight spring busts out in burgeoning, nascent grass as if Persephone herself had fled the underworld to flit past and transform the ground into vibrant, lush, impossible greens.

Oh look, a purple crocus!

Annie sighed happily as she buzzed to FU. It was hard to believe this was their fifth meeting already. She felt qualified to sit in the ladies circle and assume her place as a professional homeschooler.

There were the standard announcements. Evelyn gave a spiel about their grass-fed beef. The only drawback, aside from the exorbitant price, was that you had to commit to at least a quarter of a cow. Annie would have to buy a stand-alone freezer if she wanted to feed her family organic meat. She was tempted to give Evelyn the business, since she'd been so generous with her generator and showers during the power outage. But Dan would go ballistic at the extravagance when they were saving money for Cara's tuition.

There was a prayer request for Diana's neighbor who was let go from OBS and had two kids in college. The only career options remaining in the state were to apply at Ben & Jerry's or start another microbrewery.

Diana added, "By the way, for those who are interested, we brought organic eggs again. They're on the table up front."

Annie dropped six bucks in the cardboard shoebox and nestled two cartons of eggs in her giant canvas bag then returned to her seat. A cow was out of their price range, but at least the Mulligans could afford eggs and support a local farm.

Christine's husband had also been laid off from the Organization of Business Systems. Vermont's largest private corporation with four thousand employees had been incrementally downsizing over the years to roughly four hundred. Christine wasn't at the co-op today; she was at home with the new baby, Henry. Annie guessed she was playing hooky because she wasn't ready to deal with all the sympathy the ladies wanted to smother her with because of the layoff.

"This is the second time her husband was let go. Maybe Christine will start looking for a job herself."

"She shouldn't have to, she just had a baby," Evelyn argued. "Americans don't value motherhood enough. You get more respect for working outside the home than raising your own children. Even if you work in a daycare watching other peoples' kids."

Annie nodded in agreement. She was nothing when she stayed home with Cara and Willy. When she was merely a mom, total strangers would ask her to sign up for their bake sale, or carpool Tristan to soccer games, or ask her to watch Leaf because their babysitter bailed. But her status skyrocketed once she resumed teaching other children. Annie could have blue Play-Doh crumbled in her hair, a soiled diaper hanging out of her bag, utter the words "preschool teacher," and under its spell, folks would bond to her like Super Glue, befriend her on Facebook and urge her to advance their three-year-old up the school's waiting list.

"It's ridiculous," Diana added. "Our government has so little respect for motherhood it will actually pay for abortions so you can quit being a mother. And they use stem cells from those aborted babies to make vaccines."

Annie's morning porridge began to curdle in her belly.

"Reminds me of *Soylent Green*."

She didn't know much about chemistry, but Annie perceived a bad reaction as bile, soured milk, and salad dressing from lunch battled in her gut.

"What's *Soylent Green*?" asked Paloma.

Annie pushed herself off the metal folding chair and angled towards the restroom while the other women continued chatting.

"A dystopian science fiction movie from the '70s."

Annie was not a sci fi fan. She was relieved the bathroom door was made of heavy solid wood and could muffle that conversation.

FORTY-FOUR

WITH A CELL phone plastered to her ear, Cara walked towards the common green in their neighborhood that had wooden playground equipment. "Grammy, I have a question for you." Cara stepped around the shallow pools of melted ice on the pavement. It would've been handy if she could've brought this up to her mother, but she would've dug and dug until Cara spilled more than she wanted to. As it was, Cara didn't have nearly enough privacy, what with all the homeschooling.

"Yes, dearie."

"It's about a friend of mine? She's in a tough situation; she's about to graduate and she just found out she's pregnant and she wants to get rid of the baby so she can go to college and get her boyfriend back, and I know you've worked for Vermont Right to Life for years, so could you give me some ideas on how to convince her not to have an abortion?"

Cara heard the rattly whoosh of breath being sucked into an ancient throat. "Are you pregnant?"

"No, it's my friend!"

"Was it that boy John who did this to you? The one who jogs all the time?"

"I'm not pregnant. I swear to God. It's my *friend*."

"Can you put your mother on the line?"

"I'm not home. I'm at the playground." There was no safe space at her house. Even her bedroom was risky because her mother might come in without knocking, no matter how many times she asked her not to. Cara plunked down in one of the yellow half-bucket seats dangling from chains, dug her toe into the brown wood chips, and pushed her swing backwards.

"Playground?"

"Yes, I swear. I'm at the playground." Even to Cara, it sounded like she was lying. She looked around. The playground was empty since the kids it was built for were now in high school or college or taking a gap year in Europe. "You have to believe me. I called because I thought you could give me some advice to give my friend."

"Okay, dearie. Here's what you tell your friend: 'Refuse to choose.'"

"Say what?"

"That's what Feminists for Life say: 'Refuse to choose.' Refuse to choose between a boyfriend and a baby. Refuse to choose between a child and an education. You can have both." Grandma paused for a breath. "I'll be honest with you, dearie. This is going to be challenging. I'm not saying you can have it all at the same time. And Cara, this is very important."

"Yeah?"

"Get an ultrasound."

"You mean, my friend."

"Yes, your *friend* needs an ultrasound. Here's where science helps us. When girls see their babies on the ultrasound screen, 78% of them decide to keep the baby."

Grandma took another big breath. "And Cara, another thing."

"Yeah?"

"Thank you for calling me. I'll do everything I can to help. What do you want?"

"I want everything to go back the way it was!"

"Oh dearie, once you're pregnant, there is no going back. You have to look forward."

"I'm not pregnant! It's my friend! And it's not fair because her boyfriend still gets to go to college like nothing happened and she's stuck with a baby!"

"Life isn't always fair, but it sure is beautiful."

"But men and women are supposed to be equal!"

Grammy began clucking as if Cara were a squalling infant. "Tzh, tzh, tzh," she cooed.

This failed to pacify Cara. Her breath steamed out, hot and loud.

"Women don't need to lose their children to be equal to men. We already *are* equal in deserving dignity and respect. But if anyone tells you that men and women are the *same*, well, you can be sure they're spoon-feeding you from a big ole pot of malarkey stew. Remember how hot and tired and huge your Aunt Mary Ann got when she was pregnant with the twins? While your Uncle Brian was out playing beach volleyball every weekend?" *Humph*, her grandmother scoffed. "Men and women are never more different than when it comes to pregnancy. All the more reason we women need to rally around each other when the men walk away. So you take good care of yourself, dearie, and let me know if you need anything."

There was no getting through to her. Cara slumped in her bucket seat swing. "Okay."

"And can you do me a favor?"

"Yeah."

"Have your mother call me?"

"Okay." *Not a chance.*

"We love you Care Bear."

"Love you too. Bye."

Cara stood up from the swing and kicked the playground wood chips angrily. The brown pellets sprayed around her. *Grownups keep saying, "Life isn't fair."* Kick. *But it should be.* Kick. *Life should be way more fucking fair than this.*

FORTY-FIVE

After her mother called, Annie lurched into the bathroom and leaned over the toilet, but nothing happened. She was empty.

Could it be? Her precious daughter, pregnant? No wonder Cara started smoking at school, she was in big trouble.

Annie avoided the vanity mirror, terrified of what might reflect back at her. Feeling weak, she grabbed the edge of the sink with both hands and leaned over until her head almost touched the mirror. What to do?

She marched to the kitchen and picked up the phone to call Dan.

No.

She set the phone back in its cradle. She didn't want to burden him with this while he was so far away, working hard in Cancun, saving entire companies from computer disasters. He might hop on an overnight plane, drive their Subaru down Mapleville's byways until he found John in his gym shorts loping along in even paces on the side of the road, park in front of him, jump out of the car, grab him by the throat, and throttle him.

Annie's hands were in tight, shaking fists. Her jaw was clenched, grinding her teeth. She had to calm down. She couldn't call Dan in this state. Besides, before strangling John, Dan would want proof.

That's it. She would be logical like her husband. She would buy a pregnancy test.

Annie grabbed her purse and got in the car. On her way to the pharmacy, she spotted Price Chopper and impulsively swung into their parking lot. She would pick up some beer because she needed help and Dan wasn't available, but Sam Adams was. She grabbed a carton of Escape Route lager, then slinked her way to the Health and Feminine products aisle. She scooped up a pregnancy test and veered left, making a beeline toward the checkout.

As Annie steered toward the shortest of the long queues, she spied

Purnell cruising by with her cart. If this were a musical, the ominous opening chords of Beethoven's Fifth would pound through the auditorium whenever Purnell came onstage. *Dum dum da dum! Dum dum da dum!*

Annie pivoted to stare at the magazine rack next to the Snickers and Skittles. *Anti-abortion Activist Bombs Texas Clinic.* Annie felt the hairs on the back of her neck prickle as if they, too, heard Purnell pause. She leaned forward as if engrossed in the article.

Purnell accosted her. "Hello, Mrs. Mulligan. How is Cara doing?"

Annie swung around, feigning surprise. "Why, hello, Ms. Purnell. Cara's fine. She's homeschooling, learning a lot."

"What about socialization?"

"Cara is ... socializing a lot, thanks. And how are you?" Purnell's shopping cart contained fat-free frozen dinners and diet sodas and ice cream made from skimmed milk. Her food was as processed as her shellacked gel-topped nails.

"I'm fine, thank you." Purnell's beady eyes zoomed in on Annie's cart. Highly visible through the open mesh wire, a lusty six-pack squatted next to a pregnancy test. No food. No can of peanuts or red-hot wings to camouflage her loot. Just booze and a possible pregnancy.

Annie did a mental head slap. She could at least have propped a bag of potato chips or Doritos on top of them. Annie grabbed a random newspaper, *Voles Die in University Experiment*, and slapped it on top of the pregnancy kit. "And how is Mr. Day?" she chirped.

"Fine, thank you."

"Nice catching up. See ya!" Annie smiled brightly before turning back toward the newspapers. *Global Birthrate Declines.* "When Stanford professor and butterfly scientist Paul Ehrlich wrote *The Population Bomb,* predicting millions would starve to death during the 1970s, he triggered ..." Annie snagged a Snickers bar and dropped it in her cart, as if she weren't done shopping and had actually come here for groceries. She waited until she could no longer hear *Dum dum da dum* in her head, then replaced the newspaper into its slot.

Annie nudged her cart into a line, which had grown even longer while Purnell detained her. *Why wasn't Purnell in school where she belonged? Who the heck is she to look down her nose at my beer when she's supposed to be at work, harassing kids at CHU to fill out forms?*

Susan Towne came breezing by the checkout line. "Hello, Annie."

She felt an instantaneous prick of jealousy that Susan's daughter was successfully on track for college while her own was navigating the murky waters of accepting enrollment at Coolidge University while simultaneously keeping her expulsion and homeschooling top secret. Annie had been avoiding Susan for weeks and now she overcompensated for her guilty conscience with an enthusiastic, "Hey."

"How's Cara?" Susan ventured.

Through an unwritten woman code, both parties tiptoed carefully around the subject of Cara's mishap at CHU. Hopefully Susan had no clue about a baby on the way. If she knew, she probably wouldn't let Olivia hang out with Cara anymore. Which was a moot point since Cara was already grounded and couldn't hang out with Olivia. Except for prom shopping. Annie had graciously made an allowance for that, hoping Olivia would be a good influence on Cara.

"Good, Cara's good. How's Nelson?"

"Good, still looking. How's Dan doing in Mexico?"

"Good, loves the weather. Likes to rub it in how hot and sunny it is down there." Annie laughed lightly. "Are you taking a day off work?"

"Teachers' strike."

The very day Annie learned that her daughter was pregnant, school was out of commission and she ran into Purnell and Susan. That was one of the problems with Vermont. Everyone knew everyone. Annie could buzz to the country store to pick up eggs and discover the guy in front of her ordering a maple creemee with sprinkles for his kid is her gynecologist, who the week prior took his annual official peek at her hoohah.

"Right. The strike." Annie had heard about the union bargaining with the school board on the radio, but it barely registered now that her kids weren't attending.

Annie saw Susan's eyes track down to the pregnancy test in her cart. Susan gave a sly smile. "Ooh, got a surprise for Dan when he comes back, eh?" She winked.

Better that she thinks I'm pregnant than Cara. Annie shrugged her shoulders. "We'll see." She gave a goofy smile.

"That'll be quite an adjustment for Willy, being the baby of the family, huh?"

"Well, I'm not certain. Hence the test. It could just be menopause kicking in." Annie was impressed at how seamlessly the lie glided out.

"Menopause! Don't get me started. Sometimes in the middle of the night I have to strip off my clothes *and* the covers and then Jerry freezes. My hot flashes are so bad that when I clean house I get sweat pooling in the fingers of my rubber gloves."

By the time Annie got to the head of the line and said bye to Susan, she'd heard about her memory loss, weight gain, lagging libido, sagging breasts, and, the shining star: hot flashes, which were like a Finnish sauna, except without the rolling-in-the-snow afterwards to cool down.

Annie's entire body was rigid. She could be doing Kegel exercises without even meaning to. Not that she didn't care about Susan's hot flashes. Of course she cared! Annie appreciated the heads up so she would know what to expect when she careened into The Change. But ever since her mother called, Annie was dying to know whether Cara really was expecting, or not. The uncertainty gnawed at her. Just standing there, worrying, she could be generating extra cortisol, which prematurely ages your skin, and even if she were, indeed, a grandmother, Annie certainly didn't need any more wrinkles or gray hair.

As soon as she got home, Annie put five bottles in the fridge and one in the freezer for fast chilling. She was already looking forward to swigging that beer after The Talk. She grabbed the pregnancy test and climbed the stairs to Cara's room. Annie knocked lightly.

"Come in."

Cara was sitting on her bed with her knees propping up her laptop.

"Sweetie, we need to talk."

"What's up?"

Annie shut the door securely behind her and scooched next to Cara on the cozy plaid flannel duvet. She put one arm around Cara's shoulders and leaned close, resting her head against Cara's. "How are you feeling?"

"A little hungry."

"Oh, good! You're not nauseous?"

"No. Are you?"

Smiling, Annie turned to look at Cara. "No." She tenderly swept a strand of Cara's hair behind her ear. "Sweetie, I have to ask. Are you in trouble?"

"Yeah, duh. Got kicked out of CHU."

"Anything else?"

"Well, I'm having trouble with algebra. But you know that already."

"Is there anything else? Anything you want to talk to me about?"

Cara's eyebrows did that puzzled wiggly thing.

"Do you want to talk about your boyfriend? Is John in any trouble?"

Cara widened her eyes and she shrugged, palms up. "Haven't heard from him. I'm grounded, remember?"

Wordlessly, but with her eyes brimming with motherly love and genuine concern, Annie held out the pregnancy test to her daughter.

Cara stared ... realization flickered ... and her eyebrows smacked into her hairline. "Did Grammy call you?"

From there the entire conversation turned into a total shriekfest. Cara screamed about her lack of privacy and respect, and insisted she wasn't pregnant, and that John had actually dumped her weeks ago, which was news to Annie, and would she just stay out of her business anyway because she didn't know an effing thing about Cara's life!

"Mom, you're fired!"

By then Annie was inching backwards towards the door, clutching the unwanted pregnancy test, wondering where she had gone wrong and where was Dan while all this shit was going down? Lounging on a beach? Knocking back beers? Watching *Sherlock* reruns on TV in an air-conditioned five-star hotel? So unfair!

And who was right? Grammy or Cara? Who was wrong? Her mother or her daughter?

FORTY-SIX

"No man, for any considerable period, can wear one face to himself and another to the multitude, without finally getting bewildered as to which may be the true." ~ The Scarlet Letter

Cara sat at the kitchen table, rereading the words but she had trouble comprehending because her mother kept interrupting from the living room.

"Love this dress! Love. It. Cara, check out this gown! Why didn't Olivia and Nate post photos? I wanted to see what Olivia was wearing. Guess I'll have to wait til tomorrow. OMG! I've never seen Taryn look so ... so ... feminine. Even her makeup looks on point... Gah! Now *that* neckline is way too low. What was her mother thinking?"

That evening, when everyone else from Camels Hump High School was prepping for the prom, Cara had vowed not to torture herself by going on Facebook. But this was worse—her mother tormenting her with a running commentary as she scrolled down photo after photo. She was so off-point it was painful.

Her mom had been sickeningly solicitous ever since Grammy called. Even though she insisted she wasn't pregnant, her mother kept offering saltine crackers, flat soda, and soft pats on her back. Feeling guilty for shrugging off her mother's pathetic outreach, Cara shouted back, "Whose dress are you talking about?"

"Gillian Hans. That must be Steve's granddaughter. Did he see that on her? She's about to pop out!"

Cara stared down at her open book, begging Hester Prynne to do something, anything, to distract her from her major FOMO. Or Dimmesdale. Why won't he man up? How about Chillingworth slays them both with a long knife to end her misery?

It wasn't Gillian's gown she wanted to see, Cara was dying to see what

Olivia and Zach were doing. She was tempted to stalk them on Facebook, but that was Ashley's job. How could the girl trust such a hot guy at a prom?

Was Zach a player like Nate ... would he ever get a girl pregnant, then dump her?

No. Not Zach. He wouldn't do anything that douchey.

No matter how much she tried not to, Cara couldn't help picturing Zach and Olivia. Chatting, dancing, getting close together. Hitting it off? Slow dancing?

Please.

God.

No.

When Cara's phone bleeped, she grabbed it, expecting a text from Olivia, but it was Taryn.

Taryn: Nate says Olivia is pregnant? WTF???!!!

Taryn: Olivia is pregnant???

Cara: What is Nate doing there??? He told O he wasn't going!

Taryn: He came with someone else. He is totes wasted. Is it true? Is O preggo?

Taryn: Nate tackled Zach from behind!

Taryn: Asshole.

Cara: Zach?

Taryn: No, Nate!!! Btw, Zach is super cute!

Cara: Is Zach ok?

Taryn: Zach ok, he hit back. Nate crawling on floor. Barfing. UGH!

Taryn: Where did you find Zach? Does he have a brother, haha??

Cara: How is Olivia???!!!

Taryn: O crying. Danielle and I bringing her to girls room. Gotta go.

Cara texted Olivia but got no response. She called, but Olivia didn't pick up.

Cara to Taryn: TELL HER TO CALL ME!!!!

"Jeesum crow. That dress is so short. Is that Danielle? How can she dance in that?"

Cara ignored her mother and focused her eyes like laser beams on her phone.

"I'm going to sue that school for kicking you out and not letting you go to your own prom. You were on the committee! Cara, the balloons and streamers look perfect. Come look!"

Ugh! Her mom was so invasive. Cara's laser beams weren't working—no one was texting back. Everyone was silent. Except for her mother.

"Taryn looks adorable. Did she cut her hair?"

Cara slammed *The Scarlet Letter* shut, grabbed her phone, and snuck out the back door. The dogs whined to come out and she quietly opened the door for them, hoping her mother wouldn't notice. She walked in circles, from the patio to the arbor to the patio, repeatedly calling Olivia, leaving messages, and waiting for a call back.

Why did Nate go to the prom? He's messing everything up! Poor Olivia! Poor Zach! He had no idea what he was getting into! Ugh!

She stopped circling to stare at her phone, willing it to ring or bing or zap her a photo.

She wanted to call Zach and explain and apologize but he had no cell phone. And first she needed to hear from Olivia, to make sure she was okay.

Cara pictured Nate, trashed and slurring, bragging about the baby to the entire room, putting Olivia on the spot, humiliating her …

Olivia is crying, Zach steps in between them, he tells Nate to shut up, Nate all stupidly studly puffs up his chest, says, "what's-it-to-you?" and macho-nacho shoves Zach, who smoothly deflects it with one of his epic black belt defense moves, then Zach steps back, winds up, executes a wicked spinning kick and his foot makes contact with Nate on the side of his stupid bull-headed head and BAM! Nate's on the floor! Crawling! Where he belongs, that major, major douchebag! The crowd erupts with whistles and cheers and applause! Zach gazes around the circle of prom-goers, searching, searching, yearning to lock eyes with Cara, spots her, he rushes to her—

Cara's phone rang. She swiped to accept and shouted, "Olivia? You okay?"

"Nate told everyone! The entire freaking school knows!"

"Okay, Via, it's gonna be okay."

"Easy for you to say!"

"Where are you?"

"I'm with Zach."

"Where are you guys?"

"In the parking lot. I couldn't go back to the dance, but I don't want to go home yet. My parents will wonder why I'm back so early."

"How about I meet up with you somewhere?"

They quickly settled on Green Mountain Scoop and Zach agreed to pick Cara up at her house.

"Hold on," she said, "I need to ask my mom."

From the back stoop, she opened the kitchen door, held the phone to her belly to muffle the sound and called to her mother, who was still in the living room sponging off Facebook for a life. "Mom, can I go out with some friends for ice cream?"

"No, you're grounded," she yelled back. "Remember?"

"It's Olivia and Mrs. Boucher's son." Cara stepped aside to let the dogs wedge through the door opening, then she followed them in to the house.

"Olivia and *Zachary*?" This roused her mother from the sofa and she scurried to the kitchen. "What happened to Nate?"

"I missed the prom entirely, Mom. Can't I at least get a creemee?"

Cara could see her mother soften with sympathy. "All right... They're both good kids."

"Yes," Cara spoke into the phone. "See you in a few."

"Do you need cash?" Her mother fetched her purse from the counter and pulled out her wallet. She handed Cara a ten-dollar bill.

"Thanks." Cara took the money gratefully. But it rankled—the way her mom admired Olivia, who was pregnant and lit the joint which triggered her exile.

"Have fun, Care Bear."

But her mom didn't trust her, even though she wasn't hooking up and stayed clear of drugs.

On the other hand, how could she blame her mother? She didn't know the truth because Cara had fibbed. Her stupid little lie about the weed was so believable that now her mother believed she was a total stoner. And thanks to Grammy, her mother suspected Cara was pregnant, despite explaining that John had dumped her and they hadn't been fooling around anyway.

Everything was so messed up. While she was sitting unaddicted and unpregnant in her kitchen on a Saturday night doing homework, Olivia got to slow dance with Zach and then watch him take down Nate!

Cara jogged upstairs. She switched out of her shorts and top and put on a cream-colored sundress spangled with pink and blue flowers. She pulled her long brown hair into a half pony. She didn't want to overdo it, but she didn't want to drab them down either. She knew Olivia would be stunning in that frothy green dress she had helped pick out. And Zach had to be looking swag in his prom duds, since he could look smoking hot in an ordinary tee shirt and jeans.

She looked in the mirror. The pale fabric made her complexion look pasty, the sickly fish-belly color of skin that had seen zero sunshine for eight months straight. She needed a golden tan to rock this sundress. She slipped it off and stepped into last year's prom dress. She zipped up and stepped in front of her mirror assessing critically. The blue ruching flattered her waist and eyes, but the dress screamed Trying Too Hard! She felt stupid. She was way too overdressed to be Olivia and Zach's third wheel. Ugh. She sighed and switched back to the original flowered sundress.

Cara waited on the front porch steps so Zach and Olivia could avoid her mother. But as soon as the Boucher car turned into the driveway, her mom joined her outside.

Zach stepped out of the car and it suddenly looked small next to him. He sauntered up the flagstone path towards the porch. He'd taken his suit jacket off and whatever tie he had worn. The sleeves of his light blue shirt were rolled past his elbows. He combed a hand through his wavy brown hair which only highlighted the careless tousled look. His nose and cheek were scraped and swollen yet he managed to look perfect anyway.

Damn, I should have worn my prom dress! Olivia's seen it of course, but Zach hasn't!

"Hey Cara."

Cara pressed her hands into the wooden steps to brace herself as her heart thudded into her lungs. She tried to look normal and nonchalant. "Hey."

Zach said, "Hello, Mrs. Mulligan. I'll get Cara back in about an hour."

Her mom gasped. "Your nose!"

"The dance floor was crowded and I accidentally ran into someone," he explained. "Do you have any arnica?"

"Arnica?"

"My mother uses that on us kids all the time. Takes the swelling down. How about some ice instead?"

"Sure."

While her mom went into the house to fetch ice cubes, Cara arched her eyebrows at Zach and pursed her lips skeptically. "You ran into someone."

"In more ways than one." He whispered *shh* with his finger to his lips. "Wait 'til we get in the car."

All she wanted to do was stare at him. Lucky Olivia got to look at him all night. And who knows how long the luckier Ashley had been seeing him.

Cara had to say something.

Anything.

"Did you have good time?"

This time he arched his eyebrows and scrunched his lips at her skeptically.

Afraid of the answer she whispered, "Nate?"

But Cara's mother came back and Zach turned his attention to her. She passed him a hand towel and a bucket full of ice asking, "Is this enough?"

"You don't have any more?"

Her mom looked down at the bucket and apologized. "I'm sorry. I dumped the whole ice bin in." Then she looked up and saw Zach smiling at her. She rolled her eyes. "I sure hope that's enough!"

"No worries. My nose isn't *that* big."

FORTY-SEVEN

Cara climbed in the back seat and Olivia got out of the front seat to scoot in next to her.

"I'm so sorry," Cara told her as Zach reversed out of the driveway.

"Why did this have to happen at the prom? No one was supposed to know, but now the entire school knows." Olivia's face was damp with tears.

Cara wrapped her arm around her shoulders and pulled her friend close. "Like I said before, it'll all work out."

"Hold up." Zach took the towel of ice off his nose and inspected Cara through the rearview mirror. "You knew about the baby?" His eyes looked inward, as if he were counting backwards to determine if she knew two weeks ago when she asked him to take Olivia to the prom.

While Cara paused, trying to figure out how to respond, Olivia answered for her, "Of course." She squeezed Cara. "She was the first one I told. Actually, the only one until I told Nate."

Zach's eyes narrowed. He removed his ice pack and opened his mouth as if he were going to say something.

Cara cringed, waiting for him to call her out.

But he didn't. He let that slide and instead asked Olivia, "Your parents don't know?"

"God no—they're Catholic. They would kill me."

Zach raised his eyes skyward. His breath puttered out between pressed lips. "Everyone always says that, but parents never actually do that. Yeah, it'll be a shock at first, but you have to tell them. How can your parents help you if they don't even know?" He put the ice pack back to his nose.

"He's right," Cara chimed in. "Besides, your mom works at the school. She'll hear it soon enough anyway. Better for it to come from you than from—" Cara, paused, wondering who would have the nerve to tell Mrs. Towne.

"Ugh. I can't. I just can't." Olivia fished in her clutch for more tissues. "I can't tell them. Nate wasn't even supposed to be there, he ruined everything!"

"What the heck happened?" asked Cara.

"Nate was tanked. He didn't like me dancing with Zach and he went ballistic. He told everyone I was pregnant and then he sucker punched Zach. Got him from behind." She looked at Zach in the mirror. "I'm really sorry about your nose."

"No worries. I've had worse at the gym."

"Then what happened?" Cara asked his reflection in the mirror, eager to hear more.

Zach shook his head, "Not worth talking about."

Cara turned to Olivia. "What happened?"

"Nate hit Zach, tackled him from behind, and then landed on top of him. Somehow Zach elbowed him off and next thing you know Nate's crawling on the floor, completely wasted, Zach standing over him."

Cara turned back to Zach. "Did you hit him?"

"No."

"Kick?"

As if the question pained him, Zach shook his head.

"I thought you were a black belt?"

"Can't hit a guy who's down."

"But he got you from behind! That's not fair!" Cara's body was rigid with rage, her fists clenched tight and hard. Nate deserved a major whupping!

Olivia made a face. "He was on the floor, puking. It was pathetic."

What a letdown. This wasn't nearly as epic as the takedown that Cara had pictured in her head. She knew Olivia felt sorry for Nate. But Cara wanted to smack him herself for being such a wuss and taking it out on Zach.

"That's why Nate broke up with me, you know," Olivia told Zach. "He was scared. He wants me to get rid of it, but I wasn't ready to do that and he freaked. He's normally not such a ... he's just ..." She stared out the window. "He's not ready."

Olivia wept some tender new tears while Cara assured her again, that she was doing the right thing by keeping the baby. "Refuse to choose between Nate and Pearl."

"Who's Pearl? That girl he was dancing with?"

"No, your baby."

"You named my baby?" Olivia squealed.

"Just a nickname," Cara backed off instantly. "Refuse to choose between Columbia and your baby."

"It's not that easy!" Olivia wailed.

"If you tell your parents, they can help," Zach said.

He was like an intrusive chauffeur looking in the rearview mirror and talking back to them from the driver's seat. The kind of chauffeur who uses his right hand to steer and his left hand to hold a wad of ice on his nose. And who is incredibly handsome despite a bruised nose.

If Olivia told her parents about the baby, Cara hoped she'd also agree to tell the truth about the weed. Then Cara would be free to go back to CHU and graduate on time. It wouldn't be too late to get into college and get her life back. "She's the size of a plum by now."

"She?" Olivia's voice rose a notch.

"Just a guess," Cara mumbled.

Zach assured Olivia that if she didn't feel ready to raise the baby, she could put her up for adoption. "Thousands of couples are looking to adopt. My mom would adopt your baby. She loves babies."

The thought of Olivia's baby being Zach's little sibling was so extra that Olivia and Cara rolled their eyes at each other. Olivia burst out laughing, which quickly turned into sobbing. Cara pulled her close and let her cry it out and Zach drove silently, giving them space.

At the ice cream parlor, Zach and Cara ordered creemees. Feeling uneasy and queasy, Olivia opted for ginger ale. They drove to the village green. Zach took out a blanket from the back of his car and spread it out on the grass and they ate their ice cream while he held the ice pack to his cheek and nose.

Cara plugged them with questions and they filled her in. She wanted to hear more about Nate's tackle and the barf and then they worked their way back to the dancing.

"Who was Nate with?" Cara asked.

"Someone from another school. I didn't recognize her."

"Of course she's from a different school. No one from CHU would have the nerve to go to the prom with him when he's been your boyfriend for the past three years."

"Yeah. I'm sure she'll need to hitch a ride home from someone tonight, because he's too wrecked to drive," said Olivia. "Actually, Nate will need a ride, too. He better not try to drive himself."

"Someone will drive him," Cara said.

"Ya think?" Olivia's eyebrows folded in worry.

"I bet they had a designated driver," Cara assured her. "Did John show up?"

"Who's John?" asked Zach.

Cara immediately regretted asking the question. *What do I care if he went to the prom?* Did she only go out with him because she was sick of being alone whenever Olivia and Nate went on a date? Cara hated to think she used John just to have a boyfriend ... but did she?

Cara locked eyes with Olivia, silently pleading with her to cover. "He's a friend of ours," said Olivia smoothly to Zach. "And no, he wasn't there," she told Cara.

Then they started talking about who was wearing what and that's when they lost Zach who lay back on the blanket, closed his eyes and balanced the ice pack on his nose.

"Cara, you were right," said Olivia. "Zach has some pretty sweet dance moves."

"Ten years of ballroom dance lessons," complained Zach.

Cara sighed, "I'm jealous you got to dance with him."

Still on his back and underneath the ice pack Zach asked, "You like dancing?"

"Sure."

Zach plunked his ice pack in the bucket, stood up, and held his hand out to Cara.

She put her hand in his and allowed him to pull her up. He smelled manly and strong with a fading whiff of spicy aftershave. "What about music?" she protested.

"I've got my iPod," Olivia said. "I got a song for ya." She smiled knowingly at Cara.

The volume from the slim device was pitiful and the earthy night air swallowed up the sound waves, but as soon as Cara heard the opening notes she immediately recognized "Perfect" by Ed Sheeran. She turned her head and smiled gratefully at Olivia, who winked.

Cara stumbled in her sandals so she kicked those off. She tripped on a tree root and wobbled, but Zach's strong arms held her steady. "Sorry!" she apologized. *Why didn't I start dance lessons at age four like Olivia?*

His warm and appreciative eyes made her heart bubble and her limbs feel fizzy. Swoosh went her heart. Swoosh.

Despite the slippery wet grass underneath her bare feet, and the tingle that zinged from his hands to hers, and the jolt in her chest when he smiled at her, she felt safe and secure in his grasp. He drew her slowly around the green and she trusted his arms and floated.

The song was perfect ... except way too short.

When it ended, Zach picked her up, swung her around, set her on the blanket, smiled, and gazed at her with his sparkling root beer eyes. Then he dropped his hands from her waist and the spell was broken.

They folded up the blanket and climbed back in the car. As they drove away from the green, Olivia said, "You can drop me off first. I'm right on the way to Cara's."

He escorted her to her front door and paused.

Cara was dying to know what they were saying. In the car she faced straight ahead, straining to use her peripheral vision to spy on them.

Turning towards Olivia, he said something, picked up her hand and kissed it.

She said something.

He said something.

Then Olivia relevéd up on tiptoe to kiss him on his uninjured cheek and slipped inside her house.

As soon as she was home, Cara would grill Olivia for details and get her unedited version of the entire evening, from the pickup at her place in her gorgeous dress, to the slow dancing at the prom, to this unexpected goodnight kiss at her door!

FORTY-EIGHT

When Zach got back in the car, Cara had already switched to the front passenger seat. He drove the short distance to Cara's house without speaking. She fingered her cotton sundress, afraid to interrupt his force field of silence. The spell was most definitely broken.

When he reached her driveway, he turned off the engine, but didn't get out. She ventured a glance at him. The outdoor light on their garage shed a dim light on his face. He didn't look happy.

"Cara, what the heck was that?"

"What?"

"You set me up with a girl who was pregnant and you knew it and didn't tell me? And her boyfriend shows up?"

"Ex."

Zach put a fist to his forehead. He looked as if he wanted to punch something. "Okay," he said with exaggerated patience. "Ex-boyfriend. So they broke up. You know what this means?"

"It means Olivia is screwed." *Where did* that *come from?*

"No, it means this guy has to man up. He has to help take care of the baby, not take me out."

"Okay, I'm sorry he jumped you. I had no idea Nate was even going to be there. I knew he was an asshole, but I didn't know he was that big of an asshole."

"You don't have to swear about it."

Cara stared at Zach. Nate was the douche who dumped Olivia because he got her pregnant, but she wasn't supposed to swear about it?

"Do you want your little brother to swear like that?"

From the guy who had a girlfriend but kissed Olivia? And had turned on the charm when he danced on the green with Cara?

Zach continued, "What about her being pregnant? You should have told me about that. What if I dropped her?"

"I saw you dance with your sister Charlene—you flipped her all over the place and didn't drop her. Plus, Olivia knows how to dance—she's captain of the dance team!"

"But she's pregnant. I could have accidentally hurt the baby! Why didn't you tell me?"

"I couldn't! I promised Olivia I wouldn't tell anyone. I *wanted* to tell you. Believe me, I wish I could have told you. I wish I could tell everything! I'm so sick of everything being a lie— keeping this stupid secret, it's totally messing up my life!"

Zach drew back and studied Cara. "This isn't just about Olivia's baby, is it?"

"NO! YES!"

"Yes or no? Which is it!" Now they were both shouting. Zach paused and lowered his voice. "Give me a straight answer."

Silence.

"You can trust me."

Cara studied him. "Can I? Sometimes I don't even know who you are. First you're one person—you go to church and help your mother and visit nursing homes with your dog and chew me out for swearing. But you change completely when you're around Eric and he brags about home-schooling and all your double dates with Ashley and Emily. And you just kissed Olivia even though you have a girlfriend!"

"On the *hand*," he defended himself.

"What about Ashley!"

He looked down and shook his head. "I'm sorry."

"You don't have to apologize to *me*, you should say sorry to *her*!"

Zach cleared his throat, still facing the floorboard. "No, I need to apologize to *you*." He turned his head to meet Cara's gaze full on. "I should have told you earlier." His eyebrows lifted in apology and his mouth slid into an embarrassed half-smile. "There is no Ashley."

"What?"

"Eric and I were just messing with you."

"Say what?"

"We don't have girlfriends, we made them up."

Cara gaped at him. Ashley was a fake out? How dare he fool her like that for weeks!

"It was stupid. And I should have owned up to it earlier." He sighed and ran his hand through his gorgeous, wavy hair. "Everyone thinks homeschoolers are a bunch of geeks, so when Eric told me about your senior project, we pretended to have girlfriends so we wouldn't look lame in your report. Totally stupid. I'm sorry."

Cara was mega outraged, but even more, she felt deliriously happy that he didn't have a girlfriend! He was available! Now she was free to crush on him big time! This was a game changer!

He looked piteously contrite, and adorable, like their puppies when they had caught them plowing through the candy from their Easter baskets. Despite her anger, Cara's heart melted a little.

But then she was puzzled on top of being super mad and ecstatic. "Wait, what project?"

"The community service project that seniors have to do to graduate from CHU. We heard yours was about homeschooling and we wanted to look impressive for your report."

They must have heard her mother blabbing about her studying homeschoolers. Once again her mother's "help" had backfired. Ugh. "I'm not doing any project."

"Then why are you spending so much time at the homeschool group? How are you going to graduate from CHU?"

"I don't know!"

"Cara! What is going on? I deserve the truth!"

"You just admitted you lied about a fake girlfriend and now you want the truth!"

"It was just a prank, no harm done. But you set me up with a pregnant girl who has a psycho ex-boyfriend."

He assumed his little charade was no big deal because he had no idea how much Cara liked him. She never would've risked setting him up with her gorgeous, newly single best friend if she'd known he wasn't linked to a girlfriend! However, he wasn't to blame for believing she was spying on them, that was her mother's fault. "The truth is ..."

Cara paused. He got points for *not* being a two-timer. But, he lost points for fooling her in the first place. She chewed her bottom lip.

On the other hand, he already knew about Olivia's baby. That's what started the insane sham to begin with. Could she trust him with the expulsion story?

Zach looked at her expectantly, waiting for her to explain. Would it really ruin everything if she told him what happened? Was the truth that treacherous?

It would be a major relief to finally tell someone. And didn't he deserve to know? Look at his sterling nose—now all swollen and red. It had to hurt big time. She couldn't help feeling responsible for that.

Cara sucked in a deep breath. "Here's the deal. The reason I joined the homeschool group is because I got kicked out of Camels Hump for smoking weed in the teacher's bathroom and—"

Tap tap.

Cara yelped and catapulted above her seat landing back down hard and awkwardly.

Her mother was knocking on the windshield. "Hey, you two! Want to come in for a bite to eat?" Her mother peered in through the windshield with an overlarge smile on her face. "Or something to drink?" The garage light cast her face in shadow. Her disembodied head looked fake and creepy like a plastic doll's.

Zach immediately got out of the car. "Thank you, Mrs. Mulligan. But I'm not feeling my best." He pointed to his nose and flashed her a rueful smile. "I hope you understand."

She softened visibly. "Of course, Zachary. Another time, then."

"Sure."

He walked around and opened the passenger door for Cara who stepped out, trying to catch his eye.

"Wait, there's more," Cara whispered.

"I'm sure there is," he replied, refusing to look at her.

Willy came barging out of the house holding a flashlight. "I heard someone busted your nose!" He aimed his beam of light at Zach's face.

"Nah." Zach felt his nose with his fingertips. "Didn't even break. Yours was way more sick."

Willy shrugged modestly. "It'll start to turn colors tomorrow," he said encouragingly.

"Thanks, dude." Zach gave him a fist bump. He handed the towel and empty bucket to Cara's mother, said thanks, and folded his six-foot frame back into the car.

"Bye," said Willy and her mother, waving cheerfully as he slowly pulled out of their driveway.

Zach stretched his arm out the window and gave a polite salute back.

Next to Willy and her mother, Cara stood—mouth open, but speechless. She wondered what Zach thought of her now. First he believed she was snooping on the homeschool group for her senior project. And now he thought she was a stoner? Why did her mom have to interrupt them before she had a chance to explain that she was covering for Olivia? And he had no cell phone for her to call and explain it all. Cara glanced balefully at her mother who was gleefully shouting bye bye to Zach.

Annie set down the bucket and dropped the towel in it so she could wave with both arms. This is when pom-poms would come in handy. Earlier that evening she had tried "socialization" with Cara over Facebook, but her daughter was decidedly unsociable. Then she had allowed Cara to go out for ice cream with Zachary and Olivia, hoping their good habits would rub off on her. Olivia was headed to Columbia to begin her lucrative STEM career. And Zachary was smart, handsome, helpful, and came from a good family. Why wasn't Cara more hospitable to him? Does she not know how to flirt? Or at least give a smidgeon of encouragement to a guy?

Annie gave a final shake goodbye to Zachary and looked over at Cara, who stood immobile, impassive, staring at nothing. No pep, no zip, no smile. Annie hated to admit it, but her daughter would make a dreadful cheerleader.

FORTY-NINE

"So how was Green Mountain Scoop?" Annie had been dying to ask last night, but as soon as Zachary drove away, Cara grumbled *tired* and *bed* and fled upstairs and slammed the door. Annie had to wait to hear the juicy details about the after-prom jaunt until they were in the car after their weekly Sunday morning rush-to-get-ready-for-church.

"Good," said Cara.

Annie didn't care about the creemee. She wanted to know how the prom went and why Cara wasn't attracted to Maggie's son. After all, Zachary seemed perfect.

"Who punched Zach?" Willy piped up from the backseat.

"There was no punching. He bumped into someone," Annie told the rearview mirror. Then she flicked her gaze towards Cara, "Did you all have a good time?"

"Yeah."

"Cara," whispered Willy. "What happened to Zach?"

"Nothing," said Annie. "He knocked into someone. Give your sister some peace." She tried again to engage her daughter. "Did Olivia have a good time at the prom?"

"Yeah."

"Good," said Annie.

Except ... it wasn't.

It was supposed to have been Cara's big prom night. For months, for years even, Annie had planned on taking her darling daughter shopping for a beautiful dress for her final prom. On the big day, Olivia was going to come over so the girls could do each other's hair and nails. And Annie was going to invite Susan and Jerry over so they could celebrate the girls' last high school dance together. And she would open a bottle of wine and they would reminisce about the girls' silly crush on Mark in middle school and how they caught the girls making prank phone calls to him and had to put the kibosh on that. And then there was the first time the girls dabbled with makeup and came out of the bathroom looking like hookers. And she and Susan would have laughed until they got all teary-eyed and hugged each other and sobbed on each other's shoulders, bemoaning how time flies, while Dan and Jerry rolled their eyes and uncapped more beers for themselves.

And then they would have to wipe their tears because John and Nate would join them for dinner. Dan would have grilled steak, the cleanest dinner possible so the kids could keep their clothes impeccable. And then Annie would take photos of the four best friends in the back yard in front of the arbor. Cara and John made a lovely couple. Olivia and Nate, too, of course. After the kids cruised off and Susan and Jerry went home, she and Dan would put on their special song. They would slow dance and Willy would roll his eyes and escape to his bedroom while Annie and Dan made out in the living room.

It was going to be perfectly magical.

But no. Dan was in Mexico. Nate didn't come because the It Couple apparently broke up, although Cara refused to explain why. Ditto for John. Olivia couldn't come over because Cara was grounded. Susan and Jerry didn't come for drinks because Olivia didn't come. Annie didn't bring Cara shopping at the mall because she couldn't go to the prom. No gown. No photos. No memories.

All Cara got was a measly ice cream cone. And something must have happened there because Cara repelled her every inquiry.

They filed into church, but Annie couldn't stop herself from dwelling on last night. She glanced over at Cara, who was biting her lip, looking pale and preoccupied. *Could it be morning sickness? Please God, NO!* Annie closed her eyes in desperate prayer. She had such fervent hopes for Cara's life. A baby would mess up her plan.

Fr. McHolland read the gospel. "I am the good shepherd: the good shepherd lays down his life for his sheep. The hired man, since he is not the shepherd and the sheep do not belong to him, abandons the sheep as soon as he sees a wolf coming, and runs away, and then the wolf attacks …"

Afterwards they went downstairs for coffee hour where Cara and Olivia huddled in the corner and ceased talking every time Annie came over offering refreshments. She tried doughnuts and small Dixie cups of apple juice, but was met with "No, thanks," and silent pauses. So Annie returned to Susan and was forced to admire more photos of Olivia and Zachary on her friend's cell phone.

In the car on the way back, Willy asked, "Guess what? When wolves attack lambs, they grab them by the throat. Know why? 'Cause that way the lambs can't yell or make any noise at all and the wolf gets away with their prey without scaring the rest of the flock. Isn't that cool?"

"Yeah," said Cara. "Wicked cool," she said listlessly.

"Ew," said Annie. This reminded her of *The Silence of the Lambs,* which Dan had talked her in to watching one night. Years later she still regretted it and blamed him for her visual flashbacks. "Where'd you hear that?"

"Joey told me. He found out when he went on a field trip to a sheep shearing farm. Can I get together with Joey today?"

"Ew." Annie was stuck on the image of a lamb dangling from a wolf's jaw.

"I got my homework done already."

"All right. I'll call Mrs. Boucher when I get home."

Annie was distracted. She recalled her chat with Olivia's mom. Whatever happened to Nate? Even Susan didn't have a good answer. And of course she didn't ask her friend, but Annie kept wondering, why did Zachary ask Olivia to the prom? Why didn't he ask *Cara*?

When Annie called Maggie to see if Willy could go over, she learned they were busy; they had invited their parish priest over for dinner. But Maggie said Willy could come on Tuesday to do science experiments with Joey.

Annie whipped up another batch of chocolate chip cookies to get through the week while chatting on the phone with her mother. Then she prepared lesson plans for the upcoming week, including arranging a study date for Willy to go to Paloma's house on Thursday for a unit on Ethan Allen and the Green Mountain Boys. Paloma assured her she had plenty of tricorn hats and promised to take pictures for documentation.

She graded Cara's art homework. Annie had worked at a preschool long enough not to make the newbie mistake of asking, "What is it?" Besides, she was pretty sure it was a painting of their neighbor Steve's shed with a happy little tree next to it, and the bobbing white blobs above had to be clouds. She gave it a happy A.

Annie updated her grocery list. She needed more chocolate chips and beer.

Then she sorted through the mail that had piled up on the kitchen counter and found a letter from CHU. It wasn't like the huge packet she received weeks ago. This was a normal white business-size envelope.

Maybe they were reinstating her daughter? Cara could go back to high school, Willy could go back to middle school, and Annie could go back to preschool, where she belonged! She couldn't wait to start receiving a paycheck for teaching again. Annie zipped the envelope open and eagerly scanned the notice.

The Camels Hump Union High School Board has reviewed your request to reenroll your daughter, Cara Mulligan. We commend Principal Day and his adherence to school regulations and safety guidelines, and advise you to seek elsewhere for Cara's education ...

By loyal decree, the school board had backed up the principal's decision to eject Cara. With a sickening jolt, Annie realized she was stuck homeschooling Cara for seven more weeks. And if she homeschooled Cara, she would have to homeschool Willy as well, because how could she justify sending him to school when Cara got to stay home and study in her pajamas all day long?

Annie lifted the magnet pinning the grocery list to the fridge. She plucked a pen from the decoupaged coffee can that doubled as a pencil holder and scribbled *vodka* at the top of her list.

FIFTY

WHY GET OUT of bed if your life is just full of fiascos and you'll just screw it up more if you climb out of your comfy flannel cocoon? Annie rolled over and burrowed her head under the pillow, creating a nest, closing her eyes, banning the daylight.

She wished she had a giant pink rubber eraser to eliminate all her mess-ups—mistakes such as not signing Willy up for Tae Kwon Do when he was five years old. And failing to teach Cara to Just Say No to drugs and to sex. And Annie's last semester of college, aside from the diploma and the Bruce Springsteen concert.

Being a good mother meant getting your kids into college and getting married before starting a family. Cara couldn't possibly be knocked up. Right?

But if so, Annie would walk beside her daughter, every step of the way. She wasn't about to throw stones; she had her own secret boulder dragging behind her like an invisible ball and chain.

Head still buried under her pillow, she blinked her eyes open and spotted the bottle of acetaminophen on her night table. It was a large generic container bought in bulk to save money while treating her monthly PMS. She had a major headache. She sat up and reached for the bottle. She aligned the childproof triangles and pried the cap off. She poured white tablets into her cupped hand.

Scratch. One of the dogs was signaling breakfast time. She ignored it. The dogs could wait for Willy to wake up and feed them.

Annie sipped from the water bottle on her nightstand and knocked back two pills, wishing they were for insomnia so she could sleep through her failures. She wished she could put them all behind her and pretend it never happened. Erased. Her story would end as neatly and succinctly as closing a book shut with a tiny *thwoosh.*

Scratch. Scratch.

Annie realized she overreacted the day her mother called to say that Cara was expecting. Her mother had been surprisingly supportive, pledging help with finances and baby booties, promising the full force of her Right to Life Committee. As if a committee can help breastfeed a newborn at 3:00 am.

Annie had panicked because she wasn't ready. Grandmothers were supposed to be wise. And for the past couple of weeks, instead of getting older and wiser, Annie felt herself getting stupider. She was clueless. She was faking it. If she were assigned a scarlet letter on her breast, it would be a big fat "F" for Fault, Fraud, F'd up.

Annie slumped against her headboard, waiting for her headache to disappear.

Scratch. Scratch.

The clock radio glowed 6:37 in red. Back when she worked at PAL, she would be halfway through her shower at this time. But she had stopped setting her alarm the day she got fired.

Staying in her pajamas all day long wasn't good enough. She wanted to stay in *bed* all day. She would stay here until Dan came home and took over the homeschooling and cooking and grocery shopping and brushing the dogs. She was sick of it. No one appreciated her. When Annie approached the dogs with the prickly brushes, they promptly tucked their tails and scooted away in different directions in a concerted effort to thwart her. Willy didn't care that she bought him organic bread for his peanut butter and jelly sandwiches. Cara didn't care that she left her job at PAL to homeschool. In fact, Cara seemed to resent it.

Another claw ratcheted down her bedroom door. She didn't want Dan to come home and find trenches scraped into their bedroom door by their dogs.

She counted to three and swung her legs over the side of the bed. "Come on, Annie," she coached herself. "Gimme a U, gimme a P, what's that spell?"

Crap.

This is why Annie didn't make captain of the squad. She was better at encouraging others than motivating herself, and leaders need to be self-directed. Plus, Annie had held back from screaming at basketball games in order to save her voice for song, not realizing that her future college loans would necessitate ditching her singing aspirations for a practical career in education. Now Annie channeled Cheryl, her high school cheerleading captain with the long hair and high ponytail and low barking voice, perpetually hoarse. "Up, up, UP!"

Annie pushed herself off the snug bed and shoved her feet into her slippers. She shuffled to the kitchen, Moe and Curly tagging after legs, wagging their tails in anticipation. She measured out cupfuls of dog kibbles for the retrievers.

What the hell. She was already up. Might as well put on the coffee. At least they had electricity today.

FIFTY-ONE

After breakfast, Willy begged to go outside and Annie agreed as long as he found a bug for her to photograph to submit to the state homestudy office. Cara had clomped up the stairs to her room to work on her history. Or so she said. Annie wasn't sure what to believe anymore.

She held the answer key open on the kitchen table with her left forearm and sighed as she X'd Cara's algebra mistakes with a red pen. She wondered if maybe she should try unschooling? As much as she tried to teach by marking Cara's math mistakes with a bright red X, Annie's heart just wasn't in it today. Annie had run out of exclamation points. Her life was one big question mark.

Maggie's son had been so gracious and gentlemanly on Saturday night. Funny, too, joking with her about the ice cubes, pounding it with Willy. But Cara was silent and standoffish. She just stood there gaping when he drove away. No wonder Zachary took Olivia to the prom. Not only was Olivia a bright and lovely girl, she probably actually conversed with Zachary instead of staring with her mouth open. Annie would have relished un-grounding Cara for the entire evening to allow her to go to the prom with Zachary, but who could blame him for picking her best friend instead?

Annie still hadn't mentioned the pregnancy-possibility to Dan. She might as well spare Dan the distress until she knew for sure. The day Annie tried to give her the pregnancy test, Cara had insisted that Grammy got it all wrong, that Cara wasn't pregnant, it was a friend. Annie tried to draw the girl's name out of her, but Cara got all types of nasty-angsty, in the name of friendship and promises. Hormones exploded out of Cara like lava.

Annie had thought she mothered her children well. She had spent years honing her child-rearing skills at the preschool. They loved her there. And Cara used to be delightful—high grades, popular, and on important committees at school. She used to have such a bright future ahead of her!

But no longer. No graduation cap and gown. No stately Pomp and Circumstance for Cara.

She scratched out another scarlet X on Cara's homework. Dan was right, Annie didn't know diddlysquat about homeschooling. All she was good for was wiping kids' noses and backsides. The kids at PAL were supposed to be potty-trained, but the truth was, sometimes parents lied a little in order to get their kid admitted. Sometimes there was an accident and Annie had to deal with number two. Sure it sucked, but not nearly as much as watching Cara throw her life away on drugs and getting expelled and maybe having a baby.

But no. She couldn't even manage to keep her PAL job. She wasn't even good enough to clean up crap.

Annie put her head in her hands and pushed out a slow breath. Not only was she completely incapable of changing the world one song at a time using the Murphy Method, or one child at a time now that PAL fired her, apparently she couldn't even get one child back on the college track. Cara could hardly be in more trouble. If Annie answered to a principal, he would fire her from homeschooling. Any way you sliced it, Annie was an utter failure.

Losing her daughter was worse than losing her preschool career, and giving up her *change-the-world-one-song-at-a-time* dream. Mothering was the most important job she ever had.

She had promised to take good care of Cara. She was desperate to redeem herself. How did she screw it up so royally? Annie needed a new answer key. Not for annoying algebra, more than anything, she needed an Answer Key to Life.

Annie put her red pen down, picked up the phone, and punched in Maggie's number.

"Hello?"

"Hi Maggie. This is Annie. Do you have a minute?"

"Sure. I'll just hand the little ones some math manipulatives—that'll keep 'em happy for a bit."

"Speaking of math, Cara's having a real hard time with her Algebra 2. Do you think it's okay if she just skips it? She's almost graduated already."

"You want to drop algebra from your curriculum?"

"Um. I was considering it. Someone told me it was okay at this point."

"You're teaching more than just math. You're teaching logic and perseverance and discipline and beauty."

Beauty? Annie's voice shrank, "So I can't just let it slide?"

"You can certainly slow it down and make sure Cara understands the concepts, but I wouldn't drop it. That would show her that math isn't important."

"See, that's the problem." Annie sighed. "How can I make sure she understands the concepts when *I* don't even understand them?"

"Do you want me to ask Zachary if he would help her? He's a whiz at math."

Annie's face brightened. Her lips eased into a smile and she felt her eyes widen. She suddenly felt light and airy, as if her lungs grew three sizes bigger, as if she could shatter glass with her voice alone. "That's a marvelous idea!"

"No problem. As I say, he loves math."

"Fantastic!"

"I have a question for you, too. You've heard about the buffer zone in front of the abortion clinic, right?"

"That protesters have to stand thirty-five feet away?" Her mom, the devoted Right to Life volunteer, had harped on and on that "they" had no right to "impede our free speech."

"Right. There's a hearing in Burlington tomorrow night about the ordinance and I wondered if you'd go with me."

"Didn't a clinic just get bombed?"

"That was Texas. Vermonters aren't violent. The most we get are screams and swears."

"Um."

"The meeting is at the town hall, not the clinic. The message we want to get across is that when a girl gets pregnant, she should be showered with love and support. Every abortion is a sign that we, as a culture, failed that mother, we failed to keep her and her baby safe."

"Um."

"You don't have to say anything. Just showing up on our side tells them there's opposition to it. We have other speakers lined up to give testimony." Maggie paused. "Listen Annie, if you don't feel up to it, that's okay."

How can I say "no" when she just volunteered her son to tutor my daughter?

Annie gulped and squeezed her eyes shut. "So long as I don't have to say anything, I guess I can come."

FIFTY-TWO

"SERIOUSLY? TUTOR ME in math?" Cara yelled.

"He can help. Scored a perfect 800 on his math SATs."

"Are you trying to ruin my entire freaking life?"

"I thought you liked Zachary?" her mother said. "You always hang out with him at Faith United."

"Aaagh!" Cara stood up, threw down *The Scarlet Letter,* and stomped up the stairs.

"I'll ask him not to bring his pattern blocks!" her mom's voice called to her back.

"GAH!"

Cara stormed into her bedroom and slammed the door so hard it rattled on its hinges.

Algebra 2 was challenging enough when she could think straight. How could she possibly do it sitting next to the guy who assumed she'd been investigating him and his homeschool tribe for a senior project and then set him up for a prom only to get tackled by Nate? And who believes she's a stoner, thanks to her mom interrupting their conversation.

She wouldn't be able to explain to Zach that it was Nate's weed, not hers, with Willy and her mother sitting right there at the kitchen table with them. All sitting around the table together doing homework like nerdy homeschoolers are supposed to.

Cara was going to have to spend a humiliating hour juggling x's and y's and their stupid coefficients in front of Zach the let's-do-calculus-for-the-sheer-fun-of-it genius who would realize what a complete and total moron she was when it came to third degree equations. It didn't matter if Zach loaded their nine-passenger van full of pattern blocks, or left them all at his house. Neither would solve her word problem.

Cara pressed her hands to her head and massaged her temples. She refused to sit here and mope. She changed into her sports bra and tee shirt and shoved her feet in her sneakers. Maybe running in the fresh air would generate an idea.

She didn't ask permission to run. After all, her mother didn't ask Cara's permission before lining up Zach for a tutor!

She paused at the front door to yell defiantly, "I'm going for a run!" then she stepped outside and sucked in a tankful of air.

She was a solid member of the track team, emphasis on *was.* But winning comes and goes; it depends on your competitors. Cara liked to focus on what was in her own sphere of control. Her arms swinging, her legs pumping, her lungs expanding, her blood charging, she jogged her way into a sustainable stride. She ran for the rhythm. She ran for the woods. She cut through the opening in the obsolete fencing around the wooden playground equipment into the mini forest in the back of their neighborhood. She wanted to run and run and leave her math behind and forget about her mother's distraught face, longing for Cara to be normal, healthy, and drug-free.

Stupid pinkie swear.

Cara wanted to go back to CHU and be normal. She wanted to run for their track team and beat Essex Junction at the state meet and hang with Olivia at the cafeteria and library. She wanted the prom back so she could go. She was even willing to listen to Mr. Shullin's droning lectures.

Cara pounded through the path, putting her arms out to knock the slim branches out of her way, ducking under the larger ones.

She didn't worry about the "assault" accusation; no one believed that except Purnell. But she wanted to tell John to his face that she wasn't a stoner. Not that she wanted to get back together with him. She was over him. Way over. But she wanted him to *know.* She wanted everyone to know. Not about Olivia's baby—about her innocence.

Cara's breath was fast and dry. Without realizing it, she had sped up her pace. She slowed to a trickle and started walking, enjoying the spongy pine needle path, and the tree branches giving her shade, and the delicious fresh smell of the bounteous birch and maple leaves. Her social studies teacher had told them that the Japanese culture values the healing aspect of nature and had a word for it that roughly translates to forest bath: *shinrin-yoku.* That's what Cara needed. An internal, cleansing bath.

Now that she knew Ashley didn't exist, the stakes were higher. Zach was unattached! Her heart soared just thinking about it!

Of course, she was still peeved that he duped her ... on the other hand, it was kinda cute that he was so eager to impress her that he made up a fake girlfriend. Cara couldn't wait to tell her own girlfriends about it. They would be as outraged and tickled as her. It's so lonely liking a guy all by yourself.

Cara hadn't told Olivia she was crushing on Zach because of Ashley. How lame is that to stalk a guy who has a girlfriend? Now the blind date was over and done with and Olivia had assured her the kiss on her hand was all a pity move. Now Cara was free to gush all over Zach to Olivia.

She recalled the night of the prom ... she'd never seen him in formal clothes before. It made him look older and she had caught a glimpse of the man he was going to be. She remembered the feeling of his hands holding hers as they danced on the green. They'd never been so close and she felt what being his girlfriend would be like. Her entire body longed to go back to that moment in time and fall into the enclosure of his strong and steady arms.

Without polynomials getting in the way.

FIFTY-THREE

"ROADKILL!" MAGGIE SHOUTED. "What do you think it was?"

Annie had played scads of car games in her youth, including the insidious Gotcha Last poking game that her brother Brian always won. And she had taught her own kids the Quiet Game (whoever talks first loses). But she had never heard of this one.

And when her family had played car games, it was to pass the time during interminable road trips when they were supposed to be enjoying their vacation, driving from Vermont to Washington, DC breaking only for pit stops. Tonight she and Maggie were simply buzzing to Burlington for the buffer zone meeting.

It was twilight and Annie hadn't been paying much attention to critters in the road. She had spotted a dark lump, but was too busy dreading the upcoming powwow to give it any thought. What if a newsman thrust his microphone in her face and asked what she thought of the new regulation protecting women's health clinics?

Maggie steered her van to the shoulder and put The Barge in park.

Annie figured she better play along or they would be walking in late to the council. Maybe this was one of those alphabetical games. "Chipmunk?" she guessed.

"Nah." Maggie shook her head. "Too big. Let's check it out. Can you get the rubber gloves out of the glove compartment?"

Annie wondered why rubber gloves were necessary for looking at a dead animal. Do the cooties jump on you like fleas? Was she in danger of trichinosis? Or a flesh-eating disease? Would Dan return in two weeks and find half of Annie's face rotted off?

"We have plenty," said Maggie. "Grab a pair for yourself." Annie wondered why Maggie had an entire box full of latex gloves in her car. Then she remembered, in her previous life, Maggie had been a nurse.

Maggie unbuckled her seat belt. "If it's a skunk we'll leave it."

Annie nodded in agreement. "Good call."

"We ran into one of those last year. The kids don't need to dissect another one."

Dissect?

Maggie got out of the van and opened up the hatchback. She extracted a ratty shower curtain. "Come on!" she called.

They picked their way back in the dusk on the side of Cheesefactory Lane. Maggie looked both ways for traffic, then darted to the middle of the road where the mound lay. She bent low to peer at it. "Woodchuck. Kids will love this."

"You sure about that?"

"See the flat head and the fat body? Like a giant squirrel. That's a woodchuck, all right."

Annie had not been questioning the animal classification.

Maggie set the plastic curtain next to the body and lugged half the carcass onto it. Then she carted the other half onto the plastic while Annie avoided looking at the bloody squashed animal. "Can you help me carry it to the car?"

Annie was glad she'd pulled on gloves. She lifted her end of the litter. The mangled clump was surprisingly heavy. They placed Chuck carefully in the back of The Barge and sped off towards Burlington.

Cheerful by nature, this elevated Maggie into a really good mood. "This'll be great for science. Do you know how much they charge for owl pellets and frogs for dissection?"

Annie had no idea. "Is this legal?"

"We're doing the town a favor. No one wants to run over that, especially if they have kids in their car."

Annie had stopped pretending that Willy was going to return to Chittenden Middle School and had already filed the necessary paperwork with the state to homeschool the rest of the semester. The school had dropped the ball on its student safety campaign and didn't deserve to instruct her sensitive son. Dan wasn't happy about it, but he was in Mexico. Willy had stonewalled him as well as Annie, refusing to disclose the names of the bullies. "Could Willy do the dissection with your kids?"

"The more the merrier. There's plenty of woodchuck to go around. I'll see if Paloma's girls can make it and ask her to bring her camera. I'll put him on ice until we're ready."

When they got to the town hall, Maggie pulled into the parking lot and slid right into a spot. "Hm, I'm surprised it's not full."

They got out of the car and Maggie introduced Annie to Verona, Agnes, and Dave. Verona told them the door to the town hall was locked. "We've been here fifteen minutes, waiting."

They looked over at the Channel 4 news team who were congregating around a tall guy talking on his cell phone. Annie recognized Suzy, a pretty blond with lots of makeup, from seeing her on TV urging viewers, "Get the score, with Channel Four."

"Let's check it out," said Verona.

They casually moseyed over. The tall guy slipped his cell into his pocket. "Sons a bitches," he reported matter-of-factly. "They moved the meeting to Burlington High School."

"Why'd they move it?" asked the guy with a black oversized video camera slung around his shoulder.

"They said they'd need the extra room for the crowd."

"The crowd's *here*," said Suzy.

There were eight of them shuffling around under the streetlight. In Vermont, that qualifies.

"Yeah, they didn't get much public testimony," said the guy with the cell. "No sense rushing over there. By the time we get through the stop lights, they'll be wrapping it up and moving on to the next item on their agenda, senior housing."

"Looks like we won't get this story."

"Excuse me," said Verona. "Did they tell you when the next meeting is?"

"Two weeks."

"And is it going to be at Burlington High again or back here?"

"Good question," said the guy. "They didn't say, but I would check their website."

"I would call the council chairman the day of, to make sure they don't pull another switcheroo on us," said Suzy.

"Thanks," said Verona. "See you next time."

"See ya." The Channel 4 team sauntered off to their cars.

Verona turned to Maggie and the others, "At least we weren't the only ones who didn't know they changed venues."

Apparently Annie was the only one relieved to miss the meeting. She hid her smile by holding a tissue to her face and pretending to blow her nose.

FIFTY-FOUR

"MOM, WE'RE OUT of tampons. Can you go to the store and get some?"

Her mother froze, clutching the baking sheet between mitted hands. "Do you have your period?"

"Yeah."

"Thank God! Cara, that means you're not—"

"MOM!" Through clenched teeth, Cara squeezed out, "Willy's upstairs. He might hear you. And I already told you I wasn't."

Her mother glowed. She set the cookie sheet on the stove. She shut the oven door and pressed her hands together in prayer position, her lips moving silently above the quilted mitts.

"So. Mom. Can you pick up more tampons?"

She opened her eyes and blinked. "If you're not pregnant, then who is?" she whispered.

"I can't tell."

"Do I know the girl?"

"Not telling."

"Is it Taryn?"

"Not telling. Can you get more tampons, or not?"

"Are you sure we're out? Did you check the bathroom drawer?"

"Yes."

Not only had Cara inspected that drawer, she had swiped all of the tampons, including the pads, and tucked them safely in her sports duffle that she used to use to haul back and forth to track meets back when she was in school.

"Just use a pad."

"We're out of those, too." Cara had also filched the emergency supplies in her mom's pocketbook.

"How can we be out of everything so suddenly?" Annie plucked the potholders off her hands.

"Sorry, I used them up. It's a heavy flow this month." It's not that Cara liked deceiving her mother.

"Extra heavy 'cause you're late." Annie smiled knowingly.

"Right. We don't want any leakage." But little did Cara realize back when she took the heat for the Restroom Disaster, that she would eventually need to fabricate a story for her mother about a tampon shortage in order to get a private moment with Zach so she could explain the real reason why she was kicked out of school. The lie did double duty by convincing her mom that she wasn't preggers. A bizarro way of telling truth through fiction.

"But Zachary is coming soon to help you with your math. I want to be here when he gets here. I made him chocolate chip cookies."

"All right. I guess *I'll* have to go to the store to get the tampons." Cara closed her math book and stood up in slow motion.

"No, no. You should be here when he comes. *I'll* go to the store."

"All right. If you think that's best." Cara sat back down. "Can you bring Willy, too?"

"Willy? He doesn't want to come buy tampons."

"He needs a book from the library for his science project."

Cara knew this because she had previously talked to Willy about stalling at the library for as long as he could. He readily agreed after she had offered him five bucks.

Like most old people, her mother didn't realize that whatever information Willy supposedly needed from a book could be retrieved much faster from the internet. Cara had learned that if she said "book" or "library" to an adult, the Pavlov-dog-like response was "Yes," especially if talking to a teacher.

"Okay, but I need to get out of these pajamas first." Her mother untied her apron and hung it on its hook.

Annie skipped down the hallway into her bedroom. She pulled off her PJs and got dressed. She had been fretting about how to break the news to Dan and her parents and Maggie and Susan about Cara's condition. She had already decided to tell Wendy first, her safe person, to get her advice on how to tell the others. But now she wouldn't have to!

Secretly Annie suspected Cara's friend Taryn, who wore a lot of black, like a goth. She had a heavy hand when it came to mascara and eye shadow as if trying to court attention, which worked, since most girls sported a more relaxed and natural look. Make up was unnecessary since Vermont girls were naturally beautiful, especially her own daughter.

In her euphoria, Annie discovered she had automatically zipped herself into her "date" dress. The one she hadn't worn for five weeks since Dan was in Mexico. The blue slinky sheath that he said made her eyes look "stunning." She stood in front of the mirror.

Hell no. She looked classy and sassy, but way too dressy for an afternoon in Vermont. She disrobed, tossed it on her bed, and started over. She pulled on her standard preschool teacher outfit, a colored tee shirt and black pants with sufficient spandex to sit cross-legged on the rug at circle time. This time the mirror told her she was too loud and bright. Annie wanted to go incognito. Not that it mattered what she wore to the pharmacy or library, but she had agreed to join Maggie outside the clinic later.

Annie had been dreading it ever since Maggie talked her into it in the car with Chuck on the way back from the buffer zone meeting they had missed. As much as she hated going, she felt compelled. Annie wanted Zachary to tutor Cara in math so she could graduate and get into college. She would do anything for her daughter. Annie stripped again and flung her preschool attire onto the bed.

She decided on the most nondescript clothes possible, a staple in every American woman's wardrobe: a white tee shirt and jeans. She peeled Dan's top from his side of the bed and took a big sniff. She needed all the testosterone she could get. Then she wedged herself into her skinny blue jeans and tucked in Dan's tee, sucking in her breath to shove all the extra length in. She checked the mirror again. She had to admit she looked pretty hot considering the top was three sizes too big and the jeans were two sizes too small. But when she bent over to tie the laces on her sneakers, she couldn't breathe. Annie needed to be as comfortable as possible for this awkward afternoon.

She pried herself out of the dark denim, grunting as she stepped on the pant legs one at a time for leverage. She settled for her mom jeans, the ones that were so stretchy and baggy she could wear them to the gym, if she went to the gym, which she didn't, because who has time to work out when you homeschool? For extra protection, she slipped on her dark, oversized sunglasses. No one would recognize her. If her own mother's car tootled down Union Street, she wouldn't notice Annie.

FIFTY-FIVE

Cara winked at Willy as he followed their mom out the door. After they drove off, she dashed up the stairs into the bathroom. She surveyed the dark smudges under her eyes. She had stayed up until 1:00 am the previous night going over today's math assignment so that she would know how to do it in front of Zach.

She brushed on some mascara hoping that would draw attention away from the bags under her eyes. She dabbed a sheen of gloss on her lips. She unwrapped her hair elastic and shook her messy bun out. She fluffed her hair with her fingers and studied herself in the bathroom mirror. Yes, she would leave her hair down. If the math got too hard, or Zach got too gorgeous, whichever came first, she could shield herself by draping her hair halfway across her face.

She went to her bedroom and peeled off her tee shirt. She had set out an outfit on her bed earlier that day. She had selected a feminine coral-colored short-sleeved knit top. It was soft and stretchy, like comfort food for the skin. And it was loose enough not to show underarm sweat. Zach would be here any minute now. She shivered and scrambled into her clothes.

When Zach arrived, he petted the dogs, and carefully inspected Curly's shaved leg. "Healing nicely."

"Yeah."

"Let me guess, hated the splint?"

"Of course."

Cara offered Zach cookies. She offered him milk. He washed his hands before sitting down and snacking.

Cara turned the volume down on her iPod and asked, "What kind of music do you like?" While putting off the algebra, Cara was seeking a segue to the conversation about getting expelled from CHU that her mom had interrupted the night of the prom.

"Classic."

Cara nodded. She liked the golden oldies also. Her parents had an entire CD set of the 1960s. And another 10 CDs from the '70s. "Beatles?"

"Bach. He's mathematically satisfying."

What does that even mean? And why does everything have to come back to math? "I can take a hint." Cara rifled through her textbook to her current lesson.

"I wasn't talking about your algebra. I meant I can practically *see* the chord progressions in Bach's compositions."

She wasn't sure what that meant either. But she could see the progression of Zach's facial structure. That was mathematically satisfying to her.

Zach sat next to her and opened up a spiral bound notebook which had calculations in neat formations on the right page. On the left, slanted crosswise against the light blue parallel lines, was a scrap of handwritten words. Cara studied the angular handwriting, absorbing Zach any way she could. Even his cursive was man-gorgeous. Cara leaned closer to read.

Abruptly Zach flipped the page to a fresh sheet, keeping his hand splayed protectively on the notebook.

"What was that?" she asked.

"Nothing."

"Do you write ..." Cara paused, incredulous, "... poetry?"

Zach coughed. "I just—" he held a fist to his mouth to smother another cough—"scribble some ideas now and then." Cough, cough.

"I thought you were a math genius?"

"They're not mutually exclusive. Ever heard the quote from the writer Jorge Luis Borges? 'Art is fire plus algebra.'"

"Can I read your poem?" Cara leaned towards his notebook searching for cursive words appearing backwards through the thin paper.

Zach cleared his throat again and folded his notebook on the spiral spine, math side up. "It's not ready. Let's get to your algebra before your mother gets back."

By the time Cara finished her third problem, she was smiling confidently. "Is this one right?" Cara asked, sliding her notebook over to Zach.

She was pretty sure it was correct since it looked like the same answer she got last night before double-checking with her mom's answer key, which Cara carefully slipped back underneath the dining room hutch. She had never cheated before, but she didn't feel guilty because one, her mother forced her to take these precautionary measures by recruiting Zach as tutor, and two, it's hardly cheating when it's not even a real school.

"Let's see." Zach didn't have the answer key as her mom did, and his book was completely different, so to check her solutions he worked them out one at a time in his notebook in pen.

Who does math in permanent pen? While he hummed a tune, probably Bach, and calculated his way through the equation, Cara sighed happily. She had already successfully showed him correct answers for the first two equations. She tucked her hair back behind her ear.

"That one's right, too," said Zach. "My mom told me your mother said you were having trouble, but you're getting all these right. I don't think you need my help with math." He ran his fingers through his luscious wavy hair and cleared his throat. "But I wanted to talk about what you said the other night."

"Me too."

"Cara, if you need someone to talk to, or some help with drug—"

"I'm okay." Cara was relieved at the chance to set him straight.

"No, really, you can call me anytime."

"You don't even have a cell phone."

"You know what I mean. I got your back."

Cara's heart felt as cozy and fuzzy as her sweater. She smiled at him. "Thanks, Zach, but I don't need help. I wasn't the one—"

"Here we are!" Cara's mother barged through the kitchen door waving aloft a small plastic bag with "Pharmer's Market" printed on it. Willy followed behind, shrugging with his palms up. Sign language for, *I dawdled as long as I could.*

"I got the—" Her mother spotted Zachary sitting next to Cara. "I got the *medicine* you need. She's not contagious," she rushed to explain. "She's um, on medication. It's, um, it's just a fungus."

Cara's eyes narrowed into slits.

"A fungus ...of the..." she paused. "Toe. Anyway," she briskly changed the subject, "thanks for coming over to help, Zachary. How's it going?"

"Fine, Mrs. Mulligan. She got every answer right so far."

"Really?" She slid her gaze sideways towards Cara. "That's terrific. Good for you, Cara! You get an A for the day."

Cara felt her face heat up. She flicked her hair out from behind her ears and let it cover her cheek.

"I tried to get back as fast as possible, but Willy needed some book at the library that he insisted was crucial for his science project," she rolled her eyes, "but they didn't have it so we had to fill out a form for the inter-library loan and it took for-e-ver."

Willy nodded to Cara.

Cara could read the word "TAMPONS" blazoned across the box through the flimsy see-through plastic shopping bag. Her mom followed her gaze. She secreted the bag behind her back and grabbed the plate off the counter and held it under Zach's nose. "Would you like some cookies?"

"No, thank you Mrs. Mulligan. I've already had five. They were delicious."

"Chocolate chip. Help yourself." She set the plate on the kitchen table next to his math book. "Willy, get him a napkin, please." She moved sideways towards the hall. "Um, Cara could you come into the bedroom a minute. I need help with, um ..." She glanced around for inspiration. "Pulling up my shades."

"Would you like me to help you with that?" Zach started to get up from his chair.

"No! No, that's okay, Cara can get it." Her mother locked eyes with Cara and jerked her head towards her bedroom. She bustled down the hallway and pulled Cara into the master bedroom. "Here are the supplies you need," she whispered, pressing the bag into Cara's hands.

"Toe fungus?" Cara complained.

"I had to think of something!"

Tampons were arguably less embarrassing, but Cara didn't want to waste time arguing. She slipped into the bathroom off the hallway, shut the door, and waited. She had never timed herself, but figured two minutes would be sufficient to pretend to take care of feminine business for her mom's benefit. And for Zach's sake, to pretend to be swabbing anti-fungal cream on her toes, then putting her socks back on.

Annie hurried back out to the kitchen. She plucked a pen from the coffee can that had photos of preschoolers shellacked on it, an end-of-year gift from a previous class. The desk drawer was sticky so she yanked hard. Scraps of papers vaulted out, fluttering softly to the floor.

"Let me help you with that." Like a ninja, Zachary was already crouched on the floor. He scooped up wads of paper and handed them to her.

"Thank you! These are the kids' grades."

One piece of paper had swooped underneath the desk. Zachary stretched out his long arm and retrieved it. He glanced down and read aloud: "If a Butterfly Flaps its Wings in Brazil, Will my Mom go on a Talk Show in Georgia?" She had given Willy an A+ for the title alone. Unfortunately, now Zach was staring at the grade she had given herself for listening to Willy's rambling report: Annie A++.

Annie felt her cheeks heat up. After she had stopped receiving paychecks from PAL, she needed to incentivize herself. She suddenly recognized how pathetic it was to reward herself with a pointless grade on a scrap of paper.

But Zachary didn't need to know this. "Oops, my mistake." Mortified, she plucked the paper out of his grasp, crossed out her name and quickly penned in Willy's. She pulled out a clean scrap of paper and scribbled the date followed by, *Cara, Algebra 2, A+.*

Instead of wedging them into the drawer, she raked the papers together on the top of the desk and pinned them in place with a ceramic mug. She would need these at some point to document Cara's transcript before she could matriculate at Cool U. "I'll sort through these later, right now I'm off again. I'm meeting your mother at the clinic in Burlington."

She didn't want to go, but Maggie had assured her that she didn't need to say anything, just stand there, silently, holding a poster.

Zach nodded. "It's a good cause."

"This is my first time and I'm a little nervous. That's so brave of your mother to go there every week."

Assuming he was encouraging her, Zachary said, "What good is our freedom of speech if we're afraid to speak up, right?"

"Right." Annie managed a weak smile. She slung her purse on her shoulder and left.

Cara returned to the kitchen. "Willy, do your homework upstairs so Zach and I can study at the table, okay?"

"Aw," groaned Willy. "I was just about to show Zach something."

"You can show him another time." Cara rotated until her back was to Zach. She held up two fingers in front of her chest for Willy to see.

Willy put his hand below the table with three fingers extended. Cara nodded.

"Deal." Willy grabbed another cookie and trotted out.

"Would you like any more cookies?" Cara asked Zach.

"I'm good." Zach shook his head no. "Have you tried lavender or tea tree oil for your toes? That's what my mother swabs on rashes."

Cara could feel heat emanating from her cheeks to her forehead. Her face probably matched her coral sweater. She flipped her hair halfway in front of her face. "I'm good. The—" she couldn't bring herself to say *fungus*, "it's almost all gone."

"Speaking of lavender, maybe it would help with, uh." Zach shifted in his seat and cleared his throat. "With smoking? Lavender is calming."

"Ugh." Cara buried her face in her hands.

"I'm sorry," Zach apologized. "That was stupid. It'll take more than lavender, I get that. I'm sure your parents are helping—"

"Ugh," Cara moaned.

"I understand if you don't want to talk about it now. We can get back to your algebra."

"No, it's not that." Cara looked directly at Zach. "Here's the deal."

FIFTY-SIX

A SILVER PRIUS rolled noiselessly down the street. As it neared, the passenger side window slid silently down. A gal with her hair wrapped in a black and white batik bandeau leaned out the window and screamed, "You don't care about these girls—all you care about is a fucking blob of tissue!" She jerked her middle finger up and stuck her arm out the window as the car cruised north on Union Street.

Stunned, Annie stopped singing. She marched into the street and opened her mouth to yell back at the commuter: "Of course we care about these girls! And we're saving babies, not blobs!"

She shouted in her head, but no sound came out of her throat. Annie worked her jaw muscles back and forth and eventually clamped her lips together.

She turned her head and watched the trio of singing women. Jean was wearing a long wispy skirt trailing around her ankles. She probably shopped at the same thrift store as Diana. Agnes was in no-nonsense sport clothes, black leggings and a navy zip-up. Maybe she was planning to go for a run after this. Maggie had unbuttoned the light pink cardigan she wore over her light blue polo as the afternoon warmed up. She swayed slightly, eyes closed, singing to high heaven. Jean and Agnes chimed in with their gazes directed earnestly at the clinic. None of them paid attention to The Finger jabbed out the car window.

The ladies had all the right words, but they were flat. They needed Annie's soprano to hike it up a notch. She plodded back to them and joined their singing, sustaining the last note with her strong vibrato.

They were standing across the street from the old red brick schoolhouse, which had closed when two schools consolidated due to a dwindling population of students. An enterprising entrepreneur had invested in it, converting the building into a health clinic.

She wondered what Susan would say if she saw Annie here, singing churchy songs in the middle of Burlington. Would she turn her head and drive by, politely pretending she didn't see? What would Wendy say if she saw Annie protesting in front of the Women's Health Clinic? Hand her a perfume called *Choice*? And Dan? Would he wrap his arm around her protectively, usher her into his car, and exhort her to get back home to teach Cara about the Civil Rights Movement?

Before the ladies started on another song, Maggie said, "Here comes Verona."

"Sorry I'm late. I had trouble finding a parking spot." Verona fanned out the posters she had brought. One featured a photo of five pudgy infants of different ethnicities plopped naked and diapered in bottom-heavy seating positions. Scrolled above the babies' heads were the words: *It's a baby, not a choice.*

These kids were unbelievably adorable. Annie wanted to hold one now. Especially that biracial baby in the middle, capped with a layer of mulch-colored spongy hair. She reached for it, but was too late. Jean had already grabbed the sign, without even glancing at the photo.

Verona handed Annie the last placard, which had an ugly stick figure drawing in garish comic book colors of a pregnant mommy with a speech bubble above her oversized head with words crammed into it in childish handwriting: *Life is Beautiful.*

"Do you want to trade?" Annie asked. But Jean, chatting up Agnes, had switched topics from ultrasounds to mammograms and didn't hear.

"Remember," Verona cautioned. "We bring peace and prayers. Not arguments."

Yeah, how do you argue with The Finger anyway?

Verona looked at Annie. "Your free speech ends there. The buffer zone officially begins here." She pointed down to the curb.

Annie hopped onto the sidewalk edged by grass. "Sorry. I'm new at this."

Verona smiled ruefully. "We're all new at the buffer zone law. That's why it's in the news."

Annie checked out the news team assembled several yards away to the left. Suzy was standing in front of the cameraman, speaking into a microphone, with the brick building across the street serving as backdrop. A polite distance past Channel 4 stood two cops in beige and drab green uniforms.

Annie looked up the sidewalk. A woman in a sweater set and pressed slacks headed towards them. Uh oh, it was Carol Van Horn.

Annie stepped backwards ... trip, trap, trip, trap ... to distance herself from the demonstrators. She whipped her poster behind her back, fished her cell phone out of her back pocket, and bent her head to stare at it.

"Annie?"

She slipped her cell back in her jeans. So much for sunglasses shielding her identity. "Hey Carol."

"How ya doing?"

As if Carol cared! This was the busybody who ratted Annie out to Leslie who fired her from PAL! "I'm good, thanks. How are you?"

"Fine, thanks. What brings you to town?"

Annie looked around. "Um. Just, you know, enjoying the sunshine. Maybe walk down to the Waterfront."

Carol scanned past Annie's shoulder at the protesters and cops and news team. "What's going on?"

Gripping her poster behind her back, Annie turned her head. "Hm. Looks like there might be a protest." She swiveled back to face Carol. "How about you? What are you doing on this gorgeous day?"

"Doctor's appointment," Carol answered.

Annie's stomach clenched. Was Carol going to the women's clinic across the street? *My God, could this day get any worse*?

"I better get going," said Carol. "Don't want to be late. Nice seeing you."

"You too."

Annie watched sideways through her sunglasses and breathed a sigh of relief when Carol didn't cross the street, but continued down the sidewalk, the protesters and news team and cops each in turn stepping onto the grass, parting for Carol to pass through.

Of course Carol was too preppy to go to the health clinic. She was wealthy enough to pay out of pocket for plastic surgery for her nosy nose.

Annie pushed her sunglasses back on to her own nose and traipsed back to her group, letting her poster dangle by her fingertips. How on earth did her life come to this? Not for the first time, she cursed algebra. If it weren't for Cara's struggle with numbers, Annie wouldn't have to be here. Wondering how soon she could leave politely, she checked the time on her phone.

If Dan were here, instead of sunny Mexico, he could have helped Cara with her stupid equations, and then Annie wouldn't owe Maggie a favor for volunteering her stellar son. Annie blamed math, then Dan, then Maggie. She began casting blame onto Zach and Cara, then caught herself. Of course this wasn't their fault—they were just kids!

"I can't help feeling that we're praying at the wrong end," said Maggie.

"That's the front door right there." Verona pointed towards Women's Health Clinic across the street.

"I don't mean the wrong end of this clinic, I mean the wrong end of the problem. We should be praying for these girls before they even *get* pregnant. We need to reform sex-ed classes in school, and if they refuse, we should pray outside the *schools*." Maggie shook her head. "They teach kids to have sex, and then everyone acts surprised when girls get pregnant."

Ugh, the only thing worse than trying to demonstrate anonymously in downtown Burlington, would be doing it in the schoolyard where all the other mothers would recognize her no matter how big and dark her sunglasses were.

"It's not just the schools, it's the movies, too, pushing sex," said Jean.

"And TV and the internet," added Agnes.

"They say it takes a village to raise a child. You're right about the movies, and look, we also have the law," Maggie gestured towards the cops. One trooper was looking at his wristwatch. The other was using the curb to scrape mud off his shoes. "We have the media." Maggie eyed the Channel 4 cameraman and reporter. "We have bystanders passing by." There were two pedestrians and four cars. "And we have the abortionist, backed by politicians and federal funds." Maggie jutted her chin towards the clinic. "*Raise* a child? It takes an entire village to *erase* a child."

"Right?" Jean agreed passionately. "See what they do in there?" She plucked a brochure out of her bag and passed it to Annie.

Annie automatically took the flyer and looked down. There was a glossy close-up photo of little pink skinny limbs, severed and bloody. A small rose-colored skull, slightly smushed. A stray foot, unattached to the serrated leg.

Annie blinked, but it was too late. Blink. Blink. Blink. Blink. Blink. She couldn't un-see it.

FIFTY-SEVEN

"YOU HAVE TO tell her."

"I can't. She'll kill me." Cara swiped the brush down Moe's back. "It's my fault she lost her job at the preschool. It's my fault she had to homeschool me. She'll go ballistic if I tell her the weed wasn't mine and she lost her job for nothing."

"Let me do it." Zach put his hand on Cara's.

He took the dog brush from her and knelt next to the retriever. Gently, he skimmed the brush down Moe's reddish gold coat while rubbing the dog's chest with his left hand. He crooned, "It's okay. Just working out the snarls and furballs." Moe's tongue dangled out the side of his mouth. His eyes gazed adoringly at Zach. He panted happily.

Cara watched, jealous of her dog. Her hand still tingled where he had touched it.

Zach looked up at her. "You can't keep this a secret. It's too big. It's too important." He stood up. "Do it now and get it over with. It's the right thing to do."

Cara stood up as well. "I know it's the right thing to do for Mom. But how can I do this to Olivia? I can't betray her trust. I *promised*."

"Tell Olivia first. Let her know that you're going to tell your mother about the weed. Besides, Olivia is gonna need help herself. Her parents need to know about the baby." Zach set the brush down, bent to give a final pat to Moe, then stood erect again. "Time for truth."

Cara's chin slumped down onto her collarbone.

"Want me to go with you?" Zach offered.

Cara's head jerked upright. "No!" The only thing worse than telling her mother the truth was doing it in front of an audience.

In mock alarm, Zach backed away with his arms up, as if someone were aiming a gun at him. "Just asking."

"I'm sorry. I didn't mean it that way. It's just ... this is something *I* need to do. I'll tell my mother myself. But Olivia first."

"Promise?"

"Yes. I promise."

"Pinkie swear?" He extended his right hand, pinkie outstretched.

"Shut up." Cara slapped him playfully in the chest.

"Okay, then. I'll leave you to it."

He bent towards her. Was he going to kiss her? Here in the kitchen? With Moe and Curly watching? Willy could come downstairs and interrupt them any minute!

"Hey, Cara." He continued slowly leaning. She could smell his breath—tangy and fresh, like peppermint.

"Yes," she breathed. Do homeschoolers even know *how* to kiss?

"I'm glad ..." he paused.

Don't stop now!

He drew a breath.

Keep going!

"I'm *really* glad," he amended, "that you don't smoke."

"Oh." Blinking, Cara tilted her head back. "Thanks?"

Zach reached past her to pick up his notebook from the kitchen table she was leaning against. He scooped up his calculator with his other hand. "See you at Friday group," he said, heading towards the door.

"See ya." His plaid shirt was half-tucked into his jeans. He was tall and strong and right and impossibly handsome. She put her hand to her chest to make sure her heart hadn't oozed out.

"Hey, Zach."

He turned to look at her. "Yeah?"

Cara paused ... then plunged in. "I'm really glad Ashley isn't real." She could sense her cheeks getting warm.

"Me too," he grunted and ducked through the door before she could see if he was blushing too.

Energy surged through her like a jolt of electricity. Cara charged upstairs and grabbed her phone from her dresser. Zach was right. It was time to come clean. First Olivia, then her mother.

Cara texted: Call me after school.

She couldn't sit in her room and wait for two hours. She was zinging with anticipation. She laced up her sneakers to go for a run and was surprised when her phone rang. Olivia's number. That was fast. Maybe Olivia left class because she had to throw up in the bathroom?

"Hey Via. How you doing?"

"I can't do this," she whispered. Her voice was strained, hushed, scared.

"Can't do what?" Cara asked cautiously. But she knew. She knew what Olivia was talking about.

"I can't go through with this. I want to dance in my last ballet recital here. I want to go to Columbia." Her voice hitched. "I want Nate back."

"Do you want me to come over after school? I'll talk my mom into it, or I'll sneak out."

"I'm home. I called in sick to school. I'm going to a clinic."

"No."

"I don't have any other choice! I have to do this."

"No you don't. You can have the baby. Or, or ... you can give the baby up for adoption."

"It's not fair! Nate can go to college! He can just walk away!"

"But what about the baby?"

"Stop it! This isn't your baby! It's mine! What about *me*?"

"You're gonna be okay."

"No I'm not!" she shrieked. Olivia's voice got hard and mean. "How would you feel if *you* were pregnant?"

Cara froze. What if she were having John's baby? Could she bear his baby for nine whole months? She didn't even *like* him anymore. She didn't trust him. She shuddered.

"See?" Olivia's rage and despair lashed at Cara, smashed into her body. "Not so easy to say what to do if it's *your* life that's screwed, is it?"

Like a force field, Olivia's desperation pushed Cara backward until she hit the wall of her bedroom. Trembling, she leaned against the wall and closed her eyes. She didn't recognize who Olivia had become.

Why was Olivia blaming *her?* It was hard to think straight.

But Cara was clear on one thing, this wasn't her fault! Nate's the one who got Olivia pregnant. Nate's the one who dumped his weed on her. Olivia was afraid. That's why she was so upset; it stemmed from fear.

What had Grammy said on the phone?

Still shaky, Cara couldn't remember.

She opened her eyes and looked at the photo pinned to her bulletin board. Olivia, Taryn, Danielle, and Cara had dared each other to go on the roller coaster at the fair and they had just landed and stumbled down the exit ramp. Adrenaline was still zapping through them. Their smiles were electric. Olivia's legs trembled so much she almost keeled over, and they had all pulled her back into the fold when Nate snapped the photo.

This was no longer about Nate-guilt. This was about Olivia. "What can I do?" asked Cara. "Tell me what you want. Anything."

Olivia screamed, "I want my life back!"

She was gone.

Stunned, Cara cradled her soundless phone in her hand.

She pressed Olivia's name but the phone rang and rang and rang.

Cara texted, but knew enough not to wait for a response. Waiting was over. Suddenly it was clear what to do.

She poked her head into Willy's room just long enough to explain, "When Mom comes back from her meeting with Mrs. Boucher, tell her I had to go out."

"Aren't you grounded?" Willy asked.

"Yeah, but I have to do something first." Cara shoved her cell into her back pocket and hurtled down the stairs, two at a time, calling back to him, "I'll get back as soon as I can and restart the grounding."

Cara grabbed the keys from the basket on top of the bookshelf and swung the front door open. She yelled, "I've got my cell if you need to get hold of me, Willy!" She slammed the door and sprinted to the car.

Just that morning, Cara had received her weekly update from Baby-Bumpz and learned that Pearl was as large as a lemon and had her own unique set of fingerprints. Her vocal cords were already developed, but would anyone ever hear her voice?

FIFTY-EIGHT

"CAN I ASK you something?" A woman in an avocado green shift marched past the clinic, directly through the invisible buffer zone, and crossed the street to approach them. Her stretchy dress was the kind that had a built-in sports bra in case she had a sudden urge to do jumping jacks during her lunch break. A leather cord around her neck ended with a clunky metal peace sign, which banged on her muscular chest as she pulled to a stop a yard away. Her defined bicep flexed when she dug her fist into her waist.

"Have you ever *adopted*?" The woman shot the word "adopted" as if it were a missile. "'Cause if you've never even adopted a child, then that just goes to show you don't really care about these kids. Who's going to take care of them all?" She waved her sculpted arm in the air at the hypothetical children.

Annie took a tentative baby step backward. She was still blinking.

Jean shoved her fist on her own hip. Her arm flab jiggled indignantly. "Actually—"

Verona rested a hand on Jean's shoulder as a quiet warning. "Actually, there's a high demand for babies," she interrupted gently. "In fact, Americans—"

"I thought so. You haven't adopted, have you? You pretend you care about the girls, but you just send them back home pregnant even though they can't afford a child and taxpayers have to foot the bill."

"Get a fucking life!" yelled a young pedestrian in a floral skirt and copper-colored camisole as she sashayed up the sidewalk across the street. She raised a fist for Woman Power.

The sporty woman in avocado asked, "What the hell?"

"Go fuck yourself," called the girl.

"You go fuck *your*self!"

"Whoa, whatever happened to all your *religious shit*?" She pushed her hands against the air, as if warding off bad vibes. This gal was not a jumping jacker. Her willowy limbs suggested yin yoga.

"What?" Avocado jerked her thumb at Verona and the other ladies. "I'm not with *them*."

"You pro-choice?"

"Hell yes."

"What the fuck you doing there?"

"Talking to them!"

An old beater thumped down the road towards them. The music was so loud it made the black Chevy Impala vibrate. The bass-heavy rap overpowered the driver's words, but they knew what he meant when he thrust his middle finger at them.

From each side of the street, Avocado and Copper promptly signaled back, raising their fingers high. The younger gal upped the ante by swinging both her arms high in the air, middle fingers taut and upright. She rotated her arms for emphasis and screamed, "Asshole!"

At the top of the block, a passel of people holding banners was crossing the street, but, reaching the double yellow lines, one girl appeared to hear the commotion. She paused and pointed. This splintered the troop as some streamed past her, while others stopped. Folks started gesturing in two different directions. Cars queued up, waiting with typical Vermont patience at the intersection for the pedestrians to reach a consensus. Annie lifted her sign high and jostled it to entice the newcomers, an old cheerleading maneuver. If all these activists joined their side, then Maggie and Verona wouldn't need Annie and she would be free to go.

Finally the small cortège gathered around one tall guy with a bullhorn and filed back toward their original side. The phalanx clumped together and advanced towards them.

As they got closer, Annie could read their banners, which were so large they needed two people to hold them, one for each end: IT'S VIOLENCE, NOT SCIENCE.

Verona stepped forward and greeted the protesters. The bullhorn dude's earthy brown tee shirt had a motto imprinted in white: #NurtureMotherNature. He asked, "This the animal research lab? Where the voles died? We heard it was down on Prospect Street."

Annie wasn't exactly sure what a vole was; she imagined a cross between a mouse and a mole. She pictured a clinically white lab with stainless steel sinks strewn with velvety gray voles on trays, in jars, in cages lined with urine-drenched wood shavings. The little critters cold-still, belly up, tiny arms permanently curled in stiff rigor mortis.

If innocent little voles weren't safe, who was?

Desolation flooded through Annie, shoving nausea from her belly into her heart. This afternoon was worse than she thought it would be, and she had pre-dreaded it plenty. She didn't belong here. She yearned for peace, to live and let live. As the bumper sticker proclaimed: COEXIST. She wanted to quit this game and return home, hug Willy and Cara, pet Moe and Curly, then crawl into PJ pants and snuggle Dan's pillow in bed.

She would pass her placard off to Maggie and plead PMS. Annie sidled towards Maggie.

Verona answered, "This is the abortion clinic. You're welcome to join us here, as long as you don't cross the street."

He looked over her shoulder. "Why are the cops here? And Channel 4?" his face brightened with interest.

"Buffer zone regulation," Verona answered. She fingered one of their banners. "These signs look durable. Where'd you get them?"

Mr. Bullhorn's head was already bent down, examining his cell phone navigator, his man-bun looking like a doughnut hole plugged on the back of his head. "We're in the wrong place."

"They're waterproof, from recycled plastic," replied a girl in cut off jean shorts and a red plaid flannel shirt with the sleeves ripped off, who gazed admiringly at her sign, NO EXPERIMENTATION WITHOUT REPRESENTATION. "Not sure the name of the company." She examined the edge of the banner for a company website.

A car door slammed and Annie glanced up at the clinic's parking lot. It was Cara's friend Olivia getting out of the car.

Not only is she dance team captain and pulling in grades good enough to impress Columbia's admissions team, but she also takes the time to volunteer and join the prayer team in front of the Women's Health clinic? How courageous for such a young girl. It had only been fifteen minutes and already Annie felt like bailing.

But why is Olivia crossing the parking lot and angling towards the clinic?

"Olivia! We're over here!" Annie shouted.

Olivia turned and faced the praying ladies, and the animal rights activists, and the pro-choicers, who, done flipping off the Impala's driver, appeared to be striking up a conversation with each other.

Annie took two giant steps to the right to distance herself from the others and she removed her sunglasses, hooking them in her belt loop. "Over here!" she repeated, raising her arm.

Olivia looked, but didn't seem to see, as if she were so deep in thought she was blind. She turned her head away and continued towards the clinic. She stepped onto the concrete path snaking up to the entry.

Annie gasped. She must not know about the new regulation. "Olivia! You can't go there! It's past the buffer zone!"

She didn't seem to hear either. She continued her trek towards the front door.

"Olivia!" Annie yelled, louder, cupping her hands around her mouth to project the volume. "NO!"

Olivia didn't stop.

Annie held her breath. She was tempted to stay silent. After all, it wasn't her responsibility. It wasn't her fault that Olivia didn't know about the new law. Annie didn't have to get involved. She could let Olivia find out for herself. Or let the experts handle it.

Annie scanned the others. Jean had given up on Avocado. The animal rights activists had given up on the pro-lifers and were caterpillaring back up the sidewalk, in accordion formation, scrunching ... elongating. Verona and Agnes had resumed their quiet vigil. Maggie's eyes were closed, her lips moving, murmuring the Divine Mercy chaplet. These ladies weren't going to stop Olivia; they didn't even know her. They followed the rules and stayed sequestered on the sidewalk, behind the invisible line barricading them.

Annie checked out the Women's Health Clinic. Pots with colorful flowers adorned the front steps to the entrance. Indigo, violet, and yellow pansies bobbed in the breeze.

Annie peeked at the cops, their backs to her, angled toward each other, chatting, one guy hiking his belt higher up his hip.

She saw the news camera swivel, catch Olivia in its sight, and zero in on her, tracking her up the path.

Annie couldn't let Cara's best friend get arrested on film because of an unconstitutional regulation targeting pro-lifers. She dropped her poster and bolted across the street towards Olivia, who was halfway up the path to the front doors. Annie screamed her name and shouted, "Buffer zone!" Tires squealed a painful rubbery squeak as a car screeched to a stop to avoid crashing into Annie who ignored it and barreled onto the front lawn of the clinic, shouting: "STOP!"

FIFTY-NINE

"WAIT!" ANNIE SEIZED Olivia's arm and paused for air to rush back into her lungs. "We're over there." She leaned over, panting. Hunched and heaving, she pointed across the street to the tiny pro-life protest. By now Avocado and Copper were swinging in long carefree strides down the sidewalk, tight as sisters. Maggie and her friends were watching Annie, looking concerned.

"We're praying over there," Annie repeated, pointing.

Olivia whispered, "I didn't come to pray." Her hand floated down and rested gently on the gray pouch of her baggy sweatshirt.

Annie looked down at Olivia's hand cradling her belly. Understanding flashed, at shutter speed. She heard a whimper. But Olivia's lips were pressed tightly together. She heard another whimper. Then Annie heard herself say, "No. Olivia. No. This isn't the answer."

"What *is* the answer?" Olivia paused briefly, then answered her own question. "There is no answer." Her voice escalated in pain and her luminescent brown eyes pooled with unshed tears. "You think you know everything. But you don't know anything. You're not the one who has to deal with this! You have no idea how hard this is for me! How trapped I am! I have no choice!"

"Oh, Olivia ... I *do* know what you're going through. I understand."

Olivia shook her head and wrenched her arm out of Annie's grasp. She cried desperately, "No, you don't! You have no idea! How alone I am!"

"Yes, I do. I know how it feels," Annie pleaded to be believed.

Olivia continued shaking her head no, her expression a clash of anguish and anger.

"I—" Annie began, then clamped her mouth shut. *What would Maggie and the pro-lifers say if they found out? What would the homeschoolers say?*

"I—" *Or Susan? Fr. McHolland? Everyone at church? What a flipping hypocrite I am.*

"I—" *What if her own children learned what she had done?*

Annie couldn't force the words out. She couldn't get beyond one syllable. This is why no one had told Annie. It was impossible. Who could explain?

SIXTY

HER BOYFRIEND HAD embraced her and stroked her hair and whispered in her ear: *your future, our careers, trust me ...* He murmured the magic word *love* and she murmured back: *love, love, love ...* Her well-meaning sorority sisters chanted a Greek chorus: *right, choice, women ...* The college nurse prescribed a sanitized incantation: *clinic, help, appointment ...* Her boyfriend lulled her into compliance: *mistake, time, graduation ...* Words poisoned her food, oozed under the locked door of her dorm, infected her heart with a voracious virus: *safe, procedure, private.* Word by word by word, the spell formed an earworm that crawled into her bed, burrowed into her brain, and slithered into her soul: *body, healthcare, unplanned ...* She tried to say no, but she couldn't speak. Silence snuffed out her heart, her mind, her voice, and transmuted her into an insentient ghost until she became a bystander watching herself go through the motions in a silent movie: eat, retch, shower, shower, shower. Her boyfriend scrounged up the cash, he borrowed his roommate's funky-smelling Corolla, he chauffeured her to the appointment, he cradled her clenched fist in the waiting room, and afterwards ... after words ... driving back to her dorm, he hushed her with smooth, soothing words: *feel better, right thing, all over now.*

Not until years later did she come to realize that her boyfriend had been as terrified as she was. Did he have regrets? She never knew because three weeks later, directly after graduation, his wealthy family whisked him off to summer in Switzerland and then he went to med school out of state and she never heard from him again.

Annie asked, "Where's Nate?"

Olivia's face shifted into an implacable mask. She turned away and stepped towards the clinic doors.

"No," Annie breathed. But Olivia didn't hear. No one did.

She hadn't felt the vacuum curettage because she was as unfeeling as a mannequin when the probing tool sucked out life, aspirating amniotic fluid and placenta tissue and each nascent body part, flailing arms and legs, squishy brain, pulsing heart. Outwardly she looked the same, her stomach as flat and untouched as if it had never happened, but inwardly she bled. Drop by drop, blood clots and dark red tissue collected on the pads in her underwear. She had betrayed her uterus and it no longer trusted her. Her rejected womb rejected her; it wrested its way out determinedly, drop by drop. Shower, shower, shower ... she was trapped in the tiled bathroom watching helplessly as her body bled out. She understood why it squeezed itself out; she didn't deserve her uterus; it was abandoning her body drop by drop by drop ...

Olivia's shoulders hunched inside the gray hoodie, huddling into herself, hunkering down inside the overlarge sweatshirt with two lacrosse sticks marking an X on her back. Annie watched Olivia's small frame march towards the clinic doors.

For years after college, she spun around and walked the other way when she saw a pregnant woman. A stroller was a catalyst for tears. Her cousin's baby shower was an agonizing dissonance of tight smiles and leaching heart. Every onesie, dotted with duckies or teddy bears, made her throat clench. Aunts and older friends tittered knowingly as they warned her cousin: you'll change dirty diapers until your hands are permanently chapped ... you'll never get your body back ... you'll breastfeed the baby all night long until you finally get to sleep and then—you'll *dream* about sleeping. Ha ha ha!

She yearned for something to do with her arms; she yearned for red and chapped hands. She yearned for a swollen belly, but it was her heart that was bloated and misshapen. Her womb eventually stopped hemorrhaging, but her heart never ceased. She wrestled with sleepless nights. She dreamed about sleeping. For weeks after her procedure, she battled dark nights by getting shitfaced. Thank God for cheap beer, her go-to medicine. Her grades plummeted from A's to F's. Fortunately, most of her coursework was already done and she graduated with a B average.

She schooled herself—Don't look, don't tell, don't feel, don't think. But she couldn't stop ruminating because the answer always eluded her. She wondered if her baby would have enjoyed baking or become a singer. She wondered if her baby would have taken after her boyfriend and become a surgeon. She wondered if she would have become a painter, a researcher who cured breast cancer, or the first female president of the United States. She wondered if one day her baby would have become a mother herself?

Olivia reached the door and tugged on it. It opened seamlessly; it anticipated her with calculated attentiveness and well-oiled hinges. Her odyssey was inevitable and the Fates spooled her in with an invisible thread toward Medusa waiting within. Olivia placed one sneaker on the threshold. The entryway yawned darkly, the maw of a machine designed to swallow the fragile ballerina in the gray hoodie. Olivia slipped her other ghostly gray sneaker in the doorway.

Had identical words infected Olivia? Slithering, squirming, hissing: *yourfutureourcareerstrustmeloveloveloveloverightchoicewomenclinichelpappointmentmistaketimegraduationsafeprocedureprivatebodyhealthcareunplannedfeelbetterrightthing ...*

Olivia passed through and the heavy door shushed shut behind her back.

all

over

now

SIXTY-ONE

But it wasn't over ... it was a new beginning ... the inception of interminable suffering and questioning and guilt. Sisyphus poised, turned his endless penetrating gaze from Annie to Olivia, and prepared to roll his boulder relentlessly up and down her bruised heart for all eternity.

Rage gushed up inside Annie. A tiny, two-letter word scraped out her throat and shattered the air like an earthquake: "NO!"

Annie's body quivered with the aftershock. Sound waves reverberated through the sunny, spring air, rippling into the urban neighborhood, riffling the wings of a butterfly hovering above the purple and yellow pansies, whiffling through windows, fluttering pages in open books held by students in the local consolidated school, lifting the printed text off the paper and unfurling into the atmosphere, shifting thoughts, liberating imaginations, releasing ideas, word by word by word.

Trembling, Annie held her breath.

The door was pushed open a few inches. A pale face peered out.

Annie searched Olivia's eyes. With a splayed hand pressed against her bosom, holding her heart in place, Annie said, "That's what *I* did!"

Olivia's baggy gray sweatshirt appeared from behind the door.

"This happened to me, too."

Olivia emerged from the clinic and stepped back onto the stoop. She blinked at Annie. The girl's brown eyes were wet and wide and wondering.

"Twenty years ago. I went to a place like this," Annie jerked her head towards the clinic. Each word was etched in pain. Annie's voice was hoarse and Olivia slowly floated closer to hear.

"Everyone told me it was the right thing to do. My boyfriend. My friends. Everyone. Everyone said do it. So I did. But I regretted it. Every day. Every single day ever since. You have to believe me, Olivia. I thought I ended the problem, but it was only the beginning."

Annie stared past Olivia's shoulder. Her eyes, desiccated, saw nothing. Her vocal cords were a rust-encrusted gate, corroded from disuse, metal crunching against metal, scouring flecks of blood-red iron oxide. "For twenty years I wanted to go back to that day and live it over and do it right. But I can't. I can't go back. And now I can't get rid of this pain. Because deep down, I knew. I told myself I believed the others, but lying on my back, on that cot, I knew. I should have listened to my gut. I knew it was a baby. *My* baby." Annie swallowed, saliva lacerating her throat. Her voice, attenuating to filament. "I named her Lily."

"You?" Olivia stepped closer to Annie, her eyebrows lifted, her voice softened. "You had—?"

Annie redirected her gaze, locking eyes with Olivia. "Yes. I had—" The word was a boulder stuck in her raw, swollen, throbbing, throat. She couldn't push it out.

Olivia gestured questioningly towards the clinic.

Pain embedded deeper lines on Annie's face. She nodded. She pleaded, "Please don't tell Cara. She would hate me forever if she found out."

"Too late," said Olivia, looking past Annie's shoulder.

Annie swung around and saw Cara. Her daughter's eyes were large and round and her mouth was open, forming a perfect circle.

For years Annie had been petrified that her daughter would learn about the secret tucked deep inside the folds of her body, safe from the world, safe from her kids. Annie had dreaded the idea of Cara ever discovering the truth. In her imagination Cara would crumble in horror. Or, repulsed, walk away and never talk to her again. But what happened next was worse than what Annie ever imagined.

A tremendous *BOOM* reverberated in her ears and Annie felt the ground under her feet shift and her body lift up and stumble backwards. She screamed Cara's name and reached out to grab her, but her fingers only clutched air. Annie's arms pivoted, swiveling like propellers, trying to regain her balance ... she felt herself going down, down, down. Her head landed thud, and it was lights out.

SIXTY-TWO

ANNIE ALWAYS HOPED she would go to heaven when she died, not that she was in a rush to get there. And whenever she pictured paradise, which wasn't often, she didn't envision the flat pale heaven painted by Renaissancey masters, with the blue washed out, too insipid to claim a color or take a stand. Nope, Annie anticipated an earthy nirvana. She fancied food and flowers with an outdoor garden reception, lush with fertile fruit trees abundant with zesty oranges and lemons, planted solidly on the ground, drenched with sunlight and dappled by shady foliage, an Italian piazza surrounded by fuchsia-colored bougainvillea, with a refreshing fountain bubbling cool water and tables laden with bottles of the house vino, like the wedding vignettes that she collected on her Pinterest board, like the ad from the brochure about the cruise to the Mediterranean, which Dan had insisted they couldn't afford to go on.

In paradise they would feast on Snowflake Chocolates and Cherry Garcia and no matter how much wine she imbibed or how many truffles or ice cream cones she scarfed down, Annie would never feel nauseous or hungover or fat.

After feasting they would parade into a huge concert hall with a grand piano and an adoring audience and they would listen to Mozart jam and Nat King Cole croon. And Jesus was there, of course, in his white robe, smiling at her, swaying to the music, chiming in. His voice was perfectly deep and utterly divine.

And then Annie would get a turn at the microphone. And since there was no fear of mess-ups in heaven, Annie would be in her glory. Jesus would join her at the mic for a duet! The crowd would applaud and erupt in a standing ovation, begging for encore after encore ...

So when Annie opened her eyes and saw a cop in Vermont green and beige staring down at her, she figured she wasn't in heaven. Not that she had anything against policemen, but she was expecting Mozart and Nat. And, Jesus, of course.

She wondered if she had just died in some sort of attack. Her head pulsed with pain. All she could hear was a buzz vibrating in her eardrums. Her breath had been smacked from her back out her mouth and her lungs hungered for air. Grass tickled her arms and she dug her fingers into the ground to grab onto something.

The cop was bending over her and as his face floated closer, she recognized him as the one who gave her a speeding ticket over a month ago. *What was his name? Officer Thorn-something?* Why was he pestering her now? Did the post office lose her envelope when she mailed in her check for the speeding violation?

Thorn's lips were moving, but she couldn't hear what he was saying. She gulped in air and said, "I sent it in." The fuzzy thrumming in her ears was so loud that she couldn't hear her own words. She repeated herself, louder this time, "I sent it!"

At this, Thorn gesticulated animatedly toward his partner. His lips were jumping up and down, but she couldn't detect what he was shouting.

What's so alarming about mailing in payment? Are Vermonters expected to hand-deliver their traffic fines? Did her check bounce? Annie hadn't balanced her checkbook since she lost her job at PAL, too depressing.

Next thing she knew, cops were grabbing her wrists and pressing cold metal on them. Were they arresting her?

Her head still vibrated with a shuddering pain and an ache reverberated down her entire spine. Noise and pain blended together, boomeranging inside her skull.

Could this be hell? She had heard of fire and brimstone. But handcuffs? For driving fifty-one miles an hour on Route 15? Seriously?

Annie closed her eyes and opened her mouth to suck in more oxygen. She decided to try that visualization trick that Wendy taught her: Take deep breaths. Make your exhale breath longer than your inhale. Relax your mouth so you can smile. Now picture the happiest day of your life. *Well, there was her wedding day. And their honeymoon in the Bahamas.* That brought a smile to Annie's lips.

And then there was the day my darling Cara was born.

Cara?

Omigod! Did Cara overhear me talking to Olivia? Does Cara know I had an abortion? Will she despise me for the rest of her life?

"I'm sorry," Annie whispered, tears seeping out her closed eyes.

I'm so sorry. If I could do it all over again, I would keep you. I would keep you, Lily, forever and ever.

"I'm so sorry," Annie repeated.

"Mom!"

Was that Lily calling her? Was she going insane or was she in heaven?

Or was her hearing coming back?

Annie opened her eyes and this time she saw Cara's lovely face peering down at her flanked by Thorn and Co. Annie could barely hear her daughter shout above the ringing thrumming through her ears and heart.

"I'm sorry," said Annie.

"Mom! You saved Olivia! You stopped her from going in!" Cara's eyes sparkled and her smile glowed angelically. The sun glinted off her shiny hair and spread in rainbow prism colors circling her head like a halo. "I'm so proud of you!"

Annie sighed and closed both eyes and nestled serenely into the spongy grass. It wasn't exactly how she had pictured it. But then again, they always said heaven would be even better than you could possibly imagine.

Annie smiled beatifically. They were right.

SIXTY-THREE

After explaining the blast was from a bomb that they suspected Annie had planted, the two cops knelt next to her to investigate potential injuries. They nudged Cara aside and Thornberg held up three fingers. Annie successfully counted them off and gave her full name, but when they asked for today's date, she drew a blank. Ever since she left work at Play And Learn, she was clueless about the calendar.

"How about, who is the president of the United States?"

"Michelle Obama."

"Close enough," said Thornberg. The cops stood up and looked down at her. "On your feet."

Annie swung one leg over the other, then paused, resting. Her plan was, once her heart stopped battering her ribcage and her lungs could expand, she would flump onto her belly, then crawl up onto all fours. From there she could push herself upright. She did this all the time when circle time ended at the preschool, maneuvering from a cross-legged sit to up on three, although never in handcuffs. But she could do this. Soon. Very soon.

Mentally she coached herself: *Gimme a U! Gimme a P! What's that—*

"I'm the doctor. Let me check her out." Annie heard a voice hover above the buzzing in her ears.

A woman's face sailed into view. She peered at Annie, then gently cradled her head in place. "Follow my finger with your eyes."

This was a better plan. Annie relaxed, glad for the respite. She snuggled into the juicy grass, luxuriating in the safety of relinquishing herself into the hands of an expert. Medical professionals could harness the superpower of science to fix anything on TV's *Dr. Dempsey.* Without moving her head, Annie's eyes tracked the index finger, back and forth, up and down. Easy peasy.

"I got this," said Thornberg to his sidekick. "You go talk to the demonstrators."

Gingerly, one at a time, the woman patted Annie's legs, uncrossing them as she went. "Let me know if anything hurts."

"My head and my butt." Her hearing was returning.

"Mhm."

It was the doctor's regal French twist that sparked Annie's memory. "Wow. Small world," noted Annie. In Vermont, it shrinks to the size of a quark. "Dr. Louise?"

The woman studied Annie's face.

"You're the one who helped us when our dog was hit by a truck," Annie reminded her. "You pulled over and checked him out." Annie figured the woman didn't recall Curly because she probably stopped all the time to save animals. Like a vigilante veterinarian who patrolled the streets for accidents ... cats scared-stuck in high tree branches, dogs with porcupine needles stuck in their snouts ... What a coincidence that she was driving by the clinic at the exact right time to assist Annie.

She pictured herself, sprawled on her back in Dan's white tee, legs splayed out in her chunky mom jeans with the hidden elastic waistband, wrists awkwardly connected by cuffs, like a super-tacky, low-budget, S&M movie. Not her best look.

Meanwhile, her Good Samaritan maintained her elegant updo and understated makeup. How is it that some women have perfect hair at all times? Annie wondered if her own hair was now long enough to pull back into a shapely chignon. She'd been growing it out for weeks.

The woman nodded briefly. "Louise Higgins," she confirmed. "Was it a fracture?"

"Yup. You were right. Hairline fracture."

Louise smiled the kind of rueful sideways slide that acknowledged she was correct about the broken leg, but would really prefer no injury to begin with. "How is your dog? A golden, right?"

"Yeah!" She did remember! "Curly's fine. He hated the splint, chewed it off, but he's good now. Thanks again for your help that day."

"Of course." She turned her head back to her task and pressed a hand lightly down Annie's arm. "No broken bones for you. But you may have a concussion."

"Yeah," Annie agreed. "My head hurts wicked bad. I'm so glad you were driving by in time to help."

"Driving?" She tilted her head. "You don't know who I am, do you?"

Louise seemed curiously coy. As if there were an inside joke Annie didn't know about. This was a common suspicion of Annie's, that everyone knew something obvious that she didn't. It started in first grade when she went to the restroom and inadvertently pulled her undies up over the back of her skirt before returning to her classroom. But this time, Annie was confident. "Yes I do. You helped us with Curly when he broke his leg."

"But you don't know where I work?"

If Louise hadn't been driving, maybe she had been marching with the Friends of Voles? "Are you with the animal activists?"

"No, I don't have time to protest; I'm working."

"At Bow Wow Meow?"

"Here."

"In Burlington?"

"Right here." Louise indicated the brick building behind her. "I work at Women's Health."

"Here?"

"That's right."

"You work here?"

"Yes. It's my clinic."

Annie's head thrummed. She felt her blood pulsing, pumping, pounding, underneath the skin of her temples. Chill moisture had seeped from the grass to her tee shirt and she shivered. "I thought you were a vet."

"I considered that, but decided to go with gynecology instead."

"Oh."

There was a long pause.

Annie was rarely at a loss for words, but this time she had zero words. What's the proper thing to say to an abortionist after you've been caught protesting outside her doorstep? What does Miss Manners recommend for that?

Annie had a sneaky suspicion that she was doing it all wrong. Again. Wasn't she supposed to hate this doctor, or at the very least snub her? Instead, Annie felt grateful to her for helping Curly and for intervening when the cops tried to get her to stand up. She felt an irrational desire to impress Louise. But how was this impressive—stunned, splayed, speechless on her back?

The pause was growing, becoming awkward ... a pregnant pause.

Annie deployed her familiar preschool teacher techniques, deflection and distraction. "Who set off that bomb anyway?"

"You tell me." The doctor gave her a searching stare.

"I don't know! I swear! Was anyone hurt?"

"Fortunately no, but the building was damaged."

"Thank goodness no one was hurt. That must have been scary for you guys inside."

"Yes, it was. You never think it'll happen to your own place."

"Especially not in Vermont."

"I've heard of this in other states, real shock to happen here."

"I'm sorry," Annie said. It came out automatically, as if her default setting was an apology. She was sorry for everything—the bomb, the doctor's inconvenience, global warming ... She lifted her hands, which clanked lightly in their cuffs. Most of all, she was sorry for herself. "They nabbed me for it."

Dr. Higgins leaned back slightly and stared at Annie again.

"I don't even know how to make a bomb!"

The doctor nodded and smiled. The very idea was ridiculous. "Of course not."

"Right?" said Annie. Now that she was arrested, would the authorities outlaw her from homeschooling? If she couldn't teach, how could Cara finish high school? Or go to college? Or have a life?

"So what brought you here?" the doctor asked.

"I was. Um. I was with some friends, just a bystander." Annie sounded as nonchalant as she could, la-di-da.

Louise looked up at the tiny clump of people across Union Street being interviewed by a cop. "The protesters?" Her nose wrinkled.

Annie feared she was the worst volunteer Vermont Right to Life had ever had. Conceivably the most useless protester in the entire history of the pro-life movement. Instead of holding her ugly sign and staying behind the invisible line with the other demonstrators, here she was hobnobbing with the abortionist, who found her repulsive. She hoped her mother would never hear about this escapade.

Annie had a horrid revelation that no matter how long her hair grew, she would never be a spokeswoman for perfume. Even on her best day, she would never be polished enough to demonstrate the Murphy Method on TV. Oh sure, you could aspire to save the world one toddler at a time, but then real life crushes you daily until you find yourself flat on your ass in the grass like the lumpen bumpkin you truly are.

She launched another deflection strike. "Anyhoo. How come you work here if you wanted to be an animal doctor?"

"When I was in college, there were enough vets. I wanted to help women."

"You can still be a vet if you want to."

"Too late now."

"No, it isn't!" The cheerleader in Annie came charging out. She rocked forward a few times to get the momentum to roll into a sitting position in the grass, blinking back the pain in her skull. "It's never too late! You could volunteer at an animal hospital and see how much you really like it. And you're already a doctor so you could skip most of vet school and then take online classes—"

Unconvinced, almost patronizing, Louise smiled at Annie's enthusiasm. "I like my profession; women need me."

"Time to go." Thornberg's partner had finished questioning the bystanders and had ambled back. Each officer grasped an arm and hefted Annie onto her wobbly legs.

"Thanks for your help, Louise." Now that she was upright, Annie could see the clinic's front door, which had a three-foot jagged breach at the bottom right. "Good luck with the repairs."

"You too," said Louise. "Good luck with—" she gestured towards Annie's head, or was it her handcuffs? —"everything."

Maybe it was her hair?

SIXTY-FOUR

While her mother rested on the ground, getting assessed by a stranger, Cara dutifully gave her name and contact info to the officer, but declined any further comments. "Not until I speak with my attorney."

"All we want is your description, as an eyewitness. In your own words, tell us what happened."

"You handcuffed my mother! That's what happened! I'm not saying anything else until I get counsel!" Cara had never expected to see her mom get arrested, or to hear herself shouting at an adult. It felt oddly liberating to yell at the cops. When the uniform started quizzing Olivia, Cara advised her, "Just name and number—that's all you give."

Reinforcements had arrived to collect evidence and secure the area. When the two original cops escorted her mom to their cruiser across the street, Cara grabbed Olivia's arm and ordered her into Betsy Clunker. She wanted to follow them to headquarters, but by the time she pulled onto Union Street, she'd already lost sight of the cops' vehicle.

"That bomb could have killed my baby," Olivia whispered.

Cara looked over. Olivia's eyes were dazed. "Thank God you didn't get hit by any glass or concrete or anything."

"Yeah," breathed Olivia, "we were so lucky." Her hands formed a heart on her abdomen.

Cara didn't know if her friend meant Olivia and Cara, or Olivia and her baby. "Yeah," she agreed. "We're lucky just to be alive."

The air was freshly baked by the warm sun, which illuminated the spring-green grass lining the sidewalks of town. A soft wind ruffled burgeoning leaves overhead. An orange and black Monarch butterfly fluttered over a lawn, searching for milkweed.

Stopping at the red traffic light, Cara glanced again at Olivia who seemed to have recovered a bit. The glazed look was gone from her eyes.

In fact, they were quite focused now on aiming her cell phone camera lens directly at her belly. She smoothed the bulky sweatshirt over her imperceptible baby bump and was trying to take a picture of it, despite the seatbelt and the fact that she was barely showing.

"Olivia, since my mom already knows that you're pregnant, we might as well go all in and tell her about the joint in the bathroom. Right?"

Olivia's right hand paused a moment, the phone suspended over her stomach.

Cara pressed on. "That way she can stop worrying about me being a stoner, y'know?"

Olivia lifted her head. Looked straight ahead.

"Please, Via? After all I've done for you?"

Olivia made a what-the-hell face. "I guess." She shrugged her shoulders. "After all, I'm so screwed, what difference does it make about a stupid smoke of weed?" Olivia faced Cara. "Besides, *your* mom had an abortion. She can hardly fault me for toking up one time, right?"

"Hey. She saved your life!"

"And my baby's." *Tap.* Olivia snapped a picture of her belly.

"Right."

Olivia thumbed in a contact on her cell phone.

"Who are you sending that to?" Cara asked suspiciously.

"Don't chew me out, Cara. Nate's still the baby daddy, whether he wants to be or not."

It had been an afternoon of revelations and Cara considered telling her bestie about Nate's drunken jank kiss with her. But Olivia finally looked hopeful instead of helpless. In fact she looked surprisingly content considering she had just escaped an explosion and was still pregnant and Nate doesn't want their baby. Why disturb her peace? Besides, how could Cara spill without incriminating herself? Nah. Some things are better off left unsaid. Cara shook her head and remained silent.

Olivia asked, "So does this mean I'll get kicked out of school instead of you?"

"Let's start with telling my mom. We can figure out the school thing later. She'll know what to do. Besides, CHU can't kick you out if you're pregnant, right? I mean, isn't that discrimination? I'm sure you'd have a case."

"Hmph. Hope so." Olivia paused. "I still can't believe your mom had an abortion. She's so *old*." Olivia shook her head skeptically, then took another belly selfie. *Tap.* "I didn't think people like that had sex."

"I know, right?"

"But she must have. Else how did you get here?" Olivia looked at Cara appraisingly.

Cara and Olivia had been BFFs since fourth grade and had shared a lot, including a crush on Mark with the beautiful blond hair flip in fifth grade. But Cara did not want to share an image of her parents having sex with anyone. Not Olivia. Not even herself.

Cara turned her head to face the road. "Ew. Can we not?"

Straight ahead was Lake Champlain, glittering silver with the glorious spring sunshine skittering off it with shiny snatches of glare. The glassy ECHO museum full of amphibians and reptiles was on their left, the green tree-lined bike path on the right. "I took a wrong turn." Cara put her blinker on and pulled to the side of the road. She turned to Olivia. "Do you know where the police station is?"

SIXTY-FIVE

AT THE PRECINCT, a friendly dispatcher offered Annie a baby chick. Her eyes glistened at the unexpected kindness of this stranger. With her wrists still awkwardly cuffed, she accepted the tiny fuzzy ball. The peeping bird was fluffy and full of life and quivering breaths. Annie was tempted, but declined the free chickadees politely.

"Anne Mulligan." Her name echoed in the small room. Thornberg was back, standing in the doorway as solid and stolid as a statue sculpted from granite, the Vermont state rock.

She followed Thornberg into the inquisition room. It wasn't until he inquired for the third time when, exactly, she planted the pipe bomb that Annie suddenly remembered to ask to speak with her lawyer.

"Knock yourself out." Thornberg led her outside the room to an office with a desk where a policeman handed her an old-fashioned phone with a receiver tied by curly cord to the base, all the color of cement.

Annie dialed from memory, then turned her back to avoid the cop's watchful gaze.

"Hello?"

"Hi Dad. I'm in jail."

"Good one, Annie Banannie."

A beat passed.

"You're kidding, right?"

"They arrested me for violating their stupid buffer zone law!"

Her dad's voice immediately became serious and lawyerly. "Remember what I always told you kids growing up. 'Rule Number One: Keep your mouth shut.' And 'Rule Number Two: Ask to speak with your attorney.'"

"Too late!" Annie wailed. "I already told the police *everything*. I blabbed the whole way back in the squad car. They know the names of the people I was with. They know I parked in a handicapped spot 'cause I couldn't find a place to park. I even explained that the reason I was there to begin with is that Cara got kicked out of school and I had to home-school her!"

"How many times did we cover this when you were growing up here? Don't talk to the police except to ask for your attorney."

"I know, I know! But when I was little I didn't actually think I'd ever get arrested! Then when I did, I was so confused by the bomb—I think I have a concussion."

"Excellent, we can use the concussion in our defense. Wait a minute—what bomb?"

"The bomb that went off at the clinic! They think I set it."

"Did you?"

"NO! Come on, Dad. You think I know how to build a bomb?"

"Okay. Let's calm down." There was a pause. Annie could hear him draw breath in through his nose. "Here's what you do. Tell them you have a concussion and need to get checked by a doctor ASAP. And then, keep your mouth shut. Get it?"

"Got it."

"Good. Now let's back up a minute. Did I hear you say Cara was kicked out of school?"

"Um." Annie twirled her finger into the curlicue of the phone cord. "Yeah."

"What for?"

"For smoking pot."

"Annie! What the hell is going on there in Mapleville? Why didn't you tell us?"

"I didn't want you to know! I wanted to fix everything so you would never have to find out!"

"Banannie! How can we help you if we don't know what the hell's going on?"

"I don't know, Daddy. I'm sorry. Can you just get me out of jail?"

"Jeesum crow. Your mother's gonna have a helluva time when she hears this."

"DON'T TELL MOM!"

Annie was still explaining the back-story to her dad when she saw through the half-glass door that Cara and Olivia had arrived. "Thanks, Dad. Can you talk to the police for me now?"

Annie passed the phone to the officer at the desk so Mr. Glen Murphy, attorney at law, could officially request that the police release Annie from custody based on public recognition so she could go to the doctor and get her concussion checked out, and please note, she couldn't hear those Miranda rights, assuming they were recited to her, due to her temporary deafness and shock.

Within minutes, Annie was on the other side of the door.

"Hey, Mom," said Cara. She nudged Olivia with her elbow.

Olivia stepped forward and confessed that Cara had covered for her, it was Nate's weed and she, Olivia, was the one who smoked it in the teacher's bathroom. Although, truth be told, she only got one puff.

Cara was afraid she would have two concurrent lifetime sentences of no cell phone as well as being double-grounded after her mother found out the truth. For six weeks Cara had deceived her mom about the weed, which triggered her getting fired from PAL, forcing her to take on homeschooling, where she met Mrs. Boucher, who talked her into praying in front of the abortion clinic, where she was snagged by cops.

What Cara did not expect was for her mom to jump up and down in an awkward victory dance with several fist pumps in the air before yelling "Ow!" and clutching her head. She paused a moment, then lunged forward and wrapped Cara in a tight bear hug, nearly knocking her over.

Then her mother reached out for Olivia and glommed onto both girls in a long and loud hug. Her mother kept repeating, "I knew it! I knew something was fishy with your story!"

Cara smiled to herself. Her mom had completely fallen for it. But Cara allowed her mother this moment of faux I-told-you-so. Calling her out on her BS wasn't worth sucking the joy out of the air.

SIXTY-SIX

BY THE TIME Annie got cleared by a physician and returned to the house that evening, her answering machine was flickering red lights at her. Purnell had called to say they were missing Form No. VT982 listing the topics covered in Cara's Sexual Education course. There was an end-of-season sale at Vermont Flannel Company and she could go to their website for more information and a coupon. Wendy wanted to know if Annie would go see *Fifty Shades of Grey* with her that weekend.

Nothing from Dan, who hadn't picked up when she used Cara's phone to call from the hospital. Annie's own phone got squashed when she fell on her backside. Either Dan was in a high stakes meeting, or his phone died also.

It had been an exhausting day. First homeschooling, then to the pharmacy and library with Willy, the Women's Health Clinic, the bomb, the police station. From there she had been escorted to the emergency room where the experts agreed she had a mild concussion.

Mild? It felt full throttle to Annie. That was like saying she went through "mild" labor to deliver her kids.

Here's the thing about concussions. It's hidden trauma. No blood, no bone poking out, no stitches or scabs or scars. But the brain bounces away from impact then smacks the other side of the skull so it's a double whammy. Since people can't see the interior bruises, they treat you like you're normal, even when you're not.

Annie had tried not to moan like a cow in the car when Cara shuttled her and Olivia back to the clinic so they could all retrieve their cars and drive home. After reading the anti-drug literature from CHU, she was afraid to take the painkillers prescribed by the doctor at the hospital because she didn't want to get addicted and raid her neighbors' medicine cabinets. Instead, she was operating on over-the-counter ibuprofen. "You okay to drive, mom?" Cara asked as Annie crawled out of the van and stumbled to her Subaru.

"Sure." *Hell no.*

Willy, hoping to be helpful, had whipped up some boxed mac and cheese for dinner, earning an A+ in extra credit. Annie stirred the elbow noodles around in her bowl, much more interested in her Long Trail beer. She had already guzzled her treasured Hodad. By the time she listened to her phone messages, Annie was pleasantly pickled. At least Dan was safe in Mexico and Willy was safe at home and hey, she saved Olivia from a bomb, and Cara thought she was a hero for that.

With every sip Annie's heart grew three sizes larger, just like the Grinch's. Why stop at saving preschoolers and Olivia? Annie wanted to save everybody! She was a giant freaking lifesaver!

She would call Wendy back to say heck yes to the movies this weekend. She would thank her for *Mindfulness* and massages, and then nonchalantly let slip that Brooke was skipping classes. She would admit to Susan that she had been jealous ever since Olivia got into Columbia, and then she would offer to babysit once Olivia's baby was born. (No point in pointing out that ever since she found out Olivia was a pregnant druggie, Annie was no longer plagued with envy.) She felt so magnanimous that when she delivered Form No. VT982 to Purnell (Cara already knows about sex, thank you very much), she would coach the counselor: Stop eating processed food and diet soda. Stick with real food and water. And if you need fizz, drink seltzer.

Annie's heart was filled with benevolence for everybody. For Maggie, who came by later that evening with homemade mac and cheese, blathering apologies for the explosion. "I'm so sorry; how's your head?"

"Mild." Annie snorted at her own joke.

"In case you decide to try again, this might help." Maggie flashed her a brochure for Rachel's Vineyard, which Annie assumed was a restaurant, like Olive Garden. "I'm not hungry, just thirsty," said Annie. "How about a Long Trail?" She held out a bottle.

"No thanks." Maggie raised a hand. It looked as if she were blessing the beer.

No sense wasting a brewski. Since Maggie didn't want it, Annie took a swig.

Maggie explained, "Rachel's Vineyard is a retreat for women to heal from abortion."

Annie had the bottle suspended over her open mouth. She tilted her drink upright and froze, afraid to look at the brochure, afraid to look at her friend. Did Maggie know what she had told Olivia outside the clinic? How could she know? Annie had *whispered,* right? Only Olivia heard! And possibly Cara? Maybe? Maybe not?

Of course not!

No!

Maggie and her friends had to stand thirty-five feet away from the clinic entrance! Had the buffer zone kept her secret a secret?

"Sometimes I offer these pamphlets to the girls coming to the clinic. Outside the buffer zone, of course."

Phew, this pamphlet is definitely not for me!

Maggie set the leaflet on the kitchen table. "I hope you'll consider joining us again."

"Maybe." *Never!*.

Maggie handed Annie a tube of arnica for the concussion and declined another beer held out to her, this time blessing it with both hands before leaving.

"Bye, Maggie! Thanks!" Annie slurped, holding the rejected beer. She had already uncapped it, so she set it on the table to chug as soon as she finished the one she was working on.

The more she drank, the less it seemed to her that Cara had heard anything she had whispered to Olivia. Of course not!

Annie's head was feeling bleary and blurry and bumbling full of bonhomie. She was filled with gratitude for her dad, who had calmed her down and assured her she wouldn't be in jail "forever." And she loved Dan and would tell him never to leave her again. She wasn't like those military wives like Maggie, who could take it in stride for six months at a whack because it was their civic duty, like saluting the flag or voting in November. She couldn't wait to tell Dan about everything. She didn't need Clarence the angel-in-training from *It's a Wonderful Life,* because she had Dan and Maggie and Wendy and Cara and Willy and Susan and her parents and the nice dispatcher with the fuzzy chicks and ... that was plenty wonderful.

Plus God. Of course she could always turn to Him. In fact, she would buy herself a prie-dieu, like Maggie's, and set it up in the corner of their living room. She would start by praying for Olivia. Looking reverent, lovely and humble, eyes skyward, alert for visions, Annie would kneel there and pray for hours at a time.

Or maybe minutes.

A couple of seconds?

Nah. Who was she kidding? Her special kneeler would just turn into a coat rack. If she wanted to save others she had to start with herself, and when it came to praying on her knees, she sucked big time. Besides, how long does it take to say, "Please bless Olivia and her baby and pretty pretty please let her graduate from CHU and matriculate at college?" You could do that while brushing your teeth, and still have time to ask for a growth spurt for Willy and a decent boyfriend for Cara before expectorating into the sink.

Annie took another swig of her Long Trail. "Because life is a journey," she mused, "and we all need help along the trail. It takes a village to raise a mother, and I admit I need all the help I can get to make it up the mountain. Because," inspired by her own inspiration, she paused, punched her bottle high in the air like the Statue of Liberty's torch, "because," she proclaimed, "together we *make* the village!"

Damn that was good! She was on fire! She should be on an *At Home with Ula* episode! That audience would lap it up. They are the biggest fans of all fandom for guests on a journey.

She tried Dan's number again. He didn't pick up, but she listened to his recorded message all the way through because she missed hearing his voice, deep and rich. "Hello. You've reached Daniel Mulligan. If you're calling for International Security Support, press one. All other calls, please press two."

Annie punched two. She was going to fill him in on what was going on. Time for the truth.

But where to begin? The bomb? Police custody? Cara not being on drugs? Cara not pregnant?

No—that won't do! Annie had never told him her mother had suspected Cara of being knocked up. Dan didn't need to know every little thing her mom said.

Annie knew her time was running out on his answering machine. She panicked. She shouted out, "I love you!" but the damn beep cut her off, so when Dan played back his voice messages, all he would hear would be: "I love—!"

SIXTY-SEVEN

SEVERAL KIDS SURROUNDED the Mulligan table, which was covered with an old plastic shower curtain. Chuck was splayed out on top, spilling guts and organs. Each student had a fork and tweezers; Maggie stood nearby wielding a carving knife. Annie bent studiously over Willy's shoulder and poked at what looked like a small brown liver.

"What the—!" shouted Dan, stopping himself. He stood in the doorway holding the handle of his large suitcase on wheels with one hand, and a box with a bow wedged under his other arm.

Annie turned and saw him. "Dan!" she screamed. "Dan! You're home!"

"Dad!" yelled Willy.

Annie dropped her skewer and ran to hug him while Willy tackled him from the other side, accidentally knocking the package hooked under Dan's arm. The box flew into the tripod Paloma was aiming towards the dissection.

"Hey!" Paloma yelled, grabbing at her video camera to prevent it from toppling off the tripod. Upon impact, the box lid separated from the bottom and out fluttered a cherry red nighty, edged in black lace.

Paloma put her hand out. The red and black lingerie swooped down, landing lightly, suspended on her outthrust index finger.

Annie turned red, but not as red as Dan.

"What's going on here?" he asked. His hand formed a large circle encompassing the table, kids, and carcass.

"Science." Annie plucked the satin teddy from Paloma's hand and shoved it in the box and clamped the lid back down. "Dan, this is my friend, Paloma." She indicated the gal fiddling with her camera. Annie turned and swept her arm in a rainbow. "And Maggie and Evelyn."

"Nice to meet you," said Dan, although he didn't look convincing. He enclosed Annie with one arm, and reached out with his other to tilt

Paloma's video camera away from him and towards the table. Dan was a man who appreciated privacy.

"I didn't know you were coming home today," said Annie, clutching him.

"I wanted to surprise you."

"You sure did!" enthused Willy, latched on to Dan's other side.

"Where's Care Bear?" asked Dan.

"She's visiting a nursing home with Zachary and his dog. They'll be back any minute now."

"Who is Zachary?"

Before anyone could answer Dan exclaimed, "And why the hell is our living room painted yellow?"

SIXTY-EIGHT

ANNIE COULDN'T WAIT to be alone with Dan. He looked exotic with his bronze tan. This was the longest they'd ever been apart. She could be Mimi or Lulu or Cio-Cio-san with the complicated kimono! Or a new role play! Something Spanish and spicy to go with the red teddy he brought back! Carmen! Sí, sí!

But first, she had to get rid of her guests. Evelyn was their impromptu biology teacher for today, but now Annie took charge. "Okay, let's wrap up our experiments. Finish your diagrams and notes, then let's clean up."

As Paloma and her daughters filed out, she assured the other mothers she would send them her photos and video to forward to the state home-study office. Evelyn warned everybody not to post any pictures of the dissection on Facebook or they would incur the wrath of animal rights activists.

"Chuck was already dead when we found him," protested Joey.

"Doesn't matter. Trust me." Evelyn also advised them not to post anything on Facebook anyway because that conglomerate was mining their users' personal data for their own profit.

Maggie stayed back and helped Annie clear up the mess while Dan, Willy and Joey played with Curly and Moe in the backyard to keep them away from the biological waste in the house.

"Hi dearie!"

Had someone come to their dissection late? "Hello?" called Annie.

"Over here."

The voice was familiar, filled with memories of warm chocolate chip cookies, wool sweaters, and maternal advice. Annie leaned around the corner towards the kitchen entrance. "Mom?"

"Your father told me about the police. We are so proud of you for speaking up. Here, I made you a mac and cheese." Her mother set the casserole on the counter and planted her huge bag down on the hooked rug.

Annie introduced her mother to Maggie. Mrs. Murphy said, "Nice to meet you." Her mother's natural greeting would be a hug, but Maggie was carrying bloody body parts wrapped in newspaper. "What's that?"

"Science," Annie answered.

"The kids dissected a woodchuck," Maggie elaborated.

Her mother took a sniff and wrinkled her nose. She fetched a spray bottle from under the kitchen sink and began scrubbing the table.

She hadn't said anything, but Annie knew what her mother was thinking. "I know it's a mess," she explained. "I got behind on cleaning. I had a headache after the bomb."

"Bomb?" Her mother swung round to face her. "Your father didn't say anything about a bomb!"

"I'm fine, Mom."

Before her knees buckled, her mother plopped onto the sofa in the living room. Annie sat next to her and asked, "You okay?"

"I'm fine," she insisted. "Are *you* okay?" she asked, throwing the concern back at Annie and enveloping her in a prolonged hug, the kind with circular scrubbing on the back.

"I'm fine," Annie repeated. "The doctor said my headaches will clear up on their own."

Maggie came back from the kitchen with a glass of water which she handed to Mrs. Murphy.

"Thank you, dear." She took a swallow before addressing Annie, "Your father said the police gave you a hard time for crossing the buffer zone, but he didn't tell me about a bomb."

"We didn't want to worry you. No one got hurt. The bomb was pretty rinky-dink and the police have some evidence and are confident they'll nail the culprit soon."

"Done cleaning up?" Dan shouted as he and Willy and Joey came in the back door with the golden retrievers.

"Almost," said Annie.

"Hello Mama M," said Dan when he saw Annie's mother.

"Hello Dan! How was Mexico?"

❖

The kitchen door swung open and Cara and Zach stumbled in, laughing. Frodo bounded past them and charged up to Moe and Curly. The three dogs performed a getting-to-know-you icebreaker by snuffling backsides. Then they politely bowed downward dog to each other before playfully galloping in circles.

"Oh, Cara's here!" Grammy launched herself up from the sofa and bundled into the kitchen to wrap Cara in a warm hug.

Grammy opened her extra-large Reign Vermont handmade bag and pulled out two tiny pairs of baby booties, one in pastel green and the other in violet. She smiled proudly and also withdrew a receiving blanket crocheted in a zigzag pattern in matching yarn. "I made these myself." Eyes glistening, she held them out to Cara. "Congratulations on your baby!"

Cara's mouth fell open. She turned toward Zach.

He edged away slightly, but managed to keep his voice composed. "Your *baby*?"

Cara shook her head no, but she couldn't talk. Her jaw had hyperextended and dangled uselessly. There was so much she wanted to tell Zach. *It's not my baby; it's Olivia's. Grammy's going senile. I've never even gone further than second base. Please believe me. One more thing—I love you!*

But no words came out of Cara's mouth, which hung slack from shock.

Grammy's Irish eyes twinkled kindly. "Is this the father?" She offered her hand to Zach who, thanks to years of training, automatically accepted it, despite the bombshell. Grammy pressed her left hand warmly on top, giving him a sandwich handshake. The gesture was designed to assure him that he wasn't alone; he had the full support of the clan to back him up, complete with a nonstop supply of crocheted baby clothes and limitless maternal advice. "So pleased to meet you. I'm Angela Murphy, Cara's grandmother. The baby's great grandmother."

"Care Bear?"

Still too stunned to speak, Cara turned and saw her dad standing in the living room, head tilted, eyebrows scratching his hairline.

"Baby?" he asked.

Cara had never seen her father this tan before. Nor had she ever seen this particular look on his face. His eyebrows were crumpled and his jaw dangled down in a yawning chasm of dismay and disbelief. She guessed her own expression was identical.

Cara was dumbstruck.

Without taking his eyes off Cara, Dan quietly ordered, "Willy, take the dogs back outside."

Willy knew better than to argue. He swiveled and went back outside with Moe and Curly. Joey hustled out after him followed by Frodo.

Her mother rushed to assure Grammy, Maggie, Zach, and especially her dad that the baby wasn't Cara's; it was Olivia's.

"Oh, it was your *friend's* baby," said Grammy, tittering at her blunder.

"I told you!" Cara finally found her voice.

SIXTY-NINE

MR. DAY OFFICIATED alongside Purnell, who looked as skeptical as a bouncer outside a hot NYC club. This time Cara was flanked by both parents. Annie wasn't sure what was going down. Was there some crucial expulsion form that they had neglected to sign? Did Mr. Day hear about her arrest and call them in to chew *her* out?

"So you can probably guess why I asked you to come in." Mr. Day's jowls puckered when he smiled, like a curtain rippling into waves when drawn back. He folded his hands and rested them on the edge of his massive desk.

Annie looked at Cara. Then they both looked at Dan.

"How about you spell it out for us," said Dan.

"We have been notified that Cara was not ingesting drugs on school property, but was actually trying to convince her friend not to smoke." Mr. Day's cheek-curtains spread further apart. "Therefore, we are in a position to welcome Cara back into the school." He spread his hands magnanimously.

Her darling daughter could get re-educated! Everything was working out perfectly!

"Yes, we are very proud of Cara." Dan put his arm around his daughter's shoulders. "Sounds like a plan. When does she start back? Tomorrow?"

"Ahem," Purnell interjected. She rested her can of diet soda on the principal's desk. "Cara is able to return to our school provided, of course, that she has continued to stay current with her assignments. The teachers will need to see her work, including the tests and quizzes that she took during the past month and a half." Purnell stared at Annie, as if she knew that Cara had deviated from the school curriculum.

Annie recalled Maggie's advice, to tell the state what the student *did* learn, rather than what they didn't get around to. "Cara has been learning every day and working on each of her classes," Annie assured them. Which was true. Cara had been doing math with Zachary, chemistry at the co-op, English with Hawthorne, art with Bob Ross on TV and Spanish with Judy at Zumba. "Cara just completed her history paper. We'd be happy to submit that to her teacher."

The Civil Rights Movement: Because Emancipation Failed to Prevent Discrimination. Sprinkled with several Martin Luther King quotes, Cara argued that it takes more than legislation to change cultural attitudes. Annie had been legitimately impressed with Cara's report and was genuinely curious to see how a real teacher would grade it.

"Um."

Annie and Dan looked at Cara.

"Um," Cara said again.

"Yes?" asked Mr. Day.

Cara's eyes were full of question marks and stop signs.

"Yes?" said Annie softly.

"Um."

Dan addressed Mr. Day. "Could we have a moment to discuss this in private?"

"Of course."

Dan stood up first, Cara and Annie followed. They filed out the door and assembled in the corner of the mini waiting room, decorated in graduated shades of beige. The walls were painted a creamy-beige; the industrial rug was brown-beige. The medium-beige couch was smaller than a love seat. Either a large person could sit there, or two Goldilocks, or one sprawling, defiant sophomore about to get detention.

The Mulligans remained standing, whispering towards the potted plant with large green staggered leaves in the corner, as if recording state secrets into a microphone embedded in the glossy fake ficus.

"Care Bear. What's going on?" Dan asked.

"Do I have to come back to CHU?"

"I thought you wanted to," whispered Annie.

"I'm not so sure anymore."

Cara blinked.

She recalled her mother, in pajamas, drinking Long Trail, while reading her English paper, and scratching out a large A+ at the top.

Cara pictured herself standing impatiently in front of the class at Mr. Shullin's desk, waiting for him to sign her hall pass so she could go to the bathroom.

She remembered Willy, interrupting her painting class to inform her that it takes four generations of monarchs to complete their migration to Mexico and back.

Purnell, advising her last year not to take Advanced Placement American History because it would be "too intense" for her.

Olivia, shoulders slumped, back against the wall, sinking down in the teacher's restroom.

John, sprinting ahead of her on the homestretch when they went for a run together.

And most all, Zach ... his hands on his little sister's shoulders to comfort her, picking up Willy for Tae Kwon Do classes, whistling cheerfully while scribbling algebraic equations in pen, Zach with a bruised nose, holding his hand out to her for a dance on the grass the night of the prom.

"We only have three more weeks before I graduate. I don't think I need government school," said Cara.

Dan looked at Annie.

"Public school," she translated.

Cara enjoyed swapping out her comfy pajamas for stylish clothes every Friday to go to Faith United. She enjoyed hanging out with Zach at the homeschool group. And getting tutored in math wasn't so bad since she knew where the answer key was. Now that Zach realized she wasn't a stoner with toe fungus spying on homeschoolers for a school project. Now that Cara knew there was no Ashley!

"Camels Hump had their chance," Cara continued. She didn't really care what "value" meant in art or when was the proper time to use the subjunctive form in Spanish. And she wasn't convinced Mrs. Eckles would give her an A+ on her Scarlet Letter paper the way her mom did.

Plus, she hadn't taken *any* tests or quizzes in algebra (or history) (or art) (or English) since she walked out of CHU. She didn't want to start now, after she already forgot everything she had learned. "Can't we just keep homeschooling?"

❖

Annie glanced at Dan. She could read his face clearly. His eyebrows were saying, *What the hell?* His fists were yelling, *Are you nuts?* He was rocking on his toes, mentally shouting, *Annie, this is what you've wanted all along. For Cara to graduate at the top of her class from CHU and go to Coolidge University and become a lawyer. And for you to go back to teaching the toddlers about ABCs and colors and how not to poop in their pampers. And for Willy to quit this homeschooling nonsense and get back to middle school where he belongs. And for our property taxes to be used on our own kids' education!*

That's what Annie could read in Dan's expression, because they had been married nineteen years and she could read him like a book.

But he hadn't seen the Pendergrasts' solar power, or Hunter's Olympic-level fencing moves, or all the volunteer teachers at Faith United. Dan didn't realize how many homeschooling resources were hanging out online, like Outlier, others free for the taking. YouTube. TED talks. Kahn Academy.

He hadn't seen Willy's face the day the bullies ganged up on him. He didn't know you need a PhD in math in order to fill out the English grading rubric.

He didn't realize that their daughter still needed Annie. The PAL kids had their own parents; they didn't need her the way Cara did. Mothering doesn't magically end when your daughter turns seventeen. Mothering lasts forever and ever. Didn't Dan know that?

Parenting never ended, but homeschooling could. Could Annie keep it up? Was she willing to continue teaching for no pay and no prestige? Was she willing to risk being called a freaking geek for going to the Faith United homeschool co-op? Was she willing to take up the red pen again and beg, borrow, or steal answer keys then squirrel them away underneath her living room furniture? Could she do it for Cara? For Willy?

"Yes!" Annie answered before Dan could respond to Cara's question with some logistical obstacle like, *Where the hell would Cara get a transcript? The transcript fairy?*

Within minutes, Dan had rooted out the problem: Cara confessed that Bob Ross's voice was so gentle and mild, she fell asleep every afternoon, paintbrush in hand, her happy little trees bereft of leaves. And as for

Spanish, Cara needed to expand her vocabulary beyond *bailar* and *contigo.*

On the spot, Dan improvised a solution—a combination of home and real school. Honestly, her husband was an organizational genius!

"Hybrid homeschooling," Annie labeled it. She told Dan about Maggie's friend, Deb, who had the fencing prodigy. *Note to self: Ask Willy if he wants fencing lessons. How fun would it be to have an Olympian in the family?*

Mr. Day and Ms. Purnell looked shocked when they returned to the principal's office and informed them that the Mulligans would continue teaching at home. And then re-shocked when they requested that Cara take two classes at CHU, plus rejoin the track team.

Principal Day agreed that Cara could do track, earning her fourth varsity letter, and after proving that she had kept up, she would attend the last few weeks of classes in Spanish and Art. Ms. Purnell's eyes flickered mechanically, mentally shuffling through her inventory of forms, hunting for the correct packet of paperwork for this particular situation.

SEVENTY

CHANNEL FOUR'S CLIP of Annie accosting Olivia in front of the Women's Health clinic immediately before the bomb exploded was pirated and posted on YouTube where it went viral. Folks shared the video online with the headlines: *Anti-abortion Demonstrator Falls Flat* and *Activist Trips Over Buffer Zone* and *Protester Plans Bomb!* Viewers loved the part where Annie tried to lift off like a helicopter but landed smack on her backside. They had a special slow-motion version of her short flight. It got GIF'd. It got songified. Hours after Annie viewed it, the video's cloying melody was still stuck in her head. She caught Willy humming it and ordered him to stop.

Impish trolls posted a meme with Annie, wide-eyed and stupid-looking, on her butt, in frumpy mom jeans awkwardly splayed out on the grass, with the caption in a chunky font: KEEP CALM, DON'T BOMB. Failure was a useful theme which could be co-opted by opposing sides. The photo became known as the Mom Bomb, particularly useful for mocking helicopter mothers. It showed up on Facebook with PULLED ALL NIGHTER, above Annie's head and underneath her legs, SON'S SCIENCE PROJECT FAILED. And other captions: INSTALLED PARENTAL CONTROL APP, NOT *APP*-RECIATED. DEBATED FREE-RANGE MOM, LOST.

Annie hated how dumb she looked. That's why she went to college, to look smart. A faceplant would've been kinder that May afternoon, but no, she landed on her ass and her surprised and stupid face was enshrined for the whole world wide web to witness. Annie had dreamed of being famous for teaching children to express themselves through song with her groundbreaking Murphy Method, not for falling and failing.

Neither side wanted her; she didn't fit in anywhere. Half the internet was outraged that she bungled so badly and crossed the line. The other half was disgusted that she was on the wrong side of the line to begin with. Online ogres hated on her: "SHAME!" "Burn in hell bitch!" She was accused, tried, and lynched by the social media mob. The rage from the toxic comments was so fierce it blasted through the ethernet and her computer screen. Sitting at her laptop was like meeting face-to-face with a fire-breathing dragon whose venomous flames torched and scorched her cheeks and eyeballs.

Annie compiled a list of links to articles detailing the arrest of Jared L. Hodgkinson, an unemployed out-of-stater who was in Burlington for an RV sale. He was caught on security camera footage planting an explosive in the terra cotta flowerpot on the clinic's front steps. He meant to trigger the bomb in the middle of the night when no one would get hurt, but accidentally butt dialed it in. So he said.

Hodgkinson hadn't been a part of their peaceful protest; he wasn't really pro-life and he wasn't even a Vermonter. His social media ramblings indicated he was a democracy-loving, gun-toting socialist; he was anti-Semitic, yet pro-Bernie. Both sides of the aisle agreed on one thing, Jared was certifiably unstable.

Sick of being blamed for his insane plot, Annie copied and pasted links and quotes in the comments section of every Mom Bomb meme she saw, proclaiming her innocence over and over and over.

But it was like wrestling a Hydra; by the time Annie posted a link, seven more sites had popped up showcasing that dumbass meme. It was hopeless; she was helpless.

Desperately she devoured the news to see if any article divulged what she had privately told Olivia. Despite her notoriety, her secret was safe, so far.

Meanwhile, her father continued to defend her for the charge that she violated the buffer zone regulation by crossing the street to talk to Olivia. "You crossed a line, Annie. Quite literally, you crossed a line into their precious safe space." He snorted. "Instead of shutting down free speech, those weenie SOBs need to put on their big girl panties and learn to debate."

Her case was still pending and her dad warned her it could take up to a year to clear. When he saw Annie's reaction he assured her that he was "extremely optimistic."

"I hope so," she replied. "I don't want that on my record."

They were both heartened when a similar bubble zone law was ruled unconstitutional in adjacent Massachusetts.

Annie distracted herself by shopping. She wanted to get the most perfect gift ever for Olivia's little bambino. She scoured several baby departments, picking up striped sleeper suits and gray onesies and setting them gently back down. At the Flying Pig Bookstore she browsed the shelves in the picture book section, missing her job, missing messy finger-paints, mostly missing Nora. She hoped Leslie realized how important playacting was for Nora.

Then Annie unearthed a vintage volume of nursery rhymes. She loved Mother Goose and flattered herself that she was instilling a lifelong love of poetry in her preschoolers whenever she recited the sing-songy verses. This book had a quaint old-fashioned rhyme she had never heard before.

Triumphant, Annie purchased the book, wrapped it in a soft organic-cotton blanket, and proudly stashed it in her closet, awaiting Olivia's baby shower. Maybe Annie couldn't halt trolls from trashing her online, but she certainly recognized a treasure when she found one.

When Dan brought the kids to Lake Champlain on Saturday afternoon, Annie stayed home. She ran her fingers up and down the piano keyboard until they found the chords that matched her mood and blended with the rhythm of the nursery rhyme. The haunting melody was much more wistful and complicated than the G-major "Butterfly Song" she had composed for her preschoolers. After hours of trial and error and tears, she was satisfied. She never showed it to anyone.

Lily's Lullaby

"Hushabye little lamb, I canna sleep
Wolves at the door, hunting for sheep."

"Hushabye little mum, no more for to weep,
Wolf's on the floor, I'm safe at the keep."

"Hushabye sisters, my story don't tell."
"If we could confess, all would be well."

SEVENTY-ONE

When Cara's name boomed over the loudspeaker, Annie's heart fluttered like a butterfly prodding open a chrysalis. Cara rustled gracefully in cap and gown across the stage to receive her diploma. Annie's eyes watered. She reached over to clutch Dan's hand in joy. Her job was finished and she had succeeded. Despite the obstacles, and there had been several, including Chemistry, Algebra, *The Scarlet Letter,* the Civil War, and well, most of homeschooling, actually ... their daughter had achieved her goal—graduating with honors from Camels Hump Union High School!

Now Cara could go to college, become an attorney, and have a prestigious career. She might become the first female president of these United States! After all, several presidents started out as lawyers!

During the celebration at home afterwards, Annie stood on the back deck like a queen surveying her kingdom. They had decorated the yard with flowers and streamers and balloons in blue and green—Cara's favorite colors. Dan manned the grill and served up platters of hamburgers and hotdogs. Kids were running around blowing bubbles and shooting squirt guns. Annie noticed the homeschoolers congregating on one side of the patio and the public schoolers chatting on the other.

She introduced Wendy to Evelyn and soon they were agreeing on the risks of social media for teens. She introduced Paloma to her parents, then left before they started in on the bucket list. She introduced Maggie and Susan and they swapped contacts so Michelle and Charlene could babysit for Olivia's baby as soon as it was born.

They finally got to meet Maggie's husband, Rich. It turns out that he liked poker, too, and next thing you know he and Dan were recruiting others for a game next week. It's adorable how quickly guys can buddy up. All it takes is one hobby in common. Rich took over barbecuing while Dan restocked the cooler with more ice and drinks from the kitchen.

By the end of the party, all her compartmentalized worlds were intersecting and overlapping like a big, beautiful Venn diagram with Annie and her family smack dab in the middle.

Annie was in her glory, beaming, passing out hors d'oeuvres, and humbly listening to folks rave about Cara. When she presented the three-layer cake to the guest of honor, Annie enthusiastically led the throng in singing "Congratulations to you" to the tune of "Happy Birthday."

She and Dan had told Cara she wasn't grounded anymore and could invite anyone she wanted to the party, including John. Annie noticed that he didn't show up.

She also spotted Zachary whispering to Cara under the shade of the lilac bushes and it looked like a folded piece of paper popped out of the greeting card that he gave her, but when Annie asked Cara about it later, she brushed it off saying, "It's nothing. It's a poem." Nevertheless, Cara blushed and refused to share it.

Annie had bopped back into the house to fetch the watermelon from the fridge when the phone rang. It was Leslie, the president of Play and Learn Preschool. "We heard that your daughter did not ingest drugs on school grounds and so we would like to offer you your teaching job in time for you to head up our summer program—"

"Yes, I'd love to!"

Annie got her job back! Annie got her life back! Finally, everything was going back to normal!

SEVENTY-TWO

After the Townes recovered from the shock that Olivia had a baby out of wedlock, rather than Nelson, they set up a nursery in her older brother's bedroom. He had already moved out the previous year after graduating from college with a degree in political science and a forty-five-thousand-dollar student loan. Olivia visited him daily at his new residence in the basement. Nelson looked forward to playing the role of cool uncle in between filling out job applications online.

Olivia complained to Cara about the video of the intervention outside the women's health clinic. She wanted to create a cocoon, a buffer zone of anonymity for her baby. Privacy is precious. Some would say priceless.

But Cara helped Olivia leverage her new online status to negotiate a plan to delay enrollment for a year at Columbia. Olivia also registered for three online courses through the Community College of Vermont so she would have plenty of time for the baby, while keeping her education ongoing.

Annie took credit for introducing Wendy to Olivia at Cara's graduation party. Her friend immediately got in on the act and crusaded for Olivia to remain enrolled for the last three weeks of school, overriding the onerous ZDZD regulation. Wendy also escorted Olivia to birthing classes. She said Olivia quickly mastered the Kegel exercises. Of course, thought Annie, after fourteen years of ballet, the girl could flex muscles in her sleep. Wendy and Olivia wound up getting matching butterfly tattoos on their ankles.

At her baby shower, Olivia received oodles of adorable baby gear to put in the nursery. She thanked Annie for the book of nursery rhymes and Cara for the voucher for free babysitting.

Olivia continued to wait for Nate to come back.

And wait.

Meanwhile, she read pregnancy books, baby blogs, and selected names for their child: Nathaniel for a boy. And if it was a girl, she would call her Lily Olivia. Lily O for short.

SEVENTY-THREE

Cara was still eager to be an attorney like her grandfather. What if someday her mom got arrested again? She took a summer job showing tourists how ice cream is made at the Ben & Jerry's Factory and banked the money for Coolidge University. Her parents took out a home equity loan to make up the shortfall for her first tuition payment. And Cara practiced her cross-examination skills by convincing Mr. and Mrs. Boucher to get a cell phone for Zach before he drove off to St. A's and dropped off the landline phone grid.

Zach promised Cara that the upcoming homeschooler's Swing Dance was more fun than a prom. Way more.

Cara spent her mornings, afternoons, and evenings daydreaming about her first kiss with him. She wondered if it would be his very first kiss ever. When would it happen? And where? Would it be at that no-doubt dorky homeschool dance? On a hike up Mount Mansfield? In The Barge? No! No! No!

Perhaps at the Burlington Waterfront under a zillion sizzling stars?

"Mom, what if I step on his toes?"

"You're not going to step on his toes. C'mon, I'll take you shopping." Annie shouldered her purse and breezed to the door.

When Zachary had invited Cara to the homeschool dance, Annie was almost as excited as Cara! Her darling child had missed her senior prom, now justice had been served and Cara had a second lease on her social life. Annie would go all out for this homegrown shindig.

Cara's lips and eyebrows puckered with worry.

"When your dad gets home, you can practice dancing with him. C'mon. Get your shoes on." Annie turned to Willy. "Wanna come?"

He looked at her as if she were nuts.

"Right. I'll ask Mrs. Boucher if you can hang out with Joey while we shop."

Instead of the mall, Annie decided to drive Cara to the boutiques in downtown Burlington. The dilemma was that Cara looked fabulous in every single dress she tried on. She was toned from all that running. She had her dad's stunning blue eyes and, Annie liked to admit, her own chestnut colored hair. Cara made each gown come alive with her youthful glow.

Annie asked, "Which one do *you* like best?"

"The pink."

"Me too." It was a feminine '50s era style, cinched at the waist, with a flowing skirt. Perfect for a swing dance.

Annie suggested grabbing take-out for lunch so she would have time to go to PAL that afternoon and start prepping for the summer preschool program. As they pulled out of the drive-thru with the bag of food, Cara offered, "I can come to the preschool and help organize if you want."

"You would do that for me?"

"Sure."

"Thank you!" Annie steered right out of the parking lot and zoomed happily towards the mountain, the state's stalwart sentinel, a silent witness to human foibles and frailty. Rock-solid and never changing underneath the season's trappings, today the mountain donned reassuring shades of jolly green.

Fee-fi-fo-fum, ready or not, here I come!

Between the parking lot and the school door, Annie heard an odd high-pitched sound. *Eek.*

She caught Cara's gaze; she was equally mystified.

Eek.

They tracked the intermittent sound to the tall grass beyond the playground. A frog was periodically shrieking in terror while its hindquarters were trapped in the jaws of a snake.

EEK! Now Annie sounded the alarm as well.

It was one of the grossest sights she'd ever seen, and she'd witnessed plenty of disgusting organic material emitting from body parts at PAL over the years. Her fingers trembled as she googled the number for Vermont Fish and Wildlife. When the expert answered her call, Annie explained the situation and asked, "How do we save the frog?"

"How much of him is in the snake's mouth?"

"Up to his belly!"

"He's already a goner. Nothing you can do."

"But!"

"That's nature for ya." Annie thought she heard the guy snicker to a coworker as he hung up his phone.

"There's nothing we can do," she informed Cara, who was crouched down, filming the ingestion with her phone, looking for all the world like a wildlife photographer for National Geographic.

"Willy will love this," Cara breathed in rapt fascination.

Annie wondered if it was the same snake that had shed its skin inside the school back in March. At least it was outside now. And with a frog clogging its gullet, there was no way it could slither through a small hole. There was no going back. The kiddos were safe.

Inside the preschool, the cheery red, blue, and yellow colors of the cupboards and curtains were familiar and comforting after that sickening scene in the yard. Annie smelled crayons and Play-Doh and the homemade cleaner made from lemon essential oil, which was emanating from the potty room.

The book of fairy tales illustrated by Tasha Tudor had toppled off the shelf. On the cover Little Red Riding Hood scrutinized the wolf disguised in a white mob cap tucked in granny's bed. Annie picked up the picture book and put it back on the bookcase next to John Churchman's *Brave Little Finn*. Annie enthusiastically supported local artists, although like many Vermont luminaries, these authors were imports from out of state.

She fetched water from the sink and set the cups at the kitchen table for each of them. The elfin chairs magically transformed Annie and Cara into giants. They hunkered over the low trestle table and unwrapped the waxed paper which had kept their food not too hot, not too cold, but just right.

Cara munched hungrily on her hamburger.

"Cara." Annie waited until she looked up. "I want you to know how proud your dad and I are of you."

"Thanks, Mom."

"I really mean it. You have done so well at CHU, and then homeschooling. And with track and your friends ... the teen years aren't always easy, but you've managed them beautifully."

"Thanks."

"I just have one question."

Cara set her burger down and leaned back in her itsy-bitsy chair.

"Why didn't you tell me about Olivia? All that time I thought you were messing around with drugs and John. I was so worried about you."

"I know Mom. I'm sorry. I really am, but I couldn't tell." Cara's eyes were luminously earnest. "I wanted to, but it wasn't my story, it was Olivia's. I had to wait until she was ready."

"You didn't trust me."

"God, no." Cara leaned forward and stretched her hand across the table to clasp Annie's. "Nothing like that. I wanted to tell you, but I promised not to tell. It was all for Olivia."

Annie smiled. Her eyes watered and she feared her throat, swollen with aching gratitude, would emit an ugly frog-croak if she attempted speech.

This is one of those heart-to-heart mother-daughter moments I've watched in Hallmark movies!

This vivacious daughter of hers was way beyond grades. An "F" or "D" could take nothing away from this brilliant young lady with the extravagantly lavish heart who was willing to lie and homeschool and risk her entire career for weeks, all to benefit a friend. An A+ could add nothing to Cara that she didn't already possess.

Annie swallowed and stared in complete love and wonderment. She whispered, "Thank you, that means everything to me."

Cara's face was shining with fresh optimism and vitality and energy.

If time had a remote control, I would press pause and revel in this moment. This feeling of uttermost relief that all is well in the world. This is what makes life beautiful, right here, right now ... this connection with Cara, joined together in peace, singing our heartsongs, our voices blending together in a fermata of beautiful harmony—

"Can I ask you a question?" Cara asked quietly.

"Sure. Anything." She was a mama lion cuddling her little cub. She could practically hear herself purr.

"Why didn't you ever tell me about your abortion?"

Annie's hand slipped silently out of Cara's grasp. "Excuse me." She launched herself up from the low chair. "Sorry, I need the bathroom." She waved her hand towards her cup of water. "Went right through me."

With a few giant steps Annie reached the potty room and shut the door behind her.

SEVENTY-FOUR

CARA DID HEAR *me tell Olivia.*

This was the conversation Annie had been avoiding for twenty years. This was precisely what she didn't want to talk about. She had swaddled this secret, tucked it safely in its silent cradle, guarded it vigilantly, hushed it with a pacifier and smothered it with blankies when it became too noisy.

She had never told her girlfriends back home, or her father, and especially not her mother. The only ones who had known were her boyfriend, who never called after graduation, her college roommates, who tried to cheer her up with ice cream and flowers, an anonymous priest in a confessional in Philly, who absolved her soul, but not her heart or psyche. And a year afterwards, Dan, who needed to know why he had to inch incredibly, incrementally slowly in their make-out sessions, and to his everlasting credit, didn't dump her right then and there.

And the abortionist knew.

He knew.

He could snuff out life, but not memory.

How could one tiny choice create this piercing, potent legacy?

Alone, she had nursed this memory for twenty years. She'd never had to share it. The only reason she had divulged her secret to Olivia was to prevent her from making the same mistake. Saving someone from endless remorse was the only conceivable reason to ever, ever talk about this darkness with anyone.

Years ago while sharing a bottle of wine and discussing the patriarchy and glass ceiling, Wendy had explained that she had had an abortion. "Two, actually." Wendy held up two fingers, making a peace sign. "One to finish school and one to keep my career going. What a relief." Annie was murderously jealous of Wendy who regarded her choice with gratitude, not anguish. While her friend sipped her expensive rosé, Annie's entire world had tunneled into two options: scream insanely or snuff that grief.

She didn't scream.

Annie leaned her back against the chilly bathroom wall and closed her eyes and breathed out.

She couldn't chat about this with her daughter.

Cara was her fresh start, her do-over. Annie had vowed to do everything right for her. She had prepared the nursery with quilts and afghans and stuffed animals, and left the house when Dan painted it so toxic fumes wouldn't go anywhere near the child developing deep within her. She had read every baby book she could get her paws on. She had given up coffee and beer and roller blading. And then, the week before her due date, she and Dan made love every morning, because she'd read that sex could trigger contractions and she was desperately eager to meet her little one. She had been tenaciously protecting Cara ever since.

Annie's phone rang and she slipped it out of her pocket. She didn't recognize the number, but answered in case it was Willy calling. In a dull voice she asked, "Hello?"

"Hi, this is Jeffrey, assistant to the producer of *At Home with Ula*. Is this Anne Mulligan?"

She was stunned into silence.

"Hello?"

"Yes, it's me. Annie."

"I'm calling because Ula saw the news clip with your intervention outside the women's clinic and she'd like to have you on her show. We're onsite in Burlington and we had a last-minute cancellation and we're hoping you'll agree to come on the show and talk about your experience."

She couldn't breathe.

"Hello?"

"Yes, I'm here." Annie pushed against the cold tiled wall and stood up straight, at attention.

"We can film the story at your home tomorrow."

"Tomorrow?"

"Yes, we're already on location in Burlington. You live in Mapleville, right?"

"Yes."

"Your story will resonate bigly with Ula's audience. So, what do you say? Can we count on you?"

Annie loved *At Home with Ula*. It was her favorite show! She'd always imagined being on TV! She'd always wanted to make a name for herself! This was her chance! This was her dream come true!

Ula would believe her that it was all Hodgkinson's fault. Annie had nothing to with that explosion! Nothing! Ula would understand the monstrous injustice of the Mom Bomb meme! Ula would set the story straight and help Annie explain herself to the evil internet trolls on both sides. Ula would reframe the event with her sweet southern charm and everyone would believe her. She could explain herself to all women at once. All across America, in the privacy of their own homes, folks would tune in! They would listen! Oh, to be heard! Oh, to be understood!

And she could bring the Murphy Method to millions of viewers! What a triumph to have immediate access to moms all over America! Her singing system could change the lives of zillions of kids! Think of all the good she could bestow on the world!

Annie's mind jumped to her closet to mentally choose what to wear during the taping. She had a silky blue long-sleeve blouse that hid arm jiggle and was cut to the most attractive level of cleavage on her. And black pants, of course, the stretchy ones to be comfortable. Her hair, *dang!* She wished it were long enough for an elegant updo; instead it was in a hideous growing-it-out-stage. But she could add volume and bounce with her curling iron and—

"So?" he interrupted her reverie.

"Yes!" she gushed. "Yes, I'd love to!"

Bleep!

Her phone alerted her that Cara was calling in.

SEVENTY-FIVE

"CAN YOU HOLD a minute?" Annie asked Jeffrey. "I have a call coming in."

He agreed and she tapped her phone. "Cara?" she asked.

"Mom? You okay? I heard you talking in there."

Annie's face prickled with embarrassment. Cara probably assumed she was talking to herself. "Yeah, I got a phone call," she explained. "Sorry I'm taking so long, I'll be right out."

"Okay."

Cara, her perfect, precious daughter, ready to get back to their mother-daughter moment.

Waiting at the table ... for her.

Waiting ... to listen.

Waiting ... to learn.

Annie pressed both shoulder blades against the tiled wall for support.

Did she want Cara to see her on TV talking about—?

Annie wouldn't mind modestly admitting to saving Olivia from a *bomb* and she would love to place the blame for that explosion squarely and righteously on Hodgkinson.

But.

If Ula started questioning her, with that smooth, sweet, insistent, southern drawl ... there's no way Annie could keep her secret hush-hush. If Ula could reel in Tiffany and induce her to divulge her husband's ultimatum about babies—when he was wedged smack dab next to her on the loveseat—then surely Ula would wheedle it out of Annie that she had had ...

She would break down on TV.

Another precious dream snuffed out.

Annie couldn't stay up. Her body melted against the wall, slipping down, sliding into a crumble. Her butt plopped on the floor, her legs flopped uselessly in front of her. The frigid floor tiles prevented her from sinking into the dark pit lurking below.

Who cares about those trolls hollering online? They didn't watch Ula's show anyway. Those millions of moms could teach their own kids to sing *Row, row, row your boat.* Ula didn't need Annie. Jeffrey could get someone else to fill in. Those viewers vegging in their living rooms didn't need her. Cara needed her.

She tapped her phone again.

"Hello?" asked Jeffrey.

"Yes, I'm back," said Annie. "But I can't." She grimaced from the pain, the visceral ache of saying "No" to her lifelong aspiration. "I can't be on your show."

"Do you want a little more time to think it over? We'll come to your house, it doesn't matter what it looks like. We can prep one room, one corner—"

They thought she was declining because her house was messy? "No, it's not that."

"We're very interested in your story. We'll feature it on Mother's Day. We'll call it," and she could practically see his hand swipe the title through the air, "Annie's Choice."

They had it all planned out and pre-scripted?

Hold up—he said "choice." Did they know what she had told Olivia? Did they already know what she had done twenty years ago? They couldn't possibly have audio of what she said to Olivia! Right? Was her secret still safe?

Annie felt panic stir in her gut. Adrenaline and cortisol suddenly coursed through her bloodstream, colliding in her arteries, and her heart began to thud, thud, thud. "Choice?" The word tumbled out of her mouth. *Trip, trap, trip, trap.*

"To cross the buffer zone. Your decision to intervene."

They didn't know! Relief flooded Annie. Her lungs relaxed. Her limbs loosened. Her body melted into the tiled wall, the tiled floor. *Breathe, Annie, breathe. In for four, out for seven.*

"Hello?"

"No. I'm sorry. I can't talk about this on TV."

"Have I mentioned our compensation?"

She squeezed her eyes shut. Money. Ugh. To get paid for her choice?

Repulsed, her abdominal muscles twisted in revolt. Darkness flooded her mind. Her vision became fuzzy. His words became distant.

"... So contact us if you have any questions."

He said he would text his contact info and to call, text, or email any time of the day or night, preferably before tomorrow morning at 9:00 when they wanted to start the cameras rolling.

"I can't. Thank you. I'm very honored. You don't even know how much I want to, but I can't. But please tell Ula I'm her biggest fan."

"You can tell her in person tomorrow."

"I can't."

"When you change your mind, *again,*" he chuckled, "give us a buzz."

"I'm sorry. Tell Ula I love her show. But I have to go. Bye." Annie clicked off.

It was time.

Cara had waited long enough.

SEVENTY-SIX

I CAN'T GO on national television and talk about this.

It's time to talk to Cara.

I push myself up off the floor. My legs feel as wobbly as if I'd run a marathon, not that I ever ran one. Or ever will. Not me. It'll be a win if I can straggle back to the table. I'll give myself an "E" for Effort if I make it back.

The door is plastered with prints from Mary Azarian's *A Farmer's Alphabet* so the preschoolers can keep learning even while propped on the potty. Large ABCs in chunky black and white rustic woodcuts teach the folksy, homespun wisdom of the farm: Apple, Barn, Cow ...

I turn the knob and the door yawns open. *One, two, buckle my shoe. Three, four, close the door.* I take baby steps towards the kitchen, inch by inch by inch.

There's Cara, sipping her water, brushing a lock of hair back from her face, patiently waiting. She sees me and lights up with her wide-open smile. So young, so innocent.

I don't deserve this daughter. My breath escapes with a whoosh. I want to wrap her in my mama bear embrace. I'll squeeze her tight and never let go.

If she asks who I was talking to, I'll tell her it was Susan. No, Cara's too close to Olivia. Maggie? No, because Cara could ask Zachary. Anyhoo. I'll figure it out. No one ever needs to know that Ula called me. I'm good at keeping secrets.

Five, six, pick up sticks ... I draw myself up, head erect, ribcage at attention, shoulders back and down. I suck in a walloping huge breath, dragging air up from my diaphragm. *In for four, out for seven ... In for four, out for seven ... Seven, eight, lay them straight ...*

I know exactly what to do. I'll sit at that table, face Cara head on, look directly into her beautiful blue eyes and ...

... ask ...

... ask ...

... about Zachary.

Yes, that's perfect! She'll love talking about him!

And then, tomorrow, I'll spend the whole day prepping Cara for the dance! I'll do her nails, open my new bath gel and let her be the first to use it. I'll share my perfume and my jewelry. I'll blast Cara's favorite music while I curl her hair. I'll ask Dan to mow the lawn and freshen up the yard. He can man the grill and we'll have something simple but hearty and clean, like steak. We'll invite Maggie and her husband over for dinner and I'll whip up some festive margaritas, but not for the kids, because Zachary will be driving later. I'll buy fresh flowers for the arbor and they can pose underneath the colorful blossoms. She'll look gorgeous in the new dress we just bought. And before they go, I'll take a zillion pictures of Cara standing next to Zachary, smile by smile by smile. I'll load them all on Facebook as soon as they leave. I'll compile them into a photobook, print it out and we can admire it for years and years to come. This will be Cara's senior prom. They'll be voted king and queen of the prom! They'll have crowns and sashes and everything. It will be as magical as Cinderella's ball. Yes, it'll be absolutely enchanting!

And we'll all live happily ever after!

ACKNOWLEDGMENTS

I AM ABSOLUTELY honored to thank the following for their encouragement and expertise: To local writers group members, Margaret Grant, Kari Jo Spear, and Chris Sims; to the Burlington Writers Workshop and its founder Peter Biello, and especially those who read the entire rough draft of this novel, Mark Hoffman, Grier Martin, Hannah Powell, and Al Uris; to editors Laurie Chittenden, Rachel Carter, and Dave Dickerson; to Richard Ljoenes for the outstanding book cover; to the teachers and homeschoolers who educated my children and me from preschool to college and beyond; to the Vermonters who inspire me; to all of us who live with regret (my heart goes out to you); to Kathy, Peggy, Maureen, Rita, and all my family and friends. And to Tom, for providing the time and freedom for me to pursue my passion.

Kelly Bartlett has survived seventeen years of homeschooling and thirty-five Vermont winters without a single arrest. The author of SILENCED, she enjoys writing fiction and To Do lists, which are sometimes identical. She would be delighted to give you an A+ for reading this book and extra credit for sharing it.

Made in United States
North Haven, CT
08 October 2022

25191614R00217